The Trinity Conspiracy
~ Book One ~

I0565270

Journey
of The
Dead

A.C. Townsend

Published by Scratch Pad, LLC

ISBN-10: 0615949517

ISBN-13: 978-0615949512

To Steve

*for your unwavering faith in God and in me
and for tempering the most difficult of times
with appreciation and laughter.
I am thankful that we will spend eternity together,
because one lifetime would never be enough.*

In Memoriam

Sgt. E. John Ellis, USMC
(1925 – 2008)
8th Amphibian Tractor Battalion
1st Marine Division
who generously shared his memories
of World War II
and of the battle in which he fought
on the island of Peleliu.

Trinity Families

The Davenport Family

Ray Davenport, age 42. WWII veteran and farmer from Kentucky.

Belva Jean Davenport, age 39. Ray's wife.

Sarah Jane Davenport, age 16. Ray and Belva's daughter, who chronicles her family's experiences following the Trinity Test.

Ben Davenport, age 12. Ray and Belva's son. Sarah's brother.

Lucy Martin, age 35. Belva Davenport's sister. Deceased.

John Calvin Davenport, age 46. Ray's brother. WWI veteran and farmer from Kentucky.

Mary Elaine Davenport, age 45. John's wife.

Callirrhoë "Callie" Elaine Davenport, age 22. John and Mary's daughter.

Sylvia Forester, age 87. Mary Davenport's aunt who lives in Texas.

The Pendleton Family

Clayton Michael Pendleton, Sr., age 49. Drifter and absentee father living most recently in California.

Clayton Michael Pendleton, Jr., age 25. Clayton's son, known as Michael. Also a drifter.

Christine Pendleton, age 23. Clayton's daughter and Michael's sister. Teaches school in Nevada.

Freddy Pendleton, age 11. Clayton's son. Michael and Christine's half-brother.

The Lake Family

Robert Lake, age 32. Factory worker and photographer from Utah.

Joy Lake, age 29. Robert's wife, originally from New Mexico.

Catherine Lake, age 12. Robert and Joy's daughter.

Elisabeth Lake, age 10. Robert and Joy's daughter.

Kenneth Rhodes, age 17. Robert's friend and an aspiring photographer. Traveling with the Lake family.

David Hensley, age 17. Kenneth's best friend. Traveling with the Lake family.

Desert Springs Church Youth Group

Tom Westfield, age 26. Youth minister at the Desert Springs Church in New Mexico.

Sybil Westfield, age 24. Tom's wife.

Russell Winter, age 18. Member of the youth group. Preparing to join the military.

Arlene Brooks, age 17. Youth group member and Russell Winter's fiancée.

Will Blackwater, age 17. Member of the youth group. Preparing to join the military.

Rachael Knight, age 15. Youth group member.

Nathaniel Harper, age 16. Youth group member.

Toby McCallister, age 17. Member of the youth group. Preparing to join the military.

Abby McCallister, age 17. Youth group member and Toby's twin sister.

Maria Ramirez, age 14. Youth group member.

Vernon Sheppard, age 18. Member of the youth group. Preparing to join the military.

Gilbert Fitzpatrick, age 18. Member of the youth group. Preparing to join the military.

Prologue

I once had a beautiful fatherland.
The oak tree grew so high; the violets nodded gently.
It was a dream.
~ Heinrich Heine

January 1943

"Mein Gott!"

Captain Helmut Reiger lay prone against the crest of the ridge. Soviet tanks patrolled the eastern perimeter of the forest before him, drowning out the labored growls of lesser engines and urgent commands that ricocheted across the clearing in the tongue of the Motherland. A cavern penetrated the mountain that walled the north end of the glade. Russian soldiers swarmed the area, vague apparitions ghosting through the snowfall, guarding the site against discovery by their enemies.

A ragged band of soldiers stood motionless twenty feet below the ridge. As dawn thrust gray daggers into the shroud of chilling darkness, Reiger signaled them to join him. Fourteen tattered Nazis crept up the frozen embankment, advancing to peer warily over the rim.

A T-34 beetled away from the enigmatic lair pulling a flatbed on tracks. A sleek, black cuneiform, roughly fifty feet long, crouched on the flatbed. The front of the object tapered to a point, while the rear presented a row of jagged angles, the two outermost suggesting tips of wings sculpted seamlessly from the body of the craft.

"Was ist es?" a Nazi hissed.

Moments passed before a fellow soldier ventured a barely audible guess. *"Etwas das fliegt?"*

The men exchanged uneasy glances before looking to their captain. Reiger made no response as he committed every detail to memory: the disconcerting cache, the several hundred Soviets on skis and on horseback, the heavily loaded supply trucks emerging from the mountain to mobilize like stars around a bizarre sun. He shuddered as a KV-1 thundered past the embankment against which he and his soldiers lay camouflaged by the snow. Fear was palpable in their eyes, in their muffled breathing, but at least it was not a scent, Reiger thought, or they would have been discovered and dead by now.

The Soviets swiftly abandoned the clearing. The T-34 and its extraordinary burden melted away among the foothills along with its companion tanks, GAZ's, and heavily-armed escorts. Silence fell as the sun stole reluctantly over the horizon and began its languid journey west.

Reiger waited until the Russians were an hour gone before advancing to the cavern. His soldiers searched every crevice before regrouping against the trees, lost for an explanation. The mountain offered no evidence of previously guarded secrets. The trampled snow indicated only that troops had recently passed through the clearing.

Not a single match, not a scrap of food. Nothing to ease the desperate needs of a human scavenger. Reiger turned his back on the site and exhaled warmth into woolen palms, wishing for the hundredth time he possessed the resources with which to build a fire and feed his men.

Attempting to realize Adolf Hitler's Operations *Blau* and *Edelweiss*, the Nazis had begun their advance into the Caucasus Mountains on 28 June 1942. In the beginning, they had gained tremendous ground. The Maikop oil fields, though virtually destroyed by the retreating Red Army in accordance with Stalin's scorched earth policy, were taken on 8 August, and the Swastika flag had been planted atop Mount Elbrus by the 21st. Hitler was greedy for the Soviet Union, intending to complete his conquest by taking the rich oil fields at Grozny and Baku as well as the coveted city of Stalingrad. Despite warnings from his field marshals that there were not enough forces left of the *Wehrmacht* to accomplish these goals simultaneously, Hitler insisted that concurrent battles would be fought and must be won. But war in the Caucasus turned quickly against the Nazis, and word had it that Stalingrad not only refused to fall but had mounted a devastating offense. Weeks became months wasted on ignorant blunders, time and potential lost to the whims of a madman adrift in his own imagination.

Here in the foothills east of Novorossiisk, the war raged long and hard, the ground gained and yielded worth its weight in blood. The once solid Army Group A had been cut asunder by Soviet forces of unanticipated strength, divided, deprived of resources, and divided again. Hitler had further weakened the Army by drawing away portions of its strength to assist the diminishing forces at Stalingrad. Army groups advanced into the mountains or fought to hold their hard-gained positions at the *Führer's* fancy, ordered to stand and fight in the face of insurmountable odds with recourse neither in retreat nor surrender. Troops were initially refused permission to withdraw even when standing their ground meant certain death, and Hitler mandated that his generals should die at their own hands rather than submit to captivity by the *Führer's* enemy.

Inevitable defeat by the Red Army and 'General Winter' finally forced withdrawal of the German forces westward out of the Caucasus. Retreat was an unremitting nightmare of attacks by a relentless Russian offensive amidst brutal weather conditions, exacting heavy losses of men and equipment.

Following the conflict in which Reiger's *Kompanie* was destroyed, fifteen Nazi survivors found one another in a pine thicket above the battlefield. As the highest-ranking soldier, Reiger automatically assumed command, and the others were glad to let him. Their clothing was inadequate for the bitter Russian winter, though they added layers of warmth by stealing from the dead. They had consumed the last of their food. They carried rifles, but little ammunition. The January air slit mercilessly through their flesh until it ravaged their very souls. Some had spoken of suicide.

Providence, however, had seen fit to give them a mission.

"Achtung!"

The indomitable mentality imposed by their *Führer* made being a soldier more important than being a man. At Reiger's cry, the Nazis fell in line to follow the Soviets' trail.

Though he was desperate to ascertain their location and to appropriate supplies, Reiger wondered bleakly what his wretched group could possibly do against the several hundred members of the Red Army in whose wake they cautiously advanced. Survival depended upon reuniting his soldiers with the *Heer,* yet Reiger feared the path they now pursued would lead to capture or death. Worse was the nagging certainty that he and the men under his command were already presumed dead by their own. Collection of each fallen soldier's *Erkennungsmarke* was not an option in the aftermath of the battle they had survived, and there would be no other indication that these few had cheated death.

The swath the Soviets had cleared through the forest was wide enough to land a small plane, but the frozen ground was unforgiving. The snow and the terrain forced them to move so slowly that the Nazis faced a greater risk of overtaking their quarry than of being left behind. Remembering the lair from whence it came, Reiger was loath to let the disturbing black wedge out of his sight, lest it disappear into the landscape without a trace, leaving imagination to challenge the memory. As hours dragged by, he assigned his soldiers in shifts to maintain surveillance of the Soviet procession.

Reiger observed as the Soviets relaxed their vigil long enough to eat. Later he cast about the site for abandoned scraps to share with his own men. He considered the Russian cavalry horses, bitterly remembering how his own army had slaughtered their mounts when Hitler's promised supplies never materialized and the soldiers were left to starve. He shivered inside his jacket and glanced at his battered troops, who wore layers of dead men's clothing over their own uniforms. Reiger closed his eyes against the vision of the half-naked, bloodied corpses of his fellows freezing to the ground in the wake of the last battle – such disrespect to the valiant dead! – but they'd had no other recourse against the frigid cold. He hugged himself against the horror and sank to the ground with his back to an unyielding oak for the brief time he had allotted. Rest offered little reprieve from his formidable obligation.

He pondered the hidden storehouse and the foreboding black wedge it had concealed. A ripple of fear ascended his spine and stung the nape of his neck as he scanned a lifetime of knowledge for information that would explain the Russian apparatus and found himself wanting. Was it a weapon, one perhaps capable of inflicting a whole new level of devastation? Or was it, as one of his soldiers had suggested, an aircraft? The enemy's shortage of combat planes was common knowledge among the German troops, and as far as he was aware, the *Luftwaffe* boasted no planes that resembled this object. If the Red Army possessed superior technology that would enable them to win the war, they would surely have put it to use before now – unless they had developed a weapon so terrible as to warrant its deployment only as a last resort.

As the tedious journey continued into the third day, the climate gradually changed. It was still cold but no longer freezing. The ground thawed to a heavy, frosted muck, while the wind blew harder against their advance. Reiger was startled when their bearing occurred to him. The Russians were headed for the coast.

Reiger attempted to determine their destination. The Black Sea, of course, but at what point, he knew too little of the area to guess. Novorossiisk was impossible, occupied and embattled, and the retreating Germans had been headed toward Krymskaya and the Taman Peninsula. This meant the Soviets would have to approach the coast farther south. The dark cuneiform had not appeared to possess the traits of a floating or submersible vessel, but nothing was beyond Reiger's imagination by now. Still lost, but no longer hopelessly, he signed encouragement to his fellows and they, deadened to any notion beyond placing one foot in front of the other, continued each to follow the man before him.

Several hours into the third night, the Soviets reached the shore. Reiger gave his men leave to collapse in the undergrowth while he advanced alone onto the open expanse stretching outward to the sea to learn where the Soviet secret was to be kept. Though darkness cloaked his presence, Reiger knew that alone would not save him should he inadvertently stumble into a roving Russian guard. With no respite between the tree line and the water's edge, Reiger dropped to the ground and crept closer on elbows and knees, one limb at a time, begrudging even the rasp of his own breathing. He pressed his *Erkennungsmarke* tightly against his chest to prevent it from jingling on its chain, though it should scarcely be heard above the commotion of tanks, trucks, horses, and the surprising clarity of voices. He forced himself along, drawing suicidally close. The vibrations of enemy activity pounded through his jacket as he flattened against the ground. Concentrating his gaze forward, Reiger attempted to discern what the Russians were doing and how they were accomplishing any effort with so little light to penetrate the oppressive winter night. So gritty-moist, so clammy-cool, and Reiger fought the need to cough. He pressed a glove over his nose and mouth and focused on the enemy's activities until the wind tortured forth hot, salty tears. As he raked cracked knuckles across his eyes, Reiger's vision captured peripherally a detail that had escaped direct scrutiny. His heart raced as he made out the ominous silhouette of a cruiser lurking in the fog, now briefly visible, now a wraith upon the water.

Reiger returned to his troops, helpless to hide his dismay. They received his account dully, mind and body struggling to process any perception beyond simply acknowledging commands, and regarded him with the expectation of soldiers awaiting their next orders. Reiger stared back at each of them in turn. What now, indeed? And where, and how? What were fifteen weary men against the strength of hundreds? The burden of the war, the loss and separation engulfed Reiger suddenly, draining his resolve and aging him in a moment with overwhelming regret. He dropped heavily to the ground among his fellows and stared into the suffocating black of the moonless night. Voices carried across the beach, subliminal reminders that he had a job to do and was tragically incapable of fulfilling his own command.

He had hardly lowered his head into his hands when a presence eased alongside him, sat hard against him.

"Shall we proceed, Hauptmann? Follow them still?"

Albrecht Gohritz's black eyes glittered with intensity as they accepted the anticipated brunt of Reiger's incredulous glare. Reiger curved his lips into a smirk, attempted a mirthless laugh that emerged as a whimper. What were they to do, swim the forbidding waters in pursuit of a Soviet cruiser? Better yet, perhaps his dirty, frostbitten, exhausted men could each over-power a healthy, hardy Soviet soldier and take his uniform, slip onto the cruiser under the guise of a Russian! No one would notice the haggard German face, the cracked and bleeding lips, the gaunt frame that rattled loosely within the clothing like a bean in a hull. As Reiger's eyes dilated from his mental exertions, Gohritz tried again.

"They must load the aircraft onto the ship, Hauptmann, as well as the supplies they brought on the trucks. Perhaps they could load us at the same time."

Notions darted at Reiger from all directions, muddling his thoughts even as he tried to make sense of Gohritz's logic. His men were in agreement, then, that the apparatus was meant to fly, and he could think of no argument against their assumption. So why didn't the Russians just fly it to their destination? Reiger shook his head in a physical effort to focus. That was not the issue at the moment. There would be time later, he hoped, to revisit such theories. A decision waited now for or against Gohritz's outrageous suggestion.

Reiger looked into the faces that silently surrounded him, humbled by the determination that flickered in each pair of unwavering eyes. He was sorry he had allowed them to see him considering defeat. And yet his heart pounded in mute protest. This wasn't his war, wasn't their war! The order to destroy a nation's humanity and possess the land was the edict of a tyrant gone mad. Reiger glanced at Gohritz and steeled his resolve. He had sworn an oath to render unconditional obedience to Adolf Hitler, vowing that he would at all times be prepared, as a brave soldier, to give his life for that oath, to which he was bound by an incontrovertible sense of duty and of patriotic pride. He sat for a moment and absorbed sounds that had become so commonplace that they faded into the subconscious – sounds of war, brutal and merciless, clamoring incessantly from distant locations all around. Reality offered no resolution, no compromise, and no alternative but to fight.

Strengthened by their faith, Reiger led his soldiers along the perimeter of the beach. He kept Gohritz by his side, studied the situation through the younger man's eyes, and recognized opportunity he had not seen before. He sent his men forward in pairs to slip past the constantly patrolling Soviet guards, to disappear among the supply trucks, to melt into the pallets and bundles as undetected shadows in the thick, miserable darkness – curse become blessing – until he alone remained. They would succeed, he resolved, or they would die, and they would do so in the name of their *Führer!* Reiger chose his moment and ghosted into the darkness to join his soldiers.

Several hours later dawn broke reluctantly over the Black Sea. A frozen sun cast wistful beams across a stretch of shoreline bereft of life save for the mists that swirled the reach where the sea met the land. An ethereal curtain of fog lingered over the water, wafting in memory of the Soviet cruiser that had vanished into the night, and into myth.

April 1945

Merrill emerged from the building at a dead run and accomplished a good thirty feet before his knees buckled and he went down on all fours, vomiting violently onto the turf. Under any other circumstance, he would have been embarrassed by his reaction, but he was far from alone. Yet if there wasn't time to accommodate a sickened stomach, neither was there occasion for empathy between soldiers. Sergeant Merrill regained his feet, spat in defiance, and marched angrily past rows of gray, pitifully emaciated corpses, back through the doorway to Hell.

Merrill had been a medic since the war began. In mopping up the human aftermath of countless battles, he thought he had seen it all, but he had never encountered horror the likes of which confronted him now. He paused just beyond a stack of decaying bodies piled under a stairway and touched fingertips to wall, bracing against the miasma that enswathed him as though his own guts were rotting from the inside out. The fetid odor, once breathed in, permeated and assaulted the senses. Merrill could taste the smell, and again his stomach gripped as bile rose sour to the back of his throat. He gagged it down and faced the job at hand. Men were dead and dying, and no small effort was required to distinguish one from the other. The men of the 104th Infantry Division were taxed beyond their ability to carry out such extensive and unimaginable duties. Soldiers and medics worked feverishly side by side to introduce mercy where justice had been denied.

The first body Merrill approached was to all appearance dead, yet small wheezes of putrid air struggled in and out of the skeletal remains. A soldier brought a board, and Merrill transferred the living corpse onto it for removal to a field hospital. He moved on to the next body automatically, trying not to think about the hundreds still waiting, about who they were and why they were here and the warped justification for the torment they had endured, about the relief for those whom death had freed of their agonies and what lay ahead for those who survived. It was someone else's job to identify the living and bury the dead, someone else's job to pray for God's mercy. Too late for most, Merrill thought bitterly. God's children had found no mercy here.

Until now.

Feeble hands reached out to Merrill, and cadaverous survivors spoke with weak voices in languages Merrill could not comprehend, but he understood clearly the meaning of the tears that flowed down their ravaged faces. He didn't try to hide his own as he clasped hands, lifted bodies, murmured reassurances in a voice that he hoped relayed comfort, and moved on to the next, and the next, and the next.

Most of the victims appeared to be Polish or French. They were political slaves conscripted to build Hitler's *Vergeltung* rockets, the V-1 and V-2 flying bombs, in the tunnels beneath the Khonstein Mountain a couple of miles away. Of the six thousand prisoners warded at the Mittelbau Dora concentration camp in Nordhausen that April, five thousand remained only as corpses in various phases of decomposition. Over the previous two years Death had freed the enslaved by thousands as they were tortured, beaten, and starved into macabre, skeletal caricatures of the individuals they had once been.

During the past month, the camp had been partially evacuated. Prisoners were taken on forced marches, which few survived, to other camps. Mittelbau Dora's Nazi oppressors had abandoned the remaining prisoners when they fled from Allied advance the day before.

Faced with massive burials they could not hope to accomplish alone, American soldiers visited the town of Nordhausen and compelled more than one hundred male civilians to the task. Trenches were prepared on a hillside near the camp, and the deceased thousands were buried there. "Unknown but to God," the chaplain murmured time and again, praying over countless victims of hatred as their bodies were interred in now-holy ground. Nordhausen was not a major camp in comparison to Buchenwald, Auschwitz, or Dachau. The little crematorium installed at Mittelbau Dora, working at full capacity, could only cremate one hundred human bodies per day, and the SS staff responsible for the process had not kept up with the death rate among the prisoners.

The 104th Infantry Division, the Timberwolves, reeled at suffering and anguish carried beyond what any of them could have conjured forth from the depths of their worst nightmares. A few words from the Division's official song played through Merrill's mind, the verse declaring they would lead the way through hell onward to victory. Victory for the Timberwolves, yes, many times over. Victory for the United States of America. But victory for these before him meant enduring a battle for survival such as Merrill had never fought, beyond the agonies they had already endured.

He would see them forevermore, pitiful dead and half-dead men in dirty striped uniforms. He would feel the heart-wrenching sadness as they reached for him, their wasted hands desperate to touch hope. He would never escape the cries of tormented souls, the wounds on their bodies, the indescribable filth in which they existed, and the odor, the everlasting odor, the smell of death and worse than death. Surely the devil himself avoided this place, unable to bear the horror within. Merrill saw his feelings etched on the face of every soldier he encountered. Voices echoed disbelief as liberators shared stories of inconceivable brutalities found in every building across the camp.

By late afternoon Merrill had encountered several German prisoners among the living. He was aware that any German whose actions were considered treasonous to the Nazi movement was imprisoned and sentenced to work among the other political slaves at Mittelbau Dora. He was not surprised, then, when he approached yet another prisoner who was obviously losing his battle with time, and the man began speaking to him in German. Merrill was taken aback, however, when the man gripped his hand and raised his voice as though desperate to be heard. Merrill looked into the man's face and found his gaze drowning in black eyes that glittered with the determination of a soul that desperately needed to survive, all the more because its vehicle was very nearly expired. Merrill called out to Walters, a fellow medic, for an interpretation of the prisoner's persistent babble. Walters communicated briefly with the victim before turning to Merrill.

"Sergeant, this man was a Nazi soldier," Walters said. "He served with Army Group A during Hitler's attempt to take the Caucasus. He insists he has information that we must hear."

"Take him out and get him in line for medical

attention," Merrill said. "He can talk to someone later."

"He doesn't want to be treated until he has shared his story."

Merrill hesitated at those determined black eyes. "He won't make it if we wait much longer. Take him outside where we can breathe, and you can tell me what he has to say. Has he told you his name?"

"Gohritz, Sergeant. Albrecht Gohritz."

Less than an hour later, Merrill and Walters sat down by Gohritz's pallet to hear a bitter personal account of survival, triumph, and betrayal that had occurred two years before.

April 1943

He did not understand the message and had neither the desire nor the time to try. Reich Marshal Hermann Goering glared imperiously at the men before him and snapped his fingers at them as though they were dogs. They lowered their eyes, hung their heads, and shortened their spines in concession to that judgment – and very bad dogs indeed. He had demanded to know the nature of the letter he alternately brandished in one hand and crumpled in both, and his subordinates felt the wording so obvious as to risk insult in spelling it out further for a man who commanded their very lives at his disposal. But Goering had momentarily spent his wrath. He cleared his throat, unwadded the page, and read it, aloud, again. It was brief and to the point.

A Soviet cruiser sat dead on the waters of the North Sea. It had been brought from the east coast of the Black Sea by Soviet sailors under the guns of a dozen Nazi soldiers. These soldiers were requesting a tow into the port at Wilhelmshaven.

Goering raised his eyes from the page to study the German soldier presented to him as living proof that the letter and its implausible suggestions were not a hoax. He had not questioned this one yet, had hardly acknowledged his presence. Unlike the cowering, bootlicking assistants who had brought him to Goering, this young man stood stoutly at attention and fearlessly returned the Reich Marshal's gaze from within dark, penetrating eyes that gave the impression they saw and understood far too much. Writhing inwardly under the soldier's equanimity, Goering returned to the letter.

There was an apparatus aboard the ship that was of tremendous military importance to the Soviet Union and, therefore, to Germany. How the soldiers arrived at this conclusion was not explained. They were, however and subsequently, requesting their message be forwarded to none other than *der Führer* himself, it being imperative, the letter insisted, that Adolf Hitler study the potential of this object personally. The soldiers desired to present the apparatus, the cruiser, and the Soviet prisoners to the *Wehrmacht* and then return to active duty.

From the rigid men before him, Goering had gleaned further detail. At dawn the Russian vessel had been spotted by a U-boat but not fired upon because it sported, of all things, a homemade swastika flag. German sailors had surrounded and boarded the cruiser. They listened to a brief explanation, took a letter from one *Hauptmann* Helmut Reiger, and then left the cruiser and its occupants under heavy guard, although in its disabled state, it wasn't likely to disappear. Uncertain how to handle the unique situation, *Kriegsmarine* officers had passed the letter around and up, each new recipient eager to unload the responsibility on the next until, at last, it deteriorated under the harsh treatment of the Reich's indignant second-in-command.

Goering had been advised of the incident by telephone and, scarcely believing it, delegated the situation to adjutants to determine the nature of the dilemma and resolve any related problems. This necessitated that the minions, who to a man had no intention of taking the Soviet millstone around their necks and drowning in the ensuing accountability, fly to Obersalzberg to personally deliver their account of the event and the letter. For irrefutable proof, they also brought a Nazi soldier from the cruiser – the young man who stood before him now, calmly awaiting questions or orders at Goering's pleasure, and who could provide explanation enough, should Goering give the soldier leave to tell his story.

At the moment, he simply was not in the mood to hear it.

Goering paced the length of his office, sweating uncomfortably beneath the layers of his uniform, his mood put to the worse by the untidiness of it all. His rant had demonstrated the shameful transparency of nervous procrastination, and the resulting embarrass-ment only increased his frustration. He paused as logic finally superseded displeasure: the cruiser wasn't going to go away without his personal intervention. The *Führer* had already found cause for contention with Goering. He would be livid if implications reached him that the Reich Marshal had neglected to respond appropriately and with haste to the discovery of a Soviet vessel in the North Sea.

Still ignoring the Nazi soldier, Goering quizzed the cringing messengers again about the alleged piece of unique equipment that the alleged *Hauptmann* Reiger had brought on the allegedly hijacked ship. While the sailors who boarded the cruiser and met with *Hauptmann* Reiger had been informed of its existence, only two officers made visual contact with the proof. It appeared to be some type of aircraft.

That cleared Goering's mind. As a World War I ace pilot and current commander of the *Luftwaffe*, he was automatically interested in any type of enemy aircraft. And if shielding Hitler from unnecessary interruptions at this stage of the war was paramount, keeping this particular message from him could be especially critical since the failure of the *Luftwaffe* to perform in accordance with Goering's promises was the very reason for Hitler's current annoyance with the Reich Marshal. Poor offensive judgment and inadequate defensive forces had undermined the integrity of the *Luftwaffe* and the reputation of its commander, destabilizing the close bond he had shared with Hitler for years. If the Soviets had managed to acquire an aircraft of superior quality, it would be in Goering's best interest to safeguard that information, and thus himself, from Hitler.

There was also the possibility that the whole arrangement was a lie. The deception of a ship flying an enemy flag in order to gain access to the enemy harbor and stage an attack was as old as sailing itself. *Hauptmann* Reiger might be nothing more than a duplicitous Soviet attempting to lead his crew into Wilhelmshaven and inflict a crippling blow to the port.

He would have to go and see. Goering crumpled the letter in frustration once more. He turned on the messengers and glared at them, at which they stiffened their flimsy spines and pretended away their apprehension. He ordered them to forget everything they had seen, heard, and shared with him about the matter as he dismissed them from his presence, confident in and repelled by their groveling obsequence. He went to the telephone to arrange for a surreptitious visit to the North Sea. Nazi soldiers or Soviet sailors, these men were lacking in political sense if they honestly believed they could convince him to bring a Soviet vessel into a German port, regardless of the circumstances. He couldn't trust anyone else to follow through with the assignment when he wasn't even certain what the assignment should be. Goering would go himself, quickly, and resolve the situation, quickly, and return, quickly. And he would personally escort the dark-eyed soldier back to his comrades on the cruiser.

Helmut Reiger had not for a moment believed that their *Führer* would acknowledge him personally. He was astonished when the Reich Marshal's appearance proved that the letter had made the desired impression more emphatically than he had dared to hope. Reiger conducted Goering and the men who accompanied him on a tour of the vessel, ending with a presentation of the unique craft that had traveled all the way from the Caucasus foothills. Goering was dumbfounded. His amazement and that of the men with him momentarily struck them all silent, and then Goering exploded into action. He evicted everyone from the immediate premises except for himself, Reiger, and Albrecht Gohritz, the young soldier of whom he had finally inquired a name, if nothing else. Goering minced warily about the craft and studied it from every angle, though he refused to touch it, all the while firing questions at Reiger, who had twice related the history of the thing as he knew it.

Reiger was beginning a third repetition in response to Goering's demands when the Reich Marshal interrupted him mid-sentence and walked out. Goering departed the Soviet vessel in favor of the ship that had carried him to it and retired alone to a cabin swiftly arranged for his private use to consider all that he had learned.

So it wasn't a lie. Reiger was a true Nazi, a captain, just as he had said. The dozen men under his command obviously held him in reverential respect. Though the Soviet cruiser had left the Black Sea coast with fewer by far than the usual complement of eight hundred and fifty men, the Nazis were still hopelessly outnumbered. By Reiger's account, he and his men had carried out what amounted to no less than a massacre of enemy forces during their first few days aboard the ship, losing only three of their own in the conquest. They left alive only enough Soviet sailors to conduct the ship to its destination. Ten weeks it had taken them to reach the North Sea, in the midst of a world war, when the seas and waterways were cluttered, embattled, and jealously guarded, when the Atlantic was thick with Allied convoys. They had, in effect, assigned themselves a suicide mission and accomplished the impossible. Goering wondered that these incredibly reckless, splendidly brave soldiers had achieved their goal at all. They were, all of them, a tremendous credit to the Reich. Too bad, Goering decided, they could never be honored for their accomplishments on behalf of Nazi Germany.

Goering was terrified of the ominous black craft

within the cruiser. That it was a mystery made it more extreme a threat. Horten should see the thing, Goering thought. Reimar Horten's passion was realizing his personal concept of a flying wing – an airplane consisting solely of a wing that would contain all systems required for its operation as well as room for passengers and cargo. Goering supported Horten's experiments and efforts toward bringing this concept into viable use. Now a detail vaguely teased from the outskirts of memory. Horten had shyly mentioned years ago that his obsession with flying wings began early in his childhood, when late one night he had witnessed such an object sail silently over his home and disappear into the southeastern horizon.

Goering swiftly set plans into motion. He needed a hiding place, and the Kohnstein mines near Nordhausen, currently undergoing expansion for use as a bomb factory, immediately came to mind. Yet here was another need for haste: if Dr. Wernher von Braun were to encounter this baffling object, he would doubtless be intrigued. As it was, manufacture of the V-1 buzz bombs and V-2 rockets was forever relegated to second priority beneath von Braun's ambitions of developing rockets for the purpose of space travel. Far from nourishing such idiosyncrasies, Goering had no use for grown men who wasted time on unrealistic whims when there was urgent work to be done. It would be a simple matter to ensure that Dr. von Braun stayed occupied with other pursuits for a few weeks.

At Goering's directive, the aircraft was transferred aboard a German ship to Wilhelmshaven, where it was removed under cover of darkness and transported across Germany amidst a military convoy to be hidden away in the tunnels of the Kohnstein Mountain. The Soviet crew, the Nazi soldiers, and the German sailors who assisted with its removal were incarcerated in cellars beneath the port city, purportedly for their own protection. Goering's original plan was to execute them all outright, but something in Reiger's demeanor made him feel small, and something in Gohritz's eyes made him feel exposed, and these insecurities made him want to punish both men and their companions for inestimable strength of character to which he could not begin to aspire.

There would be more, for he had sent German prisoners aboard the Soviet vessel under the direction of a Nazi crew to scuttle the cruiser and sink it beneath the waters on which it rested. Goering had ordered that the prisoners go down with the cruiser. The supervising crew would join the others in the cellars. Silence would reign over an event that, if never recorded, could never be proven to have happened. If rumor leaked from an unsecured source, a conspicuous absence of evidence would absolve Goering of responsibility.

The Reich Marshal costumed himself with care, put on his jewelry, and went to Berchtesgaden. A month sped by, lost in the business of celebrating Hitler's birthday, of consorting with those who sought his favor, of flaunting his wealth and vaunting his deeds and carefully reading the signs in order to avoid making a wrong turn deeper into the bad graces of the *Führer*. The war raged on in the distance of Goering's hazy perception, no longer a priority.

Successful air raids against Germany by the United States Air Force and the Royal Air Force were carried out in May, above and beyond what the *Luftwaffe* was capable of returning in the way of offense. Nor were there sufficient forces to provide an adequate defense. The devastating attacks and his increasing impotence as commander-in-chief of the *Luftwaffe* reminded Goering of a job he had not completed.

Counting noses in the stinking cellars was a task he assigned to a lackey, but once it was confirmed that the number of inmates corresponded with the number he had previously arrested, Goering arranged for their transfer. A guard brought requests and then demands from *Hauptmann* Reiger asking that Goering explain the grounds for their imprisonment, hasten their release, or at least make his reasoning known to them, but the Reich Marshal had no time for political prisoners. By the end of May the cellars had been emptied, washed down, and filled with the clutter of subordinate officers to whom Goering had offered the space for storage.

Hauptmann Reiger and his men were swiftly accused and convicted, without the formalities of testimony and trial, of treason in aiding the Soviet nation in bringing not only an armed cruiser but also a lethal weapon into the North Sea with intent to attack Germany at Wilhelmshaven. They and the Soviet crew who assisted in this maneuver were sentenced to spend the remainder of the war in a concentration camp among ethnic outcasts and other political prisoners. There were no legal proceedings and no records that might trace these men and their deeds back to Goering. Such details were neither a requirement nor a consideration for men who had been officially MIA for half a year.

Nor did Goering honor Reiger's request for a personal conference. He could handle neither another humiliating encounter with the brave, self-assured captain nor further scrutiny from the captain's dark-eyed comrade. Were it not for those very qualities possessed by these two men, Goering might have been so merciful as to condemn the lot of them to immediate execution before a firing squad. Instead, they were to be punished for his inadequacies. In a moment of distorted amity, he sent word to Reiger detailing the fate of the Soviet apparatus the captain had captured and brought home. He then sentenced them, with a convoluted mixture of satisfaction and vengeance, relief and regret, to Buchenwald.

The anomalous aircraft was sealed away behind a stone wall adjacent to one of the Khonstein tunnels. The slaves who completed the masonry work were promptly executed. With the craft thus entombed, the Soviet cruiser quiescent at the bottom of the North Sea, and the only men aware of its existence spirited away to concentration camps and graves, Goering regained some measure of peace to support his arrogant façade.

By late September of 1943, disease and starvation had eliminated half the survivors of Goering's self-protective measures. Before the month was out, a group of prisoners was rounded up for transport to the new work camp at Nordhausen. Among them were Helmut Reiger, Albrecht Gohritz, two of their Nazi comrades, and three of the Soviet sailors.

The German criminals assigned as straw bosses over the laborers carried out their duties with unrestrained cruelty. The valiant captain was the first of the transferred survivors to die when he stepped in to plead the case of one of his men who was being beaten mercilessly for collapsing under the weight of his load. The foreman suspended Helmut Reiger from a beam and laughed as one of the nation's anonymous heroes died of slow strangulation. Leaving the corpse hanging as a threat and an example, he then shot dead the soldier for whom Reiger had interceded.

The laborers struggled on with their duties, each hoping his death would transpire quickly and without the added suffering that accompanied the captain's dreadful fate.

April 1945

"Tell Gohritz our soldiers found his aircraft," Merrill said. "It will be taken to the United States for examination. Perhaps its origin and its purpose can be discovered, and what we know of its history can finally be recorded on behalf of Gohritz and his friends. We are in his debt. No one would have ever known it existed if not for him."

Walters led Merrill among the pallets at the field hospital to the side of Albrecht Gohritz. Merrill told the story that had been related to him by those who broke through the wall that concealed the aircraft. He spoke slowly, permitting Walters sufficient time to translate. Gohritz listened, still and lifeless but for the fire in those eyes.

Gohritz patted the shoulder of the man on the pallet beside him, shook him harder, gave an order that was not received. He turned pleading eyes to Walters and made a petition Merrill knew neither of them could fulfill. Walters fixed his gaze firmly on the toes of his boots and translated.

"This man was a Soviet naval officer, one of the hostages aboard the cruiser. Gohritz says the war made them enemies. Buchenwald made them friends. They have stayed together for the past two years. Learned enough of each other's language to communicate. Looked out for one another. Kept each other alive while everyone else around them was dying. This man became his best friend. Closer than a brother."

Merrill blinked hard, and his voice was gruff. "Tell Gohritz his friend is dead. It's time to let go of all this and go home to his family."

Gohritz spoke again, and Walters knelt beside him. The medic pulled the prisoner's wasted frame against his own substantial form and held him while the former Nazi soldier wept inconsolably. Gohritz spoke brokenly through his sobs, and Walters did his best to translate.

"His wife's mother defended her Jewish friends. Gohritz's whole family disappeared: his parents and in-laws, his wife and their infant son. When he demanded to know where they were, he was promised that if he did as he was told, he would one day be reunited with his wife and child. He believes they have long since been put to death. He has tried his best to be a good soldier and to do what was right for his country, and in return Nazi Germany has stripped him of all that made his life worth living. He has no home and no family to whom he can return."

Gohritz sagged against Walters' arms as the medic lowered him back onto the blanket. With tremendous effort, the German soldier extended his hand to the American sergeant. Merrill knelt beside him and took the withered hand in both his own and held it tight. Gohritz spoke softly.

"He says he is very grateful to you for believing his story and for locating the aircraft. It was important to him that someone know that this is the reason he and his comrades were brought here to die. He says perhaps you will learn its secrets and discover what made it more important than all their lives. He says it was good to make your acquaintance. He says thank you." Walters stood and walked away.

"I am privileged to have met you," Merrill whispered. The soldier relaxed his head against the soft comfort of the clean blanket as his eyes dimmed with long-awaited peace. Merrill clasped the former Nazi's hand as Albrecht Gohritz exhaled in relief and slipped quietly away.

Chapter One

I still clearly remember the details that caused us to be what and where we are. The beginning was instigated by an ending. Mama's sister died in Arizona, and we went to bury her and collect her things.

Daddy was a handsome man, tall and lean and tanned, with jet-black hair. He was home after a medical discharge from the United States Marine Corps. Mama was a petite brunette. Ben had her hazel eyes, but his hair was sandy red. Uncle John's hair and eyes were the color of autumn wheat, brown or gold, depending on the light. Aunt Mary was the real beauty, with black hair, blue eyes, and skin like porcelain. I was blonde and green-eyed then, different from the rest of my family. I thought I was pretty. Other people told me I was. My days were filled with such trivialities. I have learned since that very few things in a person's lifetime merit the importance they are accorded.

But such was my life for sixteen years. I felt a bit desperate then. I didn't want to just grow up and get married and have babies and get old and die. I wanted to do something special with my life, but couldn't decide what or where or how. The world was at war, and the present was so filled with work that little time was left to dream about the future. Then Aunt

Lucy died, and Uncle John asked if we would mind visiting Aunt Mary's family in Texas after Lucy's funeral in Arizona.

Daddy used to tell me that nothing ever stays the same. He was right, and he was wrong. Many aspects of life do evolve with time, but there exist immutable facts that no amount of desire will change. Certain actions, once committed, can not be taken back or erased. But I digress. The first domino was tipped at a decrepit little diner in New Mexico...

July 1945

The sun dropped out of sight behind the café, turning the ramshackle collection of boards into a quaint silhouette against a breathtaking canvas of violet, crimson, and fiery gold. Ray Davenport relaxed against the Chrysler and marveled that something so ugly could so swiftly be transformed into one of the most beautiful sights he had ever seen. He tilted his head in a barely discernible nod coupled with a brief glance skyward in deference to the Artist.

The pageant was interrupted by the rhythmic pounding of two boys charging around the building. One raced into the café while the other stampeded toward Ray and slid to a stop against the car, stirring an unwelcome dust. Ben met his father's steady gaze with a look of delighted self-reproach. Too old to be a child, too young to be a man, and too clumsy to walk the fence without forever toppling off one side or the other, he was at this particular moment in temporary regression triggered by the company of a younger friend.

He held out a cupped hand. "Look what Freddy

gave me!"

Ray studied the unique rock shaped like a teardrop and not a great deal larger. It was full and round at the bottom as though just ready to fall. Embedded crystals danced and glimmered in the fading light. Ray nodded appreciatively as he returned his son's treasure.

"Do you know what this is?" Ben rolled it around in his palm. "It's a Tear Stone! It's very rare. It has special powers, and it will bring me good luck for as long as I own it."

Ray chewed his toothpick and observed the coquettish twinkle of the evening's first star. "Why do you suppose Freddy would give away something so valuable?"

"Because," Ben defended. "Because..." He thought hard for a satisfactory answer. "Because he's my friend. That's why!"

Ray smiled toward the sky and tossed aside his toothpick. "Well, then, be careful not to lose it. Is Mama ready yet?"

"I don't know." Ben trotted toward the café. "I'll go see!"

The inside of the shack fulfilled the testimony of the exterior. Night air rose through gaps in planks pieced loosely together underfoot. Benches flanked an assortment of odd tables, and yellowed newsprint curled from the walls.

Sarah Davenport gingerly sampled a cup of coffee and found it unpleasantly potent. Her father had driven past nicer diners in more civilized areas, but the intimacy of this place felt appropriate, considering the reason her family was here. The lack of amenities did not detract from the warmth in the proprietors' smiles or the fact that the food, had her family been of a mind to enjoy it, was some of the best they had ever tasted. Sarah decided the place could not be more perfect, with one possible exception. She gave up on the coffee and turned her attention to her mother.

Belva sat quietly beside Sarah, stirring soup in silent circles. The vegetables had been churned to a dry lump surrounded by a moat of broth kept fluid by the traveling spoon. Her eyes were downcast, staring into the slow-motion chaos of grief. Sarah wished she could comfort her mother. It must be devastating to lose one's only sister. Sarah thought of Ben. At twelve years old he could be really irritating, and most of the time she just wanted him to leave her alone. But he was her brother, after all, and – she wrinkled her nose – she did love him in a way and it would, if she were honest, absolutely crush her to lose him. But Sarah and Ben were together every day. Belva had not seen Lucy for more than ten years. Sarah wondered what her mother missed so much.

The door burst open, and a boy galloped through. He plopped down on a bench beside the only other people in the café, an attractive older man and a plain, brown-haired woman young enough to be his daughter. The three exchanged quiet banter and a moment of laughter as they rose to leave.

Across the table from Sarah, Uncle John gulped the last of his coffee and winced at its bitterness. He winked at his wife, Mary, and gave her knee an affectionate squeeze. "I'm going out to the car with Ray. You ladies come on out when you're ready."

John nearly collided at the door with Ben, who flew past him to alight beside Mary. "Look what I have." Ben held out his hand to his mother. "Look!" he insisted as Belva stared into her bowl. "It's a Tear Stone. See?" Ben reached across the table and grasped Belva's wrist. He uncurled her fingers from around the spoon and laid the exquisite, glistening teardrop in her hand.

"Freddy gave it to me. He's my new friend. See, that used to be a real tear," Ben explained. "And guess how it turned into a rock." He looked eagerly at Sarah and Mary to make sure he had their attention before he continued.

"A long time ago there was a girl who got into trouble. Freddy said she was cursed after she ran away from her tribe in the mountains. Her family found her, but by then she had been turned to stone, and where she had cried, there were stone tears at her feet."

Ben pointed to the perfect teardrop lying on Belva's palm. "And that's one of them! Can you believe it?"

No, Sarah thought, but rather than burst his bubble, she asked, "Where did Freddy get it?"

Ben grew impatient. "I don't know where he got it! That's not the point! The point is, the girl was sorry she ran away, and so her tears were given special powers for anybody who found them."

"What kind of special powers?" Mary played along, lifting the delicate rock from Belva's hand.

"I don't know that, either. I haven't figured them out yet. I'm going to go ask Freddy. Daddy wants to know if you all are ready to go."

Belva rubbed her eyes. "We'll be right there."

Mary gave the stone to Sarah. "Pretty," Sarah said, and would have offered it back to her brother, but Ben had gone. Sarah sighed and dropped the rock into her purse.

Outside the darkness was almost complete. The evening was unpleasantly dusty and stale. Black clouds drifted overhead, eclipsing the stars. Ray and John stood by the Chrysler talking to the couple who had been inside the café.

As the women joined the group by the sedan, Ray drew them into the conversation. "This is my wife, Belva. There is John's wife, Mary, and that's my little girl, Sarah Jane."

"Daddy, I'm sixteen!" Sarah pleaded.

"Nice to meet you all," the man responded in a deep, pleasant voice. His handshake was firm, and a wide smile exposed perfect white teeth. "Clayton Pendleton," he announced. "My daughter, Christine, and my youngest son, Freddy."

Sarah smiled, imagining what he must have looked like when he was younger. With his salt-and-pepper hair, dark skin, and ice-blue eyes, Clayton was strikingly handsome. But Clayton had to be even older than her daddy, and Ray was forty-two.

They were talking about the car. "Five years old and in good condition," Ray said. "It belonged to Belva's sister, Lucy, in Tucson. Lucy passed away last week. The car is Belva's now. We're going to Texas to visit Mary's aunt, and then we'll drive home to Kentucky."

"Where in Texas are you headed?" Clayton asked.

"Up near Amarillo," John answered.

"We're crossing the desert, too," Clayton began, but Freddy enthusiastically interrupted.

"My dad is a world-famous hunter! But he catches animals alive. He's hunted everything there is to hunt, and people call him from all over the world to come and hunt with them, don't they, Dad!"

Clayton laughed softly and shook his head. "Oh, no," he informed the Davenports. "Not hardly. I'm working for a California company that provides reptiles for picture shows, carnivals, and laboratory studies. They want desert rattlesnakes, and New Mexico is a sure place to find them. Besides, I've been meaning to visit old friends in the area.

"I had to make a small detour to pick up Freddy." He tousled the boy's hair. "He and his mother live in California, too, but she finds it convenient to take a trip every year about the time I'm supposed to get Freddy for our two weeks together.

"Christine's a school teacher. She lives in Nevada. My other son, Michael, is going to meet us in Carrizozo. It will be a family reunion for us. I don't get to see my kids very often, and having all three of them together at once is a real treat."

"July is the perfect time," Christine added. "School is out, and I was able to leave my volunteer duties for a few days."

"Since we'll be going the same direction for a while, it would be nice if we could travel together." Clayton nodded toward an eleven-year-old Ford pickup that had seen better days. "It belongs to the company, so it's a free ride, but I worry that it'll fall apart before I get the job done and get home. I know my way around New Mexico pretty well. I'd be glad to lead the way. We could stay together until Carrizozo, and then your family could continue on to Texas."

Ben was immediately at Ray's side. "Can I ride with Freddy? I promise I'll behave! Please?"

Ray heard Clayton fielding the same request from Freddy. "The problem I see is that Clayton's truck only has room for three people. If you go with Freddy and Clayton, where's Christine supposed to sit?"

"She could ride with us, Daddy," Sarah suggested shyly.

Clayton nodded. "That's fine with me, if you're sure you don't mind."

Ray gave Ben a look.

"I'll be good, Daddy, I promise!" He and Freddy raced to Clayton's truck. John and Mary climbed into the front of the Chrysler with Ray while Belva, Sarah, and Christine arranged themselves in the back.

Thunderstorms made driving a challenge through the night. Clayton and Ray pulled over several times to wait out a series of downpours. The weather and the limitations of the rattletrap truck made for tedious progress. Clayton didn't stay with the main highway, but led them on a meandering trail of less traveled roads, some that were little more than rutted lanes, causing Ray to wonder if following Clayton Pendleton might have been a mistake. The women kept up a steady stream of conversation for the first couple of hours before drifting off to sleep, leaving Ray and John to the tense and unsettling journey.

Just after four o'clock the Ford coughed, exhaled wearily, and coasted to a stop. Ray eased the Chrysler to the side of the road. He and John stepped out into the dampness and joined Clayton in front of the truck, where steam poured from under the hood and fluttered away in the darkness. Clayton rammed his hands into his pockets and stared in resignation for an endless moment as the predicament sank in. He produced a wry smile as he turned to Ray and John.

"Well, thanks for sticking with me this far. Just stay

on this road. Eventually you'll drive into Carrizozo. From there you can get back onto the main roads." He held out a hand, palm up. "At least it has stopped raining."

"We aren't going to drive off and leave you and your family," John objected. "Not out here in the dark in the middle of nowhere."

"I was going to ask a favor," Clayton said. "There's a woman near Carrizozo who rents rooms out of her house. Her name is Sandra Crowe. That's where we're going to stay, and Christine told Michael to meet us there. If you'd stop by the place and leave a message for Michael, I sure would appreciate it. He can come and get us, and we'll see if we can get ol' Pounce running again." He grimly patted the truck's fender.

"How would we tell him where to find you?" John peered out into the darkness. "There's nothing here!"

Clayton spread his arms theatrically toward the great wide open. "Welcome to the Jornada del Muerto! The Journey of the Dead Man." The hairs on the back of Ray's neck stood uncomfortably at attention, but Clayton shrugged off the prophecy. "Not much to see, but interesting if you've never been here. The Camino Real, one of the three great trails of the American West, stretched from Santa Fe to Mexico City. Ninety miles of it led across this desert. Settlers found nothing but sand, lava rock, and sun. There was no water, no shade in which to rest. Many people died attempting to cross this desert during the seventeenth and eighteenth centuries, thus the name."

The women emerged from the car, curious about the delay.

"That doesn't look good," Christine observed,

47

watching wisps of steam waft from beneath the truck's hood.

"It isn't, sweetheart." Clayton sighed. "Sorry about all the problems. This isn't exactly the vacation I promised you kids."

"That's all right, Dad." Christine linked her arm through his. "It's enough to just be a family for a while."

At Clayton's nod of permission, Freddy burst from the cab of the pickup, followed by a bleary-eyed Ben.

"Gosh!" Freddy exclaimed. "The truck's tore up! Are you going to fix it, Dad?" He turned to the others. "My dad can fix anything! Wherever he goes, people bring stuff to him to fix, don't they, Dad!"

Clayton shook his head slowly, staring into Freddy's face until the boy turned away and boxed playfully at Ben. "No." Clayton answered everyone but his son. "I don't fix things. I've never understood mechanical contraptions. I know more about catching rattlesnakes in the desert than I do about fixing whatever's wrong with Pounce." He gave a short laugh and bounced a look off Ray. "And that's not saying much." Clayton walked to the other side of the truck and stared off into the night.

"Hey, let's explore!" Freddy urged, but a word from his father cut his flight short.

"Just wind down a little," Clayton ordered. "It's at least another hour 'til daylight. It'll take longer than that for the Davenports to drive to Carrizozo and leave a message for Michael to come get us, and I'm quite certain that nobody is going to drive by and find us before then. We'll stay right where we are. You can play here around the truck."

"We're not leaving your family out here," Ray

stated. "And all of us won't fit in the car. I wouldn't mind driving into Carrizozo myself, but I don't want to leave everybody else stranded while it's still dark. We don't even know exactly where we are. We'll stay put until the sun comes up, and then we'll take a look at the truck and decide what needs to be done."

Yawning and stretching lapsed into peaceful silence interrupted only by the restless fidgeting of the two youngest members of the group.

"Maybe we could walk for a while." Belva's suggestion startled them all.

Mary agreed. "The boys could burn up some of that energy, and a walk would be a good way to wake up so early on a Monday morning."

Ray was too relieved to hear his wife volunteer a comment to argue. He unlocked the trunk. Mary tossed her handbag inside and shook out her mint green sweater. Belva reached for her blue one, pausing to caress the patterns of a quilt before walking away with Mary.

Ray stared at the contents of the trunk. All of Lucy's personal effects were contained in a suitcase and two cardboard boxes, tangible memories guarded by the wraith of Belva's grief. Atop one of the boxes, in lieu of a lid, lay the quilt. It was one of many that Ray's mother-in-law had stitched by hand and bequeathed to her children when she died. Belva's were stored in a cedar chest. Ray wondered what Lucy had done with her inheritance and if she had chosen to keep this particular quilt for a special reason or if it was simply the only one she hadn't discarded or lost along her restless, winding way.

Ray picked up a flashlight and handed a second to

John before closing the trunk and pocketing the keys. He and John returned to the truck, where Clayton kept a wary eye on the boys. They set off into the desert a short distance behind Belva and Mary. Freddy and Ben ran as far ahead as the adults would allow.

As she walked across the unfamiliar terrain, Sarah tried to remember her mother's sister. She had been six and Ben only two years old the last time any of them saw Lucy. Sarah remembered a slim, vivacious woman with dark shiny hair, big doe eyes, and a wide smile. Lucy smelled like strawberries and laughed as though everything were an absolute delight. She brought gifts for people she didn't even know. Sarah's was a little glass figurine, milky white, of a lady in mid-curtsey. Lucy had blown in on a Friday morning for three days of joyous turmoil and whisked away the following Sunday afternoon.

Belva had cried when Lucy arrived and was silent for days after she left. The following years brought sporadic reminders of Lucy's existence via birthday cards, letters at Christmas, and wedding announcements from various addresses in different states. Lucy never found the answer that would have completed her incessant metamorphosis. A chameleon, Belva used to say, in continual transformation. A butterfly, Sarah thought, flitting from one temptation to the next in determined celebration of the sadly short life with which she had been gifted.

Now Lucy was dead at thirty-five years old. The apartment manager told them Lucy had been drinking a lot. The doctor said her heart just stopped. How, Sarah wondered, does one's heart just stop? Surely it can't decide to quit all by itself. There has to be a reason.

"Penny for your thoughts," Christine offered.

Sarah smiled and held out her hand.

Christine laid a nickel on her palm. "I don't actually have a penny," she said with mock seriousness. "You can owe me four more thoughts."

"I was just thinking about Mama's sister." Sarah glanced covertly over her shoulder. "I'm trying to understand how Mama feels and why it hurts her so much that Aunt Lucy died. I know Lucy was family, but we hadn't even talked to her for more than ten years. Mama acts like she's lost her best friend in the whole world."

"Perhaps she has, in a way," Christine said. "Growing up together, she and Lucy knew things about each other that nobody else could have known. Like my brother and me. We've only spent a few days together since he was seventeen and I was fifteen, but I still love him and take comfort in knowing he's out there somewhere."

Sarah thought about that. She guessed it made sense. But now Christine had sparked her interest in the Pendleton family. "Are you married?"

"No." Christine smiled wistfully. "Guess I haven't met the right man yet. Or maybe I haven't taken the time to try. I've stayed pretty busy most of my life."

"Do you live with your mother?"

"I've been on my own since I was sixteen." Christine glanced back as Sarah had done. "Mother and Dad weren't exactly a match made in Heaven. Mother was timid and painfully insecure. Dad was charming and handsome and romantic – and still is – but he traveled a lot and never held a job for very long. He didn't keep in touch with us when he was away. He didn't send us enough money, even though he knew Mother couldn't provide for us, because she didn't have the courage to go out and get a job. Dad left for good right after I turned twelve years old. He had a girlfriend in California. He married her and they had Freddy.

"But Michael, my older brother, is so talented! He can sing and dance, he can design and build anything, and he's devastatingly handsome, just like Dad. Michael left us when he was seventeen. And he's been just like Dad ever since, except he hasn't married yet. All that talent and potential, thrown to the wind." Christine shook her head sadly.

"After Mother remarried and moved out, I cleaned people's houses after school to earn money for food and rent. Several weeks before graduation, one of my teachers recommended me to a scholarship committee. I went to college on that scholarship and became a teacher myself."

"You have a lot to be proud of," Sarah said. "I'm sixteen, and I can't imagine having to live alone and take care of myself right now."

"You could if you had to," Christine assured her. "And you'd do just fine. Struggles really do make you stronger."

Far behind them, Christine's father was becoming acquainted with Ray and John. Clayton indicated Ray's left arm. "What happened, if you don't mind my asking?"

"Peleliu." Ray answered as if the word provided explanation enough, but Clayton shook his head.

"Never heard of it."

"Most of the world probably never will." Ray stared straight ahead into the past. "It's an island in the

Pacific. About two miles wide, maybe six miles long. Coral and caves. A handful of bloody ridges. Hotter than any furnace. I can't imagine Hell being worse.

"My buddies and I were on the beach one evening last October. A Zero flew in low, strafing the ground. I lay still until the bullets stopped coming, until the sound of that engine faded completely away. I should have been dead. They wrapped me up and sent me to a hospital ship. Told me they were going to amputate my arm above the elbow. I said okay. An arm ain't nothing. My buddy lost his life. I lay there and stared at his empty eyes while they scraped up my arm. He had twin babies at home he never got to see. I'd been grousing because that day was my daughter's birthday, and I wasn't home to share it. All of a sudden missing a birthday wasn't a big deal. God willing, I'd be home later to see my family every day.

"When I woke up after surgery, the arm was still there. They had to fuse the bones at the elbow because the joint was shattered and most of it was left behind on the beach. My arm healed at a ninety-degree bend. Doc said the hand would be useless, but he was wrong about that. I'll never stretch my arm out, but my left hand works pretty good. I can grip things."

Ray stopped abruptly and stared at the sky. "Y'all hear that?"

"A plane," John said. "It's just an airplane. That's all." John gave Ray's shoulder a reassuring nudge.

"Two of them," Ray said uneasily. "Can't see their navigation lights for all the clouds." He followed apprehensively as his brother continued walking.

"Did you go, too?" Clayton asked John.

John shook his head. "I went to France in 1918,

when I was nineteen years old. Spent two years with the Civilian Conservation Corps in the thirties. This time around, all my service is close to home. My farm connects with Ray's. Belva and Mary look after each other, but Mary has gone through some rough spells with her heart, and I feel that I should be with her. We have a daughter, but Callie is going to college and working part time. Mary and I didn't want her to sacrifice building her future in order to stay home with us. Responsibilities that come with taking care of a family will land on her shoulders soon enough. What about you?"

Clayton looked away. "Four-F. Heart murmur. I'm forty-nine now, but my health kept me out of the military when I was young enough to join."

"People are needed just as badly on the home front in countless ways," John said. "Belva's been doing factory work. Mary tends our garden and organizes drives for everything from scrap metal to silk stockings. The kids have participated in efforts to sell bonds. There's so much to be done."

"Yes," Clayton said. "There sure is. I've held several jobs since the war started. I like to do different things. Like you said – there's so much to be done."

A short distance ahead, Mary stopped and peered at her watch. "It's five-thirty," she told Belva. "We've covered quite a distance, and I'm getting thirsty. Before we left the diner I filled our thermos with water, but I left it in the car. Let's round everyone up and head back."

"Sarah! Ben!" Belva called out to her children. Turning back to the approaching men, she reached out a hand to her husband. "Ray…"

The world erupted without warning. Blinding light and searing heat instantaneously magnified as a concussion rocked the earth and tumbled her occupants like chaff in a gale. Ray's last thought was for his wife as Belva was swept helplessly away with the blast. Ray collapsed and was propelled along, blindly writhing in agony at being skinned alive. Frying without the benefit of death, he protested with manic screams of horror and disbelief while the world ruptured ablaze, incinerating his life and a desert realm that lay, expendable, in the line of fire.

Chapter Two

◆•▸◑•✵•◐•◂◆

Robert Lake eased through the intersection and pointed the DeSoto toward the state line. A glance in the back seat assured him that his two little girls were sleeping at last. Their mother sat beside them staring out at the passing scenery, but Robert knew she wasn't admiring the landscape. Bitter resignation clouded Joy's beautiful features. She was angry because of something Robert had done, and Robert was miserable because he had done it.

"Are we there yet?" Kenneth joked, and Robert laughed along with the seventeen-year-old who was half the problem. The other half was Kenneth's best friend, Dave Hensley. No, they weren't the problem. Robert sighed ruefully. *He* was the problem, because he had invited them on this trip without consideration for his wife and her family. 'Fess up, old boy. You really blew it this time. He raised his eyes again to the rearview mirror.

Joy's expression had not changed. Robert glared to himself as he contemplated a bonfire comprised of camera equipment, but he had to admit that a shred of his anger was also directed at Joy. She hadn't exactly been a picnic lately. She never spoke to him anymore except to make him aware of his myriad shortcomings in excruciating detail. Was it any wonder that he chose to spend his precious little personal time on photography? It was certainly more pleasant than the reception waiting at home.

"Pass him, then," Kenneth suggested, leaning away from Robert's stormy expression.

"What? Oh." Robert realized he was tailgating an elderly man who was obviously in no hurry to reach his destination.

"Be careful," Dave warned. "He's taking the whole road."

The boys waved as Robert sped past the old gentleman in his impeccable Packard.

"This is exciting. I've never been to New Mexico," Dave said out the window.

"I bet we get swell pictures of the desert," Kenneth said. "I'm going to send some to Dad."

Dave was more apt to take apart and reassemble the camera than to avail himself of its intended purpose. But he also liked the idea of mailing pictures to his father, so he agreed with Kenneth. "That would be keen. I wonder what Dad's doing right now."

Robert smiled sadly at the ensuing conjectures. The boys' fathers had been sent in opposite directions to fight for their country. Kenneth's dad had crossed the Atlantic, though cryptic letters were careful not to betray his exact location. Dave's father had joined the battle in the Pacific. The separation and uncertainty were harder on both boys than they would ever admit.

Though only thirty-two, Robert received a defer-ment from the draft because his work at the factory was vital to the war effort. In addition to putting in as many as sixty hours there each week, Robert worked as a freelance photographer when he could find the time. Photography was also Kenneth's hobby, and it became common for Robert to invite the young man and his best friend along on outings that might include a chance to take pictures.

When Joy requested a trip to New Mexico to visit her family, Robert scheduled a week off work. He felt it would do them both good to get away. A vacation would benefit the girls, too. The time he spent with his family had dwindled from hours to minutes each day, until entire weeks went by in which he barely spoke with his children. Since last Christmas he had experienced a similar relationship with his wife. On those rare occasions when he had the time and wanted to talk, Joy would respond with succinct answers directed at the nearest wall. Tension descended like winter clouds, darkening their days and chilling the fragile remnants of a once-passionate love. The further Joy withdrew, the more Robert avoided contact, and the more reticent he became, the further his wife withdrew.

Joy had opened up a little when she learned Robert really was going to take her to see her family. One of her sisters was pregnant for the first time and nearing her due date. She might even give birth during their visit. Joy and Robert had talked about that, enjoyed their first real conversation in months that was actually *about* something, and then...

And then, this very morning, their lights and predawn preparations attracted Kenneth's attention. As Robert stowed his camera and a couple of suitcases in the car, Kenneth crossed the driveway between their houses to ask where he was going. Robert still wasn't sure exactly how it suddenly came about that Kenneth and Dave were accompanying his family to New Mexico, but he winced as he remembered the expression on Joy's face when she came to the car and saw what was taking place. She didn't say a word. She simply retrieved her handbag from the front seat and climbed into the back with the girls. And the split-second, smoldering look that passed from her eyes to Robert's was a lesson in hurt and anger he would not soon forget.

The girls were also unhappy with the situation. Elisabeth shot him a reproachful look. Catherine smirked and turned away in disgust. Yep, he had really messed up this time. And it wasn't over yet. Joy's parents had never been fond of Robert, and now he was bringing two strangers for them to accommodate on a family visit. The boys had brought bedrolls so they could sleep on the screened porch, and Robert knew they wouldn't cause any trouble. Joy's mother might handle the situation politely, but her father – Robert shuddered.

Movement from behind caught his attention as Joy lay back and closed her eyes. As she drifted off, the lines of frustration and disappointment faded, and her face softened until she looked as she had when they first met. Back then her ardor and innocence had awakened his innermost desires. She could still make him feel things no other woman ever had, even now when she was desperately unhappy with him. Robert's grip on the wheel tightened as he tried to remember the loss of their love.

Joy was a stunning, raven-haired beauty when she married her knight in shining armor, a striking young man with golden hair and eyes as clear as the October sky. Robert knew she saw him as a hero who would bring to fruition her every dream when he swept her away from rural life to the big city, where an endless variety of breathtaking events would keep her happy ever after. Robert had tried hard, perhaps too hard, to make her dreams come true. Despite the brutal economy, he had bought her a nice house in a nice neighborhood and a car. He worked long hours to pay the bills and to keep his wife well dressed and entertained. Catherine was born after their first anniversary. Elisabeth came two years later. Things had gone well for them right up until the war.

Now, thirteen years and twenty pounds later, a bitter Cinderella lamented her tarnished dreams as her knight spent more time at the factory or in the company of his young friends than with her and their daughters. Joy discovered retaliation in the use of silence and a contrived peace in shutting her mind against the war, against her marital problems, against her rebellious children. The gulf between Robert and Joy widened every day. It was killing Joy's love for Robert. It was breaking Robert's heart.

Catherine and Elisabeth awoke and bickered in the back seat until Catherine was enraged and Elisabeth was in tears. Their tantrums woke Joy, but she made no move to discipline her daughters or assuage their anger. The girls sulked in petulant silence when Robert considered aloud the merits of stopping the car and removing his belt.

Thus was the journey accomplished and, early in the evening, the destination achieved. Robert parked the car in front of his in-laws' home. The house was small and had only recently been equipped with electricity and indoor plumbing, but it was comfortable and well kept.

Robert stepped out of the car and indulged in a luxurious stretch. Kenneth and Dave followed suit, while the girls raced to the porch and argued over who had touched it first.

Joy emerged from the car slowly until her mother appeared at the door. Then she fairly flew to the house and flung herself into her mother's arms. Robert and the boys ascended the steps to the porch as Joy's father strode out of the house.

Folks knew Joy's father as Sonny. The word was more amiable than the man. Robert held out his hand despite the blatant animosity that he knew from experience would reward his efforts. Small black eyes snapped disapproval as Sonny deigned Robert a short jerk of a handshake before turning to his youngest daughter. Joy slipped out of her mother's arms and laid her head on Sonny's shoulder. For her, he gave his best effort to forming a smile. He held the grimace a moment longer for the benefit of his granddaughters and concluded with a dismissive observation of Kenneth and Dave as he stalked back into the house.

Robert felt the sting of censure and resentment. Though Sonny's wife was a white woman, he desired that their daughters marry local men of his choosing, sons-in-law who each boasted some strain of Navajo blood. Four of the five girls complied. Joy alone had married a stranger. Robert was regarded as an intruder and a thief, for he had taken Joy so far away that her family only saw her once a year. Though it had been Joy's idea to elope, Sonny felt his daughter was too naïve to be held responsible. He blamed Robert instead for taking advantage of a girl who was too young to make decisions that would accomplish her best interests.

"And who are your friends?" Joy's mother wanted to know. She held her hands out to Kenneth and Dave. Robert breathed a sigh of relief and tried to ignore Joy's piercing gaze as his wife and daughters followed Sonny inside.

"Kenneth Rhodes, Dave Hensley," Robert indicated. "Boys, say hello to Joy's mother, Jessamin. There isn't a finer lady on the planet." Robert hoped that was true. Though Joy and her mother were forever and bitterly at odds, Jess had always treated him fairly.

"Except maybe for Joy," Kenneth interjected, earning a patronizing smile from Jess.

"Kenneth is our neighbor, and Dave is his best friend," Robert explained. "Kenneth is going to enlist as soon as we get back to Utah. We're proud of him, but we'll really miss him."

Jess nodded soberly. "You heard, did you, Robert, that Eddie was killed?"

Robert had not heard. He carefully voided his face of expression. Jess nodded again and raised her hands to her cheeks in exaggerated woe. "This war," she moaned. "It's taking the best of our men. Who will be left to us when it is over?" She stepped around Robert and pulled open the screened door.

Robert ushered the boys ahead, pausing for a gulp of fresh air before catching up. No, Joy had not told him that Eddie was dead. How did it make Sonny and Jess feel to know that, had Joy gone along with their plans, their daughter would now be a widow? Would they rather she be Eddie's widow than Robert's wife? And what about Joy, he unwillingly continued as he stepped into the living room. After thirteen years as Mrs. Robert Lake, would Joy prefer to be Eddie's widow right now?

Robert was suddenly afraid that his marriage might be in far worse trouble than he had allowed himself to consider.

Evening drifted slowly into nightfall. Sisters and brothers-in-law came and went with multitudes of children. They were all delighted to have Joy home again, and Robert was relieved to see her transform into the happy, animated woman he knew and loved, though she ignored him completely. Various family members extended Robert the obligatory greetings, beyond which he was excluded from the catch-ups and remember-whens, an outsider to the point that Joy's sister neglected to set a place for him at supper. Joy blushed furiously with embarrassment as she tried to remedy the situation with as little commotion as possible, rising from her chair and handing Robert a plate instead of arranging a place for him among the others at the table.

As the family began passing bowls without making room for him and the boys to reach between them, Robert quietly set the plate beside the sink and led Kenneth and Dave out to the DeSoto. He drove to a small diner near Carrizozo, where they silently consumed soup and sandwiches. Upon their return, the boys went for a walk. Robert sat alone on the front porch until darkness fell before walking through the group of men in the living room, past the crowd of women in the kitchen, and down the short hallway to the room he and Joy would share. When he heard the guests departing, he slipped out the back door and washed up at the pump behind the house. It didn't take long, but by the time he returned Joy was sitting on their bed brushing her glossy black hair, and Catherine and Elisabeth were rolled in blankets on the floor.

"The girls always sleep in the living room when we visit," he gently reminded his wife.

Joy did not look up. She continued brushing. Her answer was quick and rehearsed and devoid of emotion. "They will sleep with me tonight. You can sleep on the back porch with your friends."

He gazed at her for a moment, loving her, aching for her, wondering if she felt anything for him at all. When it became obvious there was nothing more to say, Robert knelt beside the blankets on the floor and kissed his daughters goodnight. Catherine shrugged away, but Elisabeth hugged him fiercely. She studied him with large, grave replicas of his own eyes, pleading for everything to be made right. She was scared, and Robert wished he could console her. But he was scared, too.

At the door he remembered, "I don't have a blanket or a pillow."

Joy turned her back as she laid her brush on the nightstand. "Guess you should have brought a bedroll." She blew out one of the oil lamps her family still used despite the luxury of light switches, and darkness enveloped the room. Robert pulled the door closed on the three most important people in his life and made his way toward the back porch.

Jess was wiping a few remaining crumbs from the kitchen table. She looked up as he passed. "G'night, Robert."

Robert lifted his hand in a brief wave and kept walking.

"Robert, wait." Jess stepped out the front door and returned with a tattered quilt. "Here." She grinned. "You might need something to keep you warm before the night's over."

Robert stared at her incredulously as the hateful truth settled sour into the pit of his stomach. He was fully aware that Joy's whole family deemed him a nonentity, but he had considered Jess a friend. Her betrayal cut viciously deep as her features revealed the deception that mocked his trust. He took the quilt and strode out the back door.

Kenneth and Dave were laying out their bedrolls. "Hey, boss." Kenneth smiled cautiously.

"Hey, fellas," Robert bantered. "Got room for an old hound dog to bed down for the night?" He pushed open the screen door, leaned back, and hurled the quilt as far as he could across the back yard, knowing it would be found there in the morning and hoping his action would provoke a response.

Kenneth and Dave exchanged serious glances. Robert had been treated shamefully all evening, but who would stoop so low as to offer him a filthy quilt on which a mangy old dog had recently died?

Dave peeled apart his bedding, and Kenneth followed his example. By the time Robert latched the door and turned around, the two young men had laid out blankets for him to sleep on and under and had rolled their extra blue jeans together for a pillow.

Robert tried to smile and failed miserably. "Thanks, fellas." He lay down and closed his eyes and pretended to sleep through the long, lonely night.

That first day established the pattern for those that followed, though Robert gained two more allies. If Joy had no time for Robert, she also made it clear that she had no time for their children. Left to their own devices, the girls gravitated to their father, who was overjoyed at the opportunity to reestablish a relationship with them.

He and his daughters, along with Kenneth and Dave, went for long walks in the desert, took photographs, and played games in the yard.

Robert contemplated Catherine and Elisabeth with rapt amazement as they played. Both had been graced with his golden hair and intense blue eyes which, set against their mother's smooth, dark skin, made for two extraordinarily beautiful girls.

At twelve years of age, Catherine was already a knockout. She learned early how to get her way, to talk herself into or out of any desired situation, and to project the illusion that she was better than her peers. She was already developing a figure. More than once Robert had seen grown men ogling Catherine. He dreaded the future, for Catherine would soon be both old enough to choose among her many male admirers and crafty enough to have her way with them without getting caught. But for now Catherine was still a child, though a bitterly rebellious one, patronizing and sarcastic in response to the absence of her father and the silence of her mother.

It was physically obvious that ten-year-old Elisabeth was Catherine's sister, but the resemblance ended there. Elisabeth was a petite girl, quiet and patient, who never drew attention to herself if she could help it. Her behavior rarely earned a reprimand. When it did, punishment usually had the desired effect on her. She was thoughtful and compassionate, serious and deep.

And both girls were very intelligent, Robert bragged to himself. But if life were a theatrical production, Catherine would be the leading lady while Elisabeth coordinated details behind the scenes.

He watched Kenneth and Dave closely in the presence of his daughters and was pleased with the big-brother roles they automatically assumed. Forgetting their initial resentment, the girls enjoyed the extra attention as well. By the end of the week, the five of them had become their own little family of outcasts, enjoying their vacation in spite of constant rebuff by Joy's aloof relatives.

Try as he may, Robert failed every attempt at communicating with his wife. Half the time he didn't know where she was, and in her parents' home she was constantly surrounded by family members who took it upon themselves to throw obstacles across the emotional miles that already separated Joy from her husband. Robert endured the separation because he knew it would be short lived. He would work on his relationship with Joy when they returned home.

He welcomed the long-awaited arrival of Sunday night. In the morning he and his family would drive back to Utah, and he would have all of Tuesday to spend with them before returning to the factory on Wednesday. He could hardly wait to be alone with his wife again. He wanted to hold her, hold her and stroke her back and smell her hair and feel her breath warm on his neck, and there was so much he wanted to say.

Robert went into the room Joy shared with their daughters to get a fresh shirt from the suitcase. He knelt and kissed Catherine and Elisabeth, who were already asleep. He rose from the floor and watched Joy, unapproachable as ever as she sat on the bed briskly brushing her hair. He tried to think of something to say.

"We'll leave right after breakfast in the morning," he ventured. "That way we can make it back by dark. I'll even stop somewhere and buy us dinner before we get home, so you won't have to cook that late…"

He trailed off and stood awkwardly across the room from his wife. Joy had stopped brushing her hair and was staring straight ahead at the opposite wall. Robert studied her profile in the dim light and felt hope receding as nausea teased through his bowels. There was no emotion on Joy's face and none in her voice when she spoke.

"I won't be going with you." She resumed brushing, slowly and deliberately.

"You…but…" Robert stammered.

"The girls will be fine. They can stay at your mother's while you work, or you can find a housekeeper. Or – " She gave a sharp, coarse laugh. " – maybe Kenneth can take care of them for you."

Robert went weak when he realized his wife was not only leaving him, but was also walking away from their children.

"Why are you doing this? If you're mad at me, fine, I understand. I deserve it. But how can you do this to them?" He pointed at the blankets snuggled on the floor.

"As long as their needs are met, they aren't going to care anything about who makes the sacrifice," Joy retorted. "And I'm tired of making that sacrifice, for them and for you!" There were tears in her eyes as she flung the brush down on the bed. "Here I have people who love me, who enjoy being with me. My sisters care about who I am and how I feel. In Utah all I have are two kids who couldn't care less about me as long as they get what they want. And I guess I have a husband, although you'd never know it because he's been at work constantly since…"

Robert allowed the silence to build while he studied the scuffs on his shoes. He looked up at Joy, watched her sob angrily as she examined her hairbrush. His voice was soft and level and strong.

"Joy, you and I do not have a single problem that could not be solved with a little effort on both our parts. Weaker marriages than ours have survived stronger storms than this. I know it must have been nice for you to be the center of attention for a week, to lay down all your responsibilities for a few days. But that's not real life, and it won't last forever, no matter where you are or who you're with.

"Just because I'm not able to spend a lot of time with our daughters doesn't mean you can't take them places, do things with them, enjoy their company. They need to know that you care about them and want to be a part of their lives. As for my job, you're right. I have been working from dawn to dusk six days a week, ever since the war started. But at least you know where I am. At least I am able to come home to you every night, and you don't have to panic with fear that I have been killed in a foreign country every time you see someone delivering a telegram on our street.

"I love you, Joy. I know I'm not perfect. There are things I need to change, and I'm willing to do that if it will bring us closer together. But I can't change what's going on in your heart and your head right now, because a lot of that doesn't have anything to do with me. Some circumstances are beyond our control, Joy. But I didn't set out to make your life miserable. I never intended that we should have to spend so much time apart. I didn't bring you to New Mexico for a week so your family could treat me like a criminal and destroy what was left of our marriage.

"And I didn't start the war against our country. Or against you."

Robert stepped out of the room and quietly pulled the door closed. Joy continued to cry into her hairbrush. Catherine and Elisabeth opened their eyes as soon as their father had gone and searched each other's faces for a solution to a problem they didn't understand.

Robert reached the back porch, curled up against his makeshift pillow, and pulled the blanket up over his head. Kenneth and Dave studied their friend's back as it heaved under the weight of muffled sobs. At a loss for how to respond, they shared a silent prayer for him and tried to sleep.

Robert, sickened and stunned at Joy's rejection, was eventually lulled to sleep by a chain of thunderstorms. Peace eluded him even then, for his dreams wove intricate dramas that were equal parts desperation and terror, suggesting resolutions to his dilemma that were more horrifying than the problem itself.

While being devoured by a particularly hungry nightmare, Robert felt hands on his shoulders and heard Joy crying out his name. In those nebulous waking moments, he looked into her face and thought he was still dreaming. She backed away as he sat up, and he saw that she was genuinely upset.

"What is it, darling? What's wrong?"

"The girls!" Joy was trembling. "Robert, they're gone! I found a note on the kitchen table. It's from Catherine." She thrust a scrap of paper into his hand. Robert clicked on a flashlight and scanned the brief message.

By now Kenneth and Dave were fully awake.

"What's wrong, boss?" Kenneth asked.

Robert turned to his friends, frightened and angry. "Catherine and Elisabeth have run away." He reached for his shoes.

"Run away! But why?" Dave wondered as he and Kenneth buttoned their shirts. "We're going home in the morning."

Robert looked at Joy, who looked away. He consulted his watch. "It's four o'clock. We don't know how long they've been gone, but I can't see them getting very far. It's a black night, stormy and wet, not exactly ideal traveling conditions for two children on foot. Let's just check around the house first."

A thorough search of the house, vehicles, and shed revealed only that the girls had taken their sweaters and a sack of bread and cheese. Back in the living room, Robert made more extensive plans.

"We'll check with your sisters," he told Joy. "They live close enough that the girls might have gone to them."

Joy looked miserably at the floor. "They couldn't have. I never took them with me when I visited. I always left them with you." She raised pleading eyes to her husband. "They don't know where any of my sisters live." Tears rolled slowly down her face.

"Then all we can do is look until we find them. Listen to me now." Robert took Joy gently by the shoulders. "Kenneth, Dave, and I are going to drive out to the desert. We spent a lot of time there last week, and the girls really enjoyed it. You search the property again. As soon as daylight comes, ask your parents to help you canvass the neighborhood. Search all the yards, cellars, and sheds in this area. Knock on every door and ask if anyone has seen them. Will you do that?"

Joy met his eyes through her tears before leaning into his arms. "I'm sorry," she whispered against his chest. "I'm so sorry." She began to cry in earnest.

Robert clasped her close for one excruciating moment. He caressed her arms and held her inches away, touching his forehead to hers. "I'm sorry, too, sweetheart. I'm sorry I have left you so alone. We'll talk about everything later, okay? Right now we have to find our babies." He offered an encouraging smile. Joy nodded and wiped her face. Robert turned to Kenneth and Dave. "You fellas ready?"

"Ready, boss."

The boys pulled on their jackets and followed Robert out the door.

Chapter Three

I learned from my own experiences and from listening to regrets voiced by others that taking things for granted is a flaw of human nature. There was a time when a man and a woman walked in the physical presence of our almighty God. They knew the color of His eyes, felt the sound of His voice, touched Him – touched Him! And everything – Everything – was not enough.

We are incapable of fully appreciating the astonishing miracles through which we live and breathe each day. For every gift we recognize, there are benefits without number that we fail to comprehend and for which we are, therefore, ungrateful. Tragedy brings out the truth that many of our grievances are merely unappreciated blessings. Too late we realize that we could have been rejoicing instead of complaining.

Pain brings awareness. Sorrow brings perspective. Loss brings appreciation for how beautiful those days really were, clouded then by the present, now clear and bright in the light of retrospection.

And so we lament that we did not seize those moments and live them with passion, and we promise to live with focus in the future. But the best of intentions can be derailed by distraction. For many, the present continues to slip past unnoticed, occurring right in front of a world of people who are walking forward while looking back.

Joy stared vacantly out the window, seeing only the repercussions of her self-centered behavior. She had been deliberately mean to her husband and daughters. She had hurt them because she could and had allowed her family to revile them as well. She hardly noticed when her mother entered the room.

"I told your papa what happened." Jessamin sat next to Joy on the sofa and crossed her arms over her housecoat.

Joy kept her vigil, tense and silent.

Jessamin patted her on the leg. "He said it's to be expected. Those girls don't want to be with that man any more than you do. Of course they'd run away from him. But they are his children. I mean, they look like him. It's only proper that they go away with him instead of staying here."

Joy turned slowly to her mother, her eyes smoldering to life. "Catherine and Elisabeth are my children, too," she responded evenly. "And Robert is my husband, whether you like it or not."

"What I like and don't like don't matter where you're concerned," Jessamin returned. "Never has, as I recall. But you're the one who asked if you could move in with your sister instead of going back to Utah with that man. You're the one who didn't want those little girls around anymore. He's out there looking for them. He'll find them, and then they'll leave. You can start over and have the kind of life you should have had in the first place. It's a little late, but you've still got your looks about you. It shouldn't be hard to get you married right. You can have a family with your new husband and forget all about what used to be. We'll just not mention that man and his children anymore after today."

Joy stared incredulously at her mother. "Got it all figured out, do you?"

Jessamin nodded reassuringly. "I think Sonny already has a man in mind. Won't be the same as if you'd married Eddie, but good enough."

Joy sprang to her feet and raised her hands as though warding off an invisible evil. "I don't want to hear any more of this. You act as though I were a foolish child!"

"You were that when you ran off with a man you barely knew. Now that you've come to your senses, we can fix you up right."

"Oh, can you, really?" Joy shook her head in disgust. "Running away with Robert wasn't foolish. But I have been foolish this week for forgetting all the reasons I chose to elope in the first place. My only mistake was forgetting the truth. I married Robert because I love him, and because he truly loves me. I didn't marry him just to escape an abusive home."

Jessamin stood, her face twisted with rage. "You think you've done so much better? Those girls treat you like you're nothing. You let them get away with whatever they decide to do, and they despise you for it. Look what they've went and done now – run away in a strange place, where they don't know anybody. Anything could happen to them!"

Joy looked Jessamin in the eye. "I still have a chance to make things right. As soon as Robert finds our daughters, I will return with my family to our home in Utah. I was wrong to consider staying here. Robert is right. We don't have any problems that can't be resolved."

Joy turned back to the window, tired of participating in the endless battle. Jessamin muttered nastily under her breath, but Joy didn't waste time wondering what was said. She neither needed nor wanted to know.

"When the sun comes up, I'm going to ask your neighbors to help search their outbuildings for Catherine and Elisabeth," Joy said. "You and Papa can help me if you so desire. Three people can cover more territory than one."

Before Jessamin could answer, a violent thunder shook the earth. The women reached for each another as the floor shuddered under their feet. The windowpane fractured. Dishes rattled on kitchen shelves, and Jessamin cried out at the sound of glass shattering against the floor. The tremor concluded an instant after it began. Time froze for a moment of utter silence that Jessamin disrupted as she fled to the kitchen to see what damage had been done. Joy was peripherally aware of lights coming on in houses throughout the neighborhood.

Sonny staggered from the bedroom rubbing his eyes. "What was that?" he demanded muzzily.

"Mama and I had a fight," Joy answered. She saw immediately that her weak attempt at humor was wasted on Sonny. "I don't know what it was. Do you think it could have been a bomb? It cracked the window. I think some dishes are broken."

Sonny ignored her references to both the world war

and the family conflict. He ambled toward the kitchen, paused, and turned to study Joy. "Your mama loves you, you know."

Joy met her father's eyes briefly before turning away from the man who had also loved her, but not enough to intervene on her behalf and put an end to the emotional and physical abuse she had endured at her mother's hands right up until the day she fled to Utah with Robert Lake.

"I'll see if I can get anything on the radio," she murmured.

The hours between dawn and noon passed in a frustrating and fruitless search for two children whose disappearance was overshadowed by speculation regarding the unidentified quake that had jarred the neighborhood awake at five-thirty that morning. Sonny put an arm around Joy as they climbed the porch steps at midday.

"Try not to worry," he offered. "Robert must have found your little girls by now. If not, he's surely close to tracking them down."

Joy was helpless to hide her astonishment. Sonny had never spoken Robert's name or indicated the slightest faith in her husband. Catherine and Elisabeth were generally referred to as her husband's children, as though Joy had not conceived and carried them to birth. Sonny squeezed her shoulder and pulled away. He had conceded to the fullest extent he was capable.

Joy had forced her emotions into submission since Robert walked out in search of their daughters nearly eight hours before. Now the tears came despite her efforts to repress them. She withdrew to the bedroom and sobbed her anguish into a pillow. She crept to the bathroom and splashed her swollen eyes with cold water before joining her parents in the kitchen. She had barely settled into a chair when her brother-in-law charged into the house.

"Vicki's in labor!" he exulted. "The midwife's on her way!"

Jessamin immediately began putting food away, but Joy stopped her. "You two go to Vicki. I'll take care of things here."

"But you have to come with us," Jessamin argued. "It's Vicki's first baby, and she's your sister. She needs you there!"

"Tell Vicki I love her," Joy said, "but right now I have my own children to think about."

Jessamin stalked out of the kitchen without another look at her daughter. Sonny studied Joy's face for a moment as though memorizing her features. He lowered his eyes as he left the room.

Joy spent the afternoon pacing from one window to the next. She listened to the radio, but no news was broadcast about the mysterious disturbance that had awakened the neighborhood before dawn. She packed all their bags, even Kenneth's and Dave's, so everything would be ready to go when they returned. As shadows lengthened across the yard, Joy curled up small against the arm of the sofa and prayed with all her heart for her husband and his friends to return with her daughters.

It was after midnight when a knock at the door brought Joy awake and off the couch in one motion. She charged across the room and flung the door open, stopping short at the sight of two military policemen standing in the dim glow of the front porch light.

"Good evening, ma'am. We are looking for Joy

Begay Lake, wife of Ethan Robert Lake."

Joy tried to swallow the lump in her throat and choked on it instead. Coughing provided an excuse for the tears. "Where is he? Did he find our daughters? They ran away early this morning. Two little girls, ten and twelve years old, blonde hair and blue eyes. Robert went to search for them in the desert. His friends were helping him, two teenaged boys, Kenneth and Dave..." Joy leaned against the doorframe and sobbed, weary of walling away her fear and beyond caring who knew it.

One of the men cleared his throat. "We have found your family. They are alive." He paused as Joy cried out with relief. "Mrs. Lake, a munitions dump exploded in the desert early Monday morning. You probably heard the blast."

Joy nodded vigorously. "It cracked one of our windows."

"Your husband and children were in the vicinity of the explosion when it occurred. They all sustained injuries for which they have been hospitalized. They need your assistance and are asking for you. We have come to take you to them."

"Where are they?" Joy smeared the tears from her face. "How badly are they hurt?"

"I regret that we cannot offer any more detail. Your husband indicated that four family members and two friends came here to visit relatives. You should pack all of their belongings as well as your own. You'll need to remain at the hospital with your family."

"I've already packed." Joy laughed, verging on hysterics. "Our bags are just inside the door. Where is your car?"

The question went unanswered as the first man

reached through the door and passed suitcases and backpacks out to his companion.

"I need to leave a note for my parents." Joy would have stepped inside, but one of the officers intercepted her.

"You can call them later."

"No, I can't. They don't have a telephone." The man frowned, and Joy found herself hesitant to contradict him further. "My sister has a phone! The whole family is at her house anyway. I can call them from the hospital."

Joy followed the military policemen into the blackness beyond the front porch, around the house to the car crouching silently in the back yard. Two more officers waited in the front seat. Joy climbed into the back with her escorts, asking questions they were unable or unwilling to answer. As they pulled away, she fell silent, eager to be reunited with Robert, Catherine, and Elisabeth, and even anxious to see Kenneth and Dave. They were alive, if not completely well, and they would fill in the missing details for her. Tomorrow she would call Vicki's house with the news and learn all about her new niece or nephew.

An hour went by in the quiet night. None of the men spoke. Joy gazed upward at the pale sliver of a quarter moon until she drifted off to sleep against the car window, subliminally disturbed by glimpses of the desert in the darkness and a nagging intuition that eluded clarification. Something felt very wrong …

Chapter Four

Callie Davenport stared critically into the mirror. Emerald eyes stared candidly back. Habit urged her to frown upon her freckles, but the reflection appeared perfectly content with the features it possessed. She pulled a brush one last time through cinnamon waves, tucked wisps from her face with a few discreet hairpins, and smiled that what had been cosmetically tragic at fifteen was good enough at twenty-two.

"There's my girl." Sylvie turned from the sink and reached for a hug when Callie entered the kitchen. "Love you," she said. "What would you like for breakfast?"

Pleading absence of appetite would generate enough food to feed herself and half a dozen like her. Callie requested ham and biscuits and, upon customary rejection of the offer to do for herself, settled for perusing the *Daily News* while her mother's elderly aunt prepared the meal.

"What's the latest?" Sylvie worked the dough with experienced hands, savoring the pleasure of company in her small home.

"War and rumors of war," Callie sighed.

"One might expect that," Sylvie gently reproved.

Callie laughed softly. "Sorry. It just seems like this

war has gone on forever. There's another article today suggesting that Hitler and Eva Braun have escaped to Patagonia, but Argentina's foreign minister says he wouldn't harbor Axis war criminals."

"Bah!" Sylvie punched the dough with a vengeance. "I think Hitler's dead, and that naïve little lady died with him. Don't you think so?"

"I don't know what to think, really. The big story is about the U.S. and British Pacific Fleets bombarding Japan at Hitachi. And listen to this: one article reports unconfirmed rumors that Stalin might be bringing Japan's conditions of surrender to the United States – that he might be acting as an intermediary between the two countries. Right next to that is a little note saying Tokyo has a counter-strategy ready to attack the United States."

Sylvie applied a rolling pin to the dough.

"Looks like traveling is going to become even more complicated. The Office of Defense Transportation has laid claim to all passenger trains for the armed services."

"As well they should." Sylvie nodded.

"... 'avoid all unnecessary trips,' and so forth. I agree. It's just that with car travel so difficult because of gas and rubber rations, travel by rail or bus is the only option for some folks. At least we'll be driving home in a car. Mama said Aunt Belva inherited her sister's car. Daddy and Uncle Ray have plenty of gasoline stamps, so that won't be a worry."

"I wish you could stay longer. I get so lonesome here all by myself, and when you leave it'll be ten times worse. Don't tell your mama I said that. She worries about me enough as it is. Rose – she plays piano out at the church – she says animals are good companions. She talks to that terrier of hers like it was a person. It goes everywhere she does, except to church."

"You should have told me! I could have helped you look for a pet last week. Now there isn't time. Mama and Daddy will be here this evening, and we go home day after tomorrow."

"I'm not looking for one, really. Animals are cute enough when they're little." Sylvie rubbed flour off her fingers. "And nothing but mischief as they grow up. Sure can get attached to them, though." She smiled reminiscently. "And they do have a way of driving off the lonelies."

Callie watched her great-aunt cut perfect rounds from the dough. As Sylvie slid the pan of biscuits into the oven, Callie abandoned the news and helped herself to a cup of coffee.

"I can't believe it's Wednesday already."

"Neither can I. Cal, would you do me a favor this morning? Rose is going to take me to town in her car to buy groceries. Would you walk down to the farmer's market and pick us out some vegetables? It's only a few blocks, and you can take the wagon so you don't have to carry a lot of awkward packages home."

The thought of pulling a child's wagon made Callie smile. "I'd be happy to," she answered, hoping fervently that she wouldn't run into any handsome fellows while in possession of the wagon, and remembering instantly that most of the handsome fellows in her age range were fighting a war.

"I'd like to make a couple of pies," Sylvie said. "See if Beeler has any Gravensteins. The green, not the red ones. I'll make applesauce, too."

They left together after breakfast, chatting for a

while beside Rose's Studebaker before going their separate ways. Callie walked past a factory and a row of houses, along a narrow stretch of paved road, and finally to a small clearing off a dirt lane. Here local farmers offered the abundance of their gardens and orchards for sale in baskets and crates.

All the locals knew Sylvie had family coming to visit. They were generous almost to a fault. Before Callie could protest, her wagon overflowed with more produce than she had intended to buy.

She thanked her great-aunt's friends profusely and was gradually tearing herself away from multiple conversations with folks who loved to talk, when a slight movement about the wagon caught her attention. She stared as a tiny ringed tail disappeared into her bag of apples.

"Is that thing still around?" Lloyd Houk reached into the bag and yanked out a gray tiger kitten. It inserted needle-sharp claws into his fingers in an effort to hang on and spat with all the vigor a predator of such inconsequential size could muster. Lloyd yelped in pain and flung the kitten to the ground, kicking at the air where it landed as it darted under Callie's wagon.

"Whose is it?" Callie wanted to know.

"Harley Pruitt drowned a whole mess of 'em in the crick." A woman motioned toward the woods behind them. "That one must've got out of the sack."

"*Drowned* them? *Kittens?*" Callie cried. "Why would anybody do such a thing?"

"Can't afford the extra mouths to feed, honey," the woman said indifferently. "Farmers do what they have to do. No sense in keeping animals around that nobody wants."

"I'll get rid of that last one." Lloyd spoke around the perforated finger he still held to his mouth. "I've got a .22 in my truck. Bet I can get it with one shot!" He grinned at his friends.

"No, you won't." Callie stepped in front of her wagon. "I'm taking it home with me."

"You gonna take that thing in a car all the way to Kentucky? That's too much trouble," Lloyd advised, "and Sylvie don't need no cat."

"I believe that would be her decision." Callie knelt in the grass and attempted to coax the kitten out from under her wagon. It cowered and hissed at her approaching hand. She plucked a poppy and swished the stem temptingly past the kitten's hiding place. On the third pass, the kitten leaped upon the proffered prey. Callie stroked the miniscule interloper as it turned to bite, then suckle at her fingertips. She lifted the kitten to her chest, where it kneaded the front of her blouse and offered what would mature into a purr. With a nod of farewell, Callie turned the loaded wagon around and headed home.

By the time she reached Sylvie's cottage, Callie was perspiring freely and had tucked the kitten back into the sack of apples. After unloading the produce, she draped a towel inside a basket, transferred the kitten into it, and placed it in a corner of the kitchen. She wrote a quick note and laid it beside the sleeping fur tuft, delighted with the prospect of Sylvie's joy upon finding her new friend. She then put away her purchases and rinsed a handful of lettuce leaves to eat with lunch.

Callie answered a sharp knock at the door with the joyful anticipation of reuniting with her family after a week apart. She was startled to find four military policemen on Sylvie's front porch. She pushed open the screen with a tentative, "Yes?"

"Sylvia Adeline Forester?"

"She isn't here. May I help you?"

"Are you Callirrhoë Elaine Davenport?"

"Yes."

"Daughter of John Calvin Davenport and Mary Elaine Judd Davenport?"

Apprehension pervaded Callie's abdomen with an unpleasant tingle.

"Yes. Would you like to come inside?"

The men trooped into the small living room and stood rigidly among the dainty trappings of Sylvie's lace doilies and china trinkets.

"Miss Davenport, when do you expect Mrs. Forester to return?"

"Not for a couple of hours. She's shopping with a friend."

The men traded glances, reaching a mutual decision that required no discussion. "Miss Davenport, there has been an accident in New Mexico. A munitions dump exploded Monday morning. Several people were injured, including your parents. We have come to take you to them."

Callie shook her head, verging on panic. "New Mexico on Monday morning – I don't understand."

"Your parents and their companions were traveling through New Mexico on their way here."

"But they had planned to stay in Arizona through last night," Callie said. "They were going to leave before daylight this morning in order to arrive here this evening."

"Apparently their business in Arizona concluded

more quickly than they had anticipated, so they began their journey Sunday evening, which took them into New Mexico early Monday morning. The desert region is used by the military for a variety of purposes. The explosion was an accident, but your parents were nearby when it occurred, and they sustained injuries."

"What kind of injuries? How badly are they hurt? Are they going to be all right?"

"We don't have any details, Miss Davenport. We were just asked to escort you to them. They would very much like to see you."

"But why haven't you notified me before now?" Callie demanded. "I could already be with them. Why didn't you just call, instead of coming all the way here to tell me in person?"

"Perhaps because of the military's involvement with your parents' accident, Miss. I wish I could share more information, but we are just following orders."

"It'll only take me a minute to get my things together. But Aunt Sylvie..."

"You can call her later," came the edict. "We need to go now."

Callie hurried to the guest room and hastily packed her bags.

The MPs loaded Callie's few possessions into their car and covertly scoured the house to ensure that no evidence of their presence or her departure with them would be left behind. Callie wrote a brief letter to her aunt explaining her absence and promising to call. She propped it against Sylvie's Bible on the table by the lamp. As soon as her back was turned, one of the MPs crumpled the note and tucked it into his pocket. When the MPs felt certain of their anonymity, they rushed

Callie into their car and rolled away along the dirt lane behind the factory away from town.

The only signs that Callie Davenport had ever been to Sylvie Forester's house were lettuce leaves wilting on a towel by the kitchen sink and a basket in the corner containing a striped gray kitten and a note that read, "Hi! My name is Mischief."

Chapter Five

New Mexico had proven an arid experience in every way and not worth the trade. As undesirable as the job in Colorado had been, it at least provided a regular paycheck that in turn afforded regular meals. Michael glowered at the ever-changing view approximately three feet beyond each step he made.

"Could you tell me where to find Sandra Crowe..."

Excuses usually presented themselves at opportune moments. The latest had arrived in the form of a plea from his sister to join their father in Carrizozo. It was easier to walk away from work than to request time off when he had again fallen into his employer's disfavor. There would be other jobs wherever he ended up. Opportunities abounded to perform menial labor for inadequate pay. Michael shifted his backpack and kicked a small pebble from the path, grimacing with satisfaction as it bounced and rolled frantically beyond the range of his wrath. Respect for his authority, bled from a stone. Sometimes Michael found his own company utterly contemptible.

At the moment, 'contemptible' felt a fair description of his entire life. He sought refuge in thoughts of his sister, and he grasped what comfort remained from her belief that he was the chosen beneficiary of every advantage God ever handed down. Christine clung to her faith in Michael well past the proof of such folly. No one else knew him and managed to love him anyway.

"...Mrs. Sandra Crowe. I don't know her address..."

Christine envied his inherent talents, the personal lack of which left her feeling slighted by her Creator. In stark contrast to his unremarkable sister, Michael possessed an easy confidence, a sparkle that drew people to him as surely as a magnet drew steel. He learned too late that popularity fostered dependence on the illusions it created which, in turn, subliminally robbed him of the security and commitment of reality.

"She lives around here somewhere..."

Christine earned perfect marks in school and babysat their mother instead of going out with friends. Michael struggled through summer courses to earn a diploma. Christine raised a dozen different vegetables in a tiny patch of garden. Michael raised as many kinds of trouble. In the end he could no longer stand his mother's despair and his sister's resignation. He packed what few belongings he could claim and set out upon a never-ending peregrination, taking for granted that he would find himself somewhere along the way.

"... a pretty big place, from what I've been told. She rents rooms to people..."

There were detours, he acknowledged to the tobosa sagging toward the road, coarse and gray with age. There were tangents that led for miles and years in unprofitable directions. There were bad guesses and foolish choices. There was, always, ignorance that left him angry and defiant at the blatant evidence of his incompetence.

"… maybe she married and changed her name. Can you direct me to anyone in the area who has rooms for rent — anyone at all?"

That Michael had invested minimal effort into locating his father's friends before giving up was not as important as being able to truthfully say, omitting how little, he had tried. Christine had said the desert was their father's destination. Michael had not bothered to ask where the dirt road from Carrizozo ended before hitchhiking westward, and now he was sorry. The sun was hot, the area unpopulated, and Michael carried neither food nor drink. He had assumed he would have encountered sources of both by now. The last of the cottonwoods were an hour behind him. Empty desert stretched to the horizon. And the road had diminished to little more than a footpath.

"My dad and sister and brother are supposed to be staying with her. Have you seen any other strangers around town? They should have arrived Monday. I'm running a little late."

He had been gone for two years when their mother abandoned Christine for a new husband. Michael wondered how his sister had been able to cope without giving up and giving in, like he had done in reaction to far less pressure. But Christine had accomplished her goal of a college education. She now had a worthwhile career, a nice place to live, and genuine friends. She had a life that meant something.

For all the wondering and wandering he had done, Michael had yet to arrive at the elusive destination that was himself. He once got up the courage to attempt college, from which he fled to factory work and then door-to-door sales. He had run from the war, wondering how any man could be expected to die before he learned to live. He drifted from one odd job to the next, periodically walking out on another employer, apartment, town. Genetics blessed Michael with his father's good looks. Women enjoyed his company briefly as they searched for some semblance of stability in his life and, finding none, drifted gently out of reach. He was a fun date, but women chose security over vanity when sorting through proposals on which to stake their vows and pledge their lives.

"...or maybe it's this coming Monday that they are supposed to arrive, and I got here early after all ..."

Uncomfortable as always when confronted with himself, Michael cast about for a less convicting subject. Christine said their half-brother was on vacation with their father. Michael hadn't been around Freddy since the kid was a toddler, and that occasion had not been pleasant. Michael's impressions of the boy came from Christine's description.

Freddy was his mother's only child, the cause of and final blow to a miserable marriage. His mother managed a traveling theatre troupe, but Freddy imagined her to be a great dancer and singer. To ward off the ostracism of schoolmates, Freddy wove intricate and impossible tales about both his parents, neither of whom could ever live up to such fabrications. Abandoned by his father, neglected by his mother, and shunned by his peers, Freddy lied to such extents that Christine feared the child had begun to believe his own fantasies.

A father's legacy, Michael thought bitterly; Clayton had produced at least one profligate to pervert each of the next two generations. Perhaps being female rendered

Christine immune to the Pendleton curse. Or maybe, he reflected, Christine was their mother's daughter but not Clayton's. Michael immediately retracted that thought. Despite their mother's pathetic immaturity, she had remained faithful to Clayton through the disgraceful end.

Memories collided like mirrored shards of the winter night his father had come home after weeks on the road to inform them that he had a girlfriend who was pregnant. Michael ached with jealousy. His father already had a wife and two children who longed for his presence and for the security of his love. Why was he willing to take responsibility for another woman and her child when there were three members of his real family who would have laid down their very lives for a precious moment of his time?

"So you've never heard of Mrs. Sandra Crowe? Not even a lady named Sandra-somebody-else who has rooms for rent?"

Freddy received the Pendleton name and little else. Too young to remember the melee that was his parents' divorce, rationed by judgment to two weeks of fatherhood each year, he rode the beggar's proverbial horses until his wishes took on lives of their own. If no one believed his twisted version of the truth, little effort was required for the boy to convince himself that he was the envy of all who knew him.

Christine had been twelve years old, Michael recalled, when Freddy was born eleven years ago. Time had sped unmercifully past. Michael could offer precious little account for his own two and a half decades.

"Thanks anyway. Perhaps I misunderstood my sister's directions. I'll keep searching."

Given over to his mental meanderings, Michael did

not automatically register the sound of a vehicle fast approaching. By the time it occurred to him to turn and stick out his thumb for a ride, the jeep had coasted past him and stopped. Four military policemen got out and turned to face him.

Michael went still. The day's hike had left his clothes dusty and smelling of perspiration. His skin prickled and itched madly in the hot, dry air. So this is where it would end – the adventures, the pot-of-gold pursuits, his very life. He wondered where the officers would take him and how long a prison term he would get for evading the draft.

"Clayton Michael Pendleton, Jr.," one of the MPs pronounced carefully.

Michael wished for the millionth time he wasn't. "Yes, sir." He waited dejectedly, wondering if they would restrain him and name his offenses or just haul him in like the miscreant he was.

The speaker strolled to within an arm's length. "You are the son of Clayton Michael Pendleton, Sr. and brother to Christine Pendleton and Frederick Pendleton."

"Yes, sir."

"I regret to inform you that Monday morning, sixteen July, your father and siblings sustained injuries when a munitions dump exploded in this desert. They were hospitalized and are in need of your assistance. We will take you to them."

Relief that he had been wrong about the MPs' reason for stopping was immediately surpassed by a new kind of fear – the dread of having to take responsibility for family members unable to care for themselves.

"Where are they?" He allowed himself to be ushered into the jeep. "How badly are they hurt? Will I have to stay with them for very long? I'll have to contact my mother and Freddy's mother."

They would be properly notified, he was told. His remaining questions slipped away unanswered. Michael was annoyed with his escorts for disregarding his need for information, though he was unwilling to demonstrate disrespect by telling them so. The thought of anyone depending on him fell just short of terrifying. The suggestion that he might be needed for a considerable length of time incited the flight response that always carried him out of range of such situations, except now there was no way to escape and nowhere to run if he did.

Michael fidgeted against mounting tension as apprehension crawled through his belly. One of the MPs offered him a canteen filled with cool water, and for a moment Michael could allow himself to believe that everything was going to be all right.

Chapter Six

◆◆◆◆◆◆◆◆

It is the darkness I remember most. Even now, when I close my eyes, my remaining senses come alive and enable me to see by hearing, touching, smelling, and tasting the air, by feeling the atmosphere around me. I make a game of it sometimes, walking without the benefit of sight, guided by the contours of the ground beneath my feet, and the children laugh and tug my skirts and demand, "Who am I, Grandmother? Which one am I?" They lift me out of the dismal waste my life would be without them and remind me that beauty and goodness can be born of the most incomprehensible horrors, like fragile green stems breaking through earth blackened by fire to adorn the landscape with newborn color. Vibrant life grows and spreads until the beauty outweighs the scars.

Miracles do not always see themselves as such, and we don't always recognize them for what they are. Miracles do not require human acknowledgment to validate their existence. It is hard to take them for granted, however, when one's daily survival depends so completely upon them.

I knew and have since known pain, loneliness, desperation, and fear. I have not since experienced darkness so thick and black and permanent that it becomes a suffocating, all-encompassing entity spreading throughout the soul to the decease of all else.

But not all else. In the blackest recesses of the deepest dark, seeds of hope take root and wait patiently for their time to grow.

Death wooed her, tempted and allured her, only to violently spurn her when she surrendered to its advances. Competition for her attention flourished among rivals long before she surfaced through myriad subconscious levels to face what reality had bequeathed to her in the wake of its own defeat. Pain greeted her first awareness, beyond what she would have believed a human could endure. She felt as if she had been skinned alive inside and out, every organ and nerve ending stripped raw and exposed. Shrieks of astonished horror echoed throughout her mind and manifested their presence in the quaking of her limbs that continued even after she lapsed unconscious from the trauma. Sedatives stilled the tremors, dulled the agony, and removed her safely and hopelessly beyond reach of herself.

She then became acquainted with the smothering black. When first she opened her eyes, she thought she had awakened to a very dark night. As minutes crept by, she came to realize it was her eyes that were dark, for she could not see. More screams filled her mind then, of anguish, terror, and rage that burst forth as a series of anxious grunts. The attempted outburst accomplished nothing. Her efforts at communicating were either overlooked or ignored.

Gradually the incessant torment became bearable. Slow healing and carefully reduced medication permitted her to remain conscious for longer periods of time. She became aware of heat and cold, for she suffered feverishly from both. Needles punctured her skin and leaked life-sustaining fluids into her veins. Tubes adhered to her arms and legs and tickled up her nose into her sinuses, daring her to sneeze with every breath. Small pins penetrated her scalp and chest from the ends of rubbery cords that snaked irritating paths across her body. Her feeblest movements encountered resistance. Padded cuffs gripped her wrists and ankles to restrain her where she lay. Her lungs labored for each gasp as though savagely constricted, their efforts rewarded by the liquid rattle of her breath. She could not swallow. Periodic bouts of choking up vile, sticky mucus kept her nauseated. The sickening taste in the back of her throat and the repulsive smell of her own skin assaulted her senses. She forgot what it had been like to live without constant pain: the burning in her sightless eyes, the skin that pulled taut as it healed, the constant internal cramps as though her abdomen were filled with shards of glass, the excruciating acidic sting, despite the catheter, of bowel movements. She delicately handled the straps that bound her wrists and learned that her fingertips could no longer discern textures and details at the slightest touch.

Dread as to the fate of her family threatened to consume her mind as surely as the unknown malady wasted her flesh. She remembered walking in the desert before dawn. Voices carried forth from the various conversations of her family a short distance behind her. Her new friend, Christine, walked beside her. Without warning a blinding flash exploded into indescribable pain of the sort to which she had awakened. What had happened out there, and where was she now? Did an enemy attack her family in the desert? Was she still in America? *Am I a prisoner of war? Are other members of my family being tortured?*

Am I?

Visitors arrived, presumably doctors and nurses since she assumed she was in a medical facility. They turned her frequently. She did well to know up from down without the benefit of sight, but she knew the direction of the door and recognized the various caregivers by their footsteps and the pressure of their hands on her body. She hadn't the strength to fight them. The savage, searing pain generated by the merest touch of their fingers to the raw surface of her limbs robbed her of breath and the will to do more than lie still in abject cooperation. She comprehended how they positioned her by the quality of audible information. Sound offered bleak salvation from the void in which she struggled to learn and discern, to know her fate.

"I'm thirsty."

She was horrified by the sound of her own voice when first she tried to speak. A gargling moan ruptured her throat and dribbled through her lips, panicking her both with its nightmarish tone and the lacerating pain inflicted by the effort. In spite of drug-induced vagueness, in rebellion against the unknown, she focused on attempting to speak. Communication became her solitary goal. It offered her a purpose for which to live.

"It hurts," she gasped, but the cry traveled no farther than her imagination. The hands finished maneuvering her about, positioning her limbs, rearranging tubes and cords about her body. They left, two of them: the one who swished softly and the one with the heavy, irregular step. She pictured them as a woman and a man who was lame. She ascribed them faces, bodies, personalities, and names. She sobbed because she could not compare her perception with the truth, but the tears fell only in her mind.

"Hello, my name is Sarah." She rehearsed daily what she would say when she could again communicate in a normal fashion. 'If' was too horrifying a concept; she could not allow herself to consider her current condition a permanent way of life. "What happened to me? Where am I? Where are Daddy and Mama and Ben?" The order in which she would ask the questions changed with each mental enactment of the scene, as did the number and appearances of the people with whom she would speak. Variety made the pretense more bearable.

Meanwhile, her world remained dark, lonely, and cruel. "Please talk to me. Say anything. 'Hello,' if that's all you feel like. Just let me hear your voice." Sarah's desperate thoughts were drowned out even in her own mind by the hums, rattles, and beeps of the monitors to which she was bound, comforting in their rhythmic familiarity, maddening in their mechanical indifference.

"What day is it? How long have I been here?"

There was no meal routine by which to discern a day from a night and thereby judge the passage of a twenty-four hour period. Intravenous fluids provided sustenance, and Sarah's caregivers did not, so far as she could tell, visit on a set schedule. She grew ever more frustrated at her inability to act or react to pain that took her breath away and to the confusion that provoked her from hysterics to helpless rage and back again with no outlet for the emotions warring in her mind.

"Why am I strapped to my bed? Will I ever be able

to see again? *I'm thirsty!"*

It was inevitable, at least in Sarah's own mind, that she would grow stronger. She tried herself often at the straps that held her fast and worked at helping her caregivers by moving with them when they turned her. Despite the drought of her throat and the scarred, drawn lips that prevented her from forming words correctly, she attempted to speak incessantly when they were with her. Often as not she was overtaken by uncontrollable coughing that tore her inside and out. Each episode left her weak and trembling. She accepted a caregiver's assistance through the trials and then rested, disheartened, until she worked up the courage to try again.

Determined as she was to speak, Sarah was unprepared for the moment she opened her eyes to shades of gray. She struggled against her bonds until pain forced her to lie still. She shouted surprise, joy, and triumph that emerged as a series of grunts from the uncooperative remnant of her voice. At last she prayed more ferociously than she had ever done, no longer lacking the faith to hope for a miracle.

"I can see you!"

She studied the fuzzy blobs that did for her what she could not do for herself. She was alarmed at her initial inability to move her eyes in their sockets. Muscle control improved with her eyesight and although she could not tell anyone of this precious progress, she knew the caregivers were too observant of her physical advancements to be unaware of her clearing vision.

"Why do you wear that bulky costume? It must be hard to move around in that thing. It makes you sound funny when you walk, like a frog hopping through weeds."

Sarah realized she wasn't just hospitalized; she was incarcerated in some sort of specialized medical facility. Her room cocooned her in spotless, antiseptic white. No windows and no clock, no pictures or shelves interrupted the glaring sterility of barren walls. Her caregivers wore white jumpsuits with gloves and hoods.

"I live in Kentucky. Where am I now? How long have I been here? When will I get to go home? Please tell me if my Daddy and Mama and Ben are all right."

Visitors welcomed for the joy of human contact were soon met with fear and dread. Their eyes, visible through clear shields in the hoods they wore, were the only human feature Sarah could see, and she eagerly stared into those little windows each time a caregiver entered her room. Her advances were rejected. No one looked at her face, responded to her attempts to speak, acknowledged the grasping of her hands or the pleading in her eyes. They checked monitors and intravenous fluids, adjusted the cuffs that bound her to the bed, flexed her limbs, moved her around and checked her over as though she were of a breed somewhat less than human. Their costumes were so concealing that Sarah could rarely be certain whether her attendant was a man or a woman.

"My skin is turning *gray*. Why is my skin turning gray and dry? I feel like a snake that needs to shed because my hide is too small for my body. I can't even straighten my fingers. What happened to my hair! I have no hair! Will my hair grow back? Oh, please let it grow back..."

Memories of medical procedures haunted Sarah from the moment she became conscious. As her awareness increased and her health improved, the testing became more frequent and invasive. She was frequently transferred to a gurney and taken to various exam rooms. Explanations were not offered. Sarah was neither able to articulate questions or protests nor strong enough to offer physical resistance. At the mercy of faceless strangers, Sarah soon stopped trying to make sense of the batteries of treatments, tests, and drugs to which she was subjected each day. She focused instead on endurance and survival.

"Please, don't. The light hurts my eyes. It leaves me with a severe headache and feeling sick at my stomach. Please, don't use the drops this time. They burn and make me blind for hours. You don't know how it terrifies me to be blind. I get so scared every time you do this to me that I will never see again."

Sarah wanted to believe her words were becoming understandable but knew her desire to share conversation heightened the potential that she was fooling herself. She had come to feel that it wouldn't matter if she could enunciate clearly because her listeners would remain deliberately deaf to her pleas.

Chemical onslaughts left her reeling with vertigo and nausea. Exposures to radiation reduced her to breathless agony, her body incinerated yet again. Costumed monsters scored incisions inside her joints, which were then forced apart to straighten her arms and legs as her skin healed. They braced her limbs and applied dressings to help the wounds form scar tissue. At each therapy session, caregivers folded, stretched, and manipulated her limbs to encourage strength and flexibility. The wounds opened and drained and bled and began once more to heal. As painful and ugly as the cuts were, Sarah at least understood their purpose.

She could conceive of no logic to justify the vulgar, brutally invasive examinations the costumed tormentors performed on her bound, naked body. When released from her restraints in the aftermath of those vile procedures, Sarah would curl up as tightly as she could against the taut skin that held her hostage and sob at the humiliation of being violated and tossed aside as though she were worthless. Her very tears turned traitorous, burning salty trails down the raw skin of her face.

"Who are you? Why are you doing this to me? I'm trying to get better, but you do things to me that make me sick again. Please leave me alone! Stay away from me! *Don't touch me!*"

Though lacking in speech, Sarah could soon raise her voice, and she began to cry out every time a costume blindfolded her, transferred her to a gurney, and wheeled her to one of the examination rooms for another round of medical procedures. Her caregivers tolerated her behavior until the day another voice cried out in response. Sarah froze, straining to listen. When silence prevailed, she inhaled deeply to call out again, but a costume cut her effort short. Sarah felt a pinprick at her wrist and knew nothing more until she awoke alone in her bed. She would have thought the memory a dream had she not been tranquillized for her efforts at communicating with another human being.

"So I'm not the only patient here." Sarah talked almost constantly during her waking hours, painfully forming each word as correctly as possible. With nothing else to occupy her time, the conversations offered the additional merit of entertainment value. "Hi, I'm Sarah!" she dreamed of informing the unknown male voice. "What is your name?" She struggled with overwhelming emotion at the realization that she might have heard her father or uncle, her brother, or one of the Pendleton family. "Oh, dear Lord," she breathed, suspended between elation and tears. She wanted so desperately to see them. Her desire for a reunion conflicted with her prayer that the others had somehow escaped her fate. Hope plummeted at the certainty that their presence here would mean they had not.

"God bless Daddy and Mama and Ben, Uncle John and Aunt Mary and Callie." She murmured the prayer each time she became sleepy, and the bittersweet longing broke her heart until she wondered if there could be a remnant left with which to feel or to love. But for the persistent hope that her family might have survived, Sarah wished herself dead. Carved even deeper than physical ruin, the degrading obscenities she suffered at the hands of her caregivers left her hopelessly wounded inside. Of these wounds she despaired to recover, for how could one heal if one could not forgive, and how could one forgive without time and distance to help her forget the worst of it? How could one forget if she was forced to remain amidst the hurt? "How, Daddy?"

Changes for better and worse crept imperceptibly into her life. She wept with relief and joy the first time a gloved hand offered her a glass of water. Swallowing proved difficult, and the liquid came right back up, but soon she was drinking as much water as the caregivers would allow her to have. She consumed her first soft food soon thereafter. Costumes unbuckled her restraints and propped her up in the bed to eat a bowl of something flavorless and orange and the consistency of warm custard.

"Carrots," she guessed. "Or sweet potatoes." She

mouthed the texture. "I hope."

Along with thin broths and mysterious puddings, Sarah received her first oral medication. When the costume held out the tiny paper cup with its suspicious blue tablets, Sarah's first inclination was to bat it out of his gloved hand and refuse the pills until he explained why she needed to take them and what they would do for her and to her. Resigned that she was in no position to enforce her wishes, she swallowed them and waited anxiously for what might happen as a result.

What happened was that a short while later a costume brought her another meal and two more pills. Costumes brought her the medicine at two intervals without meals, after which the tablets again accompanied food. When Sarah received three meals in a row, she caught on to the schedule.

"Day and night." She smiled to herself and wondered briefly if her face demonstrated the expression. "If I only knew how long I have been here! But I can count the days now, starting with this one." As the costume recorded information from the monitors onto a clipboard, Sarah removed one of the little blue pills from her cheek and pushed it under the stack of tissues in the box on the table beside her bed. "Day one," she breathed, and stuffed her mouth full of something green and wilted so the costume would see her eating.

"Spinach," she supposed. "Possibly kale." She stared at the greasy chopped leaves on her plate. "I hope."

Sarah resented the confinement of her restraints and had to make a conscious effort not to resist when a costume required her to lie complacently and be buckled to her bed.

"What kind of sense does this make?" she inquired politely of the costume as it secured the straps to her wrists. "I'm not able to even stand without assistance, so it's not like I'm going to run away. If I were as strong as you are, I still couldn't get through the steel door." She kept talking as the costume completed the routine. "May I have a drink of water? I need to go to the bathroom. Never mind, I'll just use my catheter, thank you. Why do you wear a false face? Are you a man or a woman? Do you like your job? What *is* your job? Have a nice day now, okay?"

Therapy sessions were daily trials, eased by the merit that they replaced the more invasive and painful tests that Sarah abhorred. Though she felt like a living pharmacy due to the daily barrage of pills and injections, she finally began to experience the kind of progress for which she had been longing. Her unwilling muscles and joints responded, grudgingly at first, to the therapists' manipulations until Sarah was able to stand on her own, take her first steps, walk across the room without assistance. She cheered herself on, deliriously happy at having achieved one impossible milestone. She rejoiced alone. The costumed therapists gave no indication of having witnessed her success, but Sarah was long since accustomed to their lack of humanity. She celebrated her accomplishments despite the absence of encouragement and companionship.

"Let me try one more time."

Exhausted as she became, Sarah refused to complain about the hours of physical exercise the therapists coached her through each day. The rewards included being allowed to submerge in a warm bath afterward, a luxury Sarah could hardly believe after the sponge baths the costumes had previously given her. After Sarah soaked in the bath, caregivers gently massaged warm oils into her dry, shriveled skin. At no other time did the costumes touch her in a way that mimicked tenderness and affection.

"This is so wonderful. I feel like a person again. Thank you!"

Determination and non-stop practice also proved out in Sarah's speech. The more clearly she could talk, the more frustrated she became at the deliberate inattention of costumes who treated her like a laboratory experiment one day and saw carefully to her welfare the next. Tension mounted each time they ignored her questions, comments, and greetings. Sarah did as she was silently bidden, took her medications, protested the examinations to no avail, and reluctantly submitted to being strapped to the bed when she was going to be left alone. Though a costume soon discovered Sarah's tissue-box collection of blue pills and discarded it without comment, Sarah counted another day with each evening meal and memorized the number before she fell asleep.

"Seventy-three." She allowed herself to grieve, to cry, to give in to the dull ache of loss for a while. Hope was somehow reborn with each new day.

Sarah felt it safe to assume she would never be whole again. Although no mirrors or reflective surfaces were available in which to view her appearance, Sarah knew her body had been ruined either by the explosion in the desert or by the ensuing months of treatment or both. Her skin, at first raw and pink, soon called to mind the pale ash of burned leaves. Her head felt smooth and bald, and she experienced daily problems with digestion and elimination. She improved in other ways, however, and based her hopes firmly on the notion that once she recovered to a certain extent, someone would explain the fate of her family and the life that had been forced upon her since that pivotal moment in the desert, and she would be allowed to leave this place. Meanwhile, the doctors, nurses, or scientists in costumes subjected her to medical procedures that sickened her all over again, required additional rehabilitation and recovery, and robbed her of the improvements she had struggled so hard to make. Sarah retraced her steps countless times along the road to wellness. She wondered daily how much more she could take – how much more she would be forced to take – and where and when her incarceration at the facility would end.

"You can't keep me here forever."

But it frightened her to know that indeed they could.

"What's your name? You can tell me. I'm not as dangerous as I look."

Sarah's optimistic personality and spirited disposition deteriorated further with each physical accomplishment. She resorted to taunting the costumes, harassing them, teasing them with insults, knowing full well they could understand every word she said. The longer they ignored her, the more furious she became until, at last, anger overruled better judgment.

Two costumes entered her room and blindfolded her, unbuckled the restraints, and lifted their charge onto a gurney.

"It doesn't do you any good to cover my eyes. I can tell which direction we're going when we turn corners and how many doors we've gone through. I could find my way around this place in the dark better than I could with my eyes open."

The destination was a room set up for gynecological exams. Costumes transferred Sarah to a table and removed her blindfold. One costume wheeled out the gurney while the other stayed to prepare her for their intended purposes. Sarah could never be certain what they were going to do to her until it had already been done, but this particular room was haunted by ghosts of unspeakable horrors she had suffered in the past. She began hyperventilating with panic at the thought of being forced through such ignominy again.

When the costume took her by the ankles and parted her legs, Sarah cried out in fear. When the gloved hand slid the cotton gown up her legs to expose her crotch, Sarah reacted without thought to the consequences, kicking the costume where a face should have been and launching herself off the table and onto her nemesis. She clawed at the slippery material and ripped at the hood, possessed of raging intent to expose the thing's face and make it talk and prove itself human.

The costume squalled for help, and Sarah exulted at the first human voice she had heard since the day her own cry had been answered by another. So the costume contained a woman! Sarah ripped and clawed with renewed vigor, applying herself industriously to the zipper that attached the hood to the collar. The room abruptly swarmed with more costumes than Sarah had collectively seen. They snatched her up and bore her backward onto the table.

"Get off of me! Let go of me! *Don't touch me!*"

Sarah screamed and fought until she wriggled free of those holding her down. She struggled off the table and aimed a punch at the nearest hood. The costume responded by pulling a tiny canister from a belt clip and spraying fumes into Sarah's face. She inhaled a sweetly sickening odor and was unconscious before she hit the floor.

Sarah awoke in her own bed as the costumes were leaving the room. She listened to the grating drag and the harsh latch of the heavy steel door and allowed regret a moment to chastise her by pointing out the obvious. Sarah winced at the certainty that bad decisions earned worse consequences. She stretched gingerly and rubbed her stinging eyes.

"Hey, you forgot to buckle my cuffs!" *Dummy! Don't tell them that!* "Yes, well, they have to know anyway. I can't imagine why they wouldn't buckle me in twice as tight after that."

Sarah's yawn provoked a fit of spasmodic coughing. She was startled when, as she sat up, someone supported and rubbed her back while she caught her breath. A hand appeared in front of her holding a glass of water. A real hand. A human hand with beautiful white skin and clear, almond-shaped fingernails. No glove concealed the fingers. No protective sleeve covered the lovely, flawless wrist.

Sarah turned her head slowly and gazed into emerald eyes brimming with tears, at thick waves of cinnamon hair framing a familiar, beloved face.

"Oh, Sarah!" The voice trembled, and the tears began to fall.

Sarah cried out and flung herself into the arms of Callie Davenport.

Chapter Seven

Tom Westfield moved within the depths of his dreams, turning to look at the young people who followed him into the sunset. He smiled at their camaraderie as they enjoyed one another's company. Tom's gaze lingered on Sybil, who brought up the rear of the procession. They shared a quiet smile as their eyes met in warm embrace. She had surprised him on their second wedding anniversary the previous weekend by revealing that she was pregnant. Tom could not have imagined loving her more, yet each passing day knit their hearts more inseparably as one. A child, now, *their* child – the sheer joy of it overflowed his heart.

"I had forgotten how hot it could get out here!"

"There are heavy clouds on the horizon, though. We could see thunderstorms before morning."

Tom glanced skyward, disappointed at the possibility of rain. This particular excursion was of special importance to the entire group, for five of the six young men behind him would be leaving for boot camp within the coming months. The girls who walked with Sybil dreaded saying goodbye to brothers and boyfriends. All of these young people faced the frightening knowledge that some of them might never return.

"Singing in the rain...we're daring it to rain..." Three of the girls managed to harmonize briefly before dissolving into giggles, staggering against each other under the weight of backpacks and laughter.

The dream wavered and faded. Tom grasped the illusion with the desperation of a condemned man clinging to the bars that stood between him and a death sentence even as they imprisoned him for life. He took Sybil in his arms, gently caressed a soft, blond curl from her face. No, that was wrong. They weren't alone. The elusive vision coalesced once more, a bittersweet panorama of ten innocent faces tinted with the myriad, breathtaking complexions of the desert twilight.

The teenagers begged for a camp out instead of a lock in, desiring a memorable experience under starry skies over a night in the stagnant heat of the church sanctuary. Equipped with bedrolls, ponchos, and food in backpacks, they piled into the bed of Tom's truck after the Sunday evening service for the ride into the desert. Tom drove until they were miles from civilization and parked along a scarcely traveled path from where the group continued on foot. They soon left the truck so far behind that it, too, seemed little more than a distant memory in another place and time. The barren landscape extended as far as Tom could see in any direction. All they considered essential to their lives, he reflected, became mere speculation at moments like this. Memory asserted itself as fact, even as he lacked the slightest proof of any reality beyond this moment, when nothing existed but earth and sky.

Two hours into the hike Tom looked over his shoulder and smiled at his charges. Conversation had given way to companionable silence as dusk closed around the scenery and turned their attention inward to personal reflections. They appeared weary for the walk after rising early to attend church services and going nonstop all day. Walking backward, he addressed the group. "How about it, folks, are we ready for a break?" He laughed at the resounding "Yes!"

"All right then, ladies to the right, gentlemen to the left," Tom directed. He dropped his bedroll to the ground, resisting the urge to look at his wife again. Because they were chaperones, Sybil arranged her sleeping bag among the girls while he made camp with the boys twenty-five yards away. This would be the first night of their marriage that Tom and Sybil would not sleep in each other's arms.

"Keep those ponchos handy," he said. "It won't rain for a while, but Gilbert is right – we'll be under those clouds before morning. We may not get much sleep tonight."

"We hadn't planned to," said fifteen-year-old Rachael. "Half the fun of camping is staying up all hours!"

"I don't want to see our trip ruined by the weather, though. Staying at the church might have been a wiser choice."

"Think nothing of it, Tom. There are worse things than a little rain."

Tom glanced at Toby McAllister, seventeen and about to encounter a requirement from the armed forces that he grow up all at once. Each of the boys who stood with Tom was eager to join the military in defense of the

United States, but not one of them comprehended the reality of the life that lay ahead. Strength and valor might be achieved on the battlefield, and moments later the life that boasted these traits could be brutally ended. Tom wished he were not at such a loss for words with which to send them forth. To a boy of seventeen, death is a distant dream.

The young people assembled in a circle. They sat on their ponchos and placed an assortment of snacks within reach. Conversation flowed light and easy at first but quickly grew serious as their thoughts turned to the war.

"You're only twenty-six. How come you didn't have to go?" Nathaniel struggled with 'twenty-six' but took a deep breath and enunciated the rest of his question slowly in order to best the incapacitating stutter that made.simple conversation a challenge.

"My family is dependent upon me for support. My mother-in-law is an invalid, and Sybil is her caretaker. They need my presence and my paycheck to survive. I suppose I am also exempt as a minister, but were it not for my family, I would have enlisted regardless of deferments." A third family member would need him next spring. Tom glowed inwardly. The youth group had not been informed of Sybil's impending mother-hood, so Tom quietly cherished the thought and only smiled all the wider.

Peripherally he noticed Maria fidgeting with an unasked question. Because of physical deformities, she had tended toward reclusion through most of her fourteen years. The open arms and friendly smiles of her peers at church worked the miracle of acceptance that replaced Maria's despondency with joyous enthusiasm. She retained a bashful modesty, however, especially in the presence of men. Tom hoped he could meet her halfway without embarrassing her.

"Would anyone else like to ask a question? Maria?"

Her large brown eyes dilated with fleeting terror, but the expression eased at Tom's encouraging smile. "I wondered..." She swallowed noisily and cleared her throat. "...how you came to be an orphan."

Maria had been abandoned on the church steps within hours of her birth. There were those among the locals whose lives were rooted in devoted terror of superstitions they worshipped for fear of retribution if they did not. They believed the illegitimate child born with an abnormal facial structure, disproportionately long limbs, and six digits on each hand and foot was a curse pronounced upon the young mother for her affair with a married man. Many urged that the incarnation of the curse be destroyed, but the woman who had already gone too far could go no further. She forsook the child to the mercy of strangers and left the area. She never returned.

Tom shifted restlessly in his sleep, encountering resistance from the cuffs that tethered him to his bed. He panicked against waking, against leaving the tender security of the dream. He focused on Maria, remembering the reassurance she gained from talking with an adult who had survived growing up without parents. He had experienced the same cravings as a child. Though Tom was raised by extended family, the need for filial identity and the endless unanswered questions remained. After all this time, he still took comfort in sharing his past with someone who could relate to the emotion resurrected by the memory. He drifted back to the camp site, eager to answer her question yet again.

"My father had a leg shot out from under him during the first world war back in the summer of 1918. He and Ma moved to her father's ranch in Minnesota. That's where I was born. I remember him getting around on crutches as good as anybody with two legs.

"The summer before my sixth birthday, he was kicked in the chest by a horse. He died instantly. My little sister, Esther, died the following winter of pneumonia. Ma took her own life before the spring thaw. Papaw wasn't prepared to raise a troubled six-year-old boy, so he sent me to my father's brother in Texas. Uncle Ron and Aunt Ruth counted me as one of their own from the day I moved in. They had a big family, and everyone treated me like I had always belonged there. Their middle son, Rand, became my best friend. We grew up as close as real brothers. Rand joined the service after Pearl Harbor was bombed. He was killed almost two years ago, less than a month after Sybil and I were married." Tom drew a deep breath. "So though I was orphaned, I was blessed with a beautiful family. Just like you have been, Maria, with Pastor Clay and Mrs. Fae."

"And all my adopted brothers and sisters," Maria agreed.

Tom smiled. "Who else has a concern on your heart that you would like to share?"

Moments of nervous fidgeting ticked by as shy glances betrayed a unanimous reluctance to go first. A voice finally broke the silence.

"Okay." Arlene sighed. "I do."

Arlene Brooks was seventeen, a pretty brunette with a singing voice so exquisite that Tom thought it surely put the angels in Heaven to shame. Russell Winter, the athletic eighteen-year-old seated at Tom's left, was her fiancé. Russ would leave for boot camp in September. He and Arlene planned to marry after the war ended and he returned home.

"I know we're supposed to have faith that God will answer our prayers," Arlene began. "And I try, I really do, to believe when I pray that everything's going to be fine – that Russ will come home, and we will get married and have a wonderful life together. But in reality things don't always work that way. I've seen people pray fervently for an answer they really believed in, and then God didn't provide that answer. Their faith was shattered, and they lost all hope. I don't want that to happen to me. I don't want to lose Russ. But I know that God is going to do whatever He wants no matter what, so what does it really matter if I even pray at all?"

The others waited in compassionate silence as Arlene wiped the tears from her eyes. Tom studied the dark outline of the horizon and prayed for words that would introduce the peace and the assurance that Arlene was seeking.

"Faith is knowing God, believing in Him, trusting Him completely, and accepting His will," Tom began. "Faith means opening the depths of our hearts to God, sharing our needs and desires with Him, and knowing that He is taking everything about us into consideration as He resolves each situation. Faith is a necessary foundation for prayer.

"Prayer is nothing less than conversing with God, talking to Him and listening to His response. God does communicate with us when we pray, and our prayers matter greatly to Him and to those we are lifting up to

Him. The Bible shares numerous situations in which God altered His plans in response to someone's prayer, proving that prayer does change things, and that the lack of it can allow devastating consequences."

Tom's voice softened with reverence. "God is our Father – our Dad! He listens intently to every word we say, breathes every gasp with us, harbors our emotions in His own great heart. He walks every step of life with us. He knows us and loves us right where we are.

"Our trust and belief can falter when we focus so completely on our intense needs or desires that we forget that our faith should be in God Himself, and not in the answers we hope to receive. Just like human parents, God often hears requests from His children that are not in our best interest, and sometimes the petitions we so desperately make in our limited knowledge are not the best outcomes in the grand scheme we call Life. God knows how one life and one prayer and one request, answered this way or that, will affect us, those around us, all our futures, even the rest of the world. That's why God's decisions and His timing are perfect.

"When you pray, tell Him how you feel, Arlene, just like you have shared with us. Use the same words, the same honesty. Lay your fear and your hope before Him. Talk to Him boldly, with confidence. Understand that God loves you, and trust Him not to hurt you. As you tell God how you feel, praise Him for what you know. You know that God brought you and Russ together and that He has blessed your relationship. You know that you and Russ love God and each other and that you both desire a lifelong marriage that will bless other families as well as your own. Study the Bible to learn the truth of God's word, and focus your faith on what you *know*, because feelings are inconsistent, and that makes them unreliable.

"But God is a consistent and reliable Father. Anything that is important to you is even more important to Him. Our Father God wants to share every facet of our lives. Our love and our trust matter to Him more than any of us can comprehend."

Tom concluded to find himself the center of rapt attention. Eleven pairs of eyes focused mistily on his face, clinging to his answer with desperate hope. They were all scared, he knew, and facing a fear with which he would never be acquainted. So who was he to shepherd them, after all? His own faith was solid, but himself fallible, and he had to be careful that a lack of self-confidence did not translate to others as a lack of confidence in his Savior.

Sybil met his gaze with a hollow expression. Faith did not come any easier to her than it did to Arlene. She had grown up independent and self-sufficient, and her nature urged her to resist complete reliance on anyone. Sybil had given her heart and soul to Christ. She knew God intimately. This did not prevent her from initiating frequent spiritual challenges as she strove to submit her strong will to an even stronger love. She had absolute faith in God's power. She struggled to develop more than a tentative trust in His will.

Night claimed the desert as questions, discussions, and prayer flowed throughout the little gathering and bonded the young people as family in Christ. The clouds fulfilled their prophecy, releasing their burdens throughout the night while the group huddled under ponchos and waited for the rain to pass.

Tom stirred restlessly, subconsciously attempting to disengage from the memory. He had descended too far within the depths of slumber. He who refused to relinquish the dream now found himself doomed to relive the nightmare.

A final, brief storm provided a wake-up call around four o'clock. The group assembled their belongings, crouched under their ponchos, and drowsed in the damp until the rains abated. Tom hustled the group to shake off the water and prepare for the walk back to the truck. The predawn hike would make for a disappointing conclusion to their campout, but Tom disliked soggy clothes and hair, and he knew the others must be miserable as well. He, Sybil, and ten teenagers ingested a quick breakfast of moist crackers and tepid soda. They gathered their things, inspected the area for litter, and –

Later Tom would remember nothing but heat and light – blinding fury beyond human comprehension that radiated the clothing off his body and fried his very flesh. If there were screams, he did not hear them; if others reached for him, he did not know. A torturous explosion rent the earth, and Tom released himself to death, to the end of the world as he knew it.

Chapter Eight

⟡

Anticipation mingled with dread as Josten Maslow prepared for transfer and command of his new post. He could hardly conceive of a more appealing assignment in a less desirable location.

Stacks of reports awaited study to acquaint him in detail with the nature of his various charges. He thumbed through a massive text describing the most unique subject under his authority, wondering how far he could trust a medic's account of a Nazi tale that was beyond his ability to prove. The German POW at Nordhausen had pointed his American liberators to a bizarre aircraft that had been walled away within one of the tunnels under the Kohnstein Mountain. The POW had shared an unlikely tale in which he and fourteen fellow Nazi soldiers had taken the aircraft from Soviet forces during the winter of 1943 and presented it to Reich Marshal Hermann Goering, who sentenced the entire incident to secrecy. Whether or not the rest of the deceased soldier's story was factual, it at least offered the benefit of brief entertainment. Maslow scanned the pages on his desk.

If no reports were found in Germany to substantiate

the aircraft and its capture, neither were there reliable Soviet records to confirm the disappearance of a cruiser protecting a classified aircraft on the Black Sea. A complete and accurate account of Soviet losses in the Black Sea during the war did not exist. It was likely that deliberate inconsistencies of Russian naval records due to the secrecy of this particular mission meant that the vanished Soviet ship was considered lost at sea and promptly forgotten in favor of dedicating every available resource to the defense of Russia.

Dr. Wernher von Braun, creator of the Vengeance rocket program, occasionally visited the Nordhausen facility, but he never knew this aircraft existed. Though Goering's primary intention was concealing the craft from Hitler, he was also unwilling that it should distract from the production of weapons for Germany's war. Given von Braun's outspoken dreams of launching rockets into outer space – goals for which the engineer had previously been arrested by the Gestapo – Goering determined to provide his premier rocket scientist with no additional fodder to fuel such fantasies.

Maslow paused over this detail of the Nazi's account. A twist of fate had bequeathed him Goering's concerns. In the final days of the war, von Braun and five hundred of his staff sought out and surrendered to American troops, who transported them across the Atlantic along with three hundred train car loads of V-2 rocket components. Confiscation of the aircraft was accomplished, with considerable discretion, amidst the collection of myriad V-1 and V-2 parts claimed by the United States between April and June 1945. The aircraft was covertly stored aboard the *Prinz Eugen* upon Germany's cession of the *Schwere Kreuzer* to the United

States. The *Prinz Eugen* had been towed to Boston in January.

Dr. Wernher von Braun and his staff were now teaching in White Sands, New Mexico, where they had been assigned to share with others their vast knowledge and experience in the creation and building of rockets and guided missiles. His proximity would not present a conflict for Maslow unless the Council wished to involve von Braun in research of the aircraft in hopes that the German rocket engineer might advance the investigation. Jealously suspicious of von Braun's talent, expertise, and desire to create a space program, Maslow determined at once that he alone would personally make a decision regarding the fate of the aircraft. He would take the added precaution of storing this particular report among his personal belongings until he arrived at his new post. There were only two copies. Locked away in a vault, Nazi soldier Albrecht Gohritz's incredible account of the aircraft's discovery, capture, and voyage to the North Sea would be doomed to the denial of the aircraft itself, coveted and hoarded for mystery that could yet prove unworthy of the price it had exacted of so many.

Maslow turned to the documents detailing the study of the craft upon its arrival in the United States. American scientists and engineers had reacted with astonishment and voracious curiosity. Extensive testing did nothing to quell either effect. The craft's sharp angles, gentle curves, and backswept design were uncomfortably alien. The exotic black beast was not bereft of ornamentation. Odd symbols teased the light, miniature holograms dancing between imagination and reality. The cipher could be translated no better than the craft itself could be explained.

Disassembling the structure was first in a series of hopeless endeavors. There appeared to be no way to access the interior of the craft. No buttons, levers, or knobs protruded from or were imbedded in the sleek vessel. Temperature extremes and chemical applications inflicted no damage. The smooth skin stoically defied efforts to rupture or cut through, and forceful impacts produced inconsequential dents that recovered immediately without leaving scars.

The team was on the verge of giving up the day a cryptographer, caressing yet another pattern amidst the illusive hieroglyphics, traced a combination that released a hatch in smooth silence. Caution and curiosity reigned once more as the team shrugged off the unsolved mysteries of the façade and embraced a whole new aspect of their enigma. The interior of the craft proved no less daunting. Instead of buttons that pressed, toggled, slid, or rotated, the control system consisted of a series of panels that responded perhaps to touch, possibly to sound, and of compartments that the team eventually decided must collect, store, convert, and distribute solar energy in sufficient quantities to operate all functions of the craft. Although every attempt toward the vehicle's analysis and destruction proved futile, though the researchers failed to interpret the symbols that might have expounded the entire history and intent of the aircraft, they were at last able to bring it to life. Bitter disappointment and endless frustration at the unknown variables were offset by exploration and discovery of the means by which to operate the aircraft on its most basic premise, cutting swiftly, silent and invisible, through the night air over the clean, white sands of the vast, empty desert. Something in its design or perhaps in its smooth skin allowed it to proceed undetected by radar. There were those among the scientists who suggested that the arcane aircraft might be ideally suited for travel outside the earth's atmosphere.

Creating such an aircraft would require technology beyond comprehension. Maslow knew of no country capable of doing so. He couldn't begin to fathom where or how the Soviets had stolen or found the contraption, but even that knowledge would yet leave the mystery of its origin unresolved.

Maslow paused for a sip of coffee and a moment of deliberation. The research team had approached their subject as though the aircraft were a good thing possessing secrets of a positive nature that merely wanted decoding. What if, instead, it was a weapon or a surveillance system by which a hostile government could become a remote student of American research or a spy within an obscure government facility? What if it were a modern-day Trojan horse? He frowned over the remaining pages.

There was no final report, merely an inventory of each scientist's conclusions organized tidily into tables which related only that the team understood little more about the craft after months of study than they had known when they first made its acquaintance. The unknown generated a degree of fear, which found outlet in the warning with which the research team concluded their presentation: whether manmade or, in the terms of one rash suggestion, the product of extraterrestrial expertise, such technology in the hands of a powerful communist government presented a frightening prospect for the future of the entire world, especially one still recovering from war.

Those who came into contact with the aircraft were fed the usual drivel about remote surveillance prototypes or potential archetypes for future weaponry. The variety of tales that were deliberately leaked collided with one another as planned to clog the gears of the rumor mill until no one knew what to believe. Of those who had not personally encountered the vessel, few were convinced the aircraft existed at all. Moribund rumors whispered that it had been classified as a top secret government cache and removed to an unnamed operating location upon its arrival in the United States. Curiosity found no purchase in the minds of patriots whose country was recovering from a world war, and those who knew more knew better than to insinuate that they did.

A more important goal had been brought to fruition during the previous summer. Last July America's first nuclear weapon, created in the form of a plutonium bomb, was detonated on the Alamogordo Test Range in the Jornada del Muerto desert. The resulting explosion was monitored, studied, and approved for its devastating potential. Deployment of a similar bomb less than one month later brought an end to the conflict between the United States and Japan. In the aftermath of World War II, Americans worked to restore a semblance of normalcy to their daily lives, building their futures on a mutual foundation of sacrifice, duty, and love.

Research on the unaccommodating aircraft had been crippled from the beginning by meager subsidy and staffing upon its arrival months after the devastating success of the Manhattan Project. Those who controlled the department's finances felt there was no benefit in continuing to waste money and manpower on a potentially useless variable when the country needed funding for more important projects. With 1946 well underway, the unidentified aircraft was forgotten by all but the guard assigned to ensure its perpetual presence in an unspecified hangar that was itself unsuspected by the rest of the world.

Nations struggled to grow out of the rubble of war and establish their place in the new world hierarchy. Time would soften an impact that future generations would never feel, the war to them an elder-told story that brought their imaginations alive even as their own perceptions of reality argued that the tales suffered from gross exaggeration.

There remained those, however, for whom some legends would never die, and who would forever anonymously epitomize certain unanticipated results of the government's desert project, code-named Trinity. They were the reason – not the incidental presence of the unidentified aircraft – that Josten Maslow had been assigned to govern the clandestine facility in the San Andres Mountains of New Mexico.

He set aside the volume detailing the aircraft and opened the report that summarized the wounding, detention, and subsequent research currently underway on twenty-two Trinity Test survivors and three healthy subjects acquired for comparison. The three control subjects were of both psychological and biological value, for they were relatives of the survivors. Maslow skimmed through the pages. Keloids, cancers, cataracts; all caused, surgically removed, caused and cured again. Baldness, scarring, and skin discoloration, unfortunate results of exposures to various chemical agents and experimental levels of radiation. Studies to determine the results of prenatal exposure to radiation and the effects of chemical and biological agents on reproduction had not yet been conducted. Only one of the females had been pregnant at the time of the Trinity Test, and she had not been a viable subject.

Human test subjects were sources of invaluable research. What a fortunate tragedy that the survival of these few had made them available for this purpose.

The United States government would never openly permit or justify such activities. But lurking amidst its tangled branches were certain pseudomorphic pods, a handful of operating locations that functioned below the radar of public knowledge and moral obligation. Each location answered to its own military-styled structure of administrators, who answered to an area commander, who answered to no one but himself, as long as he avoided the scrutiny of the Council to whom he sent detailed quarterly analyses. The visible government appreciated the research the Council provided without asking how the results were achieved.

The new commander of Area L was no stranger to sins of omission. Maslow tossed the report into a box atop twenty-five individual profiles that he would review another time, after he had established authority over his kingdom.

Chapter Nine

If there is one bane of human existence, one nightmare above all others, it is Isolation. Even the terrible demon Discouragement cringes like a mere imp before the dread shadow of Isolation.

It whispers from the farthest corners of the mind. You are alone. No one knows. No one cares. No one has ever felt what you feel. No one understands your fear, your pain. Your experiences are unique. They have set you apart. You are alone.

It is a lie, of course, but harder to disprove than most, for doing so requires vulnerability, a deliberate reaching out for companionship, and then the possibility of rejection – a terrifying thought! – and so we stand back and wait for a braver soul to go first.

Isolation winks at the power of Suggestion, and they toast each other with the tears of lonely multitudes who live their entire lives as acquaintances – strangers pretending to be friends.

The shield of Faith can grow heavy, but the battle is won when one recognizes her pain in another's eyes, and both reach for the comfort of that common bond.

Arlene stared with fear and dismay at the grotesque figure that sat in front of her. The creature regarded her with a similar expression. Arlene took in the hairless head, smoky eyes, and drawn, withered features. Her gaze traveled down the gaunt frame, stopping at slender ashen hands tipped with brittle white fingernails. The hands looked just like hers. Arlene stared at them and felt her soul shrivel as reality set in with a vengeance.

She knew the tragedy in the desert had left her with permanent scars. The treatments, tests, and drugs forced upon her since that day seemed worse at times than the initial scalding that ripped tortured screams from her throat until she lost consciousness. She would never have imagined surviving the succession of hideously painful and dehumanizing medical procedures that followed. She witnessed her own skin waste from a healing, hopeful pink to the pale gray complexion she and the stranger shared. Arlene had cried, begged, threatened the unresponsive medical staff. She had prayed to die. But she remained a prisoner with hope of neither explanation nor reprieve, and until now she had been completely alone.

Moments ago a warden, suited as always from head to toe, entered Arlene's room and pointed toward a chair. She obediently sat down. A second warden wheeled in a wretched caricature of a person, unfastened its ankle and wrist cuffs, removed a hood from the poor thing's head, and helped it out of the wheelchair. The warden pointed to the chair facing Arlene. The creature promptly sat. The wardens rolled a second bed into the room and positioned it against the opposite wall. They walked out, locked the door, and left the two patients staring at each other.

Arlene had gone rigid with fright until she focused on her companion's hands. Then she knew. Truth crushed her with the weight of her world, a world that would never again be what she wanted or expected it to be, as she stared into a face that she realized mirrored her own. It was a reflection she had not seen before this moment, and it was almost more than she could bear.

The other person's hand trembled as it fluttered to the ravaged face and wiped away a tear. Arlene steeled herself against the repulsive visage, but her heart melted when she looked into sad, frightened eyes that anxiously met hers with the same reactions of confusion and dread. She took a deep breath and sat up straight with as much confidence as she could muster.

"Hi. My name is Arlene. Early on the morning of July sixteenth I was camping with my friends in the desert in New Mexico, and there was an explosion. I don't know what became of the others, but I woke up here. I don't know what day it is now or how long I have been here." Arlene swallowed hard and braided her own fingers to tame their trembling in her lap. "But it has been a very long time."

Her companion drew a sharp breath. Arlene looked up to find the creature staring at her in wide-eyed astonishment. "Arlene?" The girl's voice was raspy, and she had trouble enunciating her words. "Arlene Brooks? Oh, praise God, I thought you were dead! I thought everybody had died but me. Arlene, it's me, Abby McAllister!"

"Abby?" Arlene studied the face that bore no resemblance to the pretty redhead who had been one of her dearest friends. She forced herself to remain still when the other girl reached out and touched her bald head. They gazed at one another, afraid to believe.

"Singin' in the rain…" The girl's voice broke at the effort.

"Abby!" Arlene wailed, and the two fell into one another's arms, sobbing. Months of grief and despair were abruptly and irrevocably altered by the unexpected arrival of hope.

"Are any of the others here," Abby begged. "Have you seen my brother?"

Arlene shook her head. "Like you, I thought I was the lone survivor. But seeing you gives me hope that the others made it, too!"

"Toby and Tom and Sybil…" Abby counted on her fingers. "Rachael Knight, Nathaniel Harper, Vernon Shepherd…"

"Will Blackwater, Gilbert Fitzpatrick, Maria Ramirez, and Russ Winter." Arlene spoke the last name in a whisper. Unrelenting nightmares of her fiancé's death provoked her greatest torment – the ever-present threat that she would never see him again.

"You and me," Abby finished. "How can we find out if the others are alive and if they are here? Nobody will talk to me."

Arlene shrugged. "Nor to me. I don't know. Right now I'm just happy to not be alone anymore."

"So am I," Abby agreed. "You wouldn't believe the mental exercises I have practiced just to keep my sanity."

"Oh, yes, I would!"

For the first time since they last met, the girls welcomed an occasion to laugh.

"What is the very first thing you remember after the explosion?"

"Have you been able to talk for very long?"

"Do they give you real food to eat? I get bowls of mush."

"Breakfast was pulpy. And yellow."

"Do the wardens in suits...do things to you? Medical procedures, I mean, but..."

"Yes. They do."

The morning sped past as Arlene and Abby shared their experiences within the institution and helped each other remember the lives they had led before that day in the desert. They hurried through the tasteless repast served at noon in order to have lunch done and the wardens gone so they could continue talking. After the trays were removed, however, a third individual was wheeled into the room, bound and hooded like Abby had been. Arlene and Abby needed no introduction to recognize their new roommate, who bore unusual characteristics that set her apart from other people, even in circumstances as extraordinary as theirs. The wardens positioned a third bed in a corner and once more left the girls to conduct their own introductions.

"Maria!" Arlene exclaimed.

The frightened girl cowered to the floor, whimpering in terror.

"It's okay, Maria. We're Abby and Arlene. We're still your friends, no matter how different we look. Don't cry, Maria!" Abby held the girl in her arms and rocked her as a mother would soothe a wounded child. Arlene sat on the floor beside them and took Maria's hand in her own, waiting for the storm to pass.

The tears gradually abated, but Maria yet trembled. Abby continued to hold her, humming a hoarse tune, until Maria felt strong enough to withdraw from the comfort of her friend's arms. She then hugged Arlene and wept quietly for a while longer. Cleansing tears purged the hurt, shame, and hopelessness of the previous months and offered faith a tentative foothold in a shattered life, giving her a reason to start anew.

The afternoon hours were a joyous pursuit of three friends reunited with each other and with hope. In sharing their experiences they learned that Maria's tortures had exceeded what Arlene and Abby had endured, as if her differences offered additional opportunities for experimentation and observation.

When three wardens delivered dinner trays, the girls joined hands and spoke their evening prayers. By the time the meal concluded they had discovered that there was indeed strength in God, in friends, and in greater numbers. They clung to the possibility that where three survivors were housed, more might be confined in other areas of the facility.

Maria voiced their collective musings. "If only there was a way to find out for sure."

Chapter Ten

Robert Lake reluctantly opened his eyes to familiar clinical surroundings. He lay quiet and still, allowing awareness to dissipate the sluggish haze of sleep. He prowled the room visually until his deliberate study settled on the chair. The sight of the chair incensed him: bolted to the floor, made entirely of steel, hard and cold, a repulsive bile green. Robert wanted to pick up the chair and bash it into a wall, hurl it across the room, smash it and everything connected to it into irreparable, satisfying, bite-sized pieces and crush what was left underfoot as he walked away from this living Hell and its costumed agents – and a worse fate than this to any who attempted to stop him.

He had no idea how much time had passed since the July night his little girls ran away. Lacking any method by which to record the events and set his memories aside, he resurrected and relived those critical hours every morning. He concentrated to keep the details firmly alive in his thoughts and to safeguard them from the uncertainties that inevitably blur facts viewed through the filter of time. Forgiving and forgetting the conflicts of the miserable week spent with his wife's family, Robert began his recollections with the pressure of Joy's hands on his shoulders. He focused on waking to the sound of her voice frantic in his ear as she told him their daughters had fled the unbearable concept of a broken family.

The thunderstorm hindered their search for his daughters. He, Kenneth, and Dave divided their territory in order to cover more ground in less time. The unearthly explosion knocked Robert off his feet. He was instantly aware of a pervading sickness the likes of which had never afflicted him before. Robert called desperately for his daughters, hoping they had sought refuge in a nearby canyon to escape the blast. Disoriented and wracked with bouts of vomiting, he lost his way in the dark and collapsed when his flesh began to burn as though acid were eating his skin away. Sunrise brought heat and frustration, weakness and horrific pain. He cast about for Kenneth and Dave but they, too, were lost to him. Robert became aware of a commotion and saw in the distance his children carried away by figures costumed head to toe in protective suits. He attempted to yell, but his throat emitted an abrasive groan; he tried to crawl after them, but his limbs would not support him. Robert curled involuntarily against pain that suggested his entrails were shriveling within his abdomen. As suited rescuers lifted him from the earth, he sought out the eyes within the nearest hood and made one last plea for his little girls.

Vague memories that might have been dreams recalled immobility on a stretcher and a transfer between vehicles on what appeared to be a military base. But he had never dreamed of such things before, and since the hoods existed beyond the initial cataclysm, he expected that the other experiences were just as real.

He awoke in what he assumed to be a medical facility. Robert was not blinded. He did not lose his ability to talk. His skin was not too severely burned until the treatments and massive amounts of medication which he supposed were to have induced healing plunged him instead into a nightmare of contorted agony, burning his organs like liquid fire, melting his flesh down to cool gray ash, rendering him debilitated and defenseless.

Robert wrenched his gaze from the hateful chair and contemplated the door. It was the second to hold him hostage. The other room had been smaller. His first matter of business upon arrival had been to demand that his daughters be returned to him. None of the hoods would communicate with him regardless of how vociferous he became, except to issue necessary commands when they required his cooperation. Unwilling that their silence should undermine his humanity, Robert questioned them daily about his children, about his physical condition, about the purpose of each trial he was forced to endure, about the fate of his two young friends. The longer the hoods held their peace, the louder Robert petitioned his cause until one day he heard a voice expressing similar dissatisfaction. A cry of protest shrilled out, lacking the benefit of words, and Robert answered with his own outraged roar. He thought the other voice belonged to a woman and strained to hear more. When she remained silent, he tried to call out again. A gloved hand compressed his mouth until he could hardly breathe through the hood they placed over his head in order to blindfold him when they transferred him between rooms.

He was not startled at the revelation that the facility

hosted additional victims against their will. As if to distract him from the evidence and limit the hours he might spend plotting possible reactions to it, the hoods abruptly met Robert's demands regarding his children. The morning after the encounter, a medical team strapped Robert securely to a gurney and started an intravenous drip that lowered his awareness just below consciousness. He awoke in a room similar in every detail to his previous cell, with the exception that this one was considerably larger. He could see two more beds against the opposite wall with a small gray figure in each. Leaning over one of those beds, smiling at its occupant, stood the woman of his dreams.

The scene impacted him like a fist to the stomach, suffocating him with horror. He did not for a moment believe his wife was aware of his whereabouts or his condition. If the hoods refused to discuss Robert's injuries, treatment, and prognosis with him, he could scarcely find logic in their sharing this information with anyone outside the facility. Robert's one comfort was the knowledge that if Joy was ignorant to her family's suffering, at least she had been spared their fate. The sudden reality of her presence instigated a torrent of questions begging why she was here, when she had arrived, how she had been treated, what had she been told, and did she know, please, God, did she know how long he had been waiting for recovery and release.

Sorrow that she was here battled ecstasy and desire for her soft, sweet beauty in this cold, brutal place. Robert had choked with emotion as the sight of her swept him back through thirteen years to the most cherished days of his life, when Joy's deep brown eyes sparkled with eagerness for a future with him. He had ached to make her his wife. He couldn't remember not loving her. When the country went to war, he was glad of the deferment that allowed him to stay with his family, but his intense work schedule overwhelmed Joy with the duties of mother, father, homemaker, and handyman. She devastated him with the threat of divorce. He had clung to an elusive wisp of hope when their children's disappearance swayed her to give their marriage another chance. That memory provoked emotion too great to suppress.

He had inhaled deeply, alerting Joy that her husband was awake. She came to him, reached for him, took his wasted body into her warm, smooth arms and pulled his head against her shoulder, shrouding his face with her fragrant hair. She had answered some of his questions and avoided others. Having her here, talking with her, learning that she still loved him and wanted to be with him, had given Robert his first hope of salvation since that disastrous morning in the desert, even as his heart sank under the sacrifice of her presence. He would gladly have given her up forever in exchange for the knowledge that she was safe. It was bitter redemption to see his wife sentenced to this horrible place and to learn that she was here because military police had insisted that he and the children needed her.

He was fully awake now, having accomplished his ante meridiem routine of recalling details too important to forget. He examined his surroundings for weaknesses he might have previously overlooked and relaxed at length to the peaceful rhythm of Joy's breathing beside him. She sensed his restiveness and snuggled under the sheet, squeezing her eyes shut. Robert smiled and hugged her close. Joy had never been a morning person.

The day continued to rouse around them. Robert heard whispers from behind the curtain that divided the room in half. Catherine and Elisabeth were deep in discussion as they rose from their beds. Those two were never at a loss for words. He wondered how they could find so many things to talk about when their current life offered so limited an array of topics. One face peered tentatively around the curtain, followed by another. "Good morning, Daddy," quietly so as not to disturb their mother, though they knew from experience she was already awake. Robert winked at his daughters. They giggled softly and disappeared around the concrete partition that concealed a toilet, sink, and shower. The water came on in the shower, the toilet flush was answered by a yelp from the unfortunate recipient of an extra-hot blast, and laughter disintegrated to a brief squabble until one of the girls evicted the other from the bathroom.

Joy sighed and sat up. Robert scratched between her shoulders as she stretched, and she responded with pleasant little murmurings akin to the purr of a cat.

The shower was off momentarily, and then on again. When Elisabeth joined her parents, she was clean and dressed in a pale blue shift identical to those worn daily by her mother and sister.

"Sleep well?" Joy reached for a hug. Elisabeth walked gratefully into her mother's arms.

Robert turned away so they wouldn't see his expression. Clothing was another point of contention. Robert and his family were not permitted street clothes. Even Joy, who had arrived healthy and unscathed and with their luggage in hand, was provided only plain, straight dresses to wear. Joy had parted company with their personal effects upon her arrival. Hoods had taken her family's luggage from her and locked her in a silent, lonely room from which she was removed only for forced medical procedures. By the time she was reunited with her daughters and later with Robert, Joy had become accustomed to wearing the institution's garments and to making do with what paltry toiletries they allowed her to use to accomplish daily personal hygiene.

Robert wore a loose-fitting shirt and drawstring slacks of the same light blue cotton. In addition to pants that fit and a belt, he sincerely wished for real shoes to replace the soft-soled slippers issued to him and his family. He loathed the unkempt feeling that he was wearing pajamas all the time.

Catherine emerged from the bathroom, and Elisabeth returned with her to the other side of the curtain to make their beds. Robert sat up and watched his wife pad away for her turn under the spray. He smoothed the blankets as he listened to noises from beyond the steel door, indistinct but predictable in the mornings. The hoods were making their rounds. They would deliver breakfast soon. Robert's attention turned to the running water. He paused with pillow in hand. Mindful of the children and his own physical appearance, he resisted the urge to join his wife in the shower. The thought provoked contempt. His advances would only result in frustration for both him and his wife. The explosion had rendered him incapable of following through with his desires. He punched the pillow– hard – and laid it beside its mate on their bed.

He was bitterly aware of things he had ever taken for granted: blonde hair and blue eyes and an athletic build; physical stamina, emotional strength, and general control over the things most important in his life. Masculinity. His ability to provide for his family and protect them from harm. Talent, creativity, and ambition for a brighter future for the four of them. Privacy. His own house, bedroom, pillow, his own clothes and music on the radio and whatever in the kitchen cabinets he might desire to eat. Reading the newspaper, repairing his car, making passionate love to his wife and watching her face as she drifted into exhausted, satisfied sleep in his arms. Taking photographs and feeling pride in their publication; trying to fill a little of the emptiness left in the lives of two teenaged boys by the absence of fathers gone to war; watching the metamorphosis of his daughters from adorable little girls into lovely young women.

Robert's first sight of Catherine and Elisabeth in his room had left him paralyzed with shock. They were so wasted and disfigured that he would not have known them but for two frightened voices that called out from their beds for their daddy. Robert's heart broke, and he would have wept for hours, but there was nowhere to hide his face, and he could not do it in front of them. He faced the same dilemma with the blistering rage that followed. There was nothing to attack and punish, no one from whom to exact restitution, and had he screamed his lungs clean of tormented fury, he would have frightened his family far worse than the procedures they daily endured at the hands of strangers. It was a blessing, he supposed, that he was much more stunned by their appearance than they were at his. Although Robert was aware that he was bald and emaciated with tarnished, leathery skin, there had been no reflective surfaces in which he could view his face and become acquainted with the altered features fate had bequeathed him. Catherine and Elisabeth had not been separated. They had grown accustomed, as children somehow do to less-than-ideal conditions, to the drawn, weathered faces and dark sunken eyes of their destiny. Unlike Robert, the girls held onto the hope that eventually their skin would heal, their hair would grow back, and life would again be as it once had been.

Their acceptance of their father was automatic. They were joyous in the reunion and sorrowful of the damage done, hard pressed by guilt that found them living in greater horror than that which had chased them from their grandparents' home into the embrace of a stormy night. A lesson in maturity had been thrust upon them. Catherine daily stifled her resentment and stalked out of sight. She acknowledged that running away wasn't as important as where she might go and how far, but she remained angry at the brutality of the lesson. Elisabeth, who had followed her sister's lead because she didn't know what else to do, was learning to think for herself. She daily caressed her father's face and said she was sorry. Robert made every effort to alleviate the burden of blame the girls staggered under, but he could neither erase the evidence from their bodies nor return his family to the generous life they had all taken so tragically for granted.

Joy astonished Robert with her love, though he remained subconsciously braced against the rejection he had fully anticipated and still could not believe was not forthcoming. If she was disgusted or repelled by her husband's appearance, there was no hesitation that would betray such thoughts. Joy had held Robert in her arms when he awoke to her presence. She wept for him and their daughters and talked with him for hours about how hoods took her to Catherine and Elisabeth and locked her away with them, how her daughters' physical condition and the agonies of their recovery had nearly made her crazy. She told Robert about the subterfuge through which military police escorted her from her parents' home and took her to a military base, where she was strapped to a gurney and given an injection that rendered her unconscious. She awoke in the institution. Beyond that simple explanation, she refused to dwell on questions related to her own experiences with the physical examinations and unidentified medications administered by anonymous hoods. Joy insisted that beauty came from the heart. Robert was still her husband, and if the other two packages were terribly damaged, they yet contained her beloved little girls. She slipped quickly into the pattern of taking care of them as best she could and as much as she was allowed. Though provided her own bed, Joy elected to sleep with her husband in his. Robert was overwhelmed afresh every day at the provision of such a profound blessing in such a callous environment.

Joy agreed with Robert that the medical treatments he and the girls received were not all intended to effect a cure and that some, if not all of late, were unethically experimental in nature. Though she refused to discuss the details of her own encounters, Joy cursed when she declared that she was nothing more or less than a laboratory animal to the scientists in the suits. Of a certainty, the four of them were all in much worse physical condition at the present than they had been on the morning of the explosion.

Perhaps 'worse' was not as accurate a description as 'different.'

He had to be physically restrained the first few times a team took away one of his children. Assurances that he would be permanently separated from his family if he proved unable to control such emotional outbursts persuaded him to turn a hostile back each time Catherine or Elisabeth was taken from the room. It was more than Robert could stand when his daughters returned sobbing inconsolably. They whimpered their plight to Joy, who muttered their experiences to Robert, who wondered that he could be brought to the point of craving the opportunity to kill a person for preying on his daughters in a manner unforgivable by any moral law. And not only them. He worried about Joy's constant exposure to whatever he and the girls might communicate to her, as she was the only human in contact with them who was unprotected by an encasing suit and hood. Attendants also took Joy from him at regular intervals, and although she assured Robert at each return that she was all right, he knew she was not sharing the details of her trials with him. She refused to discuss things that might upset the girls and add to the burden already crushing her husband to his knees. Robert could only hold her close and wonder. He wouldn't demand that she relive her dreadful experiences by describing them to him. Her strength and determination made Robert love her all the more, even as his hatred for the hoods that brought such agony upon his family increased the pressure that roiled beneath his façade with volcanic instability.

With each empty day, with each grueling treatment inflicted against his own wasted body or on one of his family, Robert grew more determined to force an end to the insanity that held them captive. He fought against desperation when he wondered how many days, weeks, months had been stolen from his family. The passage of time faded behind him in an ugly blur. Daily he ached at the void left in his heart by Kenneth and Dave. He wondered if they were still alive.

Meanwhile, he showered and dressed and joined his family at the sterile table and chairs that were bolted to the concrete floor. He ingested the soft, runny breakfast served by alleged human beings in shapeless cocoons. Robert moved restlessly through the day just like he had dealt with every day before, attempting to shield his wife and daughters from the impatience and rage that devoured from within as he cast about once more for any potential of escape, no matter how slim the chance might be. Dementia grinned knowingly from the shadows, a predator waxing bolder with time. Shut away from the world in a windowless room without daily news or books to read, writing materials or a clock, without music or entertainment or human voices other than their own, no small effort was required to ignore the frenzied whispers of madness.

Love kept the demons at bay and salvaged his very life. In bed that night, during the process of repeating the morning's critical study of the room, a slight movement at Robert's side distracted his attention from the antagonizing chair. He looked down at Joy's slender arm draped across the desiccated skin of his chest and felt emotion in his heart almost beyond what he could bear. He wrapped himself around the lovely creature who was his life mate, and Joy responded by snuggling into the curve of his body. Robert held his wife close and his tears inside and welcomed a few blessed hours of slumbering reprieve from the helpless rage and grief that assailed him without mercy each day.

There was a way out, a route of escape. Robert believed this if nothing else. All he had to do was hold fast to his faith and concentrate on the details of his daily life until the solution became clear. He was strong, and he was determined to bring that dream to fruition for his family when opportunity discovered the moment.

It was no longer an invalid's quest.

Chapter Eleven

―◆‣◊‣✳‣◊‣◆―

We rely on memory to provide a haven in which we can rest when we feel the need to slip the bonds of reality. We wish each other pleasant dreams, interludes that will either resurrect soothing moments from the past or weave ribbons of fantasy from imagination – nightmares, warped sequences of impossible events, people we haven't seen for a very long time, desires that cause our hearts to ache. Sometimes our dreams are dark and loathsome. Sometimes they are reminders or revelations. Sometimes our dreams are holy.

Disturbing memories occasionally trouble our dreams. Treacherous indeed is the nature of sleep that taints our refuge from a stark present by transporting us backward in time to relive an equally pitiless fragment of our past.

―◆‣◊‣✳‣◊‣◆―

The temperature reached one hundred-fifteen degrees Fahrenheit by midday. Dusk brought only a suggestion of relief from the humidity as troops wearily resigned themselves to pockmarks they had gouged into the coral. *The foxes have holes,* scrolled dully through Ray's mind, *and the birds of the air have nests,* but the marine lays his head on jagged stone in a shallow pit that he prays won't be his grave before morning.

The three-day campaign that weeks before trans-mogrified into perpetual carnage left his mind begging reprieve from a hideous nightmare that imagination lacked the ability to dispatch. Morality argued with truth as his buddies lost their minds and their lives and were hauled off the battlefield in pieces while he stepped on, over, through the putrid remains of a fallen enemy and accomplished one more stride in the general direction of success. Focus blurred on a distant commander's call for victory when warfare became an intimate, face-to-face demand that a soldier either kill or be killed or, in the end, both.

How does the tornado work, Daddy? Why did it blow that house away, but not hurt the barn at all? Did the wind not like that house?

I don't know, Sarah. Why did the bullets blow Sherlock away, but not me, when our shoulders were pressed together in battle? I felt the hit, Sarah. I felt the bullets go into his body, and I felt the life go out. I don't know why, my sweet, innocent baby girl. Everybody liked Sherlock.

He in particular, on this day, had suffered debilitating depression on top of the miserable, grueling exhaustion of war. He greeted the dawn with a heavy heart, determined not to give in to the hopeless void that consumed so many of his peers. Averted eyes and a gruff attitude convinced his companions to stay out of his way and leave him alone to think about his family. He wondered how they would spend this day, his daughter's sixteenth birthday. He and his wife made each of their children's birthdays a memorable event, but this one should be extra special. He had little to offer in the way of a gift. He scrawled a 'sweet sixteen' greeting on the sandy beach with a stick, and a buddy photographed him kneeling next to the words he ached to say in person. He had mailed the photo and a lighthearted letter to his family with a prayer that it would be received before Sarah's birthday. Uncertainty twinged in his belly, a physical reaction to emotional pain. The island dimmed in twilight's gloom, the day nearly done. He would wad himself up in a trough in the ground and sleep and dream and, God willing, wake to miss them more tomorrow.

First he traipsed to the bay and submerged his filthy carcass in the salty water. The debate as to whether he was cleaner going in or coming out was not as important as knowing he had put forth some small effort toward hygiene. It made no difference. Nothing beyond survival, taking hold of life with both hands and damning those who would tear it from his grasp, mattered in these wretched moments.

Everything stank. There was no escaping the stench of rotting corpses, of human excrement, of sweat, of blood. Water would not wash it from his skin, could not purge it from his sinuses or dilute the taste from his mouth. In compensation for that failure, the mock bath brought his family to mind. His greatest pleasure as a farmer came in returning home for an evening of rest with his family after a day of hard labor. It was heaven on earth to lather the sweat and smell off his body in a tub of warm water, to emerge clean, dress in fresh clothing, and see the desire in his wife's eyes when he took her in his arms – a promise of what they would share later, when the supper dishes were put away and the children had gone to bed.

He shuffled inland a dozen feet behind his buddies, eyes to the ground. He swatted at a lethargic bluebottle fly and paused to listen to the night noises of the natives. Darkness released the land crabs to a gory repast. The creatures' comprehensive diet included what carrion they found on the island. Of late, there had been plenty of corpses to accommodate their eclectic appetites. He shuddered and continued up the beach. The engine sounded so faintly at first that he did not notice its approach. By the time he realized the danger, it was upon him.

Porter! Get down! God, Porter!

Ray roared in terror and pain and fought his way out of the bed. Unable to claw his way through the wall, he slammed backward against it, wide-eyed and panting, as reality trickled sluggishly through the crevices of a former life and automatically sorted, as it flooded his mind, then from now. At the mercy of memory he sank to the floor, sobbing grief, horror, and rage that never seemed to lose their edge.

Belva pulled the sheet off their bed as she came to him and used the hem to wipe away sweat that was caustic to his ravaged skin. She had grown accustomed to the war dreams that violated her husband's sleep. If that were not enough, the medication and barbaric treatments that should have aided his recovery from their desert experience further diluted his spirit until he was overcome with exhaustion, courting defeat. Belva relaxed on the floor beside her husband as Ray took her in his arms and wrapped the sheet around them both. She soon fell asleep against his shoulder.

He received his million-dollar wound with plenty of change when the Mitsubishi flew in low, strafing the beach with machine gun fire. Several bullets tore through Ray's body, but only one did lasting damage, shattering his left elbow and scattering fragments of the joint across the bloody dirt at his side. He stared into the lifeless eyes of the soldier nearest him, just a twenty-year-old kid who'd married his high school sweetheart only to leave her and their unborn child at home in the name of freedom. The child turned out to be twins, and all the boy talked about was getting home to the love of his life so he could help her raise those two precious little ones. His were the most beautiful babies on earth, and the fact that he had never seen them did not change what he knew to be true.

Ray wondered who would be a husband to Jimmy's bride and a father to his children after the war.

He flexed the fingers of his left hand, curled them into a tight, hard fist. He had been told that his arm would have to be amputated. He was surprised when he awoke from surgery to find that it was still with him. Because he was last in line, the doctor told him bluntly. Had another patient needed attention, there would have been no time for intricate surgery. The doctor would not save one soldier's arm if it meant losing another soldier's life. Ray felt ominously grateful and sickened at his own salvation after a day of rigorous self-pity; with or without his arm, he was going home to be with his family. Missing Sarah's birthday meant nothing when he would again see her smile every day. Jimmy had been too busy looking forward to a reunion with his family to wallow in disappointment of the separation. When he read the letter announcing the birth of his twins, his focus did not settle on being away from his wife when she delivered. He rejoiced at the miracle, anticipating a future that would forever be celebrated without him. Ray winced as he smudged away another tear and blinked back more that crowded behind his eyes and made his head ache. Jimmy had taught him the art of appreciation, the value of hope. Ray would always argue that the lesson wasn't worth the price.

Porter!

He could still hear the young man's voice. Jimmy had been only four years older than Sarah, yet Sarah seemed so young and fresh, perhaps because she remained blissfully ignorant of a soldier's existence in the midst of a war. Funny how Ray could see Jimmy as a contemporary, while his perception of Sarah insisted that she would always be his little girl.

Ray's arm healed in a permanent bend. Belva, Sarah, and Ben devised a variety of creative therapies at home that aided in his recovery, as did a gradual increase in the amount of work he performed on the farm. Muscle control and coordination eventually returned until he was able to use the left hand again, albeit with half its original flexibility and strength.

Ray hugged Belva close when she sighed and opened her eyes. He kissed her cheek and drew strength from her smile. Ray boosted her to her feet, clasped her outstretched hand, and followed her back to their bed. Belva relaxed against him, secure in his presence. Her breathing slowed to the rhythm of deep slumber. Sleep offered the most sincere recovery, Ray thought, from the arduous medical procedures she had endured through-out the previous day.

Ray continued his private battle, worse mentally than Peleliu. At least there he knew who the enemies were, and he knew his wife and children were safe at home. He could hardly grasp the notion that here in America, secure on home soil, his family had met with disaster. His children had almost certainly died in the explosion. His wife was as worn out as he was from the myriad trials to which they had been subjected in the name of medicine. The pain, shock, and humiliation of their ordeals voided all his respect for this medical community. He and Belva looked like mutants from some distorted netherworld, and their requests for explanations were rudely ignored. Ray was especially incensed that he and Belva had been offered no information as to the fate of their children or of John and Mary and the Pendleton family.

The thugs in protective suits were now the enemy. Ray lacked the means to express the fury he felt when they sedated him to prevent his interference when they came to take his wife away. They acted as if he had no right to protect her. Ray's anger, finding no outlet or expression since even rage was subject to drugs, became a dagger in his ribs. The blade was gradually sharpened, finely honed to a cunning, invisibly thin edge every time he was held down, injected, and pushed helplessly aside as they took Belva out the door. After a number of such encounters, a voice had informed him that his wife would be taken from him permanently if he proved incapable of controlling his temper. Ray stood silently thereafter, still close enough to make the uncomfortable suits display their hypodermic weapons as they backed out of the room using Belva on the gurney as a barrier between them and her husband's unspoken threat.

Ray trembled and held on to his wife with all his strength. As far as he knew, Belva was all he had left, and he wasn't going to give her up or allow his own life to be taken without a fight. He felt more than ready for a confrontation, but held his peace for fear of potential retribution. He didn't want to die if it meant leaving Belva unprotected and completely alone. However, if he could find a way to get her out of the institution, and his efforts cost him his life, he was perfectly ready to lay it down. That was the price of war. It had been paid by many others – Sherlock, Jimmy, and Ralph, the buddy who shared a camera he wasn't even supposed to have. Ralph took Ray's picture on the beach one evening and pounced on an enemy grenade the next morning. Live warriors and dead heroes, all. *Porter*, Ray's fellow marines had called him, faster and easier to say than Davenport. Since basic training the name had been a rallying call, a battle cry, a congratulatory cheer, a jester's chant used to convey deep respect, complete confidence, jocular banter, and brotherly love.

Ray's chest heaved with emotion, but the tears had dried and gone. God help me, he prayed. He did not have long to wait. They came for Belva in the morning.

Chapter Twelve

The door swung open. Ray was immediately awake, flinging off the sheet as he got to his feet and stepped in front of Belva. The previous night's interruptions had caused them both to sleep through their normal waking hour. Ray expected suits to enter with breakfast trays. Instead, one entered pushing a gurney. A second occupied the doorway, its crossed arms and bored manner a blatant display of outright contempt that a patient might harbor thoughts of escape. The first suit stepped around the gurney and motioned for Ray to move aside. Ray drew up to his full height, crossed his arms and stared a hole through the clear shield of the hood into the eyes of the enemy. He sensed Belva standing behind him, trying to make herself small and undetectable in the corner. They both knew how these showdowns had ended before, as well as the reaction they were provoking by assuming the forbidden stance again. Ray felt stronger this morning and prayed that he wasn't merely acting out of foolish ambition. He was tired of cowering in forced obeisance to unjust circumstances and to people who, without cause, inflicted torment upon his wife and himself.

The first suit uncovered a small tray on the gurney that Ray already knew was there. It had been a long time since they had to sedate him in order to take Belva out of the room. Ray watched as the suit deftly filled a syringe with fluid that would incapacitate Ray long enough for them to remove his wife for a few hours and return her without further interference. Ray knew what would happen next. The suit would use its greater size and weight to lunge into him, pin him against the wall and stab the needle wherever it came into contact with his flesh while he flailed ineffectually against the thick, slippery garment that frustrated any attempt to take hold of the person within. Then, as consciousness slipped away, the suit would drape him across the bed and order his dispirited wife onto the gurney for whatever horrors lay ahead. They wouldn't use the aerosol tranquilizer on Ray in the close quarters of the room because Belva would likely receive part of the spray. The suits preferred her conscious for the preliminary checkups that began each day's procedures.

The first suit held the needle aloft for Ray to see and again motioned for him to move out of the way. Ray uncrossed his arms and placed his hands on his hips. As the suit gripped the needle and took a step toward Ray, an unearthly bellow shook the hall. A door slammed, and an enormous metal food cart reeled into the other suit, knocking it out of the doorway and out of sight. As the first suit hesitated and turned toward the door, Ray unleashed his desperation. He leaped forward and threw his weight upon the syringe-bearing hand, plunging the needle deep into the adversary's thigh. It pierced through the protective layers of the costume until it pricked the soft skin underneath, draining its contents suddenly and painfully in one swift, precise motion. The suit staggered away from Ray's attack. It pawed frantically at the needle, but the narcotic quickly took effect. As the suit stumbled through doorway, Ray took Belva by the hand and led her out of the room. The suit tottered across the hall, faltered, and went down against the opposite wall.

The suit pinned by the wheeled food cart spun it suddenly away and grabbed Belva's arm as she followed Ray from the room. Ray lunged in response to her scream, prepared to kill anyone who might harm her. To his amazement another person joined him in accosting the suit. They broke its hold on Belva, hurled it into the room Ray and Belva had shared, and slammed the door, locking it in. Ray cast about for more attacks, but none was forthcoming. He turned his attention to Belva. She stared, astonished, at their allies.

Ray turned to face a man who was his equal not only in height and build but also in appearance. The other man was considerably younger, Ray thought, and in better physical shape. A beautiful dark-haired woman stood a few feet behind him. She was the first healthy person Ray and Belva had seen without a suit since they were brought to the facility. Leaning against her were two pitifully disfigured children, each clinging to one of her arms for dear life. Ray focused his attention on the man, who met Ray's analytical gaze with equal respect. The stranger stepped forward and offered his hand.

"Robert Lake."

Ray grasped the hand firmly, instinctively accepting friendship and partnership. He was elated at the unexpected encounter. Robert, he sensed, was also a leader. Also a family man forced into a powerless fate whose outcome he was determined to change. Ray gave his best effort toward a smile and nodded when the gesture was returned by Robert and his wife.

Chapter Thirteen

———— ❖❖❖❖ ————

Noise, Robert had decided, would be his first offensive maneuver. If other survivors of the desert holocaust were housed here, medical overkill and intimidation had very likely driven them to the silent endurance to which he had submitted thus far. But no longer. Hoods took Catherine away for three long days and brought her back with a surgical scar across her abdomen. They forcibly removed his beloved Joy twice during Catherine's absence and injected her with who-knew-what to see how her body would react. It had been a long time coming, this arrival at the lowest point a human could achieve short of self-destruction. Robert was not about to resign his family's fate to this demon circus until their lives ended in death or in mental surrender to the madness of constant uncertainty and pain.

That there was absolutely nothing he could do about the situation was inconceivable to Robert. Determination grew with each trial. It was his destiny, his first priority as a man, to protect his wife and children. He told them what he intended to do. Joy was nervous, Catherine was excited, Elisabeth was scared, but they all agreed to use what strength they had in an effort to escape their sorry circumstances. Only to Robert did it occur that they could be making things worse.

The delivery of breakfast each morning followed a familiar routine. Robert devoted weeks of close attention to less obvious details. He had listened carefully long enough to catch the sound of other doors opening and thumping shut nearby. Soon thereafter two hoods would unlock the door to his family's room and bring in their food. This told him the rooms were virtually but not completely soundproof and supported his assumption that other people, regardless of the hows and whys of their respective incarceration, were also being held against their will. Robert hoped he could establish some form of communication with them. He had not forgotten the cry of a woman's voice that pierced his soul so very long ago.

Routine dictated that two attendants delivered breakfast. Each morning the door abruptly swung open to admit one hood carrying a multi-level tray containing four meals. While the second hood blocked the door, the first arranged sectioned paper plates of food labeled with each individual's name, disposable cups of broth, and flimsy wooden flatware on the table that protruded from the wall between four green chairs that were bolted to the floor. The first hood then took the empty tray back to the giant wheeled cart in the hall while the second locked the door. Robert knew the hoods had no reason to fear the residents. The victims were frightened and distrustful of the facility's personnel. They avoided any contact that was not forced upon them. Even though his family was quite well physically – despite their obvious disfigurements and except for suffering the side effects of extensive testing – they were neither emotionally nor mentally predisposed to fight that which was bigger and stronger than they were. Months of dehumanizing treatment had achieved the desired result. The hoods felt completely safe with their charges.

Robert counted on that.

He waited twenty-one days to allow time for Catherine's stitches to be removed and for her to heal well enough to walk comfortably. When she insisted that she felt ready, Robert explained each person's role upon tomorrow's wake up call.

They were all showered, dressed, and ready when the door swung open the following morning to admit the hood with the food tray. The hood waiting by the door turned slightly and lifted a hand in greeting to someone outside the room. It was a greater diversion than Robert could have hoped for. Emitting something between a frenzied roar and a triumphant yell, he flung himself upon the distracted hood, taking the awkward uniform completely off guard. He yanked it into the room and hurled it unceremoniously to the floor. Joy threw a cup of wet food at the server's face, coating the window of its hood with the viscous, brownish substance. It grasped blindly for her as she shepherded Catherine and Elisabeth toward the door. Robert leaped away from the hood he had tackled and called to his family. As the wadded heap struggled to get to its feet, Joy and the girls ran from the room. Robert pulled the door closed behind them, locking both hoods inside.

Joy immediately shoved the ponderous metal food cart, taller than herself, into another hood who had been distracted from guarding an open room several feet away on the opposite side of the hall. As the weight of the cart crushed the attendant against the wall, a second hood staggered out of the room, clutching futilely at a hypodermic needle lodged firmly in its thigh. Two figures darted into the hall from behind it. The food cart came reeling toward the opposite wall, propelled by the hood into whom it had crashed, who then clutched at the smaller of the couple as they fled the room. A feminine scream brought both her companion and Robert to her rescue. The two men pounced on the oversized costume, shoved it through the door into the couple's room and locked it inside. The remaining unfortunate hood had collapsed against the wall across from the door, the needle still protruding from its thigh.

Breathing heavily, Robert stepped back and looked into the face of a man who appeared identical to him in almost every way; a bit older and more abused, perhaps, by this life that was leading them. Robert was treated to a brief calculating glance, a visual strafing by a soldier who displayed confidence in himself, if in nothing else. Robert recognized the look of a man assessing a risk. He also perceived strength and resolve that matched the fervor of his own intent. The man's companion peered around him at Joy, Catherine, and Elisabeth. Her expression glowed with excitement as she glanced from Robert to her husband and again at Joy. Robert extended a hand, which the other man received in a firm grasp.

"Robert Lake." He drew Joy to his side. "My wife, Joy, and our daughters, Catherine and Elisabeth. Hoods brought us here on July 16th, 1945, after the girls and I were injured by a massive explosion in the Jornada del Muerto desert in New Mexico. They are using us for medical experiments."

"Ray Davenport," the other man responded. "My wife, Belva. That's our story as well." The lines on his face deepened into an expression of torturous grief. "We believe our children died in the explosion, along with my brother and his wife and three friends. We just want to get out of this place."

"Let's do it, then," Robert urged. The little group looked up and down the hall at rows of doors along both sides.

"And let's take all of them with us when we go." Ray spoke the words as though giving an order, and Robert was glad to follow the command. Assignments were quickly delegated and accepted by individuals anxious to perform their respective tasks, bent on successfully waging a war that was uniquely their own.

Chapter Fourteen

Elisabeth pointed out the first discouraging fact. The hood who guarded the door also kept the keys. Both guards had been shut away in the families' rooms. The guards could not get out because there was no way to unlock the doors from within. The outside of each door boasted a lock on a flat plate and a handle, but inside was a smooth, barren surface. Since releasing their fellow captives was not possible, Belva, Joy, and the children would knock on doors and try to talk with them through the nearly-soundproof steel. Ray and Robert would explore in opposite directions along the hallways in search of information in any form. A window. A clock, calendar, radio, or newspaper. A door to the outside world. A telephone. A human being with a face and a name instead of a shapeless suit.

All suits carried radios. The muffled squawking from under the sedated suit assured them that the breach had been reported. The captives hurried to use their hard-earned time before it was gone.

Ray relieved the suit of its radio and turned the volume all the way down. He needed neither the distraction nor the potential of alerting other suits to his presence before he was ready to reveal himself. He kissed

Belva, hugged her hard, and walked away raging inwardly against even this momentary separation.

It was a long way to the end of the hall. Doors lined the walls at perfectly spaced intervals. A soldier could march to the timing of those doors, Ray thought. His footsteps, muffled by soft-soled slippers, grew louder the farther he went. Though the room he shared with Belva was chalk white with murky green furnishings, the corridors he now traveled were a claustrophobic shade of beige. The walls and floor tiles were the same color, creating a uniform tunnel with line drawings for doors and ceiling vents. The lights cast a dingy yellow glow. Ray tried to shake off the disconcerting sensation that the hall was both elongating and narrowing, squeezing him into a smaller and tighter space, threatening asphyxiation as he walked beyond the supply of breathable air.

§ § § § § § §

Robert was closer to a corner than Ray, but he was surprised at the length of the corridor waiting at the turn. As his footsteps whispered loudly in the eerie silence, it occurred to him that the rooms in this area must be larger than those in which he and his family lived, because there were fewer doors spaced farther apart. Two large panels seamed smoothly together across the end of the hall without the benefit of knobs or handles. Robert frowned with disappointment. He would have to retrace his steps and catch up with Ray. Taking a closer look at the dead end, he noticed two buttons on the wall beside the panels. Arrows on the buttons pointed up and down. He stood warily before the elevator, torn between urgency and caution.

"The only way out is..." Robert stepped forward and pressed a button.

§ § § § § §

Ray turned right at the end of the first corridor and slowed as he proceeded uneasily onward. A series of solid doors sporadically indented the passage on the right. The bare beige wall extended for an indefinite distance without interruption along his left. He wondered if he was walking the perimeter of the building, if beyond this wall lay the world in which he and his family once lived. Ray continued cautiously, listening for any indication of human activity. Another thirty feet, fifty, and an alcove withdrew into the right wall. He paused for a breath of courage and stepped into the alcove to face a door set with a small glass window. Habit encouraged him to try the handle first. Finding it locked, Ray looked through the window and found himself face to face with a wide-eyed man and a woman who pressed both her hands over her mouth. Relief momentarily overcame logic as Ray's long-pent-up emotions surged with elation and relief at the sight of normal people in ordinary clothes. He tried to open the door again. The man and woman drew back in fear, and Ray could see more people through the window as he peered into the room. A second man stood several feet away alongside two more women wearing white lab coats. Acres of machinery communicated among its various components via monitors, wires, and erratic flashes of light underscored by a vague electronic hum.

The other three people gaped in terror when they caught sight of Ray. He looked into their frightened faces and felt his heart sink in the sorrow of reality. He had been so happy to see them that he had forgotten his freakish appearance. Like a child scorned on the playground for being different, Ray lowered his head and backed away. When he was more than an arm's reach from the door, he looked through the window again at the first man and woman, the only people he could still see. The man wore a pin on his lab coat that identified him as Owens. The woman's pin bore the name Scott. Ray held up the radio. Scott leaned toward Owens with a brief comment. Owens swallowed hard and approached the door. He stopped two feet short and touched the wall. Ray could not see what Owens was doing, and he nearly bolted at the sound of static alongside his left ear. He turned to face a small intercom.

"What do you want?" Owens carefully enunciated each word.

Ray glanced awkwardly at his radio.

"This department doesn't use radios. Press the button marked 'call.' Hold it down while you talk."

Ray complied. "I am Sergeant Ray Davenport, sir. I need your help."

Owens' eyebrows elevated at the unexpected answer. He stepped warily to the window for a better view of this strange being: a bald, emaciated male figure with dark eyes and horribly wasted ashen skin stretched over a bony frame on which hung the sky blue v-neck shirt and pull-on pants that were standard issue to the scientific staff employed several floors above. This pitiful creature might be a colleague who had fallen victim to one of his own experiments. He stood straight as if at attention except for his left arm, which he bent at the elbow and held rigidly in front of his body. A plastic identification bracelet encircled the left wrist. The radio was in the left hand. Surely he was human, but his distorted appearance was frightfully alien. Yet he had identified himself as a sergeant. Owens keyed the intercom again.

"What is your branch of service, Sergeant?"

"United States Marine Corps, First Marine Division, sir. I received a medical discharge for injuries received on Peleliu last October. That is, October 1944."

"And you've been here since then? What kind of injury left you like that?"

"No, sir. The war didn't do this, except for my arm." He indicated the bent limb. "My wife and I have been here since July 1945. We were traveling through New Mexico – my wife and I, our son and daughter, my brother and his wife, and another man and his boy and girl who were friends of ours. Their truck broke down, so we stopped in the desert. It was very early in the morning on sixteen July. It was still dark. There was a huge explosion like nothing I ever saw during the war. I woke up here. That's all I know." Ray paused to swallow his emotions. "My children must have died, as well as my brother and his wife. None of your suits will provide any information about them." He looked through the window into the eyes of the other man. "But my wife is here with me. A few minutes ago we met another family who was also in the desert that morning, and they look just like us. None of us knows the extent of our injuries. We know nothing about our prognoses, but every time we get better and experience genuine healing the suits make us sick again with all manner of medical procedures. We don't know what the treatments and medications are for. They won't tell us what they're doing or why.

"We are being held here as prisoners. We want explanations. We want to be healed, and we want to go back to our homes and our families. I want to know what they did with my children. You are the first person in this place who has spoken to me. Will you tell me what happened to us and why we have not been permitted to leave? Will you find out what they did with my children?"

Owens watched Ray as he listened to his voice on the intercom. Halfway through Ray's explanation, Scott lowered her eyes and walked away. Owens was silent for several seconds after Ray finished speaking. His posture remained unyielding, but his voice wavered with inflections of shock and regret when he responded.

"Sergeant, I don't know that I can help you. But I will call my superiors and relay your message. We were told that the work taking place in the next wing was classified, but we certainly didn't realize that people were contained there."

"Not by choice," Ray assured him.

"Wait right there. I'll call you after I speak with my superiors." Owens turned to go, and then looked once more through the glass at Ray. "I'm sorry that I cannot do more," he murmured into the intercom. Ray nodded. The two men stiffly saluted one another, and Ray stepped around the corner to pace the hall and wait.

§ § § § § §

Robert breathed deeply to still the queasiness in his bowels as the elevator rose. He didn't remember riding an elevator during his detention. He was always strapped to a gurney and blindfolded before being removed from his room. When the hoods pushed the gurney out the door, it didn't stop rolling until they reached one of the several exam rooms with which Robert was unfortunately familiar. The doors he had passed on his way to the elevator, he decided, must open onto those rooms.

He had pressed the arrow pointing upward and exhaled with relief when the doors slid open to reveal an empty box. As he stepped inside he noticed that the back wall of the elevator was actually another door. He wondered briefly what was on the other side as the entrance he had used sealed shut. Rows of buttons by the door were numbered B1 through B11 and one through three. The number B9 was lit. Robert pushed "one" and the car began to climb. He was surprised. It had not occurred to him that this place in which his family was hidden so efficiently away could be several stories underground.

Robert watched the indicator above the doors with mounting excitement as he rose past each of the basement floors: eight, seven, six, five. The elevator stopped at the fifth floor. Robert had no chance to prepare for this unexpected situation as the doors slid open before and behind him. Both avenues were blocked by groups of hoods. Robert's attempts to talk to them were cut short by a conclusive blast of ether.

§ § § § § §

Ray forced himself to breathe normally and to practice respectful patience as he paced the length of the corridor back and forth, counting steps, estimating distance and square footage to occupy his mind. He studied the unusual light fixtures overhead, unfamiliar with the concept of fluorescent lighting. He outlasted endless minutes before his restraint finally expired, and he cautiously turned up the volume on his radio. A voice crackled through incessant static.

"All subjects but one are returned to quarters."

Ray sped to the alcove and peered through the window. A glance confirmed his suspicions; all the people were gone. The equipment no longer showed any signs of activity. Monitors sat blank and still, their colorful, flickering screens ominously dark. Tense silence replaced the subtle drone of machinery. Despite the obvious, Ray pressed the button on the intercom and called out for Owens.

Owens didn't answer.

An icy fingertip teased the nape of Ray's neck and ushered a droplet of perspiration down his backbone. He recognized the sounds made by the congregation gathering behind him, but Ray stubbornly held onto hope until he turned to face the group of suits who penned him in the alcove.

He tried anyway. "Hello. I'm Sergeant Ray Dav—"

Anything else he might have intended to say was lost as he collapsed unconscious at their feet.

§ § § § § §

Robert clawed his way to consciousness by arduous degrees, battling nausea and panic for his wife and daughters. He realized something was wrong long before he came fully awake. It was too quiet. When at length he opened his eyes, he saw a smaller room with less furniture than the one he shared with his family. Oh, God, no, he begged. Please, not this again, the agonizing loneliness, the sickening constant helpless anxiety for his family. This wasn't the outcome he had intended.

"No," he whispered.

A presence immediately arrived beside him, and he looked into the ravaged face of the woman he had met in the hall. Ray's wife! Where, then, was Ray? Robert looked across the room for him. Belva drew a faltering breath, obviously willing away tears.

"They got mixed up, I guess. They must have thought you were Ray."

"Joy? My girls..."

"They're okay," Belva assured him. "The suits didn't do anything to us. They just shoved us back into these rooms after they released the suits we locked in." She managed a faint smile. "The suits must think we're superhuman now. Two of them held onto my arms while others brought you in and laid you on the bed." She turned abruptly and walked away.

"I guess they put Ray in my room, then, with Joy and the girls," Robert said to her back. It wasn't so much a question as a request for confirmation.

"I hope so," Belva said softly. "There is something I have to tell him. Such wonderful news, Robert – I found our daughter. Sarah is alive!"

She walked around the partition that shielded the bathroom and stayed there, unwilling that Robert should see her cry.

§ § § § § §

Ray fought to dissipate the stupor. He groggily

rubbed his eyes with a lethargic right hand and blinked rapidly against the residual sting of the spray that had rendered him insensible. He forced his eyes open and drew back, startled, from two curious faces that loomed over him, youthful renditions of his own visage. He struggled to sit up, and his companions laughed as they fled.

"Careful," came a female voice. "Take your time. I was sprayed with that stuff once, and I vomited for three hours straight. Lying very still was my only comfort until the chemicals processed out of my system. I must have inhaled half the canister."

Ray ratcheted upright, breathing hard against vertigo and nausea. He focused blearily on the speaker. "Where is Belva?"

The woman walked closer and perched gingerly on the very foot of the bed. "Belva is all right," she said. "The hoods were a little rough because they were angry, but they didn't hurt us. They just herded us back into our rooms. Four of them came in to physically hold onto the girls and me while they brought you in. You should have heard them! All this time they've barely said a word in our presence, and this morning they were jabbering away."

Ray studied her for a moment. "Joy," he remembered. "Elisabeth and Catherine." He nodded to the girls and melted at their twisted smiles. He unsteadily surveyed the room. "Where's Robert?"

Joy rose and walked the few steps to her daughters' beds. "I believe he's probably in your room with Belva. That's what I keep thinking must have happened. The hoods were confused and upset. They were in a hurry. They weren't paying close attention, and they just got it backwards. I'm sure Robert is all right. He has to be," she insisted, and busied herself fluffing pillows and smoothing imaginary wrinkles from blankets.

"But they have bracelets on us." Ray looked at his wrist. "They always check mine when they are going to hook me up to a machine or pump me full of drugs. They want to make sure they are doing all that stuff to the right person!"

"The bracelets have codes, not names," Joy reminded him. "They don't show our ages or gender or anything else. We're just numbers. It's a wonder they haven't gotten us mixed up long before now."

"When they come for one of us, or when they bring lunch, we'll tell them about the mistake," Ray said. "They'll immediately switch Robert and me back to where we belong."

"Yes." Joy agreed with forced optimism.

"But Belva's okay?" Ray accepted Joy's reassuring nod. "Did you all find out anything about the people in the other rooms?"

Joy's eyes widened and her face lit up with an ecstatic smile. "I met a number of young people who were camping in the desert with a church youth group that morning. There were several rooms of them. We told each other our names. There wasn't time to share any detail. But that's not the half of it!" Joy hugged Elisabeth close.

"Ray, Belva found your daughter. Sarah is alive!"

Chapter Fifteen

There were moments now and again in which I truly wished to die. Many were the nights I prayed to God for that peaceful and elusive repose. I received instead reasons to live: joy and sorrow and passion and pain, emotions exquisite and beautiful and individual and pure as one snowflake and then another merging together until the eye can no longer separate the first from the last, and so such business is left to memory.

There were scenes of intense harmony in those days, though I did not recognize them at the time. Loneliness was unrelenting until it ended, and then it did not seem as though it had lasted for so long. My cousin became my sister, and in her presence I regained the crux of an identity I had mourned forever lost.

Death was only an occasional consideration from that day forward. There were times it beckoned sweetly, always in the aftermath of loss. In those moments I would have traded fates with the deceased in order that I might, instead of grieving, be that for which others mourned. There were dreams in later years less realistic but more achievable that did come to pass. For them I am grateful, and I am therefore humbly appreciative that this first longing was withheld from my devastated heart.

When I acknowledge that I have been blessed beyond what I could have known to ask, I repent the desire that would have rendered me unavailable to receive such gifts. When I walk among our homes and past the schoolhouse where children of another generation are learning their history and preparing for a future none of us can imagine, I give thanks for what has become even as I bewail that fleeting glimpse of what could have been.

Her arrival was my first manifestation of hope. Thus she remains in my memory, a beloved testimony to all I once had been and a prophecy of what I had yet to become.

⧫┄⧫┄✳┄⧫┄⧫

"Tell me about the day we were going to pick blackberries, and the bull chased us back to the barn."

"It's your turn to tell me a story. I want to hear about the time you went to the movies with Bobby McFarland and had to take his little brother along."

"Nosy. I just told you that yesterday. Think of something shorter. It's almost time for lunch."

Sarah's brow furrowed with concentration. She wasn't accustomed to living in the past beyond recalling fond memories of special occasions. However, the only relief from their isolation and the uncertainty of their future lay down the path that led them here, so she and Callie frequently retreated into the world from whence they came. They sat at the table and took turns explaining how to do things that had been ritual in their former lives: sewing shirt collars, growing a bountiful garden, baking before and during the sugar ration and the advent of oleo; transforming flour sacks into blouses and feed sacks into skirts, cooking up a batch of lye soap, Callie's excitement over driving a car.

They remembered hot wood stoves and frigid

linoleum floors in the winter. They yearned for night sounds that brought summer through their open windows in the language of whippoorwills and katydids and the bass declarations of bullfrogs proclaiming supremacy over the pond. They closed their eyes and inhaled deeply for the warm fragrance of hay, the pungent odor of livestock, and the crisp scent of anticipation that sparkled in the first frost. Their mouths watered for hot, tangy cider, for salty country ham, for sweet, delicious strawberry preserves and butter melting over piping hot, fresh-from-the-oven biscuits.

They talked about loved ones, friends, and acquaintances in order to keep precious memories alive. They discussed people they desired to meet, in order to give hope a fighting chance. They told and retold countless details of their individual and mutual histories, warding off the tendency to forget as well as establishing that each girl's identity would live on in the other. Their isolated world of concrete and steel boasted a lush meadow, a family kitchen, a city street, a schoolroom, a pair of mules hitched to a plow, a tiny tiger-striped kitten, at the whim of their imaginations.

With the single exception of hypodermic needles carried by the costumes, no sharp objects were ever brought into the room. This included pencils, for which Callie's and Sarah's requests were routinely ignored. A portion of Sarah's heart withered in the absence of her beloved books. If she could not read stories, Callie insisted she recite them from the archives of her memory. Both girls thus began relating tales each had read and inventing new ones to augment their oral library. Their flights of fancy temporarily alleviated the loathsome symptoms of confinement, but the malady of imprisonment could not be wished away.

"I know this is an unusual request, but could you bring me a guitar? I play a little, and I've plenty of time to practice while I'm here." Callie had no illusions that her desire would be fulfilled, but complacency was a greater threat than a negative response. Futile attempts and probable disappointment were preferable to the certain failure of not trying at all. The lack of instrumental accompaniment did not discourage the music. Callie and Sarah sang every song they knew until they tired of familiar refrains and began making up new words to old melodies. They committed the lyrics to their catalog of memories.

"Walk me through it, step by step, as though I have never even seen a tomato, much less canned tomato juice."

"Someday I will write it down for you."

Their eyes met. "Someday we'll meet in your kitchen or mine and put up enough to last through the winter."

"While our husbands are at work."

"And our children play out in the yard."

"We'll make a day of it and fix a big supper for both our families that night."

"We'll make a blackberry jam layer cake for dessert."

"Using homemade jam made with berries we picked ourselves from the thicket near the cornerstone."

"Oh, Sarah, don't cry. It's going to happen."

"For you, of course it will, once we get out of here. You are beautiful! But look at me. If my hands are any indication of what my face looks like, I'll do well to coax people close enough just to make friends. I don't even have any hair! No man will ever love me. I'll never have a husband and children and a normal life. Death would have been the true mercy, if I had not survived the explosion at all."

"Mercy for whom?" Callie shook her head slowly. "That isn't true, Sarah. Don't ever say that. You don't know what your future holds, either, so if you're going to speak a fate for yourself, at least describe how wonderful it's going to be. That's just as easy as pronouncing failure. Anticipating good things is much more healing to your heart, mind, and spirit than giving yourself over to despair. Do what you can to keep hopelessness at bay for both our sakes."

Focusing on Sarah's trauma helped Callie suppress her personal fear and anger at the injections and examinations to which she was subjected. Callie disciplined her reactions by insisting that her procedures were much less painful and invasive than those con-ducted on Sarah. When Sarah asked about them, Callie gave her vague answers and standard reassurances that did nothing to disguise the truth or to make either of them feel better about their situation.

"If we both admit we're pretending things are better than they are," Sarah ventured, "is it still a lie?"

"We're not pretending," Callie asserted, and she refused to hear arguments to the contrary.

As desperate as they were to leave the facility, the removal of one girl from the room left the other in the company of overwhelming anxiety that the one taken would not be returned and that loneliness would again be the single, debilitating companion of a soul cut off from light and life. Every time the costumes took one of them away, the other paced the room to the beat of a terrified heart until they were reunited.

Callie relentlessly kept Sarah on the move, performing routine exercises along with her and designing new movements to increase both girls' strength and flexibility. Strength was important, she insisted, on every level. "We must be strong physically, mentally, emotionally, and spiritually, because some day we are going home. We need to be ready to live our lives to the fullest and to honor the memories of loved ones lost."

Sarah continued to count the days. She didn't know how much time had elapsed during the critical part of her recovery or how long she had lain unconscious before she began drifting in and out of awareness. From the first day she received three consecutive meals, she had mentally advanced a number every morning to amass a brutally astonishing number of days in which she and Callie had been detained. Each morning she braced herself against the cruel passage of time. "One hundred and forty-five."

Callie had lived by herself in a small room for an interminable period before being moved in with Sarah. She would never have believed she would have been held for so long, so it did not occur to her to number those frightening days alone. She echoed the number that celebrated Sarah's return to awareness. "One hundred and forty-five." The insufficient count could not tell them for certain how much time had passed since July 16, 1945, but the number did have information to relay.

"I'm seventeen," Sarah murmured. "I had a birthday, and I didn't even know which day it was."

"We missed Daddy's and Mama's and Uncle Ray's birthdays, too. Gosh, do you think it's April yet? I might already be twenty-three."

"I'll bet we've been here close to a year."

"Thanksgiving and Christmas and New Year's Day. We missed them all."

Callie and Sarah searched each other's eyes in stunned silence for answers neither could offer while the reality settled harsh and bitter into their hearts that they were literally being robbed of life. To have lost so much time to the will of strangers for a purpose unknown was more than they could grasp. They wondered how much longer it would be before the will and the purpose were satisfied.

Despite their creative attempts to make each day different from the one before, every morning began with a never-changing routine that followed an established course through bedtime. Callie and Sarah whispered and giggled through a variety of outlandish plans for disrupting the schedule, but they weren't bold enough to play tricks on their costumed caregivers, especially since there was nothing to accomplish by doing so. They did not want to jeopardize what little consideration they had been allowed. Freedom of movement around the room after being cuffed supine to a bed and companionship after months of solitude were not progressions that Sarah took lightly. She and Callie were unwilling to risk such tremendous loss and so, with the exception of occasional lapses into gales of laughter when the costumes entered their room, the girls held their peace.

"Nothing stays the same," Sarah insisted one night as she lay in semidarkness, staring at the same spot on the same ceiling. "Everything changes. Both the best and worst of times will pass."

"Says who?"

"Daddy."

"Uncle Ray is a wise man."

"He was. Callie, do you pray?"

"Of course I do. Only God can get us out of this place beyond reach of these people."

"But do you believe? I mean, really and truly believe? Mama and Daddy did, and I was taught to as well, but knowing and doing are not the same thing. I believe, but I wish I felt more confident in God. Why does He let things like this happen, especially to people who haven't done anything to deserve such punishment? It's just not right."

"Mama used to read the Bible every day. Her faith was based on knowing who God is, regardless of circumstances." Callie paused, considering her own words. "She would say that times like these are trials, not punishments."

Callie sighed and rolled over in her bed to face Sarah. "I know what faith in God is, or at least what it means to me, but I'm not sure how to explain it to you. We have tremendous faith in far lesser things. When you sit on a chair, it never occurs to you that the chair might collapse and dump you in the floor. You take for granted that it will support you. You have faith that when you turn on a faucet, water will come out; that when you flip a switch, a light will come on. You absolutely trust and believe in these things, and if on occasion one doesn't work, you automatically accept that the malfunction is an exception to the rule. One burned out light bulb doesn't make you distrust the light fixture from that moment on. You still know for certain that the ability to produce light is connected to that switch. But there's no way we will ever understand certain things. Maybe it's enough to know that God sees the big picture of our lives – past, present, and future – and knows what is best for us along the way."

"Then why this? I didn't bring this on myself! How can this possibly be good for me, or for you?"

"Maybe this isn't just about you or me – maybe we're part of something that is actually about someone else."

"But that makes no sense. Who else?"

"I don't know, Sarah. You'll have to ask Him."

"I have asked Him. He won't answer me."

"Maybe He would like to, but you're too busy talking for Him to get a word in edgewise."

Sarah huffed sharply at the ceiling and concentrated on a smart comeback, but by the time she thought of an appropriately humorous retort, Callie was snoring softly from across the room.

The following morning they learned that they weren't the only patients who plotted a disruption in the schedule. Others craved escape badly enough to risk everything in the effort.

Callie and Sarah awoke to muffled thumps of doors closing down the hall, the usual indication that costumes were on their way with breakfast. The girls arose, showered, and dressed in clean blue shifts. They were making their beds when a thunderous roar resounded along the corridor, followed in quick succession by a loud crash, a slamming door, a man's cry of outrage, and a second collision. A woman screamed, and another door slammed.

Sarah dropped her pillow and held her breath until the commotion ended. She crept to the door shoulder to shoulder with Callie and strained to hear if anything else would happen. She stiffened at the tones lilting vaguely beyond the door.

"Voices!" she whispered. "People are talking out there!"

Callie closed her eyes and concentrated on the sound. "Women," she breathed. "The voices I hear belong to women."

Hammering suddenly assaulted their door. Sarah gasped and pulled Callie away, but the banging continued with the rhythm of a fist knocking for attention. The pounding stopped long enough for a voice to call out, and the fists resumed their urgent attack against the unforgiving steel. Sarah returned to the door, raised a tentative fist, and looked at Callie. Callie nodded. Sarah rapped against the door.

From without came a woman's voice. "Hello! Can you hear me?"

Sarah went still. The voice was familiar.

Callie knocked and called out in response. "Yes, hello! We hear you!"

"My name is Belva Davenport. My husband and I were injured in an explosion. We were brought here for treatment and are being held as prisoners. We know there are others in the same situation. Can you hear me? What is your name?"

Callie muffled a cry while Sarah sobbed and ran her fingers over the door as though she could somehow find a way to make it open.

Belva rapped against the door again. "Can you hear me? Please answer me! What is your name?"

Sarah overcame the emotion that had frozen her mutely in place and began pounding frantically against the inside of the door. "Mama!" she screamed through her tears." Mama!" And again. And again.

And again.

Callie pulled Sarah from the door and clung to her, attempting to calm her as they both leaned forward to press their ears against the cold metal. Commotion resumed in the corridor. Male assertions of authority overrode feminine exclamations of protest. Doors thumped closed, but without the finality of the isolation that had ruled until only moments ago.

Callie and Sarah hugged as they wept with relief and joy. Ray and Belva were alive! Maybe John and Mary were, too. Belva had not said anything about them. Callie winced at the heartache. Oh, to hug her beloved parents close again and smell Mary's rose-scented perfume on her own cheek long after the embrace had been relegated to memory! The military police had brought Callie to the institution on the premise that her parents needed her, yet no evidence had been offered to prove that John and Mary were here. Callie had refused to accept the near-certainty that her parents had survived the desert experience only to die soon upon their arrival at the facility, but deep in her heart she feared it was true. Grief had seeped through her mind in a steady and constant flow, never permitted release until now. New hope gashed Callie's heart open with a devastation completely unexpected and beyond the clutches of her carefully determined control. Her parents might really have survived after all! But what if they lived, and looked like Sarah? And they almost certainly would. Could she stand to see them like that? Of course she could. Regardless of their appearance, John and Mary were her parents. Uncle Ray, Aunt Belva, Ben, and Sarah were her family, and she would love them unconditionally whatever the circumstances. She would give her life for them if necessary.

"Ben!" Sarah cried. "Mama didn't say anything about Ben. I hope Ben is okay. Please let Ben be okay, too. Let Uncle John and Aunt Mary be okay. And Mr. Pendleton and Freddy and Christine..."

We question our faith, Callie thought, but that doesn't diminish our ability to pray. She had not heard all that Belva said, but she had caught something about another family that Belva had seen or met, another family just like them. Excitement burned within her. She and Sarah were not alone in this nightmare. Their family was not alone! Others had suffered the same fate – a blessed curse, a cursed blessing, if ever a situation could be described in such a way.

Sarah spoke as though reading Callie's thoughts. "I wonder how many others are here."

Chapter Sixteen

Arlene had made an event of packing her memories and storing them deliberately away in the remotest corner of her mind. She did not want them easily available or so unconstrained as to reappear when she least expected. The present was difficult enough to accept without bittersweet hauntings by revenants of a history and a future forever beyond her grasp. Her parents, siblings, and friends were put away. What she had looked like before the explosion. Her goals for the coming years. She had planned on going to college to study music, both piano and voice. There would have been marriage and a family and a nice house close to town. A dog and a cat, at least one of each; she had always loved pets. Maybe a rabbit, too, and a pony for the kids. They all went into the box, these picture-perfect dreams in their polished sterling frames, and when the lid was sealed, she determined to never think on such things again. There was simply no point in punishing herself by desiring the impossible. She forced success on almost all counts. However, one memory of her past and intended future refused to be put away and ignored. He emerged in the darkest hours of night and caressed her in the depths of her dreams. His name was Russell Winter.

"Listen!" Abby hissed.

Maria paused, one ankle crossed over a knee, one hand hovering with a slipper inches above a bare foot. Arlene returned from wherever she had been and tilted her head in curiosity at Abby's directive.

Unusual noises suggested a disturbance in the hall. Silence was briefly restored only to be shattered again by insistent thumping outside their door. A woman's voice filtered through. The urgency in her tone drew them all to the door to hear what she would say. Arlene spoke for the girls, exchanging basic information with the first outsider who had talked with them since their arrival. Her name was Joy Lake, and her family's experiences were similar to those of Arlene and her friends. Such a brief conversation after so long a silence, and Joy had to move on.

The three friends looked to one another in mute apprehension, the unspoken question become yet another point of confusion with which they must contend. Should they be excited or afraid; trust that their living conditions would improve or accept things as they were? Should they allow themselves to believe friends and loved ones they had relinquished as lost may have survived after all? Could they perhaps even look forward to release from their confinement and indulge in thoughts of going home?

Abby and Maria voiced their misgivings first, willing to err toward optimism, their simultaneous chatter disrupting the cadence of their thoughts.

"Maybe Toby is here!" Abby clung to the hope of a reunion with her twin brother because she could not cope with the alternative.

"And Tom and Sybil." Maria's eyes shone. "They

were like family to me, next to Pastor Clay and Mrs. Fae. And Nathaniel. He and I grew up as brother and sister."

Clay and Fae Carter. Arlene still giggled because their names rhymed, though she wasn't quite sure why that struck her as funny. Maria had never called them mom and dad, though they had raised her from infancy. Arlene wondered why from a distance, remaining silent as her companions continued their speculation.

"Logically, they all have to be here," Abby insisted. "We all suffered the same fate out there, so it only makes sense. Were you and Nathaniel close?"

Maria shrugged. "Sort of. He didn't talk much because he stuttered so badly it wore him out to try, so when he did speak I made sure to listen carefully. I wanted him to know I was paying attention. We probably watched out for each other more closely than most siblings do. Nathaniel talked more to Mrs. Fae than to anybody else, but then so did I. She was our mom."

Arlene smiled. The Carters had been parents to a variety of strays as well as four of their own flesh and blood. They made for a colorful family, taking in children of various races over the years to share all things equal with their own red-haired offspring. Arlene's mother once told her the Carters had raised thirty children from the time they married, usually accepting the homeless without the formalities of adoption, caring for them, educating them, and loving them. Arlene wondered if Maria's mother had known this when she left her baby at the church door.

"I want to see my mother and father again, too, but I wonder how they will react to this." Abby studied her hands and glanced at Maria, who placed one of her hands against Abby's.

"I don't think people will look at me much differently than they already do," Maria murmured, with a slight movement of the sixth finger that angled oddly from the side of her hand.

Arlene sat on her bed turned slightly away from her roommates, paralyzed by the emotional turmoil raging within. The box! The box, it was no more. Its sturdy walls, constructed to protect that which was within and without, were shredded, torn asunder by the escaping contents as they were quickened by words of hope uttered in the voice of a stranger. How to rein in the memories and expectations, and where to put them if she did? The bulwarks she had erected were demolished, the borders erased. Hope laughed at her discomfiture as it teased her resignation to circumstances and dared her to give a little, just a little, in concession to Faith.

It had taken days for Arlene to become acclimated to the appearance of her friends, to be able to look at them without experiencing an automatic shudder of revulsion as she turned away. She knew Abby and Maria felt the same when they looked at each other and at her. Never having seen herself, Arlene could make believe she was not as horribly disfigured as her companions. She dreaded the inevitable look into a mirror that would prove her grossly wrong.

She dreaded even more the possibility of a reunion with her beloved Russ. For months she had desired him, wished for him, prayed and dreamed and lived for the moment she might see him again. Now that she faced a real possibility that Russ might truly be alive, Arlene could not bear the thought of that meeting. The probability of Russ's disfigurement did not faze Arlene. She loved him more than her own life regardless of his appearance. She wasn't as confident in his love for her. If Russ looked at her and turned away in disgust, even if his injuries had left him more maimed than her, Arlene did not know how she could survive that rejection.

She didn't realize she was crying until the tears dropped from her face onto her hands. Abby and Maria sat beside her on the bed and put their arms around her. They silently shared her grief without questioning its source. I have friends, Arlene thought, and her tears became expressions of gratitude. They are true friends. If Russ is alive and can't bring himself to love me anymore, at least I won't be completely alone.

The thought still frightened her, though, as well as another point that Abby had made. What would Arlene's parents and siblings think of her when they saw her in this condition? As much as she loved them and missed them, a part of her wished she would never have to see any of them again.

After the morning's excitement, the day plodded along more mundanely than usual. Time slowed to a tedious crawl even to the perception of those left ignorant of its passage by the lack of calendars or clocks. They knew noon had come and gone by the rumblings in their empty stomachs.

"The food is vile," Abby remarked. "But it's better than nothing at all. It scares me to think that they could starve us to death right here in this room, and no one would ever be the wiser."

"At least the wardens have left us alone," Maria said. "None of us has been hauled out for lab rat duty today. You know something of consequence is taking place when they don't come for me. I'm their favorite, after all."

Arlene and Abby giggled in appreciation of the joke. Like a blind person would not be affected by the darkest night, Maria had learned from infancy to live in expectation of rejection because of her appearance. Her only complaint about the horrendous damage inflicted by the explosion was the loss of her lovely brown hair. Yet she still managed to laugh and to cheer up her friends. Her sense of humor lifted their spirits. Maria's hopes reached higher and anticipated more, encouraging Arlene and Abby to also be brave.

For the first time in their lives at the facility, an entire day passed without interruption from a warden. By dinnertime the girls were ravenous, having been served nothing to eat since the evening before. Sleep finally took precedence over hunger. They said their prayers and went to bed. All three lay awake listening for a presence that confessed neither name nor identity, an uncertain spirit that manifested only in a terrible sense of dread that constricted their hearts and kindled a flicker of fear in their eyes.

Chapter Seventeen

An aura of suppressed anticipation permeated the atmosphere throughout the entire wing with an almost-audible thrum. A day without testing. A day without food. Anxiety and fear attempted to take root in soil rich with hope. They flourished sporadically only to wither as quickly as they sprang forth.

Robert and Belva conversed as though they were in the waiting room of a salon expecting a technician to open the door at any moment and call one of them out. Robert was ready to take on the hoods again in order to get back to his family. He felt sorry for Belva, who looked as though her heart would surely stop beating if she had to balance much longer between the elation of finding her daughter and the distress of missing her husband.

Ray was more comfortable talking to Catherine and Elisabeth than to Joy, and the girls took pleasure in teaching their made-up games to someone new. Ray enjoyed their company, but he was desperate to hold his wife and celebrate her discovery of Sarah. He wanted to know the extent of Sarah's injuries and the prognosis for her healing. He wondered whether his daughter lived alone or if she was granted the benefit of a companion, and if that companion was another family member – her brother, perhaps. Joy said Belva did not mention Ben. Ray hoped his little girl had been spared the medical procedures that were inflicted on his wife. He prayed that Ben and John and Mary were still alive.

Joy, having once attempted to forfeit her family, now suffered the torment of losing her husband. Within a day shades of astonishing depression stole into her mind, luring her toward a vortex of hopeless despair. She felt their insolent presence as they lingered, patiently awaiting evidence of weakness. They could not close in as long as she remembered that Robert was alive, as long as she kept faith that the hoods, though they had demonstrated a cold lack of concern for their patients' desires, should at least acknowledge the necessity of exchanging Ray and Robert back to their proper rooms. Joy participated in her daughters' games, exchanged information with Ray, and did her best to ignore the emotional darkness that her companions countered in a tug-of-war for the stability of her spirit, unaware of their participation in the battle.

Darkness closed out another day. Down the hall, Callie and Sarah went to bed in concession to the timer that would not bring the lights on again until approximately an hour before breakfast was due in the morning.

"We are poised on the brink of the unknown," Sarah said with a sigh. "That's what I would write in my diary tonight, if I were allowed to keep one."

§ § § § § §

In his own private world in the last occupied room, Tom Westfield knelt to say his prayers. Conversing with his Maker was not a problem, as there was no one else with whom to talk. Had he not believed in God, Tom felt he would have succumbed to madness by now. Unaware of the morning's commotion, not understanding why the door had not opened to admit so much as a meal all day, Tom offered his petition this night as a confident request that God would not forget him or allow him to be forgotten. As he had since his last moment with her, Tom concluded his prayer with a heartfelt blessing for Sybil and their child. He lingered for a moment on the gut-wrenching hope that their baby had miraculously survived the cataclysm. He wondered if his child were a boy or a girl and if sufficient time had elapsed for Sybil to give birth. He lay down on his bed and tried to ignore the persistent, gnawing hunger in both his stomach and his heart. He tried to not be afraid. He tried to think logically of positive outcomes, and he tried to convince himself that tomorrow would be better. Tom Westfield finally gave up trying on all accounts and cried himself to sleep.

§ § § § § §

Arlene was last in the shower the next morning. She was toweling herself dry when she heard Abby's triumphant voice.

"Breakfast is being served! I hear doors opening down the hall. I can hardly wait. I'll eat everything on my plate."

"So will I." Maria wrinkled her nose. "For once."

Arlene emerged from the bathroom smoothing her shift across her abdomen. "That proves we're desperate. Why else would we so eagerly await a plateful of what passes for food in this place?"

"You're right." Maria's smile matured into soft laughter. "Our last breakfast contained pieces of what I thought was bacon. It was brown, and really salty like bacon, but sort of rubbery. By the time I chewed it enough that I could swallow it, all the taste was gone, and the consistency made me think of soggy cardboard. I wouldn't want to know what part of the pig that bacon came from, but I don't think 'jowls' were involved."

"If it came from a pig at all," Abby put in, and all three grimaced at the undesirable possibilities.

"Even at that," Arlene said, "I think I'm hungry enough this morning to eat every bite of salty, bacon-colored cardboard on my plate."

They were still laughing when the door swung open. Three wardens entered, one after the other, each pushing a wheelchair. Three more wardens blocked the door. Arlene, Abby, and Maria were confined to the chairs, their wrists and ankles secured in padded metal cuffs. They met one another's eyes in farewell. Abby blinked back tears, but Maria's escaped down her cheek. Arlene sat very still and did not look at either of her friends again. Amidst her most ravening nightmares stalked the wraith of loneliness with its ominous threats of permanent isolation. She closed her eyes against the spirit's escape to reality and kept them closed even after a warden placed a hood over her head to render her blind to her surroundings.

The wardens transported Arlene to a familiar room and subjected her to a complete physical examination. Afterward they led her to a tiled stall that was outfitted with stainless steel implements. They bathed her, thoroughly scrubbed and rinsed her in a variety of scented solutions. The wardens dressed her, restrained and hooded her again, and pushed her swiftly along in the wheelchair on what she hoped desperately was the route back to her room. Instead the chair bumped across a threshold and stopped. Arlene heard doors gliding together and felt a stomach-tugging sensation as though the room were rising. Movement ceased with a slight jolt, and she heard the doors open. They covered a short distance and turned a couple of corners before the chair stopped again. A key rattled in a lock, and Arlene was wheeled a short distance forward. Her nose tingled in objection to mingled odors of disinfectant and paint. The warden behind her chair removed her hood. Arlene sneezed twice and stared in surprise at her surroundings.

She sat in a small, pleasantly-appointed room. The walls and furnishings were attractive in tones of dusky blue and sand, so lovely after months of algae green and chalk white. A twin bed kept company with a nightstand and a chest with three drawers. A small table and four chairs were not bolted to the floor, but could be moved about at the occupant's will. Pictures were painted on the walls in such a way as to deceive the viewer into believing that three-dimensional, framed prints were actually hanging there. An open archway offered access to another room. A clock gazed down from its position above a closed door.

The hands that loosed the cuffs from Arlene's wrists were concealed only by surgical gloves overlapped by a pale green sleeve. Arlene gaped at her caregiver, a young woman with dark hair sleeked away from her face into a tight bun. Her long-sleeved shirt and pants reminded Arlene of the surgical attire a doctor might wear. A mask covered the woman's nose and mouth. Arlene cast about the room. There was no sign of a warden.

The young woman's eyes crinkled at the corners, indicating a smile behind the mask. "Hello, Miss Brooks. My name is Helen. You'll be seeing a lot of me from now on. I am your nurse and you are my patient, so please discuss with me any changes you notice in your bodily functions or in the way you feel. You've been prescribed an entirely new schedule of medications, so you should expect to feel poorly for a few days until your system becomes acclimated to them.

"Through that doorway is another room just like this one, and a third room lies beyond that. Miss McAllister and Miss Ramirez will reside in those rooms. The three of you can still spend as much time together as you would like, but now you have the option of privacy when you feel the need. You will find a small foyer between this room and the next one. There are two doors in the foyer. One of them leads to the bathroom that the three of you will share. This door behind me, under the clock, will remain locked at all times just as in your room on the ninth floor.

"Do you have any questions, Miss Brooks?"

Arlene vaguely recalled her manners. "Nice to meet you, Helen." She glanced around the room again as she rose from the wheelchair. "Questions, yes. How much time do you have?"

Helen's eyes smiled again, but something in her expression abruptly closed. "Miss Brooks, a great many of your questions will be answered in a few days by someone far more qualified than I am to tell you what you wish to know. I am personally not at liberty to discuss issues with you that do not specifically relate to your health. I regret that I cannot be of greater assistance." She wheeled the chair to the door and turned to nod in farewell. "Make yourself at home. See what your friends are up to. Since you missed breakfast this morning, lunch will be served early, within the next hour. I will bring your medication at that time."

With that, Helen was gone. Arlene stood perfectly still, mind and emotion besieged by questions jostling for precedence.

I didn't miss breakfast, she thought. I just wasn't given any. No meals at all yesterday. A clock! It's ten-thirty in the morning. Gosh. I should have asked Helen what day it is. What pretty colors! I never want to see that other room again. Pond scum green only looks good on...well, pond scum. Helen, her name was Helen, and she talked to me, and she was so polite. Does this mean there will be no more wardens? I hope so, because if I never see a warden again, it will be too soon.

Her thoughts continued to collide among themselves until she heard voices from the next room. Abby and Maria had found each other. Arlene rushed to join them.

§ § § § § §

Elisabeth and Catherine were astonished to find themselves tended by nurses who spoke with kind voices and touched with gentle hands. The barriers of face masks and gloves were hardly noticeable after months of contact with hoods whose only human features were eyes peering through an impenetrable clear rectangle framed in a shapeless hood. The girls stared in awe at their new surroundings while the nurses slipped away before the children could recover from their surprise sufficiently to ask questions.

Left alone, they explored their surroundings. They were delighted to have a room of their own that was separated from their parents' room by walls instead of a flimsy curtain. They opened the shallow drawers of the chest and found two changes of clothes and new slippers for each of them. Extra blankets nestled in the bottom drawer, and the bathroom contained more than the usual allotment of thin white towels. Elisabeth touched one to her face, commenting on the soft texture and fresh scent that was another improvement over the antiseptic smell of everything related to their previous surroundings. Catherine didn't answer. Elisabeth turned to see why and pressed the towel to her lips with a muffled shriek. Everything in her screamed rejection of the truth that stared her, at last, in the face.

Mounted on the wall above the sink was a large rectangle of shiny stainless steel. The corners were rounded, and a decorative design was cut out of one side in the shape of a flower made blue by the wall it revealed. The smooth, unbreakable surface lacked the flawless precision of glass but rendered the details that trespassed its borders with heartbreaking clarity.

Elisabeth lowered the towel from her mouth, her impulse to flee suppressed by the restrictions of captivity. She touched her forehead and nose, traced her jawline from ear to chin with a fingertip. The image in the steel pane ruthlessly mimicked her every move. She looked in desperation at Catherine's face beside her own and watched as horror metamorphosed into denial and fury that settled as vengeful glints in her sister's eyes.

"It's only temporary." Catherine's voice trembled with fear and rage. She took Elisabeth's face in both her hands and glared into her eyes, daring her to disagree.

"We haven't healed yet. That's all there is to it. Our nurses will take care of us and give us medicine to make us well. They'll fix us back to the way we were before the explosion. Our hair will grow back. Our skin will look normal. Our eyes will be bright blue again. When I walk out of this place, I'm going to be even more beautiful than I was before I came here." She shoved her sister aside and was gone.

Elisabeth leaned against the bathroom sink and attempted to control her grief. She heard her mother's voice from the next room and wept for a moment with sheer relief that nurses had arrived with Joy and, hopefully, Robert. Ray was so very nice, but he wasn't her father, and Elisabeth felt the intense undercurrent of need in herself, in Catherine, and especially in Joy for Robert to make their family whole again. She wiped away her tears and listened closely, wondering if she could hope hard enough to make her wish come true. But it was Ray whose voice joined the others in conversation. Elisabeth pressed the towel hard against her eyes, determined to not cry anymore. When she heard the nurses leaving, she rinsed her face in cool water and patted the moisture from her skin. She stepped from the bathroom into the little foyer and looked into the room she would share with her sister. Catherine sat straight as a statue on the ottoman in front of the stuffed vinyl chair beside her bed. Her features might have been chiseled from stone. She neither looked at Elisabeth nor acknowledged her presence.

Elisabeth turned toward the opposite doorway and stood quietly, listening to her mother and Ray discuss sleeping arrangements in case their nurses failed to place Ray and Robert with their own families before bedtime.

Elisabeth saw anxiety in Ray's expression and dejection in her mother's. Unnoticed, Elisabeth backed away from need, sorrow, and dread and returned to the bathroom where she could hide her face in a towel and battle her own demons of uncertainty and fear.

§ § § § § §

Robert had ever been determined to think positively. Of late, he wondered what made him feel obligated to put forth the effort when his hopes were consistently dashed. For others, then, if not for himself, and so he forced a brave front for Belva's sake. She had weakened emotionally during the short separation from her husband. She spoke optimistically about the future, but sad eyes and trembling hands betrayed a brutal absence of the confidence she attempted to show.

When hoods restrained Belva in a wheelchair, Robert was sorry that he could not save her from the same fate that Joy and their daughters had endured so frequently. Hoods brought a second chair for him, and he surrendered once more to hope – this time on faith that he would be taken to his family. However, after a thorough cleansing and a meticulous physical exam, he was wheeled to a room to which Belva had been transferred seconds ahead of him.

"Yes!" Belva was answering a nurse. "There is something you can do for me. Ray Davenport is my husband. When suits locked up the two families who escaped yesterday, they put Robert Lake in the room with me. I believe they placed my husband, Ray, with Robert's family."

Robert quickly agreed. "That's right. Since you're

here with the chairs and restraints, would you please take me to my wife and bring Ray to Belva? We both miss our families very much, and this misunderstanding has made for a somewhat awkward situation."

The nurse called Dana smiled behind her mask. "I can't do that for you right now." She hastened to the door. "But Cheryl and I will speak to our supervisor and explain what has happened." The nurses wheeled the chairs out the door and were gone before Robert and Belva could protest further.

"At least we tried," Belva said. "At least this time our medical personnel were real people without suits, and they actually spoke to us. I asked to see Sarah. The nurse said she'd talk to her supervisor. They left before I could ask about Ben." She inhaled deeply and closed her eyes. "I don't know if I have the nerve to ask if my son is still alive."

"Believe that he is," Robert said.

"I can't imagine life without him."

"That is reason enough to hope for the best." Robert swallowed down memories of time without end before he was placed in a room with his wife and children. He had seen his little girls alive in the desert, but the unsatisfied question of whether they survived beyond that moment had left him angry and desperate. Life without Catherine and Elisabeth was more than his mind would comprehend, but the mere suggestion made him all the more determined to return to his family. "I hope those nurses speak to their supervisor immediately. Don't get me wrong; I have enjoyed your company."

Belva appeared relieved that he had changed the subject. She actually laughed. "You are a very nice person, Robert, a gentleman and a friend. But you're not

Ray, and I'm not Joy, and in this situation we need our families more than we need anyone else." She excused herself and went into the bathroom.

Robert explored the room. The new quarters offered a more pleasant atmosphere than the cell from which they had been removed. The colors were so attractive and calm that he took a moment to simply stare at the walls. He studied one of the painted scenes within its painted frame. Wildflowers sprouted from a grassy slope. A butterfly wafted toward him from the left. A monarch, Robert decided. A tiny honeybee had just landed on a pink clover bloom. Robert stood at eye level with the flowers, too close to glimpse more than a sliver of blue sky, but shadows among the petals, lighter here, darker there, suggested sunlight beating down. Robert inhaled deeply for the scent of the park in the summer and listened for laughing children, barking dogs, and chirping birds just over the hillock. He was sure he could feel the sun on his shoulders when a sound from the bathroom snapped him back to reality. Robert chided himself for getting lost in the moment and rebuffed the desire to entertain his imagination for just a little bit longer. He surveyed the room and cast one last glance at the butterfly in the frame. "I know how you feel," he informed the monarch. "It's an attractive place, but it's still a prison." He drew a forefinger from the wall across the frame into the scene. "It's still a prison as long as we're trapped within borders that were created by other people to fence us in and deny us our freedom."

He tore himself away from the picture and turned his attention to the furniture. A drawer yielded extra clothing of the same type he wore now, along with two of the pullover shifts for Belva. "Delightful," he muttered.

"At least I don't waste time each morning deciding what to wear."

He was carrying the table and chairs to the opposite side of the room, one at a time, out of sheer elation that they were not bolted to the floor, when Belva stumbled through the doorway. Even by their standards she looked terrible, her ashen skin paled to a sickly translucence. Before Robert could reach for her, Belva collapsed across the bed, curled into a fetal position, and hid her face against her knees, whimpering like a lost child.

Robert sat beside her and petted her shoulder, concerned for her health and wondering what had happened. Remembering a detail that Dana had showed them, he hurried to press a button beside the door. Within moments Dana arrived, checked Belva over and, finding nothing wrong, called Cheryl on her radio to bring a sedative.

Not knowing what else to do, Robert tucked a blanket around Belva and sat in a chair beside the bed until her breathing came even and slow, testifying to drug-induced slumber.

He looked around the room. He needed to move those last two chairs. First, he needed to use the bathroom. Robert stood slowly so as not to disturb Belva, though she was unlikely to awaken for several hours. He stepped into the small foyer and frowned at the discovery of two doors. One, he knew, lead to the bathroom, but Dana had not said anything about the other. Robert tried the handle. It was locked. He must remember to ask about that.

Robert stepped into the bathroom and closed the door. He turned toward the sink and stared as all his senses shuddered in protest of a sight similar to that which had rendered Belva prey to her own image. Robert had seen his daughters. He had seen Ray and Belva. He had studied his own hands, his whole body below his chin. Had he honestly expected to have been spared this part of the devastation, which twisted his facial structure into the visage of a grim false face? No party, this, after which the mask could be removed; no holiday, no costume ball.

Robert made his way back to where Belva slept soundly across the bed. He sank to the floor with his back against the bed, elbows on knees, ruined face in wasted hands. A new despair swept over him, a fear he had not previously encountered, a certainty that his wife was surely sickened at the very sight of him. She must be a strong woman to pretend so convincingly otherwise. Could there be so great a love as to overcome the affront of such a loathsome appearance? It was different for Belva and Ray. They bore the same scars. Joy was lovely and unscathed. She should belong to the attractive man he had once been instead of being thrust into the company of the beast he had become. Robert's shoulders heaved as an ocean of unshed tears burst forth from where they had been too long contained.

§ § § § § §

Counting one's blessings was especially important, Tom considered, when they were in such short supply. There was a time when he was certain they must number no less than the stars that glittered across the blanket of the darkest night. Now he had to sit and contemplate what things merited gratitude. The infinite collection had narrowed to a handful of tangible positives while terms that once described reality now applied to those desires that remained beyond the realm of the possible. But then, Tom believed in God, so impossibility was merely a point of view.

After a day of solitude uninterrupted even for meals, Tom felt both reluctant and relieved when two of the suited staff entered his room the following morning. He sat still as they strapped him to a wheelchair and pulled a hood down over his eyes. More medical horrors to come, he supposed, but perhaps they would at least feed him afterward.

There followed a complete physical exam. Blood was drawn, injections were given, and Tom was subjected to the most thorough cleansing of his life. He grew annoyed at the succession of showers, a variety of solutions coursing over his body before a final welcomed rinse of clear, cool water. The staff dressed him in clean clothes and again restrained him in the wheelchair. The ensuing ride felt different. The trip took longer, and he had certainly never experienced the lift before today. Tom tensed, unprepared for what he might see when his hood was removed. The scene that greeted him was the last thing he would have expected.

The room was lovely: attractive colors, comfortable décor, pictures on the walls, and furniture that intimated a hotel instead of a hospital. Tom took his time letting it all sink in, wondering if he would truly be permitted to stay. Hands touched his wrists and released him from the chair. He blinked in astonishment at a young woman standing where he expected an anonymous suit to be. Her eyes were a deep dark burgundy brown, like coffee laced with cinnamon, and tears abruptly blurred his vision as if to spare him the intimacy of looking another person in the face.

"Sybil," he pleaded, bewildered by emotional overload.

"My name is Ilya," came the gentle response. "I am your nurse." She explained her assignment as it related to Tom's healthcare, and he tried to pay attention to what she was telling him as he drank in every detail of the first person to breach his isolation. Her skin was smooth, honeyed amber. She wore a pale green uniform and a cloth mask over her nose and mouth. Her hair was black and curled tightly against her head.

Ilya's voice lilted warm and melodic, exquisite to the ears of one for whom noncommittal grunts from nameless, faceless creatures had served as communication from the moment of his arrival. Tom closed his eyes and focused on the light accent of her words, the timbre of her voice. After a moment she fell silent, and Tom opened his eyes.

"Please, don't stop. I'm listening."

The corners of Ilya's eyes tilted upward. Tom had not been so long alone that he had forgotten the features of a smile. He did his best to return the expression, urging his muscles to behave after a fashion to which they were long unaccustomed.

"That is all I was going to say," Ilya responded. Tom felt the warmth of her hands through the thin gloves as she took his arm and assisted him out of the wheelchair. "Is there anything I can do for you?" She turned the chair and followed it several steps toward the door. "Is there anything you need right now?"

Tom could not stop staring. He wouldn't be disrespectful for anything in the world, but was hard-pressed to recall his manners after so many months alone. Ilya's words, however, banished the surrealism he felt at experiencing so many new and unexpected events at once.

"My wife." It was all he could do to keep from sobbing her name. "I need my wife, Sybil. She is pregnant with our first child. If I survived, surely my wife is still alive, too. Please, if you would find her for me, bring her to me…"

Ilya's downcast eyes reflected his heartache. She lifted her face gravely to Tom's. "I'll speak to my supervisor for you." She rolled the wheelchair out of the room. The door latched behind her with a conclusive click.

Tom stood in the midst of new surroundings and wondered if he should leap with joy or acknowledge misgivings in response to the events of the past few hours. It appeared he had been granted a variety of vast improvements. A quick scan across the room prompted him to smile at the warm colors and pleasant amenities. When the blessings were counted, said and done, however, Tom remained imprisoned and alone.

Chapter Eighteen

I had thought there could be no worse moment in my life than that instant before dawn when the world erupted around me in a fury surely conceived in the very fires of Hell. There lies the conceit of such moments, both good and bad, for each desires to be the most important of its kind, remembered above all others before and since. Not so, for there are always better and worse, which renders comparison of no value.

Numerous events share the notoriety. I am asked sometimes to live them again. "Tell me a story," one will plead on behalf of all who seek vicarious adventure. But the far reaches of the spectrum, the devastating and the sublime, once survived, forbid resurrection if for no other reason than humanity lacks the language through which to convey such experiences.

"I will tell you," I begin, "about the time..." And they are satisfied, never knowing that they are learning of kinder evils and lesser miracles than actually thrive in my memory. Would that I could share the benefit of my wisdom while sparing the lessons through which it was gained! One must feel an emotion, however, in order to react with an honest expression. Life performs the greater service through stark reality than I am capable of offering from tender hands and a heart that would spare all hurt.

Yet I spare myself by not speaking that which was and inviting it to live again. There is a place in which I pour out my life across pages no one will see unless and until, perhaps, these chronicles are all that remain of me. Even thus, the shades of history lack the brilliant colors of authenticity and the corporeal dimensions through which they breathe in the mind of the survivor. The heart harbors a record of memories too vivid for the spoken word.

Callie found her voice first. "Pat," she confirmed, as if she could forget the name of the person before her. "Thank you, Pat, for talking to us. There is indeed a problem with which Sarah and I need your help. We need to find our parents. My parents are John and Mary Davenport. They were allegedly injured when a munitions dump exploded in the desert. I was brought to this place on the presumption that I would be caring for them during their recovery. Instead I was locked away alone for a very long time before your people in suits moved me into a room with my cousin, Sarah. Will you please tell me if my mother and father survived this horrible mess? If they did, I wish to see them."

"My parents are Ray and Belva Davenport," Sarah said. "I know they are alive, and I want to be with them. I also need to know if my brother, Ben, is all right, and I want to see him, too."

Pat scribbled a few words on a small note pad. Nancy, the other nurse, pushed one wheelchair out into the hall and waited for Pat to follow with the other.

"I can't make any promises," Pat said. "But I will relay your requests to someone with the authority to make such decisions.

"Who would that be?" Callie wanted to know.

"We are only permitted to discuss topics pertaining to your physical health, and nothing more." Pat joined Nancy in the hall, and the door latched shut behind them.

Callie and Sarah stared at each other, silenced by uncertainty. Sarah meandered about the room, trailing fingertips across furniture, until she had completed the circuit twice. "Well." She sighed toward Callie and sat on one of the beds. "This is definitely an improvement."

"That's what they want us to think, anyway." Callie sat on the other.

Sarah tilted her head in acknowledgement of Callie's logic even as she plunged onward with determined optimism. "But it is. Anybody would take this room over the one we've just left. And Pat and Nancy are real people, not costumes with hoods. They actually talked to us! It's such a relief to have other people talking to us. Now we can get answers to our questions, and we can know what kind of tests and medications are being used on us. Best of all, maybe we'll get to see the rest of our family soon!"

"Yeah." Callie reluctantly nodded. She opened her mouth to say more, thought better of it, and faked a yawn instead. "I'll be glad when they get here with lunch. Pat said they would bring it within an hour."

"Me, too. I'm hungry enough to eat a bear."

As uneasy with the food as she was with all other aspects of their confinement, Callie changed the subject again. "It's great to have a clock on the wall, to know what time of day it is. I wish I had thought to ask for a calendar, though. Help me remember to do that when they come back."

"Will do." Sarah flopped backward onto her bed. "I'll ask for a newspaper, too. I want to know about the war. I want to know if what happened to us out there had anything to do with the war."

"You won't find that answer in a newspaper," Callie replied. "Especially not after all this time."

"You're right. I know. But at least I can read about what's going on in the real world." Sarah abandoned the bed for a quick assessment of the dresser drawers. "Not so much as a manufacturer's label," she complained. "If they don't give me books or magazines to read soon, I'm going to forget how."

Callie examined the pictures on the walls, startled at the discovery that they were actually painted there, frame and all, by someone with a talent for three-dimensional art. The illusion was quite remarkable. From a few feet away the viewer was easily deceived. She stepped through the doorway into the foyer and encountered two closed doors. One was locked. The other swung open into a bathroom decorated in the same powder blue and sand as the rest of their new residence, and boasting yet another feature to which she had not previously been exposed.

"Well, hello," she greeted her reflection. Her titian hair had grown considerably, and it lacked the luster with which it had once shone. Deprived of sunshine, her freckles had paled. Her eyes looked older, but they were still just as green as when she had last observed her appearance in the bedroom mirror at her aunt's home. "I had just about forgotten what you look like." And then Callie remembered Sarah.

It was too late, even as Callie cast about for some

mode of redemption through which to spare her cousin the visual impact of the tragedy she had endured on every other level.

"I hear them in the hall!" Sarah called, joining Callie at the sink. "Lunch is on the way." Sarah's voice caught when saw her reflection. She went still and studied Callie's image, then her own, then Callie's again. "It doesn't do you justice." She touched the pane lightly, as if afraid it might burn her fingers. "Not like a real mirror would. Your hair is much brighter than it looks in there." Callie would have put an arm around Sarah, but Sarah was gone as quickly as she had arrived, leaving an aura of emotional agony that settled on Callie's shoulders and wrung from her the tears of Sarah's grief.

She heard activity in their room, voices, aromas, and then Sarah stood again at the bathroom door. Seeing Callie's expression, she stepped forward and hugged her close. "Oh, Cal, it's okay. I'll get better. Just don't think about it." She pulled away, wet a washcloth in the sink and applied it to Callie's face without looking into the mirror. "Nancy brought our food. Come on, it'll do you good to eat."

Callie wanted to protest. She was not the one suffering from the first look at a face marred by grayish skin and burn scars, at a bald head on which hair would likely never grow again. She hoped she was doing the right thing by allowing Sarah to deal with the situation in her own way. Callie could have handled a hysterical outburst better than Sarah's detached stoicism, as though if she postponed the reality long enough, perhaps she might never have to face it at all.

She followed Sarah to where lunch had been arranged on the little round table and permitted herself a moment of glee at being able to scoot her chair as far forward as she needed to in order to eat comfortably. They clasped hands and prayed a blessing over the meal, and ate with appreciation generated by the previous day's fast. Sarah carried her half of the conversation with optimism afforded by more pleasant surroundings, but from a distance that left Callie to struggle alone with the bitter truth. Sarah was a strong young woman. The more difficult things became, the tougher she attempted to be in response. Callie feared Sarah would break under pressure she was trying to ignore, for she lacked the experience to bend with the gale until the storm blew past.

"Sarah..."

"I have a surprise for you later," Sarah interrupted. "It's a surprise for me, too, because I didn't think my request would be granted." She chewed with determination and swallowed hard. "They still won't bring me any books, and nothing to write on or with. Nancy said maybe in a few days I'd be allowed to have something to read. I asked for anything. A shopping list. An eye chart. Nancy laughed, but I think she realizes how serious I am. You and I need something to occupy our time before we both go crazy. There are only so many ways for us to entertain ourselves, after all."

Callie fought the urge to cry the helpless tears that Sarah had walled away. If Sarah had resolved to be indomitable, Callie must not let her down. She fortified her own will against both self-pity and sorrow for another who was determined not to need it. Drawing a deep, faltering breath, Callie pushed her empty plate away.

"Checkers," she stated. "We should ask for checkers, and a chess set, too, while we're at it."

"And cards!" Sarah smiled eagerly. "I know lots of

card games. We'll ask Nancy if you can have a guitar, too. The costumes ignored us completely, but things are better now. Who knows what we might receive if we keep asking long enough. And you know what else we forgot to ask?" Sarah stood with her hands on her hips. "We forgot to ask Pat and Nancy to find out when we can leave this place and go home."

Callie had not forgotten. There were questions she hesitated to ask for fear of the answer she might receive. She nodded anyway as she stood and began to help Sarah clear away the remains of their meal.

§ § § § § §

"An assembly. What does that mean? I know what an assembly is, of course, but..."

Tom went to considerable lengths to extend each visit others made to his room and to keep his nurses talking. He had spent three days in his new quarters with no interruption save the routine of regular meals. He expressed gratitude and relief to his caregivers at the suspension of what he called scientific experiments. He thanked them for the generous room with its nice amenities. Despite his best efforts, and although Tom had lived alone for months with nothing to do, he found the isolation and boredom of his new location maddening. Tom had long ago begun performing daily exercise routines to increase his physical strength and flexibility. He sang songs, even in the dark of night, so that his spirit might escape the captivity imposed upon his flesh. He never stopped wishing for his wife, with whom he could share experiences, relate memories, or just enjoy each other's quiet presence. His request for companionship went ignored for so long that the petition slowly died on his lips. Tom remained alone, a circumstance recently amplified by the commencement of sporadic interaction with other people.

Ilya's eyes tilted up at the corners in the smile Tom had come to appreciate so much that he made jokes in order to call forth her reserved laughter. He wished he could see her face without the mask over her nose and mouth, but it was enough to be acquainted with her and with others who called him by name and thus offered respect for his humanity that he had never experienced at the gloved hands of his former captors.

"It will be at four o'clock this afternoon," she continued. "The second door in your foyer, the one that stays locked, will open so that you can join others in a common room to hear a speaker share information that is very important to all of you."

"Others?" Tom stared hard into her face. "Will my wife be there? Is this how your supervisor is going to give Sybil back to me?"

Ilya looked away. Tom resisted the impulse to grab her by the shoulders and shake the truth out of her.

"I'm not at liberty – "

"You are at complete liberty, Ilya," Tom cut in. "You have no idea what it means to have your freedom, all of it, taken away indefinitely by complete strangers who feel no obligation whatsoever to explain to you why you are a prisoner locked away from all you ever held dear. I am not permitted to leave this room. I have not been informed as to the fate of my wife and our child, and no one will tell me what happened to the ten beautiful young people who were with us. I have had things done to me forcibly in the name of medicine that most people would not do to an animal!

"I received injuries from an explosion that none of you will admit, much less explain. Between that and the so-called treatments at the hands of the experts here, my healing has left me with the appearance of a carnival freak. My wife would scream when she sees me, but she probably looks just like me!"

Tom was yelling and Ilya was crying, but he didn't care, and he wasn't through.

"What kind of experiments have you been performing on me? What have you learned from the things that have been done to my body?"

"I'm not...I can't...I don't know what treatment was provided before I became your nurse."

"Treatment. Provided. How nice. And even if you did, you would decline to answer because you are not at liberty to discuss your patient's history." Tom didn't try to keep the disgust out of his voice. "Well, then, let's talk about the future. What experiments are lined up for me in the coming weeks, months, years?"

Ilya closed her eyes and shook her head. "You're alive and doing well. I don't know why you keep insisting that such horrible things have been done to you."

"Please, Ilya." Tom lowered his voice and leaned with both hands on the back of a chair, wearied by his outburst. "My injuries obviously wrecked my physical health. Solitude has eaten away at me emotionally, and everything I've been put through in this place has certainly affected my attitude." He raised his head and looked into those lovely, sad eyes. "But none of these things has damaged my mind or decreased my intelligence. I am not stupid, Ilya, so please do not further offend my sensibilities by expecting me to feign ignorance simply to make your job easier."

Ilya unclipped her keys from her belt. "There won't be any medical procedures for at least four more days. You need a week, minimum, for your body to get used to your new schedule of medications." She walked to the door.

"What others?"

She hesitated, glanced at Tom, turned her eyes away.

"You said that at four o'clock I will be joining others. Who exactly are they, and *will my wife be there?*"

Ilya opened the door and stepped into the hallway. "You'll find out at four o'clock."

Tom turned his back on the door as Ilya turned her key in the lock.

§ § § § § §

"It's almost time." Maria nervously braided her fingers as her feet tapped a light dance on the floor.

Abby glanced up from the other side of the table where she sat none too patiently, attempting to reassemble a paper napkin that she had torn into tiny pieces. "I'm almost finished." Her voice was calm, but trembling hands betrayed her anxiety. "This is a far cry from Europe in the 1760s, don't you think?"

"Hmmm?"

"That's where the first puzzles were made. They were paper maps glued onto wood and cut into pieces."

"How on earth did you know that?"

Abby moistened a fingertip to encourage one piece of napkin to adhere to another. "Toby and I used to put puzzles together all the time. Mom and Dad helped, too, but Toby and I were really good at it."

"I won't ask how I look." Arlene smoothed the hem of her blue shift across her knees. Maria responded with a polite laugh.

Abby darted another panicky glance toward the clock. "I guess Toby and I will still look like twins." Her bottom lip quivered when she tried to smile.

Arlene walked to the table and squeezed Abby's shoulder. "Two minutes." She nodded toward the clock. Abby wadded her napkin scraps into a ball and tossed it into the wastebasket. She and Maria followed Arlene into the foyer. They waited in silent anticipation by the door.

"Are you sure there were only a couple of minutes left?" Maria finally asked.

A metallic slide and a click within the door answered her question. Hearts pounding with apprehension, the girls looked to one another for reassurance. Arlene pushed down the lever handle, stepped back, and pulled open the door. Abby and Maria huddled close behind as they proceeded into a spacious, generously lit room.

Others emerged from similar doors on three sides of the room. Many others.

"Dear Lord," Arlene breathed.

"This is like Frankenstein for real!" Abby cried in a strained whisper.

"They look like aliens," Maria answered in a small, frightened voice.

"They look like us," Arlene stated. "And we look like them."

Some hurried forth while others crept cautiously through doorways. One man and woman, coming out of different rooms, rushed to clasp each other in a hug. He squeezed his eyes shut against his tears, but she wept openly.

Arlene nudged her friends and pointed out three healthy people among the group. Two women were blessed to have lovely smooth skin and beautiful long hair, one with cinnamon tresses halfway down her back, the other with ebony waves cascading to her waist. The redhead stood shoulder-to-shoulder with a disfigured young woman Arlene judged to be about her own age. The dark-haired woman held the hands of two decimated little girls until all three leaped into the arms of one of the male victims. A very attractive man, apparently unrelated to the two women but appearing as unscathed as they, came from a different room. He walked with a terribly scarred little boy.

Any attempts that might have been made at socializing were cut short by the nurses' arrival. They herded their patients toward five rows of chairs arranged before a podium. The victims, dazed at encountering a crowd of strangers in the unaccustomed brightness of the large, entirely-white room, obediently sat where they were shown, with nurses positioned between them so that none of the roommates sat side-by-side. They faced the podium that stood at the center of the L-shaped room and waited for the speaker they had been told to expect.

The wall was recessed beyond the podium. Around that corner, facing away from the assembly, a door sealed smoothly into the wall. The door was out of sight unless one went deliberately around the corner, and no one could exit through it unless it was opened electronically from the other side. Through this door the speaker, flanked by two other men, appeared suddenly before the survivors. All three wore military uniforms, though the smooth cloth was conspicuously barren of insignia or identification. The speaker was in his thirties, slim and personable but for a disturbing lack of warmth in his golden eyes. His formal bearing bespoke a man accustomed to commanding much authority. His companions stopped two strides short while he advanced and placed his notes on the stand. The speaker looked out at the hopeful, uncertain faces of the patients intent on what he was about to say and pulled his eyes quickly back to the pages on the lectern.

He cleared his throat. "At 0530 Mountain War Time on 16 July 1945, on the Alamagordo Bombing and Gunnery Range in the Jornada del Muerto desert in New Mexico, the world's first atomic bomb was detonated in culmination of a government test, code named Trinity."

He paused for effect, but his audience appeared mystified, as though he had just spoken a language none of them understood.

"The Trinity Test provided a magnificent display of the power of atomic energy. After observing the effects of that initial explosion, our government elected to detonate a second atomic bomb above Hiroshima, Japan, on 6 August 1945. On 9 August 1945, a third was unleashed upon the city of Nagasaki. On 14 August 1945, President Truman announced that Japan had surrendered, and the war had come to an end."

Again, he paused. The room was as silent as a tomb. The expressions that stared into his face ranged from bewilderment to horrified understanding. He looked back to his notes and continued.

"In war there will be casualties. Injuries will be sustained. Lives will be lost in the battle to maintain the freedoms we value above all else. Although every effort was made to ensure that no one would be endangered by the nuclear blast in the Jornada del Muerto on the morning of 16 July 1945, we were unable to assure security as effectively as we had intended. Inclement weather temporarily grounded our observation planes. When at length they were able to take off, thunderstorms prevented the pilots from accessing the target area. A heavy cloud cover made it impossible for them to complete a reconnaissance of the desert surrounding the test site. We were therefore unaware that security had been breached. This unfortunate circumstance resulted in civilian casualties and mortal injuries with which each of you are acquainted.

"You, the survivors of your nation's Trinity Test, were brought here for treatment and recovery, as well as for observation and research into the effect of atomic radiation on the human body. Although it is tragic that you were exposed to the plutonium bomb's radiation, your participation in our experimental programs has yielded invaluable information that we could not have achieved in any other way than through direct study involving human subjects. For that we share with you our deepest gratitude."

"We weren't offered a choice!" a voice from the audience interrupted. Robert Lake raised his hand over his nurse's objections. The other victims, emboldened by his bravery, spoke out in agreement. "And if you please, who is the 'we' to whom you keep referring?"

The speaker rapped his knuckles against the podium. The group fell silent before him, and he continued as though he had not been interrupted.

"The facility in which you are housed is a clandestine stronghold. Its operations are overseen by government, military, and corporate representatives. Only an elite few are aware of its existence. Personnel who work here are not permitted to view any portion of their journey to the institution. They are relocated after their terms are served under the same conditions of secrecy. In this way we guarantee their ignorance of our location. I tell you this in order to reassure you of your safety in this facility. You will be well fed and cared for; you will receive continued treatment and the benefit of ongoing medical testing; you may rest assured that no harm will come to you from outside sources. Of these things you have our solemn promise."

"Sir! We aren't livestock, for God's sake," another man insisted, and others called out in agreement with Ray Davenport. "The primary concern for each of us is when we will be allowed to go home to our families." His companions lifted their voices enthusiastically in consensus.

The speaker frowned and waited with obvious impatience for their attention. The audience reluctantly quieted once more as he lifted a page from the lectern. "In closing, I would like to express regret to those who lost family members as a direct result of the Trinity Test. The following individuals laid down their lives for this cause."

Four names were pronounced, stunning the little group into an oppressive silence broken by muffled sobs from two of the women. One man in the back row stood, shrugging off the nurse who attempted to restrain him in his seat.

"Sir, none of us could have sacrificed ourselves for a cause we knew nothing about. Some of us were prepared to join the armed forces and fight for our country, but none of the deceased volunteered to die anonymously in an explosion, and we are not here because we desire to be. We are, very literally, prisoners. If you were ignorant to that fact, now you know the truth. If you were feigning ignorance, now you are aware that we are not willing to support the lie. You can hardly express gratitude for our cooperation under circumstances in which everything we've endured has been forced upon us. If you want to offer something in compensation for our injuries, release us and send us home to our families and friends." The young man started to sit down, but changed his mind. "Arlene Brooks, are you here?"

Arlene had recognized the voice if not the face. Upon hearing her name spoken by the man for whom her heart had broken a thousand times, she forgot all her reservations about a reunion with her fiancé. Helen grasped her wrist, and Arlene nearly dragged the nurse out of her seat as she made her way two rows back and took refuge in the arms of Russell Winter.

The speaker continued, apparently unruffled by the challenges of his audience. "I am sure gratitude for the unique and generous opportunities bestowed upon you will make physical demonstrations of protest unthinkable. When you consider your situation, you will have to agree that the benefits far outweigh the minor inconveniences you might occasionally experience as a result of certain medical procedures. You have here all that is required to sustain life. All your needs are met. Be advised, nevertheless, that any displays of aggression such as what took place four mornings ago will result in severe disciplinary action including but not limited to solitary confinement.

"Upon consultation with your caregivers in the

aftermath of that outburst, it was concluded that companionship will enhance your mental progress and diminish the mild stress that naturally accompanies some of the experiments. We have learned that physical health correlates with mental health. Boredom is inevitable in one who is constantly alone, and this could negatively affect your physical progress. The human mind thrives on the stimulation provided by communication with others. It is for these purposes that you have been transferred to the newly remodeled wing and brought together for social interaction. If your behavior is exemplary, if you demonstrate that companionship improves the quality of your lives, you will be permitted to socialize frequently."

The speaker offered a patronizing smile, bid his audience a good day and turned his back on the podium. In spite of his admonitions, the victims rose from their chairs and called after him.

"Wait! When do we get to go home?"

"Who are you? What is your name?"

"How long have we been here? What day is today?"

Strolling to the exit between his companions, the speaker paused mid-stride and turned to face the group. "I am Commander Josten Maslow. Until further notice, this facility is your home. All of your families were regretfully notified of your demise during the week following the Trinity Test. Today is Tuesday, 21 May 1946."

The victims watched in stunned silence as he turned away once more. One of his companions spoke into a radio as the three men disappeared around the corner. The door opened and closed behind them, smoothly inaudible. The whispery report of the lock resounded in their wake as thunder announces with a long, rolling echo the occurrence of lightning briefly glimpsed, as though compelled to offer some explanation for the damage done.

Chapter Nineteen

❖❖❖❖❖

Ray moved first, rising from the chair and stepping over the nurse as he reached for his wife. He drew Belva into his arms and nuzzled her ear. "Happy birthday, sweetheart."

"I'm forty years old today! What a way to celebrate." She swallowed her sorrow, unwilling to bare her heart in front of a room full of strangers. "Look! There's Callie, and that has to be Sarah with her." Belva took Ray by the hand as she turned and fairly ran in their direction.

Robert closed his eyes and basked in the love of his wife. Joy snuggled in his left arm. Their daughters hugged him around the waist, sharing their father's affections without bickering.

Arlene and Russ held on to each other as though they would never let go. The nurses, ignored as other victims approached one another, retreated to the perimeter of the room to allow their patients freedom to mingle. Reunions brought laughter and tears, while introductions prompted excited chatter celebrating the end of solitude. Alarming revelations pronounced by an impassive speaker were momentarily set aside for the blessed gratification of fellowship.

Two male victims approached Robert and Joy. They hesitated, and then one put out his hand. "Hey, boss," was accompanied by a lopsided grin. "Remember me?"

"Kenneth," Robert whispered, and the tough exterior collapsed as he threw his arms around the young man and bawled loudly, releasing the fear and rage of helpless uncertainty along with the agony of feeling that he was to blame for the presence of his family and friends in this place. Joy hugged Dave and cried with him, expressing her own burden of guilt and shame.

"Why are you crying?" Catherine demanded of Elisabeth.

"You know whose fault it really is that we're here," Elisabeth snapped.

Catherine turned her back on her sister, her family, her reality, and sat on a chair a short distance from where the others were congregating.

Five chairs down the row, Tom was not aware that Catherine had taken a seat nearby. He faced the podium blindly and alone. The commotion that surrounded him took place at a very great distance. Drowning out the voices of his fellow survivors, a cruel echo chanted the same taunt over and again. "The following individuals laid down their lives...Sybil Westfield...regret to those who lost family members...Gilbert Fitzpatrick, Toby McAllister, Vernon Sheppard...laid down their lives for this cause...Sybil Westfield...for this cause..."

"No." Tom rose from the chair. In one fluid motion he turned and lifted the chair and slammed it into the wall. "No!" he bellowed, hurling another chair after the first. His arms were suddenly heavy with weight that dragged him down. He struggled against the sudden restriction even as he went to his knees. *"No!"* His cry turned desperate, and he heard his name spoken in a way no one had addressed him for a very long time.

"Brother Tom! Please listen, Brother Tom…"

"Sybil," he begged, bargained, prayed. "Oh, God, my wife, my Sybil, our little baby…" He wept in arms anonymous but for the common bond of loss. "I'm sorry, Sybil, everyone, I'm sorry," he whispered. "Should have camped in the sanctuary. I'm so sorry." Gentle hands stroked his back. He was vaguely aware of a low voice murmuring a prayer. As his own horror subsided, he heard the sound of a girl weeping. He knew her voice…had to think…

"Abby McAllister." He sat up, leaning away from the comfort he had received and turning to offer it to another. Three girls sat one row back. Arlene he recognized because Russ stood behind her with his hands on her shoulders, and Maria he identified through traits that even now set her apart from her companions. Arlene and Maria sat on each side of Abby and held her upright as she sobbed inconsolably for her twin brother. Assisted by friends, Tom Westfield got to his feet. He turned a chair around to face Abby and sank into it. He took her hands in both of his. They leaned on each other's shoulders and shared bitter grief made bearable because neither had to weep alone. At length Abby pulled away as Tom had done and leaned back in her chair. One of the nurses who had approached in response to Tom's outrage offered handkerchiefs to them both. Abby mopped her face and blew her nose, but tears continued to flow from her eyes.

A hand gripped Tom's shoulder. A voice spoke close to his ear. "Brother Tom," was all it said. Tom stood and hugged Nathaniel Harper.

"We're here for you, Brother Tom," said Will Blackwater. Beside him stood a girl forlorn with loss, too dazed to cry, and Tom recognized Rachael Knight. She had dated Vernon Sheppard. Gilbert Fitzpatrick had been her cousin. Rachael's heart was twice broken. Tom reached out to her.

"I'm sorry, Rachael." She squeezed his hand and sat beside Arlene.

"Will there be preaching on Sunday?" Nathaniel's eyes were sincere.

Tom shook his head, unable to think outside the hurt. "My nurse brought me a Bible last week. If we're permitted to come back into this room together, it would be appropriate to have a weekly service. But who would offer the sermon? I'm just a youth leader."

"Not anymore. You're our preacher now." Will clasped Tom's hand. "And we're going to need you more than we ever have before."

Tom shuddered under the weight of unexpected responsibility as he observed a pretty black-haired woman deep in discussion with an angry teenaged girl just a few chairs away. He had seen at least three healthy people who consorted with the victims, yet were not dressed as nurses, and he wondered who they were and why they were here. More than anything, Tom wondered how these people could expect him to offer any semblance of leadership on any level when he was surely the weakest of them all.

Sarah and Callie had already identified those they believed to be their parents before the nurses separated them for the address. After the speaker's departure, when Pat and Nancy stepped aside with the other nurses, the girls hurried to meet the two couples.

"Mama, Daddy!" Sarah cried, and Callie echoed the words as she flung herself into the open arms of John and Mary. The blessing was bittersweet for them all. Callie sobbed softly as she held one parent and then the other. Sarah had to force herself to look at her parents, and she knew it broke their hearts to see what had become of her. "Happy birthday, Mama," Sarah whispered. Belva allowed herself the respite of a few tears against her daughter's shoulder.

"It is a happy birthday." Belva wiped her eyes. "I have my family back together again. I thought my children dead, but they are both alive. That is an answer to a prayer I have whispered with every breath since the last morning we were together."

"You've seen Ben?" Sarah gasped. "Oh, Mama, where is he?"

"Sarah," came a voice from behind her. She and her brother shared a fierce hug so tight neither of them could breathe. They held onto each other at arm's length and looked each other over. Sarah braced herself for the inevitable insult, but no such words were forthcoming.

"I thought I'd lost you forever," Ben said, and Sarah melted at the honesty in his eyes. John and Mary hugged her then, and she learned that Ben had been moved into their room as soon as he was able to walk without assistance. He had lived with them from that day forward. Sarah looked at Ben with new respect. Gone were the days she could pin her little brother to the floor and tickle him until he struggled from her grasp. Ten months had added height to his stature, despite the disfigurement he had suffered. The boy was fast becoming a young man.

A man Sarah did not know approached her family and shook hands with Ray. The two men gave each other a quick hug and a slap on the back. "How are you, Robert?" Ray asked.

"Better in some ways. Worse in others. Thanks for looking after Joy and the girls. They said you made a bad situation bearable."

"Likewise. I missed Belva terribly, but I'm glad she wasn't alone. Let's trade places today when they put us back in our cages. We'll tell them what we've done and dare them to argue with us."

"Politely," Robert warned, and nodded toward a handful of nurses, male and female, who loitered across the room from the victims and kept an eye on proceedings. They all sported tiny spray canisters clipped to the waistbands of their pants or to the necklines of their shirts. Ray did not have to ask what they were for.

"Robert, I'd like for you to meet my children. Thank God they both survived." Ray's voice grew husky with emotion. "Sarah is seventeen; Ben is thirteen." He drew them into his arms. "Kids, I'd like for you to meet Robert Lake. That's his family over by the chairs: his wife, Joy, and their daughters, Catherine and Elisabeth."

"Nice to meet you," Sarah said.

"A pleasure, sir." Ben offered his hand. Sarah glanced at her brother once more with amused admiration.

A young boy approached and waved his hand carelessly in greeting. "Hi, Ben."

Ben stared at the newcomer. "Freddy?"

The boy grinned. "Gee, I'm sure glad to see you, Ben! Dad and Christine are over there, and see the dark-haired guy? That's my brother, Michael. He's a traveling salesman. He works all over the world! They had to go all the way to Australia to find him and bring him here to take care of Dad and me. We didn't know if Christine was here or not until just now. Dad and Michael and me have lived together all along, but Christine had to stay with some girl from a church camp."

Ben draped his arm around Freddy's shoulders. "It's good to see you again, too, Freddy. I'm glad you and your family made it through this. Let's check out the room, and you can tell me more about Michael's job."

Ray's eyes brightened as the rest of Pendleton family approached.

"Clayton? I recognized you after I saw Ben talking to Freddy. I'm glad to know you and your family are here. Well, I'm not glad that you're *here*. But I'm overjoyed to know that you all are alive and well."

"As well as any of us can be," Clayton agreed ruefully. "It's wonderful to see you all too, Ray. You remember Christine." Clayton indicated the young woman who was sharing a hug with Sarah. "This is my son, Michael, whom we were going to meet in Carrizozo that day. I don't know why military police officers went out and found him and brought him here. They told him his family needed him, but there was nothing he could do for us then or now. Now he's stuck here, and they're using him for medical research, too. He'd be perfectly healthy if the experiments didn't keep making him sick. It scares me to think what they're doing to him – to all of us."

"That's exactly what happened to our daughter." John drew Callie close as he introduced her. "She was staying with her great-aunt in Texas, and the military police actually went there to get her with the same explanation they gave your son, that we needed for her to take care of us. They told her we were injured when a munitions dump exploded in the desert. They brought her here and kept her locked up all by herself for a long time. They finally moved her in with Ray's girl, Sarah. She tells us they've been doing those tests on her as well. Bad enough they're messing with me and my wife, but there's no reason for them to be treating Callie that way."

The conversation was momentarily lost on Callie. She caught herself staring up into the ice-blue eyes of Michael Pendleton, admiring his wavy dark hair and perfect smile, blushing under the intense expression he leveled on her as he caressed the shiny red hair, emerald eyes, and tentative smile with an appreciative glance.

Callie flinched when Mary took her by the hand.

"The nurses are going to bring our dinner to us in here." Mary's face softened into as much of a smile as her scars would permit. "They're going to let us all eat here in this room together."

Tables that lined one wall were brought out into the center of the room. The chairs that faced the podium in tidy rows were placed four to a table. Callie led Mary to the opposite side of the room, which remained unoccupied but for Ben and Freddy. The boys sat on the floor with their backs to the wall, deep in conversation. Callie counted twenty-five people: twenty-two Trinity survivors, plus herself, Michael, and a lovely dark-haired woman she had yet to meet.

"Gosh, Mama, I still can't believe this. Even after living here for the better part of a year, I still try to convince myself that I'm going to wake up and realize it was all just a horrible dream."

"I know, honey." Mary squeezed Callie's hand. "I'm

just so glad you're okay. I'm glad you decided to go and visit with Aunt Sylvie instead of riding to Lucy's funeral with us. Despite everything else, you're healthy. You can still have a normal, happy life. You look so pretty." She smiled wistfully.

"As pretty as anybody can look in a shapeless blue shift," Callie sighed, and immediately regretted the thoughtless remark. She could no longer take her physical appearance so for granted as to criticize her features for being less than perfect. She was surrounded by people who had suffered a tragedy she would never be able to fully comprehend. What did it matter if her hair styled neatly or not, when her own mother and father had no hair at all. She could hardly complain about freckles or oily skin when her complexion was healthy and smooth. Callie wondered if the other female victims menstruated. Sarah had not had a period since she arrived at the facility. Callie's still came regularly, though there had been disruptions due to her own medical experiences. It frightened her to think Sarah and the other young women might have been robbed of their ability to have children. Callie, so far as she knew, could still hope to have a family in her future.

"I'm sorry for being rude, Mama. Thank you for the compliment."

"It's just the truth, honey." Mary laughed softly and hugged Callie close. "I've always said it and always will: I've got the most beautiful daughter in the world."

"Sarah surprised me with a hairbrush a few nights ago," Callie said. "She asked one of the nurses if she could have it for me. She insists on brushing my hair for me every night before we go to bed. 'One hundred strokes for healthy hair,' she says. It tears me apart. I want to turn around and do something nice for her, but there's nothing I can do."

"Sure there is. Appearance isn't the only thing we can compliment about each other. In truth, it's the most shallow aspect of our existence. Sarah is an intelligent, creative young woman. Emphasize those things to her, along with anything else you notice: that she's good and kind, responsible and caring. Encouragement is one of the most precious gifts we can give to each other."

"Thanks, Mama. I will."

"The other is prayer. Don't forget," Mary admonished.

Callie nodded.

"Pretty paper and shiny ribbons fade and fall apart sooner or later. It's what is inside the package that counts. Here comes supper. What do you think it will be this evening? Mystery meat pâté or rubber chicken consommé?"

"Maybe we'll get lucky and both will be served." Callie laughed. "With a side of sawdust au gratin."

John held a chair for Mary as they joined others at the tables. Callie caught Michael looking at her and blushed again at the attention.

The meal had been consumed amidst constant chatter when a suggestion circulated that they each take turns introducing themselves. Ray went first, simply stating his name and where he was from, but the others would not settle for such scant detail. He and Belva talked for half an hour before the questions tapered off enough for Ray to introduce John and Mary, and thus turn the attention to them. The survivors were still talking when a group of nurses entered the room at nine o'clock to check identification bracelets and shepherd the exhausted survivors back into their respective rooms.

Family members and newfound friends hugged each other until it hurt. They shed a few more tears for lost lives and lost time and for the relief of finally coming together again. Awareness of their own injuries was insufficient preparation for the reality of similar effects in others. The sight of loved ones so horribly changed provoked a new kind of pain, fresh and raw and stinging with the salt of anger.

Any jewelry worn by the victims had disappeared along with the other details of their lives, though many were scarred with the memory of where precious metals had rested against their skin. Though all that remained was an indention around her finger, in her heart Arlene still wore Russell's engagement ring. Seeing him for the first time all over again, so different and yet so reassuringly the same, left her speechless with emotion. Russ was the man to whom she had pledged her love and her life. His was the voice that held her spellbound, the loving heart and tender touch she had thought she could not live without until she was mercilessly forced to do so. All was returned to her now with an abundance of time, if indeed the promise held true that they would soon be together every day in the assembly room. Russ still wanted her, loved her more than ever. He had told her so, both with words and with those sadly ruined but still incredibly warm eyes. Arlene felt ecstatic for herself, heartbroken for Abby, and more exhausted than she would have believed she could ever be. She and Maria sat with Abby, offering what comfort their presence might afford, until the grief-stricken girl fell asleep. They bade each other goodnight and slipped away to their beds.

Russ asked permission to stay with Tom overnight. He was afraid to leave Tom alone with the knowledge that his wife and unborn child were dead, had been dead all these many months while he prayed and put his faith into believing they were still alive. Russ's request was denied by the nurse Ilya, who insisted that she would look in on Tom while he slept.

Robert and Ray successfully exchanged rooms. Two nurses, Dana and Frank, huddled in a brief discussion while Robert and Ray prepared a defense that they were spared the necessity of presenting. Frank checked their bracelets against his chart. Dana nodded in agreement. The nurses allowed the men to rejoin their families with neither opposition to their plea nor the requirement of a delay while they sought permission from a supervisor.

Sarah brushed Callie's hair and teased her about Michael, and then cut their usual bedtime chatter short and cried herself to sleep. Callie's heart throbbed in rhythm with Sarah's muffled sobs as she wished for the millionth time that power existed within her to make Sarah whole again. She considered the events of their day and their introduction to friends who might have remained strangers, but for one fateful moment in history that had irrevocably bound their lives together.

There remained the question of their future. None of the Trinity survivors was willing to accept the verdict pronounced by Commander Maslow upon the rest of all their days. Circumstances had improved. For this they were grateful, but their status was not changed. The war was over. The Trinity Test had led to victory for the United States of America. All across the land, freedom rang loud and clear and strong.

Seven stories beneath the crags of a remote

mountain range in a lonely desert in New Mexico, twenty-five people strained to hear the sound.

Chapter Twenty

I have listened to lifetimes recited in timbres of regret. I have chronicled family histories. I have documented roads traveled and choices made long before the narrators' paths merged with mine – and that not of willingness or desire. Fate robbed us of chance and choice. We would all have wished away our desert experience, but at what expense in relationships, in the families and the futures that would never have been? We bonded with friends we would not otherwise have met. We celebrated their loves and grieved their losses along our way. What of those lives and events, had we not touched their world?

Hindsight is a whip that drives us without mercy if we risk so much as a glance over our shoulder. It lacks the warmth of Memory and the benefit of Experience, focusing only on a past we haven't the ability to change.

My friends spoke from the depths of their hearts, and I attempted to put their courage into words, but when I arrived at that point where their lives diverged from the intended horizon, I asked no more. From that point forward, I recorded their stories as I knew them. I wished to spare them the futility and hopelessness of 'what if' and 'if only.' I wished to spare myself another journey down that road too well traveled.

He had not been gifted with the dream since the day he learned his wife was dead. Tom writhed in the shaded awareness of drug-induced delirium and reached for hope, but the mirage evaporated, leaving nothing to support the illusion. The desert, the youth group, Sybil's face blurred and faded with the babble of voices whose words could no longer be discerned. Fever plaited his erratic thoughts into a kaleidoscopic whorl and abandoned him within the maze of his own confusion. He cried out in terror of the void his life had become. His garbled pleas were answered with a soothing voice and with gentle hands that stroked a cool, damp cloth across his throbbing forehead and cleansed the perspiration from his burning eyes.

He tried to get it right this time.

"Ilya." Though his vision wavered as uncooperative as his speech, he was conscious of her response. She placed her hand in his, and he gratefully clung to her. He closed his eyes against the savage pain of experimental surgery and the despair of unrequited longing. He focused on her voice and her touch, both as tender and lovely as those elegant doe eyes. Her presence was a sweet essence to him. Tom did not fear death, but he did not want to die alone.

A fluid curtain of loss shimmered across his past, cutting him off from everything he ever considered sacred or beautiful. There could be no turning back, but the path ahead vanished into the yawning chasm of a destiny unforeseen and unwanted. Tom had no desire to live another moment. He wished he had died with Sybil. His survival meant nothing without her.

If 'nothing' insinuates the grief and horror of loneliness, it also prepares one's life for a new beginning.

Tom's friends united to share his bereavement and to shine their light into his darkness, lending their strength and courage until faith could begin the healing of his heart.

Tom gradually grew aware of blessed relief from his heartache. An oasis unexpectedly sprang forth in the wasteland of his existence. Ilya became the redemptive moment that urged one more breath. She soothed him through the fever. She listened to the torment that poured forth from the very depths of his soul as anger, as tears, as illness. Even in his state of drifting consciousness, Tom was aware of the emotional war that raged inside him. He reached out with all his being to breathe Ilya's presence and to take all he could hold of the help that she offered before he should come to fear his dependency upon her and begin to mend his walls.

§ § § § § §

They might not tell the whole truth, but no one could accuse them of lying, Robert thought as he hung his head over the toilet and retched again. Nurse Dana had warned him that changes in his medication could disrupt his digestive system for a while. Robert made a mental note to ask that woman to define her concept of 'a while.' He had not slept through the night in more than a week. Catherine and Elisabeth also tossed and turned and cried out in the night, and both had lost their appetites since their medication had been changed. But at least, Robert thought as he rose dizzily from the floor, at least sickness earned them a reprieve from forced participation in Commander Maslow's experimental programs. Dana and Cheryl had taken Joy from him for a couple of hours this very morning. Joy told him upon returning that the nurses did nothing more than draw blood and give her an injection. For what, Robert wanted to know, but not every question was satisfied with an answer. He thought of the scar healing across Catherine's abdomen and worried for his family.

Lately Robert had become just as concerned for Catherine's emotional health as for her physical well-being. His oldest daughter had exhibited an attitude of overbearing confidence from infancy. Catherine until the explosion was extraordinarily beautiful, and Robert could easily believe she had been born fully aware of this benefit. She was exclaimed over, catered to, excessively spoiled every day of her twelve years, often by perfect strangers who stopped to stare at his little golden girl with helpless adoration. People forever showered her with candy, coins, compliments, eager to win the approval of one so lovely.

Catherine grew haughty and demanding, developing a personality whose ugliness clashed with the physical perfection in which it was housed. From birth she was handed her heart's desires. No exertion was required to earn or achieve any of them. She came to believe the world owed her absolute worship. Catherine relentlessly enforced this expectation and inflicted brutal punishment upon any who fell short of her demands. Robert had often winced as Catherine viciously shattered the confidence of young boys who offered her flowers or spitefully destroyed the self-esteem of other little girls who dared wear dresses that might be prettier than those in her own closet. If another child had something Catherine wanted, Catherine knew how to take possession of the coveted item. Robert lost count of the times he'd had to apologize to other parents for Catherine's deceit. He and Joy became the guiltiest parties in Catherine's crimes when they allowed their daughter's punishments to melt under the dramatic penitence she offered, complete with theatrical tears, as she promised to make restitution for her wrongs and amend her evil ways. Without fail said restitution would bow to Catherine's favor, and the parent of another heartbroken child would hold Robert and Joy responsible for the guilt of their daughter's multiplied wrongs.

Now Catherine's physical features appeared as repulsive as her personality. She at first amazed Robert by demonstrating that she had adjusted remarkably well to her injuries. Throughout her recovery Catherine's attitude settled, and she became more agreeable to her family. Robert could not help but notice that since the survivors had been relocated, Catherine had reverted back to her old characteristics of hostile behavior and self-centered conceit. He and Joy were at a loss to understand the change.

Robert didn't want his problem child to grow into a problem adult who would continue to hurt people. He didn't want Catherine to end up bitter and alone. Her adult peers already rebuffed the bullying tactics she had used to intimidate her childhood companions. Robert wanted Catherine to have friends, but he knew she must experience the desire to give from the heart. She must learn to receive graciously what others offered, instead of selfishly manipulating each gift into generating an even more abundant return. He hoped it wasn't too late to teach her how to be a friend to other people. If he was going to go there, however, he must first navigate the territory in which she had currently isolated herself. In order to do that, Robert was going to need help preparing for the journey. He turned to Elisabeth for enlightenment.

The Trinity victims were allowed access to the assembly room after one o'clock every afternoon. They could come and go between it and their living quarters until ten o'clock each night. Robert found his youngest daughter there and took her back to his and Joy's room for a chat. He was startled at Elisabeth's automatic answer when he asked if she knew what was troubling Catherine.

"Well, sure. Catherine is ordinary. She looks just like everybody else. For the longest time, she thought it was just temporary. Even now she tells me she is going to fully recover and be beautiful again. Then she will marry the richest man in the country and have everything she ever wanted. And nobody had better dare to get in her way!"

Robert's heart sank. "Is that what she really thought she would do when she grew up?"

"No." Elisabeth patiently explained. "Before we ended up here, Catherine wanted to be a queen." She giggled. "I don't know exactly how she planned to do it, but she used to tell me that if I did exactly what she ordered me to do until she became queen, she'd make me her number one personal servant." Elisabeth laughed out loud. "I used to believe her. I was really stupid."

"You're not stupid, Elisabeth. Don't ever say such things about yourself." Robert wished he had questioned Elisabeth years ago, wished he had taken Catherine in hand before she was even out of diapers to dilute her vanity. It troubled Robert that other people mattered so little to Catherine, even though she was still hardly more than a child.

"I know I'm not. I made better grades in school than Catherine did. I was one of the smartest girls in school, and I earned better marks than all the boys."

"I am so proud of you, honey. I have always been very proud of you." A thought crossed Robert's mind that made him ashamed. Everything was always about Catherine. Even now she ensured their world revolved around her. Robert experienced a brief flash of fatherly indignation. "Are you all right, Elisabeth? Is there anything you would like to talk about?"

Elisabeth shrugged her narrow shoulders. She was a petite girl, modest and quiet. She had also been very pretty, though she had never turned heads and dropped jaws like her sister did. Her dainty features were dominated by large, expressive eyes that the Creator had faithfully copied from the face of her father. Elisabeth raised them to Robert and said, "I miss my friends. I miss going to school. I miss my clothes. I wish I had my own room so I wouldn't have to share everything with Catherine. I wish I could see Sam again."

"I wish all those things, too, honey, believe me I do. Who is Sam," Robert wondered.

"He's my beau."

Robert was floored. His bashful eleven-year-old had a beau? "Elisabeth! I didn't know you had a boyfriend!"

She lowered her head so he could not see her expression. "He liked me. Sam liked me better than he liked Catherine. He thought she was mean and nasty. He said no girl was pretty enough to make up for all that. He said I was prettier than Catherine because I was nicer. Nobody else ever told me that. I liked Sam. I was going to marry him when we grew up."

Robert studied his baby girl with the sinking realization that she was a complete stranger to him, and with gratitude for the opportunity he was given, here and now, to be a father and a friend to this special young lady.

"Catherine tried to get Sam to like her instead of me, but he wouldn't, and she got really mad. Catherine hated Sam. Catherine hated me, too. She hates everybody."

"Do you really think so?"

"Yes. She used to hate anybody who wouldn't do exactly what she wanted them to do. Now she hates everybody because nobody treats her special. Merely walking into a room doesn't get her noticed anymore. Now she actually has to talk to people to get their attention, and she doesn't know how to do that. Remember what you said in the hall when you knocked down the hood and we got out of our room? You told Mr. Davenport that all of us have recovered as much as we're going to. I got really scared when you said that because I thought I'd get better. I thought my face would heal and my hair would grow back. Catherine thought so, too, and even though she knows we'll always look like this, she still insists that it's not permanent and she'll be beautiful again. Can I tell you something, Dad?"

Robert nodded sadly.

"I'm glad Catherine is ugly. For the first time, people like me just as much as they like her. Maybe even better. Used to be, I was just Catherine's little sister. I didn't even have a name. Now I'm Elisabeth. Now I'm *me*. Once in a while they call me 'Robert's daughter,' and that's not so bad. But it's nice to hear people call me by my own name, without qualifying me in reference to another person as though I were somebody's pet."

Qualifying her. Where did she come up with such ideas? Robert smiled widely at his sweet, clever little girl. She would have gone to college. She would have made her dreams come true through hard work, determination, and commitment toward what she most desired to do. Elisabeth would have loved people, and people would have loved her in return. Robert would have laid down his life right then and there to give her back that future.

"I'm sorry. I didn't mean to be bad."

Robert felt the remorse in her voice. "What are you sorry for, honey? You haven't done anything wrong."

"I said I'm glad Catherine is ugly. But I'm not, really. I don't want her to be sad. I know she's got an awful temper and treats people bad, but she's still my sister, so I should be nice to her."

Robert looked into the solemn face of the child before him and wondered who was the adult in this conversation. "Remember this for me. Okay?"

Elisabeth nodded.

"Feelings are neither right nor wrong. They are honest reactions. It is what you do in response to your feelings that is right or wrong. Do you understand?"

Elisabeth contemplated the lesson. "I think so."

"Look at it this way. The next time you see Catherine, she might do something that makes you so angry, you want to hit her."

"Might?" Elisabeth sighed heavily. "Why don't you just say she *will*…"

Robert smiled. "Your feelings are understandable. If she says cruel words or breaks an item that you value, of course you're going to be hurt and angry. There isn't anything wrong with that. But hitting her or tearing up things that belong to her would be inappropriate ways to express your feelings."

"Doing those things would lower me to her level of indecency," Elisabeth stated.

Robert blinked at her. "Who told you that?"

Elisabeth studied the toes of her slippered feet. "Kenneth."

"Kenneth?"

"One day when we were back at Grandma's house Catherine and I had a fight. The guys broke us up. Dave talked to Catherine while Kenneth talked to me. I was really upset, and he told me I could be mad without being bad."

"Ah." Robert frowned. Where had he been when this encounter took place? "Well…it's true. That's right."

He wondered once more who was gaining the greater lesson out of this discussion. He had learned what he wanted to know about Catherine. She acted as though she despised her little sister, but Elisabeth was the first person to whom Catherine would confide when she needed to vent anger or fear. Just as important as Catherine's troubles, Robert had learned more about Elisabeth than he would have believed there was to know. During all the time his family had spent locked in a room together, they had occupied themselves with lighthearted banter and childish games. But neither he nor Joy had opened themselves up for the sharing of their deepest hearts, and the girls had followed their example.

Let this point be taken, then: his chat with Elisabeth proved that it was not too late to begin having occasional private conversations with his daughters and to encourage Joy to do the same. He and Joy should get to know them now, while they were children. Soon enough they would both be adults, and then – and then? What then? He once would have predicted college, marriage, family, work, happily-ever-after for both his girls. Those might-have-beens were irrevocably erased, leaving nothing but a vacuum that could only be filled day by day. But then, the future existed for no one. Only the present offered proof of reality, one moment at a time. Anticipation, Robert decided, was what made the future appear tangible, as though the expectation existed, but simply had not been arrived at yet. Hope was a mirage in the desert of eternity.

Robert lingered on the metaphor as he hugged Elisabeth and sent her back out to the common room. Dreams, goals, intentions, saving money, making appointments – all plans laid out for a future that did not exist. How much of his present had he missed by looking forward to special moments to come, as though they were real and not merely in the process of becoming? Yet one had to make plans and follow through with them if anything worthwhile were ever to be accomplished. Robert shook his head and decided there were enough points of contention in the present to drive him crazy without entertaining what-ifs and wherefores. If he intended to look forward to any future for his family at all, it had to begin by getting them out of this place. His mind automatically cast about for a way to make that happen. Robert laughed at his own folly as he joined the others in the common room.

Dana greeted Robert with a box. He was slow to accept it until he noticed that everyone in the room had one. Joy waved from a distant table, and he hurried to join her, anxious to share with her the details of his conversation with Elisabeth.

§ § § § § §

Ray stared at the carton on the table before him as though he expected it to open on its own. The nurse had offered no explanation when she placed it there. She and two others carefully ensured that everyone in the room received an identical package. Familiarity with similar boxes left Ray wary. He reluctantly reached forward and folded back the lid, fully anticipating a tin of Spam and a slip of Maxwell House coffee, perhaps a bit of Dentyne gum and a four-pack of Chesterfields along with a book of paper matches. To his relief he was confronted not with K rations but with a deck of playing cards and items of personal hygiene that had not previously been made available to him. He leaned against his wife and peered into her box.

"Did you get chocolate?" Belva clutched a small bar with both hands.

Ray dove into his box and found his candy. All over the room, the survivors were pulling out the narrow paper-clad bars, holding them like treasure in their hands.

"I can't decide whether to eat it now or save it until later." Belva stared at the bar as though if she blinked it would vanish. Considering the unappetizing textures and questionable flavors of the foods they were served at each meal, a taste of chocolate could easily be heralded as a gift from the heavens.

Ray prowled through the remaining items in the box. There was indeed chewing gum as well as a handkerchief and a toothbrush with a tube of Colgate. He looked forward to the pleasure of brushing his teeth once more. The last item in his box was a small paperback

New Testament that included the Psalms and Proverbs. He lifted the little book with gratitude, and his heart pounded with unexpected longing to read the words inside.

Across the table from him, Sarah sat with her mouth agape as she held her own Testament in trembling hands. "A book," she breathed to Ray. "A book! To keep!" She held it up triumphantly.

Ray smiled. "Half of one, at least."

"Callie! A book…"

"Daddy." Ben approached as Sarah fled with the Testament in one hand, the chocolate bar in her other. "Would it be all right if I stayed with you and Mama tonight? Uncle John and Aunt Mary said it was okay with them."

"We'd be glad for you to. You have our permission, but your nurse will have the final say-so on a request like that."

"I know." Ben wrinkled his nose. "I hate to ask the old bag, but I will."

"Ben!" Belva reproved.

He ducked his head and laughed. "Sorry, Mama. I hate to ask *Nurse Thornton*, but I will."

Ray and Belva looked at him in surprise. "I don't think we've met her," Belva said. "All the nurses here introduce themselves by their first names."

"Not her." Ben shook his head vigorously. "Most of the nurses are young, but Thorn-in-my-side is older. Her hair and eyebrows sit really high on her head, and her eyes sweep around as if she's always looking for something to get mad about."

Ray chuckled in spite of himself. Belva shot them both a reproachful look. "Perhaps she's just unhappy,"

Belva suggested. "You're right; most of the medical staff are younger folks. I wonder how she ended up here."

"Somebody probably wanted to get rid of her. This is the perfect place to send a person you never want to see again."

"Ben, that is a terrible thing to say."

"But it's true, Mama. That's why we're here."

No one had an answer to that. A pained expression lingered on Belva's brow, and Ben looked ashamed that he had pointed out the obvious in a way that might have hurt her. Ray decided it was a good time to change the subject. He held up his candy bar and smiled brightly at Ben.

"Did you get chocolate?"

Chapter Twenty-One

"I used to take a book to bed with me every night," Sarah reminisced. "I would read until I fell asleep. I'd be awakened an hour or two later by the corner of the book poking me in the back. Mama would have already slipped into my room and turned the light out. I'd move the book up next to my pillow and go back to sleep. Most of my friends slept with stuffed animals or dolls, but I preferred books from the time I began learning to read. I could never get enough of a good story."

"The books in the assembly room will not be loaned to individuals," Nancy stated in a tone that precluded argument. Sarah had sighed over all the lovely volumes. Two shelves of them greeted her when she ventured into the common room that afternoon. There weren't many, and she devoured books quickly. She'd have them all read soon enough anyway, without the pleasure of taking them 'home' overnight. The paperback Testament alone was permitted residence beside her bed.

"A pencil and paper, then," she pleaded.

"There is a blackboard and chalk in the common room," Nancy reminded her.

"The whole point is that I want to write down things on paper that I can keep."

Nancy's eyebrows bunched together in an irritated frown. "Writing instruments are forbidden. The blackboard and chalk were provided to appease those of you who persist in requesting pencils and paper. Residents are not permitted," she explained with exaggerated patience, "to have sharp objects in their rooms, and that includes pencils. Besides," she wondered as she left. "What could you possibly need to write down and keep?"

Callie spoke up as Pat administered an injection. "Did you ask if I could have a guitar?"

Pat laughed and shook her head as though Callie were indeed a silly girl. "No."

"You said you would ask," Callie insisted. "You said someone with more authority than you would have to make that decision."

"The decision has been made," Pat snapped. "You have music every afternoon."

Callie thought of the speakers mounted high on opposite walls in the assembly room. She supposed they were connected to a radio located elsewhere in the facility, but there was only music. None of the entertaining programs with which the survivors had previously been familiar were played, and no news reports ever leaked into the room.

"The music is nice," Callie said tentatively. "It's very nice. Perhaps we could get our favorite programs, too. Bing Crosby or the Lone Ranger or Fibber McGee and Molly; Sherlock Holmes, maybe, and I know Sarah would love to hear Ellery Queen or the Shadow. Ben was a member of Captain Midnight's Flight Patrol. He had the bronze medal with the propeller on the front, the Code-O-Graph, all that stuff. We all miss our favorite shows."

Pat wrote briskly across her clipboard. "You people would rather listen to the radio than to the music you hear now." Her eyes were accusing, though Callie did not know what slight she had committed. "I don't believe such a thing will be done, but I will pass the word along."

"I suppose there's still no chance you will bring me a calendar, either."

Pat's eyes narrowed with the labor of an annoyed smile. "You don't need a calendar, Callie! There's no need for any of you to be looking that far ahead."

"I thought we were relocated because the victims were getting well," Callie protested. "I hoped the next step from here would be that we'd get to go home."

"You were moved to the seventh floor because the Trinity survivors have significantly improved, yes," Pat agreed. "It was no longer necessary for the staff to wear full protective clothing when seeing to your needs. As your health has improved, your medical needs have changed, which means that everything else has to be adjusted to accommodate those changes, from clinical equipment to pharmaceuticals to meal programs. Some of the survivors are as well as they will ever be, but our superiors prefer to advance the lot of you at the same time. If release were an option, one wouldn't go home until you were all ready to go."

"And who determines when we *will be* released?"

Pat ignored the question. "You were also relocated because certain among you made it obvious that you were becoming restless and antagonistic. It was felt that a change in scenery was advisable for you all. Our superiors believed that permitting you to interact and communicate with one another would be beneficial to your mental and emotional health, so the assembly room was an added kindness on their part. You really should appreciate the books and the music and the time you are allowed to spend with your family. People you've never even met made these arrangements so that you and the other Trinity survivors could lead as normal a life as possible."

Callie held her breath in order to restrain the bitter comments that begged release. Pat checked the thermometer that had been under Callie's tongue and pencil-stabbed little marks in a row of boxes that bordered the page on her clipboard.

"I'll be seeing you." Her voice was light, but her eyes appeared weary with the effort of maintaining a cheerful façade for a patient who forever demanded more than a mere nurse could give, or tell, or be.

§ § § § § §

Ray covertly watched his son pace the perimeter of common room. The far end of the L-shaped area where the wall recessed was seldom used. It was the narrowest section of their assembly room, making it less convenient for meal times or activities. Ben, though, had apparently taken an interest in the corner from which their speaker, Commander Maslow, had appeared weeks before.

Ben glanced around, ensuring the others were occupied. Ray's smile was bittersweet as his son slipped around the corner out of sight.

From the moment he learned to walk, Ben was an explorer in pursuit of the enticing unknown. One moment he knelt beside Belva in the garden, examining the seeds she planted and watching earthworms work their way through the freshly turned soil; the next instant he was gone. Ray would spend hours scouring the woods for his little lost son, only to find Ben mesmerized by a spider weaving its intricate web among the branches of a slender redbud or observing a beetle's erratic path around and over the comparatively mountainous obstacles that littered the forest floor. When Ray appeared, Ben would be too full of excited questions to notice his father's frustration and relief. Ray's annoyance inevitably dissolved as he answered and explained and released himself to the wonder of Ben's discoveries.

As Ben grew older it became apparent that no matter where he went or how long he stayed, he was never lost. Farm chores soon replaced playtime, but in the cool of the evening when the day's work was done, Ben was free to steal away. At such times his exuberance settled into the quiet stealth necessary for blending into his surroundings. He refined this talent until he could closely approach and capture small creatures alive. He would examine the wonder in his hands, admire fur, feathers, or scales, and release the captive where he had found it.

Ben located thickets frequented by deer. He followed the evening route of the gray fox, visited the ancient tree in which the horned owl nested, haunted the back doors of rabbit warrens and groundhog dens. He spied on gray squirrels and fox squirrels as they chattered from the safety of branches high overhead. He led his inquisitive sister to raccoon dens and showed his mother the favorite hunting roosts of red-tailed hawks. He crept alone to the cave spring where small brown bats awaited dusk, and he sat on a rock and watched their aerial ballet as the tiny mammals consumed their fill of insects.

In the company of other children, Ben played energetic, competitive games. In the presence of his family, he practiced compromise and self-control. Alone with the animals, he learned to be still. Patience, stealth, and keen observation were qualities few people knew the boy possessed, but these skills were so practiced that they might have been inherent.

Ben learned while very young to remember where he came from, and he never forgot how to find his way home.

Ray's brow furrowed at that last thought. Ben still knew his way home – he still roomed with John and Mary – but twice of late his presence had gone unaccounted for. The nurses had been surprisingly lenient in allowing Ben to spend the night with Ray and Belva or with Clayton and Freddy. More than a week had passed since Mary made a passing comment to Ray about Ben staying with his parents the night before. But Ben had not done so, and Ray had not gotten around to asking Ben where he did end up spending the night. It happened again a few nights later. Ben had asked to spend the night with Clayton and Freddy but changed his mind. However, he didn't inform John and Mary of his decision, and he didn't sleep in his own bed that night. Ray was in no hurry to press the point. There was nowhere for the boy to go, after all, so he had to be camping among his fellow Trinity survivors. Moving from room to room would never compare to Ben's childhood adventures in the forests around his home, so why challenge his efforts to enjoy what little roaming he managed to do in this place?

Ben stepped back into view and looked carefully around before joining Ray and Belva at a table in anticipation of lunch. When cleaning off the table afterward, Ray saw Ben conceal three broken wooden forks among their litter. He raised an eyebrow, but remembered his decision not to pry.

§ § § § § §

"Dana was true to her word," Robert told the men over their cards. "We all got sick during our first few weeks here. I was still having problems when Dana and Cheryl started hauling me and my family out for tests again."

Ray picked up the card he was dealt and added it to his hand. "That portion of our lot has not improved. Belva and I are more unwilling than ever to submit to the wishes of the lab staff. I know how ridiculous that sounds. It matters not whether any of us go friendly or fighting. Force eliminates the need for cooperation. The examinations we're going through now are far more threatening than anything we experienced before."

"And more humiliating." Russ laid down his cards. "I'm out. My nurse has started asking very personal questions that are downright embarrassing. I refuse to answer them. I've been wondering if you all were being asked the same things."

Tom snorted. "If those questions pertain to arousal, yes. I don't know why they are putting us through that drill when they already know the answers. Ilya told me that all male Trinity Test survivors were rendered impotent by the explosion. But recently she's been asking for intimate details and won't tell me why. She said one of our researchers would provide magazines that I could view privately for visual stimulation, after which I could report how my body responded. I told her that I am a Christian, that I don't have a wife with whom to prove if I am capable or not, and that I refuse to degrade myself in such a manner. I'm glad you mentioned this, Russ. It's good to know I'm not the only one whose nurse has taken an interest in the subject."

Robert clenched his teeth until the muscle in his lower jaw twitched at the pressure. "It's my fault," he finally said. "Joy says the nurses are putting all the women through a battery of gynecological examinations again. She and Callie are being included in them all. I...we..." He exhaled in frustration. "A few weeks ago I discovered that my ability to perform sexually was returning. I didn't think Joy would want me to touch her, looking like I do, but I was wrong. She was very, ah, encouraging. The day after we made love for the first time, Joy was taken out for an examination, and of course the nurses realized what we had done. I've been accustomed to regular physicals myself, but what they are doing to me now is the most degrading, inhuman treatment they've ever forced on me. Like Tom said, their questions are embarrassing. The handling is far worse. I get angry at being nailed to the wall by a woman who has no business prying into that area of my life, nurse or not. I become enraged at being strapped down helpless while doctors and nurses have their way with my body. When I get back to my room, Joy and the girls feel as though they have to tiptoe around me until I calm down. I don't take my anger out on them, but they interpret my silence well."

Russ sorted his losing hand of cards. "The women

have developed routines for the sake of doing more with so much time than simply watching it slip away. Meanwhile, we try to adjust to our new environment and deal with a whole new assortment of medical nightmares. Is that really all there is to the rest of all our lives?" Russ ran his fingers lightly across his scalp as he had done when he sported a head full of unruly brown locks. "I wish Arlene and I could get married," he continued. "Arlene said she'd like to have a pretty wedding, a small one, with our family and closest friends in attendance. I want that, too, but first I want to improve like Robert has. I want the ability to be a husband to my wife."

"Belva wishes she had her wedding band back," Ray said. "Her finger is scarred where it used to be. Sarah wants to write about what is going on around here. She always did journal every little moment. Ben is bored stiff. He always stayed busy, going here and there, exploring places he'd never been, learning how to do things."

"Joy and the girls want to return to our house and our friends and our possessions." Robert neatly arranged his full house on the table over Tom's two pairs. "But we will never do that. I told them the best we can hope for is to start over and build a whole new life together. Joy and Elisabeth can grasp that idea and work with it. Catherine..." He slowly shook his head.

Ray grinned smugly and displayed a straight flush.

"Hey!" Robert protested. "You didn't warn me I was playing against a pro! I thought the spoils were mine. Such as they are." He laughed at the odds and ends in the center of the table: a handkerchief, chewing gum, a half-used tube of Colgate, and other items from the boxes they received every week.

"No chocolate, though." Ray drummed his fingers on the table and glanced around hopefully. "Maybe we can up the ante next time?"

"Not as long as I'm losing," Russ said, and Tom nodded in agreement.

"To the winner!" Robert raised his paper cup of water. "And for what does the winner wish?"

"I wish for the wisdom to get us out of here."

The four men went still, hearts pounding in unison as they saw in each other's faces the depth of their dedication to making that wish come true.

Chapter Twenty-Two

And out of the ashes arises the soul, suckling hungrily for life, kicking angrily at bondage, squalling loudly to the world that – it lives! – and reaches beyond itself, for we ever want to have, to see, to be more. Whether by growth or by progress or by another word crafted so as to intimate That Which Must Be Achieved, we reach because life demands it, even as it dances forever beyond our grasp, leading us in a maddening chase from the womb to the grave.

Torture. *The word yet lurks about my mind like winter's sharp breeze chills and cracks the highest branches of the pines. How many times was my very heart exposed, violated, and returned to me empty and cold. My body was changed beyond hope of repair, but the spirit, the spirit is before and during and after and beyond the reaches of the most fearsome of our humankind. Mercenaries of the physical are helpless to touch the supernatural, for God retains that which is holy for Himself.*

"The Phoenix bird, dost thou not know him?" Yes, Mr. Andersen – you who bequeathed to this child the power of your immortal imagination – oh, yes, I know him. I know many of his kind, and I am become in specie with him in ways that would have blighted your beautiful vision. I suffer things you never knew, and another generation will be astonished by that

which I know not of, for as long as there are men upon the earth, they will never cease to search for the means to accomplish countless atrocities, each more horrendous than the last, against their own kind.

It is as if they fail to realize that there are experiences worse than death.

Callie cringed and stared wide-eyed at the wall above her head as eerie whistles floated from the loudspeakers, silencing everyone in the room. A man's voice picked up where the whistling left off, and the survivors, glancing from the amplifiers to one another, began to smile.

"I know the nameless terrors of which they dare not speak!"

The Whistler concluded his introduction, and applause erupted across the room as the program began. A small accomplishment, but the broadcast represented a victory, a request made over and again until it was granted. Callie did not forget to express her gratitude to Pat that night as the nurse ushered her back into the apartment she and Sarah shared.

Pat didn't answer right away. When she did, her voice was stilted. "It's good to see you smiling and happy," she offered. She laid aside her clipboard and blood pressure cuff and sat on the edge of Sarah's bed. "Callie, are you familiar with the Serenity Prayer?"

"No," Callie said, taken by surprise at the concession to Pat's usual formality.

Pat handed Callie a small card. "It was written by the theologian Dr. Reinhold Niebuhr. The U.S.O. had the prayer printed on cards like this one and distributed them to our troops during the war. Read it," she urged, and paused while Callie complied. "The prayer asks for serenity to accept the things you cannot change, for courage to change the things you can, and for wisdom to know the difference. Callie, I think you need to focus on that serene acceptance. All of the Trinity survivors are frequently dissatisfied, but none so much as you. You seem constantly intent on overstepping your bounds, on wanting things you simply cannot have. It would be so much easier on all of you if you would just accept your life as it is and learn to enjoy it."

Callie didn't attempt to conceal her loathing of Pat's words. She answered hoarsely around the sour lump in her throat. "No human accustomed to freedom is going to willingly accept a lifetime of torture and imprisonment."

Pat shook her head. "That's just what I mean: referring to the facility as a prison. You've got it made here, Callie! You don't have to worry about anything. Your meals are prepared and brought to you, and medical care is provided with no expense or delay. Everything you need, from clothing to personal care, is supplied for you without you even having to ask for such things. You don't have to hold a job and earn money. You don't have to study for exams and obtain an education. There is even Michael Pendleton, an attractive young man not much older than you are and unaffected by the Trinity Test, should you desire male companionship. All you have to do is take life easy and enjoy leisure time with family and friends. Your days are filled with luxury. You don't even have to do laundry or dishes! You would feel so much better if you would count your blessings instead of dwelling on those things you perceive as losses. Wanting what you will never have is a certain ticket to disappointment. Wanting what you already have, appreciating the things that are provided to you, will improve your attitude and make you more pleasant company for everyone else."

Callie was so grossly offended that she was at a loss for how to react. Her ears rang in the silence that followed Pat's advice to forfeit everything she hoped for and believed in. That her viability as a person could be so casually dismissed was enough to chill Callie to the bone. The intimation that she was too slow-witted to realize that freedom was a burden, and that being robbed of that burden should be welcomed as a good thing, left her speechless. *There is even Michael...* That was the final blow. A cow and a bull penned together would mate automatically. The flip suggestion that Callie and Michael should react to each other in like manner was the crassest dehumanization Callie had encountered, and it was more than she knew how to withstand. Pat had reduced her faith to nothing, and Callie would not allow such an attack to go unchallenged. She lowered her head but raised glittering eyes that bored into Pat's face from beneath fiery tresses, her expression akin to that of a tigress poised to spring upon her prey.

Pat bit her lower lip. Her face hardened as she took in Callie's reaction. She rose without another word, collected her things, and brushed by Sarah on her way out the door without so much as a by-your-leave.

"Gee." Sarah tossed her head. "What was that all about?"

Callie didn't move. Sarah sat down across from her on the spot of warmth that lingered in memory of Pat's visit. The rage in Callie's eyes was palpable, and Sarah waited for it to diminish. Instead of lessening, however, Callie's anger simmered so visibly as to check Sarah's usual loquaciousness. The silence lengthened, and still Callie did not move. Sarah finally asked, "Is there anything I can do to make you feel better?"

Callie's upper lip trembled in a predatory snarl. She stood, not willing to unleash her temper on someone she loved so much. "Thank you." Callie closed her eyes and breathed deeply, ashamed of the murderous inflection that tainted her voice. "You go on to bed. I'm going to exercise for a while. Please do not wait up for me. I need time to myself."

The lights went out before Sarah could reply, and the room was at once a den of shadows dispelled only by a luminous panel in the foyer. It was all the light they would have until the timer turned the others back on in the morning. Sarah stretched out on her bed. She thrust her feet under the covers and listened to Callie's defiant workout. The movements continued for a very long time. Callie fought until weariness claimed the battle and forced her to stop. Exhausted, she sank to the floor and wept in the darkness. Sarah wanted to go to Callie and offer the comfort of her presence but feared Callie might be embarrassed to know that she was still awake. She lay quietly when Callie got to her feet and marched into the bathroom. The steady rain of the shower soon lulled Sarah into a troubled sleep.

"I hope you can forgive me for my bad mood last night," were Callie's first words the next morning.

Sarah had arisen the moment the lights alerted her to daybreak. She left Callie snoring softly in the other bed. Callie greeted her with the apology as she returned from the shower and paused to drop the previous day's shift in the hamper beside the door.

"Nothing to forgive. I was worried about you. Are you okay?"

"I'm worried about all of us. Pat had a little talk with me last night before Nancy herded you in."

"I was with Christine and Elisabeth. We talked until the nurses broke us up and insisted we go to our rooms."

"I'm going to tell Daddy and Uncle Ray what Pat told me. Sarah, last night Pat gave me every reason to believe they intend to keep us here forever."

Obstinacy settled hard in Sarah's eyes. "I think we've all wondered if that wasn't the case. Commander Maslow said this place would be our home 'until further notice'. That's not what I'd call encouragement, but it left more room for hope than if he'd told us we would be here indefinitely. Seconds later he turned around and told us that all our families have been informed of our deaths. That means our confinement has to be permanent. What did Pat say?"

Callie carefully abbreviated Pat's remarks, prudently omitting some of her comments altogether. "Pat wanted to convince me how wonderful it is that we have been relieved of the efforts of making even the simplest choices pertaining to our daily lives. I didn't have the wherewithal to tell her that freedom 'from' and freedom 'of' are two very different situations. I was so upset by the time she finished speaking her mind that I couldn't say anything at all."

Sarah cast about for a shred of logic in the nurse's approach. "Surely Pat doesn't honestly believe all that."

"She doesn't have to believe it," Callie retorted. "Her job is to make *me* believe it so I'll behave myself like a good little patient, along with you and all the others.

What can we do, Sarah? What recourse do we have? There is no way out of this place. We are prisoners, and we are at their mercy. If they want to keep us here for the remainder of our days, there is not one thing any of us can do about it."

Sarah sat up straight to still the tremor that teased along her spine and manifested in a small shiver. "Our hope is all we have, Callie. Don't let go and give up on me now. We have to believe this is only temporary."

"How long can we have faith in that?"

"For as long as we are here," Sarah insisted. "For as long as it takes for all of us to be afforded our freedom."

"And if that never happens? If they never let us go?"

"Then we will achieve our freedom another way."

"But how? Look around you, Sarah. You're hoping for the impossible. It would take a miracle to get us out of this place. I don't know about you, but I'm fresh out of miracles just now."

"Miracles are in God's keeping, not in ours, and 'impossible' is a human concept by which we limit God and ourselves. I am no more acquainted with a solution to this mess than you are." Sarah balled her hands into one tight fist. "But I know, I just know, that I'm not going to spend the rest of my days within concrete block walls under these sickly yellow lights until I wither away from deprivation of everything that makes life worth living."

"Fluorescent," Callie muttered. "One of the nurses told Daddy that fluorescent lights have become very popular since the war ended. I hate their cheap, cold, artificial light. I'd give anything to stand in the sun."

A key turned in the door. "Hang in there, Callie, okay? Don't let these people steal your hope and destroy your spirit. We're not defeated as long as we hold on to our faith." Sarah picked up the card Callie had placed on the table between their beds. "Serenity." She read the prayer and nodded in agreement. "I like this."

"You do? Why?"

"Sure. We do need to pray for the courage to change the things we can."

"What about accepting the things we cannot change?"

"We don't yet know what things we can or can't change," Sarah pointed out. "And I'm not going to take Pat's word in that regard, or Nancy's, or Commander Maslow's. I'm going to keep watching and praying and hoping and believing that we're going to get out of here."

Callie smoothed away her tears with the back of her hand. "I'm not ready to give up. Not as long as I'm alive to fight." She looked at Sarah and forced a tight smile that only deepened the misery in her eyes. "It's just that I get so tired sometimes; you know?"

Sarah nodded. "I know."

One attendant entered with their breakfast trays while another guarded the door. Sarah took note of the little aerosol cylinders clipped to each man's belt. She remembered her own experience with the powerful tranquilizer and dismissed any thoughts of an outrageous escape attempt for one more day.

Chapter Twenty-Three

Mary Davenport wrote the July birthdays on the blackboard. Maria's would be on the thirteenth, and Ben's would follow on the twenty-fourth.

"Special days will be no less special because of circumstances beyond our control," she insisted. "Occasions once celebrated must be celebrated still."

"Life is what we make of it," Joy agreed. "At least the radio makes it easier to keep track of what day it is."

"I wish we could hear the news, too. Wonder why they silence the news broadcasts? It shouldn't matter to them whether we hear it or not."

"Ignorance is a weapon. Discouragement is another. We have both working against us here."

"Neither will diminish who we are unless we allow it." Mary dusted chalk from her hands. "It's so important that we keep ourselves alive emotionally, mentally, and spiritually. Physically, too, though Lord knows there were times I wished to die."

Mary and Joy stepped aside as Christine approached the board and began to write math problems for her students. "This would be so much easier with pencils and paper," she complained. "Textbooks would be nice, too. Do you know what I was told when I requested materials to continue educating our children? A nurse said we didn't need to be concerned about such things, because the children would be cared for so completely that they would have no need of a formal education. The nerve!" The schoolteacher continued to mutter under her breath as she briskly created a mathematics lesson from memory for her charges, whose parents were delighted with Christine's schooling even if their children were less than enthusiastic about the discipline.

"Being deprived of the opportunities to do the things we love really hurts," Joy told Mary as they walked away. "I enjoyed designing clothes for my daughters. Catherine wore them grudgingly, but Elisabeth appreciated my efforts. She took pride in showing her dresses off to her friends. Robert misses photography."

"John and Ray would give just about anything to be farming again," Mary said. "I enjoy puttering around in my garden and doing embroidery. And I love to cook. If I could be turned loose in my kitchen back home, I'd spend an entire day cooking up the biggest meal for all of us that you've ever seen. Genuine, delicious food, too. You wouldn't have to wonder what exactly you were eating."

Joy managed a smile, but her heart broke with the reality, unacknowledged but ever-present, that her home and possessions were long gone and that, if she were to be released tomorrow, Joy Lake had no address or bank account to which to return. She exhaled a deep breath and, with it, thoughts she could not bring herself to consider. Three female voices harmonized nearby, scattering the demons to other pursuits as Joy and Mary sat down to listen.

Arlene, Abby, and Rachael had sung together in church since they were children. The devastation of their bodies had not permanently ruined their vocal abilities, and they had recently begun to lighten the bonds of their captivity with song. Their beautiful voices blended and harmonized on melodies ranging from gospel to ballads to jazz.

Tom laid down his cards and leaned back in his chair to listen. He closed his eyes in an effort to linger on the bittersweet memories resurrected by the song. It had been a popular hymn at church. It was also one of Sybil's favorites to sing while she worked around the house. Tom would get so tired of hearing it at church every Sunday and Wednesday and at home every other day of the week that he'd covertly urge the music minister to choose a different song. Sybil's voice was as lightly refreshing as a summer's breeze. What Tom wouldn't give now to hear the simple, lovely melody of the Morning Hymn wafting from his kitchen with the aroma of coffee and bacon or fairly raising the church roof as a congregation of voices lifted those lyrics in praise. He smiled at the recollection as he joined Arlene, Abby, and Rachael on the Doxology.

Tom had taught lessons every Sunday morning since the survivors were introduced into the assembly room. Sunday School, he called it, but his teen members wanted more, and others also voiced their desire for additional instruction and inspiration. Tom procrastinated and begged their pardon. Finally he prayed, already knowing what the answer would be. On the coming Sunday afternoon he would present his first sermon to the little congregation of people who desired spiritual leadership of him. How one who felt so weak and insignificant could offer any semblance of guidance, Tom did not know. *Not me, but Christ in me...* For the God he called Father, for the Father he called Lord, he would do his level best to share the redemptive message with these people who so desperately sought salvation in every aspect of their lives.

At the far end of the room Robert sat talking with Catherine, who answered when she had to and stared stonily at her lap when she did not. He didn't know how to get through to her. Experience assured him that both he and Joy would tire of trying long before Catherine would open her heart to them. It hurt to be treated so dismissively by his own flesh and blood even as he acknowledged that a dozen years without firm discipline or clearly established boundaries left him largely to blame for his daughter's lack of empathy. The Trinity survivors had been victimized by a situation that left them permanently damaged in ways that could not be fixed, but Catherine only acknowledged her own injuries. If she threw a big enough fit, fate would bend to her will and replace the beauty it had so cruelly stripped away. Thus she had succeeded before, and Catherine was used to getting her way. Robert wondered how long it would take for her to realize that this time she would not be able to coerce or manipulate the facts to achieve a desired result. She had not appreciated her blessings when she possessed them. Now that they were forever gone, she wanted them back with interest. Surely her desire would be accommodated once she had made everyone involved miserable enough to concede to her wishes – and they all would, so that she would lift the crushing weight of her malicious disapproval and smile for them again. Not this time, Robert thought. You are no longer an exception. You are just another person. He longed for the day Catherine would recognize that the world neither revolved around her nor existed exclusively for her. Until then, all he could do was love her. If she refused to talk, he would say the words, and she could listen. If Catherine learned nothing else, she would know that her family cared for her and wanted her to experience happiness that had nothing to do with outward appearances and absolute control.

Catherine wasn't the only one having trouble with the truth. Freddy's face paled with shame as he faced Ben across a checkerboard in a distant corner. He made one weak attempt to distract Ben with anger. "Are you calling me a liar?" But his voice slipped an octave higher, betraying his bluff.

Ben relaxed against the wall with his legs straight along the floor. He crossed his feet and held Freddy's eyes with his own steady gaze. "Are you telling me you are not a liar? That what you've just said to me is the truth?"

"Of course it's the truth!" Freddy sputtered.

"Your father is a world-famous hunter and has the ability to repair anything that does not work properly. Your brother is a salesman who has worked all over the world. Your mother is an actress. Christine can speak any language known to man."

"Yes," Freddy said, but the word begged for permission.

Ben stretched and yawned, and then made as if to stand. "I want to ask Mr. Pendleton and Michael about the places they've been and the people they've met. And you know, with Christine's talents, she should be teaching us more than just English. I'd like to know another language or two, myself. That would be fun."

"No! I mean, I can tell you anything about Dad and Michael you want to know, and Christine's our teacher. We have to spend enough time each day with her. You don't want to get her started teaching more stuff. That'd be boring." Freddy rolled his eyes dramatically.

"You can't tell me everything that Mr. Pendleton and Michael have seen, because you weren't there. And learning isn't boring. I like to learn new things." Ben stood and turned to go.

"Ben, don't!" Freddy sprang to his feet and took Ben by the wrist. "Please."

"Don't what?" Ben tilted his head at Freddy, mildly perplexed and completely innocent.

"Don't tell Dad and Michael and Christine what I told you. I might have made some of it up." He looked around anxiously to see if anyone else had heard.

"*Might have* made *some* of it up?" Ben started to walk away.

"No! Okay, I made several things up." Freddy's shoulder's drooped. He slid a checker about the board with a bare toe. He glanced up at Ben, who frowned and inhaled a breath so deep that it raised both his shoulders and his chest before exploding out his nostrils and mouth in an effective demonstration of utmost annoyance. He stepped aside as if to walk past Freddy.

"Ben, please! I...look, I made everything up, okay? It's all lies, everything I said. None of it is true." Freddy dropped to the floor cross-legged with his elbows on his knees. He picked at one thumbnail with another and began to cry. "Are you going to tell on me?"

Ben resumed his seat beside the checkerboard.

"There's nothing to tell, Freddy. Everybody knows you've been lying from the minute we all met you. The things you've been telling us can't possibly be true."

"Then why are you making such a big deal out of it?" Freddy sat up straight, and this time his anger was real.

"Because nobody likes to be played for a fool, and that's exactly what you're doing when you lie. You are treating another person as though he is so stupid he'll easily believe your tales. Then he is upset with you for treating him like he doesn't have any better sense than that, and he's angry with you for trying to trick him. On top of all that, he's left with a dilemma: does he go along with your lie, let you think he believes you and that you've gotten away with making a fool out of him, or does he turn the embarrassment back on you by telling you to your face that he knows you're lying? That's a terrible thing to do to people, Freddy. Presenting exaggerations and outright lies as truth does not make people like you or want to be your friend. Instead, they shake their heads at your latest round of tales and laugh behind your back as you walk away."

Freddy didn't look at Ben. He picked at the tattered cuff of his blue pants and sniffled as he smeared away another tear. He swallowed hard several times and lined the checkers up on their edges, a row of little wooden wheels with nothing to carry and nowhere to go. "I lied about the Tear Stone. It's just an ordinary rock. You know that creek bed that ran behind the diner where we met? Remember how it was all dried up and in the bottom there was a lot of sand? I was poking around there with a stick, scattering sand off the bigger rocks, and that little stone rolled out with a bunch of gravel. I thought it was keen, so I put it in my pocket. Then when I showed it to you, and you went on about how pretty it was, I didn't want to tell you I'd just dug it out of the sand, so I made up a story and said it was a legend. But it was all a lie."

The two boys sat quietly for a moment. Freddy finally raised his head. "I'm sorry, Ben."

Ben studied his face. For once Freddy didn't squirm or look away. Ben nodded. "Apology accepted."

Freddy produced an odd little smile in return. He looked very confused.

"It was your move." Ben motioned toward the board. "I think. We've moved the pieces off their squares. Would you like to start a new game?"

Freddy stared at the board and wondered, "But what will I talk about?"

Ben arranged the discs on the black squares. "What do you mean?"

"I've never done anything exciting in my life. Neither have Dad or Michael or Christine, so far as I know. At least Christine went to college and teaches school. I'm not very smart. That's why I act silly when Christine asks me a question during our classes. I don't know the answer, so I get embarrassed. My mom works with a theater group. She stays busy with her job and meets lots of people. Your dad fought in the war. Mr. Lake worked in a factory and took pictures that were put in newspapers and magazines, and they had to travel really far to visit Mrs. Lake's family." He rolled a checker back and forth in front of his feet. "I don't have anything to talk to people about, Ben."

"Just be yourself," Ben assured him. "Conversation will come naturally. Don't work so hard to try to impress people. Listen to what they say to you and respond when you feel like it, like we're doing right now."

Freddy thought about that. He nodded slowly, spinning a checker like a top.

"I don't think you should stop telling stories," Ben continued.

Freddy looked startled.

"What I mean is, you have a gift. You just haven't been using it right. The Tear Stone Legend, for instance, is a terrific story. The only problem with it is that you lied and said it really happened instead of saying you had made up a story about the stone, and would I like to hear it. Instead of saying Michael has traveled all over the world, why don't you make up stories about a guy who travels and tell about the places he goes and the things he does."

"Like books!" Freddy exclaimed. "Except I could say them instead of writing them down!"

"Exactly. People would really like that. You have a talent for it. When we use our talents properly, they make everybody happy."

"Golly." Freddy basked in his new awareness. "Thanks, Ben. Gee, I never thought of doing something like that. I feel so bad about lying. I never thought it would hurt anybody."

"It does hurt people's feelings." Ben made the first move into a new game. "But you were hurting yourself most of all."

"Yeah." Freddy returned his checker to the board and moved in response to Ben. "So where did you learn about stuff like that? Like how to tell a story without lying and about using your talents and all."

"I guess from being around smart people. Daddy

and Uncle John are really smart. So is Mama. She doesn't miss a thing. My sister's pretty smart, too, but I'd never let on about it." Ben's naughty grin turned thoughtful. "Or maybe I would. I bet Sarah would like it if I told her that."

"People like it when you say nice things about them," Freddy agreed. "When they know you really mean it. The truth is –" Freddy made two jumps and claimed two of Ben's checkers – "the truth is, I don't think Dad and Michael are very smart. They don't keep jobs for very long, and they move around a lot. They don't have houses to live in or cars to drive. I get to spend two weeks every summer with Dad, but Mom always hates for me to go with him. Before Dad picked me up this last time, I heard her telling one of her actress friends that she was afraid I'd get hurt or that we would just disappear and Dad wouldn't bring me back. I wonder if Mr. Maslow bothered to tell my mom that I died in the desert. I wonder if she thinks Dad really did just take off with me. I miss my mom. I hope she misses me, too, but she was always so busy that she probably doesn't think about me much."

Ben fidgeted uncomfortably, too young and inexperienced to offer consolation against the lifetime of loneliness and rejection Freddy had expressed. He was spared the effort when nurses arrived with food trays. "Supper's here! I'm hungry, too. Seems like I never get quite enough to eat."

"Me, either." Freddy was still reflecting on all he had learned.

"You're ahead, so you win the game," Ben told him. "You're a better checker player than I am."

"You're a better friend than I have ever had."

Freddy dropped the checkers into their little cloth pouch while Ben stood and picked up the board. "I'm not going to lie anymore, Ben. I want people to really like me, not just pretend they do in hopes that I'll go away and leave them alone."

"And you'll still tell me stories?"

"Real stories, from now on!"

The boys laughed at the oxymoron as they approached their nurses and claimed their meals.

§ § § § § §

"Happy birthday to you! Happy birthday to you!"

Robert celebrated his thirty-fourth birthday on August fifteenth. He felt old beyond his years, and there was plenty of evidence to suggest that the occasion should be anything but happy. If Robert counted his blessings, his family and friends certainly topped the list, so he was glad to set aside his anxieties for a few hours and allow himself to be treated with extra consideration.

Birthday celebrations had become important events for all of the Trinity family. Even the nurses appeared to enjoy extending best wishes and slipping larger dessert portions to the day's esteemed guest. In keeping with their vocation, the nurses recorded daily vital signs, administered medication, and accompanied their patients to and from procedures in other parts of the institution. They were caregivers and concerned participants in the survivors' lives, but they could only become friends within the boundaries of their profession. An invisible barrier prevented them from becoming intimately acquainted with those in their care. Ever brightly smiling and cheerful, the nurses performed their duties, listened graciously to what their patients had to say, and were careful to do no more than that – to not make promises they could not keep, offers that were beyond their power to fulfill, or suggestions that might lead to future unrest.

Robert tried to appreciate Dana, Cheryl, and the others who attended to the needs of his family, but he harbored unforgiveness for them all. The medical staff regularly participated in forced experimentation on victims who were unable to defend themselves. In the aftermath of each treatment, the nurses would sympathize as they tended to the discomfort of those to whom the damage had been done. Robert knew the nurses were following orders. He felt certain that the medical personnel were given no choice but to carry out strict directives. If he could not hate them for their helplessness, he could condemn their complacency, though he resisted the urge to do so to their faces.

Dana and Cheryl were present to sing the birthday song. They quietly slipped away, dropping two sticks of peppermint candy into Robert's pocket in recognition of his special day. They could do no more.

Though there were no packages to open, candles to blow out, or cakes to cut, the Trinity survivors celebrated through what means were available to them. Mary enjoyed playing the hostess of each event, announcing the occasion and the individual to be honored. Gifts began as treats shared from the weekly boxes everyone received, but the word quickly took on a whole new meaning. A special song from Arlene, Abby, and Rachael, a new story from Freddy, or an intricate picture drawn in a corner of the chalk board by Will came to represent ways in which individuals offered a part of themselves as a gift in lieu of material packages. Robert basked in the joy of their giving and experienced yet another defining moment of excruciating awareness that he had taken the most valuable things in his life for granted throughout his years. Now, here, in the absence of freedom and choice, those things that mattered most remained at his fingertips. Such treasures brought tears to his eyes without the usual provocations of anger or fear.

"Make a wish," Mary ordered, and Robert did. Everyone joined hands to form one large circle while Tom led the group in prayer. Robert squeezed his eyes tightly shut and implored his Maker fervently for a way to gain freedom for all the Trinity survivors. It was a desire he expressed only to God, bargaining that he would gladly surrender his own life if it meant his children could live theirs in the world from which they came.

Chapter Twenty-Four

Robert glanced at the clock and sighed heavily as the speakers crackled into silence. It was almost ten o'clock, time for the nurses to arrive and herd them all back into their respective rooms. The past three months had resembled a bizarre comedy and tragedy production. The sheer bliss of interacting with the small community of Trinity survivors was countered by the horror of more invasive surgeries and intensive rounds of experimental drugs that left the patients incapacitated for days. Even with new friends and more pleasant surroundings, boredom was never alleviated. Monotony spawned unrest, and unrest generated a desire to do *something*, but here there was nothing to do. Robert stood to stretch. He paused when he saw Ben approaching with an expression that suggested trouble.

"Daddy is suffering," Ben told him.

Robert knew. Something horrible had been done to Ray the previous morning, and Ray had not moved or spoken since except to beg for medicine to dull the intense pain. Those who visited Ray in his room became frightened for him when he hardly knew they were there. Robert was sickened and angered. Ray had become his best friend. He looked down into the solemn face of

Ray's son. Ben jerked his head toward the far end of the room, and Robert followed him away from the others who were preparing to enter their apartments for the night.

"Tell Joy to tell your nurse that you are going to spend the night with Tom Westfield. Aunt Mary will say I am staying with Michael and Freddy. It's okay. The nurses never check with each other anymore. You have to come with me. There's something I have to show you and someone I want you to meet. Tell Joy now, before the nurses get here. Just trust me, Robert. There's no time to explain."

If the authority of Ben's words and the gravity of his manner were not enough to secure Robert's cooperation, the boy's use of his first name was. Robert hastened to share with Joy the directive Ben had just delivered. He told Joy that Ben needed him, and she assumed they were both going to spend the night in Ray's room. Pressed for time and lacking an explanation, Robert let her believe that, promising himself that he would share every detail with her as soon as he learned what Ben meant to do. He said goodnight to Catherine's stiffened spine, returned Elisabeth's possessive hug, and found Ben waiting impatiently just outside the door of the apartment. "What's on your mind? Where are we going?"

Ben led him to the farthest end of the room and slipped around the corner. They faced the door from which Maslow and his two companions had emerged upon the survivors' first encounter with the assembly room and each other. Ben removed from his waistband a sliver of wood that Robert recognized as a tine bitten off one of the little wooden forks that accompanied each meal. Ben used his fingernails to pry a small metal cover from within the crevice where the doorframe met the wall. Robert wondered how Ben ever noticed the tiny, inconspicuous rectangle in such an unlikely location. When the cover popped off into Ben's hand, Robert glimpsed a cluster of wires. There wasn't time to be astonished. As a chime sounded through the speakers announcing five minutes until lights out, Ben thrust the wooden tine among the wires, touching two of them together. Robert heard a metallic click, and the panel visibly relaxed upon release from the tension of the latch. Ben forced the door open with his fingertips and shoved Robert through.

"What? Where?" Robert knew he sounded asinine, and he couldn't help it.

"Ssshhh!" Ben hissed. He snapped the metal cover back into place, stepped across the threshold, and slid the panel shut. Robert experienced an involuntary chill at the ominous click of the lock tumbling into place. He and Ben stood in darkness broken only by a pinstripe of light drawn beneath the door.

Robert was stunned at the chain of events with which Ben had calmly bound him. He trembled with excitement and fear at the prospect of exploring a whole new area of the facility. The craving for escape was an ever-present torment, and the possibility of finding a way out filled him with rampant eagerness that was immediately reprimanded by reality. He wished Ray were able to accompany them, or that he was at least well enough for Robert to tell him what he and Ben were about to do, whatever that was. Robert trusted Ben, but Ben was barely fourteen years old. The Unknown introduced its constant companions of fear, hesitation, and resistance. Robert responded accordingly.

"Ben," he began.

"*Ssshhhhh!*" Ben ordered, yanking sharply on Robert's sleeve.

They heard the nurses cheerfully ushering the occupants back into their rooms. Ben held onto Robert's sleeve and counted each thump until the final door closed. He exhaled with relief as the light glowing under the door was extinguished, leaving them in total darkness.

"At least tell me where we are," Robert whispered.

"Stairwell," Ben responded. "We're going nine flights up. Be really quiet. When we get to the top I'll explain everything. Here." He guided Robert's fingers to the handrail and promptly disappeared.

"Wait!" Robert gasped. "Ben!" There was no answer. The soft-soled slippers they wore ensured that their steps fell silently. Robert blindly started up the stairs, one damp palm sliding along the handrail as the other preceded him as if to ward off whatever lay ahead. He had accomplished the first landing when Ben reached out of nowhere to grab his arm and pull him onward. Robert swallowed the startled cry as it left his throat. His breathing became shallow, and his mouth went dry. Annoyed at the scare, Robert wanted to ask Ben if there was a purpose to this escapade or if the boy was just playing games. But Ben urged him to climb the steps quickly, insisting that he remain silent. With no alternative in the unfamiliar gloom, Robert complied.

A solid door waited at each level. There were twelve steps, a turn, and twelve steps again between floors. By the fourth flight Robert was winded. He would have stopped to catch his breath, but Ben silently compelled him forward. They had ascended two more flights when Robert saw a welcome glow illuminating the next landing. It was the first door he had seen with a window. Dim light filtered through the twelve-inch-square pane from an interior source, relieving their blind advance. Music and low voices suggesting a radio rose and fell in the distance. Ben stopped and Robert, two steps behind, waited to see what would happen next.

Ben abruptly turned on Robert and shoved him backward to the previous landing. As they turned the corner, the door above them burst open and footsteps thundered upward. Robert nearly jumped out of his skin. Everything had happened so quickly from the moment he followed Ben into the stairwell that there had been no opportunity for Robert to think through the situation in which he found himself, to present questions and secure answers, to make sure that everything was under control. He felt sick with frustration and insecurity, and Ben's quiet self-assurance made it worse. The boy had a take-it-for-granted confidence in his surroundings that made his approach seem reckless, but he obviously knew what he was doing. Robert wished he did, too. He did not like being second in command, especially to one so young and inexperienced.

Robert heard a second door open on the next floor above. It had not even latched when Ben started up the stairs. "Hurry!" He grinned over his shoulder, an eerie caricature in the shadows. Robert gave an exasperated snort and trotted up three consecutive flights before Ben stopped again. Robert leaned against the wall, breathing hard. The door on the landing below flew open. Loud footsteps retraced their path down one flight and back through the door from which they originally came.

"Night security for the lab. His girlfriend is a glazed doughnut." Ben snickered.

Robert stared at him with stunned disbelief. He shook his head and rubbed his eyes and finally asked where they were going next.

"Nowhere," Ben replied. "We're here."

Ben crept to the door and stared through the little glass window for a moment. To Robert's consternation, he then grasped the knob and opened the door wide, exposing the entire landing and its trespassers to brilliant light. He grinned at Robert. "After you!"

Robert froze, helpless and scared. He was furious with himself for not taking control of the situation long before he and Ben had come this far. Now there was nothing to do but pay the price for their foolishness, and he dreaded the magnitude of its impact on all the Trinity survivors. He stepped warily to the edge of the door and peered around the frame. Ben gave Robert's sleeve a gentle tug as he walked past him into a well-lit area the shape and size of their assembly room. This place, however, looked and smelled like a garage. The air was stagnant with oily odors. Tools hung at random from a tangle of hooks along one wall. Miscellaneous equipment and materials sprawled haphazardly across a table along another. Robert surveyed the area with wonder. He had worked with tools identical to some of these in a factory during the war. It seemed like forever since he had held such objects in his hands.

Ben walked to the solitary door on the opposite side of the room. Fully half that door was glass. Ben studied the area on the other side intently while giving Robert a few moments to recover from his initial surprise. When Robert wandered over to join him, Ben immediately opened the door. Robert walked through first this time and stopped to stare open-mouthed at the sight below him.

It was a warehouse, Robert decided, that had originally been designed as a hangar. Huge doors dominated one side, through which planes could come and go. Tools and an odd procession of machinery trailed along two walls, and right in the middle of the hangar...

Robert had never seen such a flying machine and would never have imagined one like it. He left Ben behind and made his way down two flights of concrete steps to the hangar floor. He approached the unique aircraft and walked slowly, incredulously, around the extraordinary apparatus. He touched it, examined it, tried to formulate a sensible explanation. It did not occur to him to simply ask Ben. Robert had momentarily forgotten about the young man who brought him here.

As he completed his second lap around the craft, Robert looked for Ben and panicked at what he saw instead. A man, an ordinary man in a khaki uniform, appeared from a small office in the corner behind the steps. The checkered grips of a pistol gleamed casually from the holster on his belt. As Robert cast about frantically for a place to run, Ben walked from behind the opposite end of the craft and strolled straight over to the stranger. Robert opened his mouth to shout a warning, but the man smiled at the approaching figure and offered a hand in greeting.

"Hello, Ben."

"Hey, Al." The two shook hands and hugged like old friends.

Robert stared in disbelief at the uniformed gentleman and the horribly disfigured boy. They talked for a while before Ben motioned toward Robert. The conversation continued too hushed for Robert to hear. The stranger regarded Robert with caution. His demeanor was free of animosity, but Robert sensed disapproval. Robert wondered if he should approach them and introduce himself, but decided against it. Ben had obviously known this man for quite some time. In deference to Ben's trust, Robert stifled the suicidal urge to attack the man, attempt to overpower him, and take his gun. Robert couldn't lead his friends to freedom. They didn't know where to go and would be captured long before they found a way out of the facility. He could not take the aircraft. He had never flown a plane. The hangar was wide open, offering no place to hide and no way to defend himself. Robert felt horribly exposed and more than a little betrayed. He decided to keep an eye on Ben and not speak until spoken to. As moments slipped by, curiosity asserted itself in competition with determined vigilance. At length Robert compromised by warily turning half his attention back to the unbelievable technology at his fingertips while remaining alert to the location and actions of Ben and the stranger.

By the time Ben and his friend approached for introductions, Robert was full of questions. He knew the answers would be a long time coming. First he had to learn whether this man could answer them and, if so, a relationship would have to be established before he could be encouraged to discuss such topics. No one would share the information Robert wanted with a civilian. Ben might know a lot already, but Robert doubted the boy would have thought to ask the questions he had in mind. Robert suppressed the excitement and anticipation, tempered with caution and a degree of outright fear, that escalated his blood pressure and made his heart pound. He was taxed to great effort to conceal his urgency as Ben and the gentleman stopped beside him.

"Al, I'd like for you to meet Robert Lake. I've told you about Robert and his family." As Ben went over a few details of Robert's life before the Trinity incident, Robert took advantage of the opportunity to study the stranger. It occurred to Robert that this was the first healthy person, outside the three with whom he was incarcerated, that he had seen without a cloth mask. Al was an inconspicuously handsome man of medium height and build whose dark hair was barely visible below his cap. Robert found it impossible to estimate the man's age. He could have been twenty-nine or forty-nine.

Ben turned to Robert with the crooked smile he had worked so hard to achieve during the pain of his recovery. "Robert, I am happy for you to meet my friend, Alden Morrow. His sole responsibility is the security of this aircraft. He knows it inside and out better than anybody else."

Alden's expression was sincere, but shadows of subtle disappointment haunted his eyes. Robert knew Alden was concerned because Ben had brought another survivor to meet him. As they shook hands, something else caught Robert's attention. On the far side of the hangar a gentle radiance softly illuminated the floor. Tracing the light upward to its source, Robert saw a louvered vent set into the wall against the ceiling. The vent was open, allowing fresh air to circulate throughout the hangar. For the first time in more than a year, Robert gazed into a night sky filled with twinkling stars and the sliver of a new moon. As he beheld beauty lost to him so long ago, Robert, a valiant man with strength to hold his own against adversity beyond what he could ever have imagined, turned his back and walked away from potential danger to stand in the moonlight and stare at the stars.

Ben and Alden retreated to the little office to talk while Robert explored the hangar and looked at the aircraft. He occasionally approached Alden with questions that were casual enough to be answered while only hinting of the critical information that Robert was so desperate to know. He studied the warehouse from all angles and watched the sky's upended smile traipse across the vent until it orbited out of sight. Too soon Robert felt a familiar tug on his sleeve.

"Time to go," Ben said. The young man shook hands with Alden and turned away. Three hours had passed in a blur. Robert would have given anything to stay longer, but he knew Ben was right. Ben knew details about nighttime routines within the stairwell of which Robert was completely unaware. It was critical that they return before the night staff made their usual rounds to peek in on their charges. The nurses might count noses, and it would not do for them to come up two patients short. As he retreated up the concrete stairs behind Ben, Robert paused for one last look at the hangar, the aircraft, the night sky, and Alden Morrow.

§ § § § § §

Ray balanced weakly on the edge of his bed as Belva and a nurse tried to coax him into eating the yellow cream purported to be breakfast. No sooner was the first bite swallowed than Belva dove for the wastebasket to catch it and the rest of what came back up.

Nurse Frank shook his head with concern. "I warned them that they were going too far," he muttered, but he refused to elaborate on the comment and wouldn't answer Belva's frightened questions. Instead, he helped Ray to lie back onto the bed and took the breakfast tray away. Frank returned twenty minutes later to inform Belva that medical procedures on Ray were suspended indefinitely until he recovered from his "unforeseen reactions" to the previous battery of experiments.

Belva spent the rest of the morning sitting on the bed beside Ray, offering comfort and encouragement of which he remained unaware. She entreated God for her husband's life, lifting up prayers born of the deepest, most intimate love for this man to whom she had faithfully kept the vows she made before Heaven and Earth at an altar twenty years before. Lunch was served, but Belva did not eat. When Nurse Gwen returned for the tray, she directed a patronizing frown at her patient and inhaled to deliver a callous sermon. Taking in Belva's resolute expression, Gwen changed her mind. She checked Belva's blood pressure, picked up the untouched tray, and slipped from her presence without a word. As soon as the doors were opened to the assembly room, Belva kissed her feverish, semiconscious husband and stood to leave their apartment. She turned and walked squarely into Robert.

"Sorry," he said. "I knocked, but there was no answer, so I wandered on in."

"I was on my way to find you. His responses are growing less frequent. He knows who I am, but he's so far away." Belva's eyes were bright with unshed tears. "Would you talk to him for a while?"

Robert nodded, humbled by Belva's fortitude and

determination. He had been so close to giving in so many times, but he had never observed such finality in Ray's wife. Robert had seen Belva cry, had watched her hurt as she recovered from dreadful wounds. He had felt the undercurrents of strength and emotion as she battled to control her anger and her fear. He had seen her weakened by separation and loss, but nothing about her had ever suggested defeat, and she obviously did not regard it an option now. Robert twisted his mouth into the general contour of a smile and resolved to muster more of such quiet, constant strength for himself and his family. He eased past Belva, looked down at his friend, and spoke his name.

Ray drifted without direction in a fog. He was mentally exhausted, weary of constant pain and sickness, emotionally near the end of his reserves. Hope faded with consciousness. Faces and names floated before him and left him frustrated at his inability to move from the threshold to one side or the other. Belva, Sarah, Ben, John, Mary, Callie...Sherlock, Jimmy, Ralph, Buster, 'Bluster,' they'd called him...full of hot air...what was he doing here? *How are them young'uns, Jimmy?* But Jimmy didn't answer, just smiled wistfully and marched right on by. Ray did his best to fall in behind him. Jimmy looked so peaceful. Ray wanted peace, too. He had tried to be a stronghold for the family and friends who shared this fate, but he could do no more. Even his wife and children were wafting out of reach. *God, love them*, he prayed through the haze of his departure. *Be the protection around them that I can't be, that I never could.*

As Ray gave himself over to the haven that was only a breath away, his tranquility was shattered by a thunderous, military-style barrage of commands, oaths, and accusations. Ray frowned at the onslaught, resisted being dragged back into a painful, undesirable reality. Clarity elevated him beyond reach of his ghostly compatriots. As awareness sharpened, Ray's frown turned into a bittersweet smile. He opened his eyes in obedience to a direct order.

"About time," Robert snapped. "Let me tell you something, buddy, you don't check out until we all check out! Understood?"

Robert helped Belva prop Ray against a mound of pillows. "You don't have to say a word," Robert advised him. "It's probably better for you if you don't. I have a story to tell you. This might take a while. If you get tired, you let me know, and I'll come back and share the rest later. Okay?"

"Yes, sir!" A wry grin accompanied the weak answer.

Belva retreated to that background area from where women keep an eye on their men and eavesdrop on their conversations while still allowing them a sense of privacy. She couldn't quite decipher the strange look on Robert's face. Though the men spoke in low tones Belva could hardly hear, the increasing fervor in Ray's eyes testified that he was catching Robert's suppressed excitement.

"I'm going to share the information first, and then I'll tell you where it came from," Robert began. "We are housed in a secret quasi-military base in the San Andres Mountains in New Mexico. Nine floors of this facility are underground or completely encased within the mountain, and one side of the top three floors faces the outdoors. Our institution serves two purposes. It is storage space for items the United States government would rather civilians not know about, mostly aircraft and pieces of aircraft of unidentified origin. It is also a laboratory that was established for the purposes of creating and testing methods of biological and chemical warfare and researching human genetic modification. I asked what that meant and learned just enough to scare me witless. Surprisingly few people work here. Four floors are completely vacant of human activity. Soldiers and civilian personnel serve long terms, up to four years with only one week of leave every six months. As much as two-thirds of the staff are women who joined the military to serve as doctors or nurses. They are transported in and out, just like Commander Maslow told us, without the vaguest notion of where they're coming or where they've been. We aren't the only ones who don't get to hear local news. The personnel listen to national reports, but local programs are prevented from broadcasting into the facility.

"There are several aircraft stored here, but only one is capable of flight. It is a unique piece of equipment, and no one knows where it came from, but it has been flown before. The security guard is a pilot. He was a member of the team that figured out how to make her fly. A decision was made against continued use of the aircraft, and the people who worked on it were reassigned individually all over the world. Only the guard remains, and his sole responsibility is the craft's maintenance and safe-keeping."

Robert realized he was getting carried away. He paused for a breath of air and to gauge just how much of this information was sinking into Ray's consciousness. Ray was breathing hard. His eyes were bright with both fever and anticipation.

"How?" he demanded. "When?"

"Your son. Last night."

Ray closed his eyes and relaxed his head against the pillows. "I knew he was up to something. Several months ago John gave him permission to spend the night with Belva and me. I didn't find out until the next day that Ben was supposed to have been here. He never showed up." Ray's voice was raspy, but he waved away the cup of water Robert offered. "When I finally asked Ben about it, he said he spent the night out in the common room just messing around. John and I got to talking and realized that Ben has been doing that a lot. We reprimanded him. If the nurses found out, we might all lose our privileges. Ben promised to be careful. I didn't make him promise not to hide out anymore, because I know he wouldn't keep that promise. Ben always hated feeling confined and closed in." Ray tried to swallow and failed. "But what does he have to do with all the things you just told me?"

"Ben figured out how to unlock the door in the common room, Ray. He met the security officer in charge of the aircraft. The officer's name is Alden Morrow. He and Ben have become good friends. Ben says Alden gets lonesome because he doesn't have much company. It appears Alden has taken a fatherly interest in Ben, showing him around the area in which he works, telling him about his work here in the institution. I didn't talk to Alden much myself. I was too astounded at learning that Ben had found a way out of these rooms. When we returned, Ben told me what I have shared with you. He said there's lots more to tell, but we didn't have time to go over it all last night. He says we can trust Alden to keep our secret. We can't go beyond the walls of this facility even if we do escape our rooms, and Alden enjoys the company.

"I saw..." Robert's voice caught in his throat with sudden emotion at the memory. "I saw stars, Ray. I saw the night sky through a vent. There was a new moon and stars, and I could smell the air, fresh natural air."

Fatigue deepened the lines on Ray's face into narrow gullies as he considered the unexpected revelations his son had brought about.

"You have a son to be proud of," Robert said. "His attention to time and detail were flawless. I was impressed to observe such maturity and perception in one so young. I asked him how much longer he had intended to wait before sharing this information. Ben said he had not meant to tell anyone. He wasn't sure what good it would do, and he didn't want to cause trouble for Alden. But then you became so ill. Ben is really worried about you. He wanted me to see the aircraft because he thought it might be a way to get you out of here if it was necessary to save your life."

"Escape will be necessary to save us all." Ray closed his eyes. His breathing slowed with exhaustion.

"Ben will take you to meet Alden as soon as you recover."

Ray's eyes flew open. "Where is Ben? Why isn't he here with you, telling me about the new things he's learned? He always loved sharing his adventures and discoveries with Belva and me."

Robert turned away from the inquiry he had dreaded, but he would not hide the truth even though he worried how it might affect Ray. "Both Ben and Sarah were taken from their rooms before breakfast this morning, and neither has been returned."

Ray turned his head slightly to look up at the clock. It was almost three p.m. Ray clasped his friend's hand as Robert stood to leave. Belva followed Robert into the foyer.

"Belva, please don't tell anyone else about this yet. Ray and I need to discuss the situation, investigate what possibilities might exist before we go public, so to speak."

"I understand. I won't say a word. Robert, have you heard anything else at all about Sarah and Ben?"

"I spoke with Mary and with Callie. Thornton tells Mary she doesn't know anything, and Pat tells Callie that Sarah's condition really isn't any of her concern. Callie is ready to commit murder and wonders what worse these people could possibly do to her in the way of punishment if she did. She isn't serious, of course, but I recommended she not speak such threats too loudly in this place."

Belva nodded gravely. "Thanks so much, Robert."

"I'll stop by again in a couple of hours. Meanwhile, if you need anything at all, just call out to me."

Belva returned to Ray and set aside the pillows against which he reclined until he lay flat on the bed. Ray's mind overflowed with all Robert had told him. He was too weary to process so much information immediately. He maneuvered onto his side and laid his arm across Belva's lap as she sat beside him. *An airplane!* He closed his eyes and prayed for his children as he drifted off to sleep that was genuine now, because he had a new purpose to fulfill and a new promise to keep. *Just take care of my children*, he begged. *Please, please protect my daughter and my son…*

Chapter Twenty-Five

❖❙❂❙❋❙❂❙❖

They lie who self-righteously claim to believe that looks aren't everything. The adage is used inappropriately to reprimand our vanity. It does not refer to beauty, after all, but to appearance. The blithe assertion that physical appearance doesn't matter fails to take into consideration the significant impact of first impressions. Each person has standards by which others will be judged and judged again upon each successive encounter. The other person's countenance, posture, conversation, hygiene, and manner of dress all process through our minds to produce an opinion that influences our reaction. This is human nature under the best of circumstances. In the glaring light of a more public and less forgiving society, beauty – or the lack thereof – can become the shameful measure of individual worth.

I know as well as anyone that appearances can be deceiving. I learned as a girl exploring the library that I will miss out on a lot if I judge books solely by their covers. A beautiful illustration may conceal a shallow, unappealing tale. A worn, plain, or poorly kept cover may enclose a brilliant, warm, enchanting world. Exterior beauty and inner loveliness never balance completely, for perfection is merely an illusion.

When I was a child, the reactions of others to my arrival usually made me feel confident, attractive, and welcomed into their company. Later responses to my appearance left me humiliated, hurting, and filled with self-loathing. Does what we look like make us who we are? In part, yes, for how others see us bears heavily on how we see ourselves. A little girl who is told she is beautiful will grow up believing it is so. A little girl who is told she is ugly, stupid, and unwanted will grow up believing, tragically, that it is so.

In both cases it can take God years to undo the damage that was – with best intentions, or maliciously – done.

"Where did you learn to play poker like that?" Tom demanded as Ilya sorted through her winnings.

"I might ask the same of you," she said. "I didn't know men of the cloth participated in such revelry."

"Tell me what you mean by revelry." Tom stretched and sat back, contented. "And I'll tell you if I find it to my liking."

"These can go back into the basket." She arranged a portion of her prize into a neat little pile. They played for nonsense, items Tom received in his weekly box of miscellanea, things Ilya could slip to her patient without jeopardizing her standing with her superiors. She swept a generous handful of hard candy from the table into the basket. Tom retrieved an orange piece, unwrapped it, and popped it into his mouth, savoring the sweet-sour taste.

"You know I'll eat every bit of this before we can play for it again."

"Then I'll just have to bring more." Ilya smiled.

"You have a beautiful smile. How is it that you can get away without wearing a mask anymore? Most of the other nurses still wear them."

"We were told that they are no longer necessary. The choice is left to each nurse, but our patients are not considered a risk to our health anymore."

"Because we have recovered from our exposure to the radiation," Tom guessed.

"Because of a lot of things."

Tom accepted Ilya's evasive answer and allowed her to change the subject as she smiled at him again.

"So where did you learn to play poker?" she asked.

"From my uncle and cousins back home in Texas. And you?"

"From family and friends."

"How did you end up here?"

Ilya looked for a moment as though she might abandon Tom and his intrusive question. Instead she composed herself and studied Tom's expression until he laughed softly and leaned across the little table, bringing his face mischievously close. She took his right hand in both of hers and sat up straight.

"You're very nice to me. You don't treat me as though I'm different from everyone else."

"Are you?" Tom grinned.

Ilya's face registered the hurt, and she attempted to withdraw her hands.

"No, wait. Please. I'm sorry. I know what you mean and why. Ilya, you're a lovely lady, patient and kind. I look forward to spending time with you every day." A slight pause betrayed his reluctance. "Some people focus so much on being a color that they forget to be a person. Racial lines were blurred for me during the years I worked as a youth leader under Pastor Clay Carter. He and his wife raised many foster children of different races in addition to their own four. It didn't matter to them if a child was white, colored, Mexican, or Indian. Pastor Clay and Mrs. Fae loved all their little ones equally. Whenever people in the community acted appalled that he treated everybody just alike, Pastor Clay would remind them that the same holy hands of God created each and every one of us. God designed our unique features and our coloring with all the love in a Father's heart, so who are any of us to despise our fellow creations? In the Bible Luke quotes Paul as saying that God has made of one blood all nations of men who live on the earth. But Pastor Clay wasn't just following orders. He and Mrs. Fae truly loved all people without prejudice. Pastor Clay was my mentor and a dear friend. I learned a lot from him about living my faith, but the lessons that stand out to me the most are the ones he practiced every day in front of the whole community."

With a forefinger, Tom traced the slender hand that lay across his palm. "So you can stop wondering if I'm just pretending that your race doesn't matter to me. I have no use for judgments that are based solely on our God-given appearance."

Ilya stared hard into his face. "I grew up out there in your world. Not many white people can make such bold claims as your Pastor Clay and mean them."

"Not many."

"That can't have been a popular position to take. It must have cost you friends."

"It wasn't." Tom's eyes looked straight into Ilya's. "And it did."

They stared at one another until Tom attempted to

shift the piece of candy from one jaw to the other and accidentally bit down on the orange disc. The resulting crunch broke both the candy and the tension. Tom and Ilya laughed together, playing with each other's fingers and attempting to tickle the palms of each other's hands. Ilya remembered herself first and stole a glance at the clock.

"Just a little longer," Tom begged. "You know a lot about me. Give me something about you."

"A bit of history, then," Ilya agreed. She placed Tom's hand palm-down on the table and laid both of hers across it. Her expression grew abstract as she sought far-away memories.

"Rosa Ruiz de Cardona was born in Utuado in 1898. That was the year Spain ceded Puerto Rico to the United States after the Spanish-American War. Rosa's family did well for themselves despite all the changes until a hurricane devastated the island. They lost everything. Rosa was still a little girl when her parents decided life would be better in America on the mainland. They set out for the Puerto Rican coast. From there they journeyed across the Dominican Republic and Haiti to Cuba. Rosa was about five years old when they settled there.

"Travel was hard on the family. Rosa's worst memories were of time spent on the water in leaky boats that were crammed full of people all in the process of escaping a hopeless lifestyle for a chance at a better tomorrow. Rosa's mother had fallen very ill by the time they arrived at the American fort of Guantanamo. She survived because of an American doctor. She decided then that her little Rosa would someday become a doctor in the United States of America.

"The family remained in Cuba for several years.

They worked hard in sugarcane and tobacco. Rosa was seventeen by the time they made their way across the island to Cardenas. Politics were raging, and the family was more eager than ever to reach the American mainland. They arrived in Florida in 1916 and kept right on going. The war was in progress, but that all seemed very far away to them. They hired out as farm hands in southern Georgia, where Rosa caught the attention of a bold young Negro man who walked right up and told her she was the prettiest girl he ever did see. Samuel Washington was his name. He was her first love. They married six months later. Rosa's mother succumbed to a fever that winter, and her father dropped dead in the heat of the cotton fields the following summer. Rosa and Samuel moved from place to place and found work wherever they could until she became pregnant. They settled in Alabama.

"My earliest memories are of my mother telling me how her mother always wanted her to be a doctor. 'Ilya,' she'd say, 'you are the future of this family that I was not able to be. You must go to school and work hard. You must study medicine.' I was in college when the United States entered this war, so both my parents went to work in factories. They died two years apart. Since then I've been on my own. I learned long ago that a half-Negro, half-Boricua girl was not going to be looked upon with favor by society in general and by the medical community in particular, so I entered the military to complete my studies and to fulfill my family's dreams for my future." She lifted her hands in a small shrug. "That is how I came to be here."

"You have a remarkable history to pass on to your children," Tom said.

"It sounds grand to you because it all began in another time and place, but my life has been anything but pretty. I attended colored schools, of course, but being only half-colored made me the subject of much ridicule. Children can be very cruel to one another. They would say horrid things about my mother, and I wondered how they thought up such hateful words. Years later I realized my peers were only quoting their parents. I looked back and saw that my mother didn't have many friends. She never learned to speak English very well. That embarrassed her and made her shy. My father loved her fiercely. But for him, she would have truly been alone in the world. I grew up speaking both languages at home. I haven't spoken Spanish since my mother died. She's the only person with whom I shared it, anyway."

"But you've kept your dream alive. You're on your way to becoming a doctor."

Ilya gave a little shake of her head. "I haven't received the training I wanted through the military. I should have been a doctor by now, but those plans were altered for me. Soldiers go where and do what they are told. I will have to complete my obligations here and be discharged before I can return to school and continue my education."

"But you enlisted with the expectation that you would complete medical school and become a doctor; why has that not happened?"

"Half-truths from people who needed warm bodies in uniforms to fill certain jobs in certain places. Misplaced trust on my part."

Tom entwined his fingers with hers. "I'm glad you shared your memories with me."

Ilya swallowed hard. Her hands stiffened as she

drew them away from Tom. A shade of uncharacteristic sadness sketched bleak lines across her forehead and under her eyes, drawing down the corners of her full mouth and dimpling her chin. "I wish things were different, Tom."

He heard the rest of the thought in all its fatalistic candor. *But they aren't, and they are never going to be.* Tom could wish away his scars and the situation that brought him here. He could desire freedom, but outside the institution his appearance would yet deny him a normal life. If there were no other considerations, society would do its part to discourage his relationship with Ilya. It was one thing for Pastor Clay to raise colored children who called him Papa. Even that wouldn't provoke the outrage that a white man's romance with a colored woman, herself of mixed race, would cause. He contemplated the situation briefly. If the obstacles of his appearance and her obligations were gone, if he and Ilya met in ordinary, everyday circumstances – Tom frowned. They would not have met at all. Tom knew he was kidding himself to believe otherwise. If they encountered one another at a doorway or at a corner, he might have said a polite 'pardon me' as they moved out of each other's way. But there would have been no exchange of small talk, much less extended conversations while seated side by side on a park bench or in a booth at the soda shop. They would hardly have brushed against one another by accident. Holding hands and gazing into each other's eyes would have provided fodder for an all-out scandal. It was gallant to think that he and Ilya could stand up in the face of overwhelming prejudice and go right on with their lives. Truth predicted they would never have gotten as far as an introduction. Tom found that reality a bitter pill to swallow.

Speculation was pointless. He had not lived that life and would never experience such a challenge. There was only this blessing, that while they were here Ilya had allowed herself to relax and enjoy his company far beyond the realm of professional contact. However, she was only obligated to the military for two more years. Tom's stomach tightened with a terrible thought.

"You aren't leaving, are you?"

Ilya's faltering smile was confession enough that her own emotions had toppled into the jagged gulf between what might have been and what would never be. She shook her head. "I'll serve the remainder of my time here."

"What then?"

Ilya didn't answer. Tom lifted her fingers to his lips and planted a slow, gentle kiss on each one. As the last kiss lingered on the tip of her little finger, Tom looked into her face and was startled to see tears in her eyes. Ilya astonished him by drawing his hand to her face and kissing his fingertips in return. The tears began to fall as she touched her lips to the palm of his hand.

He whispered her name.

Ilya stood abruptly, overturning her chair. When Tom bent to pick it up, she took him by the arms as if to push him away. Instead of releasing him, however, she held onto his wrists and raised her face to his. Her eyes were depthless and dark and bore the scars of a different kind of pain. The arm's length that separated them might as well have been an ocean.

"Mine is a job to do, not a judgment call to make, not a situation with which feelings or sympathy are to become involved."

"I know," he said.

"I wish...I can't..."

"I know."

"I just...I want you to understand..."

"Ilya, I know how things are. I know what that means."

"You will never know what it means for me," she whispered, and was gone.

Tom stood staring at the closed door as loneliness settled heavily in the room. He picked up the chair and placed it before the table. He lifted the nonsense basket. It was flat and reminded him of an offering plate. He carried it to his bedside table and slid it into the drawer. He wondered why sometimes he could feel so close to his Creator that it seemed as though God's divine breath were wafting right across his face, while at other times spiritual intimacy appeared as insubstantial as a mirage in the desert. Tom reached for his Bible to fill the hour remaining before he would be allowed to enter the common room and visit with the others. He needed comfort, reassurance, a reason to pick himself up and continue this blind journey of Life.

First, Tom laid the sacred book on his bed and took a handkerchief from the drawer. He carried it to the table and laid it on the barren surface to absorb the tears that Ilya had shed before lifting the cloth to his face in an effort to check his own.

§ § § § § §

Arlene slipped away to her room and studied her reflection in the stainless steel bathroom mirror. "I am a withered old prune. I am ugly and afflicted, and I have no future." Ashamed of her words, she straightened as she eyed the surreal image that mimicked her every move. "I have a creative mind and a beautiful heart. I am strong and healthy. I believe my future is filled with good things. Russ still loves me. And I can sing. I can still do that."

She took a deep breath along with one last look at her appearance before crossing the foyer into the bedroom. As she did, Russ entered from the common room, holding out his arms. They met each other halfway. Arlene melted into his embrace and raised her lips to his. Russ's kiss was passionate and tasted of possession to which Arlene gladly surrendered. Time and circumstance ceased to exist for a few precious moments as Russ smiled into the face of the woman he loved. He placed his cheek against hers, whispering suggestions into her ear that made her body shudder with desire. Arlene pulled reluctantly away, bright-eyed and breathless. They stood apart for a moment to regain their composure, only to find that lingering just beyond each other's reach kindled their exhilaration to even greater heights.

A feminine voice called to Arlene from outside the room.

"Oh, yeah," Russ remembered. "They want you to sing a song. I was supposed to come and get you."

"I love you." Arlene clutched her left hand in her right, as she had occasionally done when she wore an engagement ring.

"I love you." Russ wrapped his arms around her, engulfing her in a hug. "I want to marry you. I want to be your husband, and I want you to be my wife."

"Yes." She smiled against his chest.

"Someday." Russ spoke the word as though daring anyone to argue. "Someday we will be married. I promise you that."

"Don't make promises that are not within your power to keep." Arlene gently withdrew, but Russ held onto her.

"If not in my power, then in the hands of a greater power," he insisted. "I promise, Arlene."

She studied his eyes, struck by the wonder of this incredible love surviving and increasing amidst the wasteland of their lives. Arlene had witnessed the desert in the aftermath of a harsh spring rain. She had been awed at how quickly bare ochre erupted into a floral fantasy of white, yellow, pink, and red as a new season brought life to that which had been, to all appearances, dead. Such was her heart upon reuniting with her fiancé.

"Someday," she whispered. She clung to Russ as he kissed her again.

"Arlene!"

Russ rolled his eyes in annoyance and tucked Arlene's hand into the crook of his arm. "And we'll be good little boys and girls until then," he said, escorting her to the door.

"We will," she confirmed. "Because I want our wedding night to be perfect and special and new, not just a repeat of things we've done illicitly before we were married. I want to be a gift for you that night, one that's never been opened, one that is completely and exclusively yours. And—" She narrowed her eyes in an appraising stare. "I want you to be all those things for me."

Russ paused in the foyer and gazed down at the bold tilt of Arlene's eyes, at the expectations outlined by her words, at her smile. He momentarily lost himself in the complexities of confidence and self-respect that held her ardent love and desire for him within the bounds of common decency.

"Every time I look at you, I fall in love with you all over again," he told her. "I am all those things for you. I will remain so until I make love to you on our first night as husband and wife and throughout our marriage thereafter."

Arlene felt her face grow hot. Her heart pounded so furiously she thought everyone would surely see it beating beneath the fabric of her shift. She firmly reined in her imagination, knowing her thoughts were every bit as much a spiritual matter as an emotional affair.

"There you are!" Abby welcomed Arlene. "We've been asked to sing." She threw Russ an unfortunate look over her shoulder. "Next time I'll just go tell her myself."

Russ looked away, embarrassed. Arlene gave his hand an affectionate squeeze as she moved away to join Abby and Rachel near the blackboard.

In another place and time, three young girls gravitated toward one another in Sunday School as the class belted out songs they would later sing for the congregation prior to worship service. Their efforts, now as then, were rewarded with sincere appreciation and genuine admiration from their peers. They even received compliments from the nurses who occasionally heard them sing. On this day, Arlene wanted to sing a wistful song that she alone had conceived from the hope and the longing that dominated her daily life. Everyone fell silent as the girls took their customary place under the clock. Hands clasped, heads bowed, and voices gave way to reverent silence as the girls began to sing.

O Lord our God
With strength and honor
Bless us O God
As here we wander
Your name is holy
Your love divine
Lord make us wholly Thine.

Here in my heart
Where pain and sorrow
Tear me apart
Threaten tomorrow
I look to Heaven
For blest relief
I receive rest and peace.

O Lord our God
Here in this desert
Long have we trod
Knowing our treasure
Waits beyond what our
Eyes ever see
Our hope remains in Thee.

Robert emerged from Ray and Belva's room as the song began. He moved quietly forward to listen. Small arms encircled his waist and drew his attention to Elisabeth's large, solemn eyes. Robert leaned down to her. "What's wrong, baby?"

"Nurse Cheryl brought Mom back to our room. Mom was really quiet. When I asked if she was okay, she started crying and sent Catherine and me out here. She told us she didn't feel well and wanted to be left alone."

"Okay, honey. I'll go see how she's doing." He gave Elisabeth a quick hug and hurried to his family's rooms.

He found Joy lying across their bed, sobbing as though her heart had broken. Robert lay beside her and cradled her in his arms. He kissed her face and stroked her hair while she wept. He reminded her that things were better, that there might be the potential of a new life away from the institution in their future. He told her that Ray was determined to recover. He described the beautiful song the girls just sang. He mentioned that Elisabeth and Catherine were scared because their mother was so upset. Then he asked Joy what was wrong.

Joy turned a terrified face to her husband and announced the impossible. She hid her face against his shoulder and shuddered under a fresh onslaught of tears.

Stunned by her revelation, Robert felt too weak to move. He held his wife close and forced himself to comprehend what he had just been told. As the truth sank in, he swallowed waves of nausea brought about by stress and his own reaction to recent medications. He wanted to stand and fight, to run away, to cry out in protest, to shout with ecstasy. Emotions tumbled hard in their struggle for dominance, leaving his heart bruised and numb. He tried to think, tried to feel, but he fiercely rejected the sinister thoughts that swarmed his mind in response to the quest. He kissed Joy's forehead and pulled a blanket over her as he unwound his legs from hers. He went to the sink and ran cold water over a handkerchief. He sat on the bed beside Joy and bathed her face, washing away the tears and cooling her fever. When her eyes scanned his expression for hope, he made himself strong for her. His smile offered encouragement, intimate and sincere. He watched her fall into the deep sleep of utter exhaustion. He continued to watch as her features relaxed and her breathing slowed until, at length, her hand released the tight grip with which it clung to his. He sat still, jealously guarding her, until his world shuddered back into orbit and his thoughts began to process. His heart began to break for his family's vulnerability and to harden in resentment of his own.

Robert wondered what would happen to his wife now and what more he could possibly do to protect her and their unborn child.

Chapter Twenty-Six

There was a time when a day lasted forever, yet never lasted long enough. The rooster crowed at sunrise, and I laughed toward the sound: you're a bit late, Dandy. I'm already awake! A brilliant summer day filled with animals to feed and books to read and lessons to learn culminated all too soon in a firefly-filled dusk. My brother and I captured the living nightlights and gazed at the blinking miracles in our hands, and then lifted the little creatures to the heavens and watched them take flight. We were ever humbled by the joy and the grief of watching them go.

Mama told Daddy the garden was flourishing. Yellow blooms were being pushed away by tiny tomatoes here and baby cucumbers there. Daddy responded with comments about how the crops and the cattle were coming along. My brother and I stared up through branches of prayerfully folded mimosa leaves and begged for one more minute, just one more...

We were reluctant to bed but quickly to sleep, to the deep dreamless slumber that makes the night but an instant hardly long enough to fulfill its duty of distinguishing days. Daddy convinced me to relinquish the overdrawn day by reminding me that after I fell asleep, I would awaken to a whole new one.

Then the War began and never ended, and my carefree childhood was among the first casualties. My innocent perceptions of the world abruptly matured. I began learning from a darker reality that the mutual compassion, considera- tion, and respect I had accepted as facts of life, weren't; that not everyone believed in God as a loving Father; that the people I love the most are not immune to sickness, pain, and death, nor am I. I learned that tomorrow is not always to be desired. For the first time in my life I began looking forward to sleep as a reprieve from the day, and dreading the moment when the sun's insistent rays and Dandy's proclamation would prod me awake to endure another.

Life is not always joy, not always sorrow, but must cycle the spectrum over and again. Extremes of great ease or great distress that last too long cause restless disturbances within the soul. It is the journey from ecstasy to heartache and back again that strengthens our hands to truly take hold of life, to comprehend and to love and to passionately live.

Sarah was vaguely aware of her mother's voice calling from a drug-induced distance. Considerably more distinct were the hot fingers of pain extending across her belly and penetrating deep within her abdomen. The pain produced a physical perception that did not quite register with her mental faculties. When she vomited, or when her mother placed a chip of ice on her tongue, or when a nurse checked her blood pressure, these things happened as if to someone else, and Sarah watched the goings-on from afar. Faces registered like stills from a slide show long after the visitors had come and gone: Mama and Daddy, Callie, Uncle John and Aunt Mary, Brother Tom, Dave...

I can see her...

Belva stroked a soft, cool cloth across her forehead. "What is it, honey? Take it easy, sweetie, Mama's here..."

Help her...

"It's all right..."

Stop! You're hurting her...

Memories trespassed through Sarah's mind of Maria lying on a gurney across the room, of Maria fighting as men strapped her down, of Maria crying out in terror and pain before Sarah was herself rendered unconscious. There were moments when Sarah's distorted thoughts drowned in the horrible scene, insisting it was happening in the here and now. Other nightmares visited less frequently. They, having been left farther in the past, did not resurrect with the vivid detail of Maria on the gurney.

"There, now...it's all right..."

But it wasn't all right, and Sarah lacked the ability to convey her tormented thoughts. Her attempts at speech produced a garble of gibberish that made no more sense to her than it did to anyone else. It took her back to the beginning, all the way back to the horrifying moment she awoke to find herself blind, immobilized, and unable to express herself to those responsible for her unfamiliar new world.

A nagging fear surfaced and retreated like a pendulum whose rhythm she could not quite match: something about Ben. Thornton had wheeled him from his apartment as Nancy pushed Sarah by, and they had been taken to neighboring rooms. Maria cried out, an alarm resonated from the next room, people ran back and forth rolling carts of equipment past the door...

I don't want to go to sleep...

Nurse Thornton ferociously shouted orders. Her

anger was a mask. The mask was on crooked. Sarah could see fear peeping through.

Mama? Where is Ben?

"Lie still now, take it easy…"

Mama! I'm scared!

"…everything is going to be all right…"

"How's my girl?"

…Daddy?

"She's restless, muttering and moving about." Belva bathed Sarah's forehead again. "She can't keep anything down, not even a spoonful of water. She tries to talk, but I don't think she's even aware of what she's trying to say."

Sarah turned her head away from Belva's hand and stared off into the distance. A tremendous heave of her chest produced a cry that tore Ray's heart asunder. He sat beside her on the bed, took her hand in both of his, and warmed away the cool dampness of her fingers. Ray touched his daughter's face, and his expression darkened with concern. He glanced at Belva.

"I know. I've told them. They've checked her and given her medication to bring the fever down. It will break for a while, but it shoots right back up." Belva's tone was bleak, her eyes weary from lack of sleep and complete disregard of her own needs. Barely a week had passed since Ray's life nearly slipped away. He was not completely recovered, but he insisted that Belva leave him alone in order to spend time with Sarah. Belva divided her time thereafter between her husband and daughter. Sarah required constant care. Belva agreed to share turns with Mary and Callie, but the effects of exhaustion and stress were evident in her tremulous voice and unsteady movements.

Ray massaged Sarah's hand. "Ben is back in his room."

Belva gazed at Sarah for a moment longer. She slowly raised her eyes to Ray and burst into tears. Ray made his way around the bed as quickly as his own health would allow. He sat beside Belva and took her in his arms.

"I'm sorry," she sobbed. "I have to go see my little boy, but I can't leave my precious girl, and who's going to take care of my husband while I tend to our babies?"

Ray rocked her gently and kissed the top of her head. "You're tired, honey. You need to rest. Mary and Callie can see to Sarah and Ben for a few hours. Come back to our room with me and get some sleep."

"No," Belva protested. "I have to take care of my children. Oh, Ray, what have they done to our children?"

Moments later Mary knocked softly as she entered with John and Callie. They found Ray holding Belva with one arm as she wept against his chest, and his daughter with the other as Sarah maneuvered sideways in her bed, attempting to turn and face a crisis only she could see.

§ § § § § §

Ray flinched as someone dropped into a chair on the other side of the table.

Robert's grin was laced with concern. "Aren't you supposed to remain supine until further notice from a medical authority?"

Ray grimaced. "Our medical authorities have nearly killed my children and me, and my wife is killing herself trying to take care of us all."

"I went to visit Ben."

"He's a mess. I stayed with him this afternoon while the nurse changed his bandages. His groin is grossly swollen around two scars. He can't even move his legs."

Robert winced.

"Blast it, Robert, if he wasn't already impotent or sterile from the radiation, is that what they've done to him now? Have they made him so he'll never be able to physically love a woman? And what about Sarah? What if they did a hysterectomy on my little girl? Belva says when they do that, they remove a woman's womb! What if they've made certain that Sarah will never bear children, even if she were to fall in love and marry one of the young men here?"

Robert picked at his fingernails. "I know this doesn't help right now, but before we were transferred to this floor, the suits put me through a similar procedure to what has been done to Ben. I lay flat on my back in unbearable pain for several weeks. I thought I might die. Had it not been for Joy and the girls, I'd have wished for that."

Ray gave a short nod that conveyed sympathy and a subtle lack of appreciation for the comparison.

"Joy is pregnant," Robert whispered. "Remember?"

Ray brightened. "Yeah! So maybe Ben will be able to father children, too, should he ever marry."

Robert regarded him soberly. "I don't know about Sarah, though. Catherine went through that surgery, too, before we were moved out of our old rooms. She's fine now except for a thin scar. It might be years before we find out, if we ever do, what was done to her and Sarah and what effect it might have on their ability to have families of their own."

"Tom said Maria had the same thing done to her.

She's even worse off than Sarah. At least Sarah is in her room where her family can take care of her. Maria's health has been an emergency twice in the last four days. They've had to come and take her away for the treatment needed just to keep her alive. Tom keeps asking about her. He says he wants to make sure Maria doesn't mysteriously disappear. I believe he's afraid that if she died, no one would tell him."

"After what he went through when he learned about his wife and baby, that's certainly a legitimate concern. Joy has been run through more tests and treatments in the past week than she has since we arrived here. She said she and Callie are the only women who are able to have a monthly cycle. Without that, the women are probably sterile anyway, so I don't understand why they are doing such morbid surgeries on the girls."

"Because they can," Ray snapped. "It is morally and legally wrong that experimental surgeries are performed on us and our children against our will. The perpetrators aren't even required to explain their intent. I've wondered from the beginning what kinds of experiments we were all being used for. I don't like the path my suspicions are following."

Their eyes met across the table, and Ray put into words what they both were thinking. "We have to get out of here."

"While we're still alive to do it," Robert agreed.

Ray shuddered at the unexpected chill.

§ § § § § §

"One more time," Ben insisted.

Robert thrust the tine amidst the jumble of wires

and deftly brought one against another. The lock clicked, and the door relaxed. Robert looked at Ben.

"Good. Recite the schedule to me again."

Robert patiently went over the number of flights in the stairwell, when to pause, when to hurry and, most important, when to conclude the visit and return to his family. "I'd feel better if you were leading the way," Robert told Ben, and meant it. "I dread going alone."

Ben clenched his teeth and swallowed his disappointment. "I wish I could go, too. Give Alden my regards. Please explain to him why I haven't visited for the past twelve nights."

"I'll tell him." Robert held out his hand. Ben shook it firmly. Robert took in the boy's slumped shoulders and dejected expression. "You're worn out. Let's get you back to your room." Robert stepped behind the wheelchair and rolled Ben across the assembly room toward the apartment he shared with John and Mary.

Ben displayed maturity beyond the grasp of his fourteen years, Robert thought. But then, he really had no choice. Neither a tantrum nor a sulking session would make Ben heal any faster. Besides that, either reaction would be highly uncharacteristic of the young man. Ben had the bright smile and easygoing manner of youthful exuberance, but since Robert had known him, that energy had been tempered by a healthy dose of forethought and wisdom. Robert suspected that Ray was responsible for that.

He stopped the wheelchair for Mary.

"Would you like some company?" she asked Ben.

"Thanks, but I just need to sleep." An appreciative smile wafted across Ben's face. "Have you seen Sarah today?"

"She was out here earlier. Like you, she tired quickly. She's in her room resting, but I'm sure she'd love to see you, Ben."

"I might get by later."

"Sure. You just take it easy. My boy." Mary smiled and patted his shoulder, and Robert continued toward Ben's room.

"I should move in with Mama and Daddy." Ben spoke quietly. "But I don't want to leave Uncle John and Aunt Mary. I wouldn't hurt their feelings for anything in the world. Do you think Mama and Daddy understand?"

"I'm sure of it." Robert lifted Ben from the chair and eased him onto the bed. Though Ben could sit up for short periods of time and tolerate brief trips in the wheelchair, pain would allow only limited use of his legs.

"I'm sorry I can't go with you, Robert."

"So am I. But I'm looking forward to coming back and telling you all about it."

Ben looked at Robert intently. "You'll do that?"

"You'll be the first to hear about it," Robert promised. "Then we'll go together and tell Ray."

Ben's swallowed hard and gave a quick nod. "Thanks, Robert."

"I'm beholden to you for this opportunity," Robert said. "One of these days, we all might be indebted to you for setting in motion the steps leading to our rescue."

"I hope so." Ben sighed deeply and closed his eyes. "Are you going to see Daddy now?"

"In a little while."

"When you do, will you tell him I…I mean, just let him and Mama know…"

"I'll tell them." Robert squeezed Ben's ankle. "You get some rest."

"Tell Sarah for me, too."

"I will."

By the time Robert had pulled the blanket over Ben and pushed the wheelchair to one side, Ben was fast asleep. Robert hesitated on his way out the door for one last look at the exhausted boy. It occurred to him all at once that he was going to be a father again. His heart fluttered with a fleeting hope that his and Joy's third child would be a son.

Chapter Twenty-Seven

Accompanied by countless misgivings and a surprising case of loneliness, Robert slipped into the stairwell by himself and waited, as Ben had done, for nurses to clear the assembly room and send everyone off to their apartments for the night. When the thread of light against the floor went dark, Robert turned and grasped the handrail. He took a stout breath to calm his trepidation and began to climb.

The secrets of night travel that Ben had taught him brought Robert safely to the hangar. He lurked beside the last window until he saw Alden Morrow through the glass. He then burst through the door and practically ran down the steps to the hangar floor, relieved at having achieved his destination undetected.

Alden turned toward the steps with a hearty smile that froze when he saw Robert and disappeared completely when he realized Robert was alone.

"Good evening, Mr. Morrow." Robert had decided that politeness was to be preferred over affected familiarity. He wished at the last moment he knew Alden's rank or title, but Ben had not mentioned either. He just called the man 'Al.'

Alden nodded cautiously. "Mr. Lake, isn't it?"

"Robert Lake, yes." Robert cleared his throat. "Ben couldn't make it tonight. He wanted me to tell you why it's been so long since he came to see you. He was put through a dangerous surgery the morning after our last visit, and it nearly killed him. He's better now," Robert hastened to add in response to Alden's alarmed expression. "But his recovery is going to take a while. He wanted you to know."

Alden's brow creased with concern. "I didn't even know anything was wrong. He didn't mention needing surgery when he was here. Was it an emergency?"

Robert blinked as though he had walked into a wall. "Hasn't Ben told you about our experiences here? About the nature of the medical attention we have received?"

"When we first met, he told me a lot of things. Some of them did relate to medical treatments, or experiments, as he alleged. I believed a few of his stories and chalked the rest up to a boy's overactive imagination. I asked him to stop talking about such outlandish things because I simply could not believe them. He didn't bring the subject up again." Alden shoved his hands into his pockets and studied the toes of his boots. "So what happened to Ben?"

Robert shared as much detail as he knew. He went on to tell Alden about Sarah's and Ray's surgeries, about Joy's pregnancy, about what had been done to Catherine months before. He continued talking as Alden motioned him to a corner and offered him a chair. Robert outlined what fates had befallen each of the Trinity survivors all the way back to the moment he had first awakened in the facility.

Alden watched Robert's expression and listened to what he had to say. When Robert talked himself out and leaned wearily back in the chair, Alden lowered his gaze to study the lines in the palms of his own hands.

"You've covered everything Ben told me and more. Far more." Alden propped his elbows on his knees and continued staring into his hands.

"Ben trusts you implicitly. Is he safe in doing so? Am I?" Robert gave a short laugh. "I guess it's a little late to be asking after I've told you so much."

Alden looked up at Robert. "Trust is a mutual concept, Mr. Lake." He patted his shirt pocket and leaned back in his chair with an exasperated sigh. "Years ago I smoked a pipe. I'm not permitted to smoke on the job. My shifts are so long that about all I do is work and sleep, so I'm too tired to enjoy a pipe when I'm off duty. I miss it, though." He looked at his hands again. He turned and selected a small block of wood from the pile on the table behind them and brought out a pocketknife.

Robert watched him open the blade and shave an edge off the block.

"Camillus makes good knives," Alden told him. "Like the Keen Kutter for Simmons." He held the knife on a flat open palm for Robert to see. "Camillus also makes Diamond Edge for Shapleigh and Craftsman for Sears and Roebuck."

Robert nodded at the knife, wondering if he was expected to touch it. He gingerly lifted it from Alden's hand and danced his fingertip across the sharp edge, opened and closed the second blade, and offered it back to Alden. Alden took the proffered handle and applied the blade to the wood, talking as he worked.

"The company was small until it was purchased by a German immigrant. In his hands it flourished and even produced knives for allied troops during both world wars. Isn't that ironic?"

"Glad he's on our side," Robert offered.

"Did Ben tell you how we met? Scared the hell out of both of us, he did. I stepped out of my office to see Ben staring up at my aircraft. From the back in the dim lighting he looked for the world like an alien from one of those comic books. My first thought was, sweet Mary, they've found it, and they've come back for it!" Alden chuckled and brushed curls of blonde wood from his hands.

"You mean to tell me you believe that thing is a space craft?"

"Is that any more incredible than what you've asked me to believe?"

The men considered their respective histories, their contemplations interrupted only by the sound of the blade caressing the wood.

"I have a son nearly as old as Ben," Alden said. "My wife moved out when he was still a toddler. For a while I got to see him once a month, then only a couple of times a year, then not at all. Having Ben around reminds me that I am a father, though I never had a chance to prove how good a father I could be. I've missed seeing Ben. I worried that something might have happened."

He nodded toward the hangar's occupant. "I don't know what to believe. It arrived here last February. A team of technicians was assigned to identify the craft and its purpose. I was a member of that team. We wanted to know where it came from. Our superiors said they did, too." Alden paused and looked beyond Robert at the craft. "The technology was beyond our comprehension. Especially mine. I'm a pilot, not a scientist, but I have experience with aircraft design, so I suppose it was thought I might do the project some good. I certainly tried. We all did." Alden worked his way around a small knothole in the wood.

"What did you learn about it?" Robert hoped he didn't sound as impatient as he felt.

"It is constructed of materials the likes of which none of us had ever come into contact. We attempted to analyze the skin. It defied our tests, refused to be recognized either as a naturally occurring material or as a manmade substance. If it could logically be classified as a type of metal, we couldn't decipher the compounds from which it was developed. It smooths over the vehicle like a solid membrane. The aircraft doesn't come apart. That is, we were unable to understand how it was assembled in the first place. We could locate no evidence of attachments: no seams, no rivets, nothing. It's as if the whole unit was formed as one piece. It proved impervious to chemicals and to temperature extremes. It bowed and dented instead of breaking under pressure. We did find the mechanism that opened the hatch. That was something of an accident, but at least it was progress. The thing operates via symbols on a panel that respond to touch. No buttons to push, gauges to watch, knobs to turn. None of the controls to which we are accustomed. We believe it runs on solar power and stores it, too. There is also the possibility that it uses other means to literally create its own energy. It is invisible to radar. It refuses to die."

Robert laughed. Alden remained serious.

"Through more than four months of experimenttation and study, we learned enough about how it worked to make it perform on a very basic level. Then the new area commander, Josten Maslow, got the brilliant idea that the aircraft might be dangerous. What if it were equipped with a tracking device through which an enemy could locate our government's secret installations, what if it was contaminated with a biological agent that could kill us all, that sort of thing. Never mind that two dozen of us had worked in direct contact with it and had suffered no adverse effects.

"Maslow is a genius in biotechnology, but he is arrogant with power and lacking in empathy and common sense. He went overboard with his suppositions and caused a mild panic, after which it was decided that if the craft's mysteries could not be discovered, it must be destroyed.

"It was taken out to the Marshall Islands the last weekend in June to join the fleet used for Operation Crossroads. The President wanted to see what effect atomic bombs would have on warships and aircraft. The week before that, our team was disbanded, and we were all reassigned. I was left with the responsibility of taking the aircraft to Bikini Atoll, where it was destined for destruction by an A-bomb." Alden shifted in his seat.

Robert looked over his shoulder at the aircraft. "What happened? Why did they decide against it?"

Alden's crooked smile reminded Robert of Ben. "It was placed aboard an aircraft carrier, the USS *Saratoga*. There were other aircraft aboard, but we shrouded this one to avoid the questions people would naturally ask upon seeing such an unusual apparatus. The shroud blended in with the deck. From a distance no one could tell it was even on the carrier. I flew over the target fleet prior to each detonation, and I had to look closely in order to see it at all, even though I knew it was there.

"Two atomic bombs were detonated. We dropped

Able from a B-29 on July first. On July twenty-fifth we detonated Baker underwater. I don't even know how to describe to you what that was like."

"I have an idea," Robert said, and Alden grimaced.

"It was Baker that got our girl. The USS *Saratoga* was the vessel closest to the bomb. There was an immediate pressure wave that damaged the carrier and then, within seconds of detonation, a wave nearly one hundred feet high crashed over her. The aircraft and equipment on her deck were washed overboard. Eight hours later *Sara* breathed her last and disappeared beneath the surface.

"The Navy tried to rescue the carrier but, of course, the whole area was suffused with radioactive contamination. There was nothing to do but watch her sink. I was among those investigating the site in the aftermath. I needed to ascertain, if at all possible, the fate of our aircraft. I made several passes over the area, visually sorting through debris, before I saw it."

Robert looked over his shoulder again at the object of their discussion. Sleekly pristine, it could not have endured such damage so recently. Robert wasn't aware that he was shaking his head as he turned back to Alden.

"It was floating about a mile from the lagoon, looking completely unconcerned with the history-making event that had just taken place. I traded my plane for a boat and checked it over. It was undamaged. It was clean. My superiors wouldn't believe it, but I knew what the uncooperative lady was like because I had worked with her for months."

"Clean." Robert sought a logical explanation.

"I mean that aircraft not only survived two atomic blasts intact, but without any residual effects whatsoever. There were no traces of radiation, no damage to indicate such a thing had even occurred."

Alden brought a whisk broom from under the table. He swept his wood shavings into a pile, pushed them onto a piece of cardboard, and shook them into the waste basket. He wiped his blade with an oily rag, folded the knife closed, and slipped it into his pocket as he stood. Robert followed him to the aircraft.

"You're certain it was really on the carrier?"

"As certain as I am that we are standing here with her right now."

"My apologies," Robert said. "I'm not accusing you of lying or suggesting that I doubt your allegiance to your job. It's just that..." He ran his fingers lightly along the flawless, flowing curve of the craft. "It's perfect."

"That's what my superiors think, too," Alden said. "I've been under investigation, whatever that means, since the bombs didn't put her on the ocean floor. I posited that being swept overboard removed her from the scene sufficiently to protect her from utter devastation. It's the best excuse I could offer under the circumstances. I've been assigned to guard her until they decide whether I get a medal or a demotion for her survival and, either way, what they should do about me and all that I know."

"What will they do with the aircraft?"

"Nothing. She's considered to be in storage until the day a record-keeper stumbles across her in a musty file and decides to investigate her all over again."

"And you have no idea at all where it came from?"

"During the war, the Germans stole the aircraft from the Soviets and stored her in a mine that had been converted to a bomb factory. The Americans confiscated her from the Germans and brought her to the United

States in January aboard the *Prinz Eugen*, a German cruiser that was ceded to the States during war settlements. Incidentally, the *Prinz Eugen* was also among the target fleet at Bikini Atoll. There are others tales surrounding her pedigree. It's quite possible that only God Himself knows her true origin."

"As to whether the Soviets made it or stole it from another government."

"Or found her somewhere," Alden agreed.

"How was it transported to the Marshall Islands and back?"

"I flew her." Alden's voice softened at the memory. "Have you ever flown, Mr. Lake? Throw all your expectations out the window. She's not like anything you have ever encountered. Silent. Swift. Smooth. I want so much to know more about her, but I am forbidden to do anything more than sit here and watch her. Guard duty is a joke. Who would ever find her here, in a place the world doesn't even know exists? What would they do about her if they did? I am the only one whose touch can make her fly. This assignment keeps me and the things I know secret and hidden from view."

"Who is behind what happened to me, to you, to the aircraft? Is this place run by the armed forces?"

"We are wards of a Council comprised of U.S. war and intelligence agencies, financial institutions, and corporate contractors. They all have an interest in what takes place in facilities like this one, and they all squabble as to who gets to make and enforce the rules of whatever game they are playing on any given day. Maslow is the commander of Area L, and everything here operates at his discretion unless something happens monumental enough to merit the intervention of the Council. The lack of clearly defined leadership makes true organization impossible and kills any hope for progress."

"Jaded?" Robert produced a wry smile.

"Very. So much good might be done simply by researching treasures that are destroyed outright or consigned to permanent storage. As it stands, I will not have an opportunity to fly this aircraft again or to explore the extent of the technology that keeps her operative. I will not learn her full potential, and the public will not learn of her at all."

Robert followed Alden around the craft and back to the little office. Alden stepped inside. Robert peered through the door into a tiny room crammed with a desk and several bookcases crouching under immense burdens. The desk was occupied by a typewriter and a photograph of a smiling little boy in the arms of a pretty girl.

"You read a lot," Robert observed.

"Keeps me busy," Alden responded. "And I enjoy learning new things." He reached into his pocket and removed the piece of wood on which he had been working. He held it out to Robert. "I know you can't take it with you. Just tell Ben I made him another one."

Robert took from Alden's hand a carved equine head rising from a rounded base. The knothole that ran all the way through the block stared back at him as the horse's eyes. "A knight!" Robert turned the piece over in his hand, studying the image that Alden had brought forth during the course of their conversation. "I didn't know Ben played chess."

"We play a little during every visit. One game can go on for ages. We come here to my office and take a few turns while we talk." He pointed to a board set up in the corner to Robert's left. "Ben wished for his own set, so I decided to make one for him." He took the knight from Robert and subjected it to critical scrutiny under the light. "I'll sand it and apply a clear finish later." He opened a drawer and pulled out a metal tray lined with felt on which glossy wooden chess pieces patiently awaited their summons to a game. "I still have to do the pawns." Alden glanced at the clock." You'd better get going."

Robert held out his hand. "Thank you, Mr. Morrow, for all that you have told me."

"We can share one another's burdens, if nothing else. Take care, Mr. Lake. Tell that boy of ours to hurry up and get better." He shook Robert's hand and dropped the knight into the drawer beside the tray of finished pieces.

"I'll be seeing you," Robert said. He reluctantly left the hangar behind, resisting the urge to look back at every turn until he accomplished the stairwell. He hesitated then, allowing the details of Alden's over-whelming revelations to take root in his mind. For Ben, visits with Alden were temporary reprieves from inescapable circumstances. Conversations between them were lighthearted, though weighted with the knowledge of events Ben had not been allowed to share. For Robert, this first visit alone represented a hopeful step toward orchestrating a way for the Trinity survivors to escape their oppression.

Ben knew what he was giving up by sharing his secret, Robert reflected, but Ben had not hesitated to sacrifice precious moments of pseudo-freedom when he thought his father might die. Robert was very proud of him and looked forward to telling him so.

As he crept among the shadows in the assembly

room, Robert realized he had forgotten to tell Joy where to tell the nurses he would be spending the night. He couldn't join his family. The night duty nurses would know he hadn't gone to bed with them. Of course, all of the nurses would know who had been in their rooms at bedtime. What had Ben told him? Fall back on the excuse that the nurse hadn't seen him because he'd been in the bathroom at the time. Realizing he had to be present for the two o'clock check, he hurried to unlock the closest apartment door in the same manner Ben had shown him how to unlock the door to the stairwell. He quietly let himself into the apartment shared by Will and Russ. Will's bed was empty – he was obviously spending the night elsewhere – and Robert crawled gratefully between the cool sheets. He had hardly stretched out before the hall door clicked open. A dim flashlight shone across the beds to be sure they were occupied. Russ roused groggily, rolled over, and started in alarm at the silhouette in Will's bed. He maintained his composure until the beam floated back into the hallway and the door locked behind it. Robert identified himself, and Russ went back to sleep without demanding an explanation. The Trinity captives did not always understand what Robert, Ray, and Tom were up to, but the three men were trusted implicitly and their actions, if occasionally peculiar, were considered above question.

Chapter Twenty-Eight

Will stood before the chalkboard and studied his work. Christine had allotted him a generous third of her teaching space for the project. Despite the limitations of white chalk and months deprived of the tools with which to practice his talent, Will's depiction of the holy family in crowded Bethlehem portrayed a poignant declaration of the season. Shepherds shyly approached the stable. Angels gazed down from the heavens, their hands clasped in wonder.

"Where are the wise men?" Freddy wanted to know.

"They didn't show up until Jesus was about sixteen months old." Will added the finishing touch by signing his initials in the bottom right corner of the board between the tiny hooves of a lamb.

"It looks like a tuft of grass," Freddy pointed out.

"It's supposed to," Will agreed. "I want people to focus on the picture, not on my name."

"But the work isn't more important that the person who did it," Freddy objected.

"Sometimes." Will gave Freddy a pat on the back. "Sometimes it is."

Yet another thought to ponder. Freddy sighed and slipped away.

Will took another look at the board and paused with a frown.

"Oh, don't look at it like that!" Mary exclaimed as she stopped to admire the scene. "It's beautiful!"

"Thank you," Will mumbled, suddenly shy. "I was just thinking that I don't have room to draw a second picture with a Christmas tree in it."

"We'd actually like to make a tree. We ladies have been discussing what materials are available and how we could make them hold the shape of an evergreen." She smiled brightly. "We'll come up with a way."

Will gave her a hug. "It's fun, but it's hard," he confided. "I want to celebrate the holidays, but it hurts so much to know that my family believes I'm dead."

"You don't know that for certain."

"Mr. Maslow said so. And I feel it in my heart."

"So do I," Mary conceded. "But Mr. Maslow didn't provide us with details. None of us knows what our families were told, or the fates of our homes and our belongings, our livestock and pets. In the absence of fact, we hold on to faith." She smiled encouragement at Will, and beyond him at Michael, who had approached in time to hear her words.

Michael stared at Will's artwork without really seeing the picture. He didn't know much about faith, but being thrown into the constant presence of his adulterous father, his long-suffering sister, and the little brother he barely knew had taught lessons from which he could neither run nor hide. He envied Will because Will had no family here. He knew that Will probably envied Michael his father and siblings. Life was funny. Michael had ever wanted what he couldn't have, but he had not considered that anyone but Christine might envy him anything.

344

Getting to know his father had been interesting. "I see myself in you," Clayton had told him, but not with any pride. Clayton had shared a lifetime of regrets with his adult son, with the intimation that he didn't want Michael to turn out just like him.

I already have, Michael thought darkly, and turned away from the chalk-dust couple who had just birthed their baby in a barn. There was Callie across the room, talking with his sister. Had he passed Callie on a city street mobbed with humanity, he still would have noticed her. Shiny cinnamon hair, emerald eyes, a shapely figure above the nice legs that showed beneath her shift – now there was his idea of a holiday celebration! Callie was smart, though, probably smarter than she was pretty. She spoke with him politely, as she would with any friend, but resisted his efforts to flirt his way into deeper intimacy with her. He had told Callie very little about himself, but Christine had doubtless filled in the blanks. There were few secrets here.

Michael's helpless anger at being forced into a boring, empty life was tempered by the security it offered. If he wasn't allowed to do anything else, neither did he have to decide what else to do. He could complain right along with the others, safe in the improbability of having to prove himself beyond these walls. His dreams had once destroyed his future by devouring the present. Over the past year they had decomposed to a pessimistic dust that clouded his attitude with cynicism. The only thing that remained was his general discontent with the malady of life.

Carols erupted across the room, and Michael drifted among the group to stand next to Callie. She smiled and urged him to sing. Christine had always told him he possessed an excellent voice. He joined in on the chorus and, at Callie's look of admiration, sang bolder and louder on the following verse. Afterward there were compliments and exclamations over his talent, along with exhortations that he must sing again. Arlene and Abby were particularly adamant, demanding to know why he had not expressed his ability long ago instead of quietly listening to everyone else. Michael enjoyed basking in the adoration of others. It had been a long time since he was the life of the party. The people who surrounded him now, though, were not members of a superficial crowd whose focus was on discarding reality for fun because nothing else mattered beyond that very moment. The sincerity of the Trinity survivors put him off, made him desperate to escape the genuine warmth that touched his heart in sensitive places. There was the threat of love which, if allowed, would introduce its potential for rejection. Michael was intimately acquainted with the agony and gaping depth of wounds inflicted by rejection. He saw the aftermath of its destruction on both the guilty and the innocent every day of his life. It was written all over his father's face.

Uncomfortable with their automatic respect, knowing their esteem was wasted on one who lacked any sense of purpose, Michael excused himself and returned to the apartment in which he spent so much time alone. Clayton and Freddy had both made friends among the other survivors and were rarely 'home' during visiting hours.

"What do you want out of life?" Clayton had questioned him months ago after nurses moved them into their apartment and granted them access to the common room.

I want my childhood back. And this time I want a dad who will be there when I need him. I want a mom who is strong and confident because her husband treats her like a woman instead of like a child. While we're at it, I want Christine's childhood back for her, too, so she can be free to grow up without growing old first. I want her to be a little girl instead of a parent to our mom.

"I want to be happy," Michael had answered.

"Make commitments and stick by them. Take responsibility for everything you do and are. Don't be too proud to ask for help when you need it. Don't ever fail to reach out and offer help to someone weaker than you. When you've hurt someone's feelings, even by accident, say you're sorry, and mean it. Finish everything you start. Learn something new every day. In order to learn, you have to acknowledge your ignorance, if only to yourself. Realize that life isn't a solitary trip, but a group effort; loneliness is often a self-inflicted curse. Strive to brighten the lives of those around you."

"How can any of that make me happy?" Michael didn't bother to hide his disdain.

Clayton studied him for a moment. "You tell me, then. What do you believe would make you happy, Michael?"

Michael shrugged violently and rose to pace the room. "I don't know!" He thought for a moment. "Lots of money, I guess, so I'll always be secure. Lots of friends to have fun with. A pretty girl whenever I want a little lovin'. The cash to ensure that my friends and I could always eat, drink, and be merry."

Clayton shook his head as he stood. "Security, friendship, and love are not doled out in return for monetary compensation." He had walked to the door and paused for a look back at his oldest son. "Think about what I told you, Michael. You said you want to be happy. I want you to be happy, too."

Remembering, Michael slouched in a chair and propped his feet up on the bed. He wasn't so sure of his father's belated wisdom. Friends appeared when he had a little money to spend on them, and vanished when he had none. So did pretty girls. Friends and pretty girls equaled security, at least to a certain extent. Therefore, the money to lure them both was necessary to his happiness.

He idly took paper cups from the nightstand and tossed them back and forth, stacking one on two atop three. He remembered Mary's comment to Will about making a Christmas tree. Well, this would be one way to do it. He wondered if Mary had thought of using the paper cups. He could go and ask her. But why, and why not? He shuffled the cups around like a carnival hawker with a pea under a nutshell. "Not under this one. Or this one. Or this one, either. Any way you look at it, you lose!" Michael killed another half hour before becoming frustrated that the asinine inclination refused to die. He snatched up the small stack of paper cups and stalked out into the assembly room to find Mary.

§ § § § § §

"Our second Christmas here." Sarah looked around the apartment. "I can't believe it's almost 1947. At least this year we are aware of the holidays, and we have each other."

"Mama's designing a Christmas tree," Callie said. "I told her a tree isn't important considering our circumstances, but she said those are the very reasons that it is so important. She has Tom and Christine working together on a Christmas service."

"That the meaning of the season be neither forgotten nor ignored," Sarah quipped. "Aunt Mary is right. We do have blessings to celebrate, and that's all the more reason to enjoy the holidays."

"We have things to be thankful for," Callie agreed. "For instance, the nurses are decreasing our medications. None of us is getting as much medicine as we were forced to take before we were transferred to this floor. And thank God nobody's been taken for surgery for the last couple of months."

Sarah made a face. "The nurses still haul us out for regular examinations, though, and the things they do are still experimental and unnecessary. Mama told me that Joy is getting more attention that the rest of us, and she's not even a victim! I hope they don't do anything to hurt her baby." Unexpected tears crowded Sarah's eyes.

"Robert's worried about that, too. He said the suits did a lot of things to Joy back when we were all still isolated from each other. There were things she wouldn't even talk about, because she didn't want to upset him or their daughters."

Both girls looked up at a light knock against the doorframe. Callie stepped into the foyer to admit their visitor, though they both recognized the gentle rap.

"Hi, Dave." Callie couldn't resist a knowing smile at Sarah as she welcomed the young man into the room.

"Hi, Sarah," Dave said, at the same time Sarah said, "Hi, Dave." They laughed with awkward delight. Callie moved to the other side of the room to offer them as much privacy as her presence would allow.

Dave dropped into a chair across the table from Sarah. "You look great," he said.

Sarah would have laughed at the ridiculous compliment, but Dave was serious. She risked a glance into his face and saw the beautiful person who lived inside the scars. She smiled with gratitude and elation that he saw her in the same light.

"Thanks." Dare she say it? "So do you."

They laughed again.

Dave reached across the table and gently brushed a tear from Sarah's cheek.

"We were talking about Joy," she murmured. "Robert is so concerned about her and the baby. The rest of us can't help but worry, too."

"It's okay to cry in front of me, Sarah. Just be yourself. That's how we all love you." Dave studied her with an intensity that made her bashful. Sarah's face grew hot, and she wondered if her skin was capable of betraying her with a blush. She lowered her gaze with a shy smile.

Dave drew back, embarrassed, and cleared his throat. "Arlene and the girls are going to perform a special program of Christmas songs this evening." He glanced at Callie, who took peripheral note of his discomfort and padded away to the bathroom. The moment she was gone, Dave reached for Sarah's hand. "Will you sit with me tonight?"

"Knock, knock!" Ray entered in time to see Dave release Sarah's hand. He directed an appraising look at his daughter.

"Callie's in the bathroom," Sarah explained.

"Oh." Ray exhaled. His shoulders slightly relaxed. "Oh. Well, I'm just delivering a message. Your mama sent me to ask if you'd like to join the ladies in one of their hen sessions...er, card games."

Sarah laughed outright, as she knew her father hoped she would do. "Sure, Daddy. I'll be right there."

Ray glanced at Dave, who stood and backed away from the table, never taking his eyes off Sarah. "I'd better be going."

Sarah smiled. "I'll see you at the singing, Dave."

Dave hesitated only long enough to nod, but Ray was not blind to the ecstatic grin on the young man's face. As Dave left the apartment, Ray took another look at the daughter who had become a young woman even as he had taken for granted that she would always be his little girl. The transformation left him feeling suddenly unsettled.

Callie emerged from the foyer as Sarah linked arms with Ray. Sarah beckoned to her. "Want to join the others in a game?"

"In a little while. I want to read the last chapter." Callie held up a book.

Sarah gasped. "We aren't supposed to have those in our rooms!"

Callie shrugged. "What're they gonna do, imprison me for breaking a rule?"

Sarah giggled, but Ray's laughter included a gentle admonition. "You never know what they might do to us, Callie. I don't blame you for borrowing the books. Just don't make it obvious you've done so."

"Sure, Uncle Ray. I'll be careful." To Sarah, she said, "Tell Mama and Aunt Belva I'll be out in half an hour or so."

Ray walked Sarah to a table that was occupied by a group of animated women. He kindly declined their invitation to sit and chat. He kissed his wife and then slipped away to John and Mary's apartment where Robert, Ben, and Tom were already deep in discussion.

"Area L," Ben was saying. He pushed out a chair for Ray. "Al said the agencies behind the institution use a numerical system of classification. This time they used a Roman numeral. He said there are several facilities like this one, but not all of them are in the U.S."

"I wish we knew more about Commander Maslow," Ray said. "He carried himself with authority, like one who is obeyed without question. He was unaccustomed to challenge. That much was evident by his reaction to our comments during his speech. That leads me to believe he was once a high-ranking military officer."

"You think maybe he's a colonel?" Ben asked.

"No," Ray said. "I can't imagine a full bird supervising a place like this."

"Al called him a genius in biotechnology, which could suggest that he is a civilian official working for the federal government," Robert said. "Whatever he is, he's not a very considerate one. Alden's a good man, though. Tom, are you sure you wouldn't like to go with one of us to meet him?"

"Three people moving around among twenty-five are enough," Tom cautioned. "The fewer who go, the less chance we have of getting caught by our nursing staff. It might be better for Alden's peace of mind as well if the number of people going back and forth is limited."

"That's true," Ben said. "But there are only four of us who even know about Alden. Well, six counting Mama and Mrs. Lake. One more visitor shouldn't be a problem."

"Thanks, Ben. Nevertheless, I feel better focusing

my energies on the Trinity family right now. Do you honestly believe there may be an opportunity for us to escape this place?"

"There is the aircraft." Robert shifted uncomfortably. "Alden doesn't know much about it, but he has at least flown it a few times."

"He showed me the interior three nights ago," Ray said. "There isn't much room. Four healthy people would find it an adequate fit. Six people our size could get in, but it wouldn't make for the most comfortable ride."

"I'd be ready to try anything, were it not for Joy," Robert said. "I don't want to drag my feet on any plan that might come together, but my wife's pregnancy is my primary concern. I don't know how safe it would be for her to travel. I know she wouldn't make it far on foot. I won't take off on an uncertain venture and leave her and the girls behind. Unless a foolproof plan comes along, I am unwilling to take Joy away from the only medical care we have, such as it is, until after our baby is born."

"I can't argue with that," Tom said. "The way I see it, either we all go, or none of us do."

"We might not all be able to leave at once," Ray said. "Especially if it comes to taking that aircraft out of here. A few of us would have to escape and get help to force the release of the others."

"Where would we find help?" Ben wondered. The men silently pondered his question until Ben leaned forward and told them something they didn't know. "Al's been submitting records to the Council again. This is the second time he's been ordered to do so. He photographed the aircraft from every angle and copied all the notes he and his team recorded about it. He wrote out his own observations and turned in a complete report of how the aircraft survived its visit to the Marshall Islands. Al says the agencies who share custody of this institution are discussing plans to build a replica of the craft. They want to see if by making one themselves, they can discover things they still don't know about the one upstairs."

Ray, Robert, and Tom stared at Ben. He shrugged. "I went upstairs last night. Al has almost finished my chess set. The reports have slowed him down." Ben stretched and stood gingerly. Though he was no longer in pain, a certain amount of stiffness lingered from the surgeries he had endured in September. "We need to pay close attention now. If Al's superiors begin showing sincere interest in the craft, we may have to plan our exit sooner than any of us expected."

"Where are you going?" Ray asked as Ben walked away.

"I promised Freddy a game of checkers, and I ought to spend some time with Mama. I've hardly spoken with her for several days."

They watched Ben leave. Ray shook his head. "I have to remind myself that he's just a fourteen-year-old kid."

"A very smart and grown-up kid," Tom said.

"Nope, you're both wrong. I hate to disagree with Ben's own father, but Ben is a quick-witted young man. He might be all the more mature because most of his time for the past two years has been spent in the company of adults, but he has grown up. He's no child and doesn't deserve to be treated like one." Robert shook his head ruefully. "I'm going to have to eat those words, I just know it."

Ray laughed. "I was wondering if you had taken a

good look at Catherine lately."

"She's a tough one. Elisabeth is so quiet and smart. She's even-tempered, easy-going, a real pleasure to be around. With her petite size even at eleven, it's easy to see her as a little girl, no matter how grown up she acts. I'll have to be careful to treat her with more consideration as she grows older. But Catherine is thirteen going on thirty and a real handful. She's too hot-tempered to let Joy and me ignore the fact that she's growing up. I'm glad she's taking on womanly proportions, despite all we've been through here."

"It doesn't seem to have interfered with the children's growth," Tom agreed. "I noticed yesterday that Freddy is getting taller. He wants to be masculine and broad-shouldered like Clayton and Michael. Freddy described his mother as a slight woman, though, and it appears he got his slim build from her."

"Well, gentlemen, I guess we'd better return to the assembly room before the others think we've been hauled off to the lab."

"No one has questioned our meetings," Tom said as they stood. "I can't help but feel guilty keeping a secret of this magnitude."

"Don't," Robert said. "There are those among us who might do something rash if they knew what we know. As you said about limiting Alden's visitors to only three, it's best that only a few of us share this information. If an opportunity arises to escape, we have to be ready to seize it. If no chance presents itself, we may eventually have to make our own."

Their hearts raced with excitement and determination as the three men rejoined their fellow captives in the common room.

§ § § § § §

"Dave really likes you," Callie observed Christmas night.

"He hasn't much of a choice," Sarah brooded. "It's not as if he has an unlimited selection of women with whom to explore the opportunity for romance."

"What's that supposed to mean?"

"It means that if we were out there in the real world instead of trapped inside this place, Dave probably wouldn't look twice at me."

"Nor you at him? Is Dave not what you have in mind when you think of dating?"

"No!" Sarah turned to Callie. "That's not what I meant at all. Dave is nice. I really like him a lot. It's just that…"

"You'd like to know if he would have asked you out over all the other girls in school."

"I don't want a boy to like me because I'm the only girl available. I don't want a man to feel that he got stuck with me because he wasn't able to marry a woman he really would have wanted."

"Dave isn't stuck with you. He has other choices. He could be spending time with Abby or Rachael, but he prefers your company. That's no different than if the two of you were in the same school or church group."

"But what if we had not ended up here? Dave and I would never have met, and he'd be dating a girl who really and truly struck his fancy over all the other girls he knew. Instead, he's having to settle for one of only three girls available to him."

"What if Mama's family had never moved from Texas to Kentucky? She would not have met Daddy, and they would both have married other people. What if Mama had been able to have babies of her own? She and Daddy would never have adopted me. What if Lucy had not died? None of our family would be here. You can drive yourself crazy with what-ifs. Questions like that accomplish nothing, Sarah. They distract you from what is and taunt you with insinuations that your life might have turned out better, *if only*."

"When you put it that way, I sound pretty foolish."

"Not foolish. Just scared. Would you go out with Dave if none of this had ever happened? I don't know what he looked like before, but based on personality alone, would you enjoy his company?"

Sarah thought for a moment. "Yes. Yes, I would. Dave is a kind, considerate person. He is honest and sincere. He makes me laugh. Looks aren't as important as those things."

"Then don't find it so impossible to believe that he feels the same way about you."

Sarah contemplated the conversation as she and Callie turned down their beds and took turns in the bathroom. "Thanks, Cal," she finally said.

Callie took in the brave smile that defied the burden of baldness, of scars, of a life permanently altered by a vicious twist of fate. She hugged her cousin close as the lights automatically dimmed, glad her expression had not revealed the what-ifs that plagued her as well. She despised the horrible thoughts that rose unbidden in her mind. *If my parents had not gone through the desert that morning, I would not be stuck here. If they hadn't told anybody about me, the MPs would not have known to come after me. I'd still be free. Thank goodness I didn't take the trip with them. I don't think I could bear to live if I looked like Sarah. At least if we ever get out of here, I can have a normal life.*

It sickened Callie to admit such traitorous feelings to herself. She loved her family with all her heart. She would never betray any of them, not even with words. She prayed that God would soften the resentment that sometimes constricted her emotions.

By the dim glow of the foyer light, Callie took one last look into the drawer that held her parents' Christmas gift to her: twelve bars of chocolate they had saved from the boxes they received the first day of every week.

"We know how much you love chocolate," Mary had told her.

The gift represented a sacrifice, six weeks that her mother and father had gone without the single luxury the Trinity victims were allotted. Chocolate was the only tangible taste of sweetness that graced their lives. Callie's parents had sacrificed for her sake from the moment of her conception. Twenty-three years ago an unmarried teenaged girl had delivered Callie into the world and released her into the arms of strangers who gave the infant a name, an identity, and the foundation of a loving family on which to build a successful life. Callie was both humbled and horrified that she could take such gifts for granted and never even know it.

She slipped into bed remembering the Christmas tree that Mary and Michael had made from white paper cups; the beautiful songs Arlene, Abby, and Rachael had sung, and how attractively Michael's voice had complemented theirs; Tom's reading from the book of Luke, and his incredible insight into the heart of Christ; Will's artwork that he painstakingly recreated every three days, erasing one lovely illustration from the blackboard and drawing another. Callie closed her eyes and saw again the eclectic cast who presented the Christmas play. Joy was a Navajo Mary with child. Maria was a Hispanic Mary after the birth in Bethlehem. Nathaniel portrayed the Ethiopian magus, after which he uttered an observation in his slow, faltering speech that touched the hearts of all within the sound of his voice.

"Race doesn't make us different anymore. Look at us: I'm not colored, you're not Mexican, and you're not white.

"We're all just the same hazy shade of gray."

Chapter Twenty-Nine

❖❖❖❖❖

There are memories that intrude upon my thoughts unexpectedly, recalled by a scent or a sound or an uncommon brilliance of light upon water. They invade gently, beguiling my spirit with the breathtaking clarity of yesterday, and I willingly surrender a few heartbeats to their ephemeral dance while life goes on without me. I catch up and do not explain what caused me to fall behind. Such visitations, and their price, are secrets of the soul.

Light and color spread a visual feast that I will ever insatiably crave as one who eats but is not filled. Autumn is my favorite time of year, when the forests in all directions erupt into such joyous strains of color that even an old woman is helpless but to dance with the song. The crisp boldness too soon falls prey to cold, damp months of barren monotony, and I live those days blessed with hope because I know this season of slumber will end.

There inevitably comes a day when I decide I can not bear the dreary burden for a moment longer. My downcast eyes distinguish the purple seam of a plump crocus bloom lifting up through the snow, or the pink and green beads of a hyacinth ready to burst into a shower of scented bells, or the yellow thread in a blade of grass that is about to birth a daffodil, and I realize that Winter's lease has expired. She is packing her things even as Spring begins the redecorating of her new, if temporary, lodging.

The forsythia blooms. The fragrance of the crabapple sweetens the breeze for miles. Memory merges with reality. I smile again. Life goes on.

Joy sank her nails into Robert's arm and pinched hard. He yelped at the rude awakening and sat up straight before his eyes were fully opened. He turned muzzily to his wife.

"Whadja do that for?"

"The baby's coming."

Robert went weak. It had been twelve years since Joy spoke those words about Elisabeth. The announcement skewed his mental processes. He took a bleary moment to right himself.

"Lie still. I'll notify the nurses."

"No!" It wasn't a plea; it was an order. Robert hesitated, confused.

"Mary has been a midwife before. She has agreed to help me."

"But it's barely April. The baby isn't supposed to be here for two more weeks! You'll need a nurse, honey."

"As big as I am, I think they estimated my delivery date wrong. Catherine and Elisabeth were both born within a week of their due dates. I think this baby is on time, too. I don't want medical personnel in here until after I've delivered, Robert, please. I'm afraid of what they might do to our baby. I want to stay here among my family and friends. My contractions aren't too close together yet. In less than two hours, the staff will bring our breakfast. When we've eaten and our trays have been collected, you can bring Mary to me so I can get on with having this baby."

"Buh...ah...what do we do 'til then?" Robert felt frantic. How could she be so calm?

"Will you rub my back for me? Please?" The tension in Joy's voice brought Robert back to earth. She was going to have his baby, and she was hurting. She needed him. Robert helped her sit up and gently massaged her back.

"Talk to me," Joy ordered.

"Okay," Robert agreed. "About what?"

"Anything. I don't care. Tell me how we're doing."

"I'm hanging in there," Robert said. "You're doing great."

"That's not what I mean." Joy took a deep breath. "Get my mind off me. Talk about someone, anyone, everyone else. Talk about good things."

Robert tried, and yawned. "Good things..."

"You've been weaned off your daily drug regimens. So has everyone else. It's a huge blessing that none of our people is taking medication anymore. You still have weekly physicals, but the worst of the medical stuff appears to be over."

"At least for the moment." Robert slid his hands up to Joy's shoulders.

"The small of my back, please. That's where I'm cramping."

"Sure, sweetheart. I'm sorry."

"What else?"

"Our privileges were increased after Christmas," Robert ventured. "We can go to the common room right after breakfast. We aren't confined to our apartments for half the day."

"The food is better," Joy added. "We get vegetables instead of puréed orange stuff and stringy green lumps and that spongy yellow mash…"

"I never did figure out what that was. I couldn't even decide what it tasted like."

"Like spongy yellow mash." Joy winced.

Robert massaged more firmly. "There is the calendar Christine keeps propped in the chalk tray. And the radio is no longer so rigidly policed. Occasionally a national news program actually gets played before someone catches it and turns it off."

Joy didn't reply. Robert allowed his thoughts to wander as he continued to rub her back. She was right that a number of benefits had been granted with the arrival of a new year. While the improvements were deeply appreciated, they also provoked a new urgency among the survivors to find a way out. The little group feared for their lives in a way they hadn't before. Instead of macabre death in the name of science, they dreaded living out the decades that stretched before them as captives confined to a series of small apartments with never again a glimpse of green grass and blue sky. Ray, Robert, and Tom calmed the troubled waters as far as their influence could reach, even as each frequently retreated to deal privately with his own raging desire to escape and to ponder the disconcerting secret that might make it possible.

They all made the same petition of their nurses each day. Some pleas for release were greeted with laughter, others with indifference or scorn, but the answer was ever and irrevocably the same: the facility was their home, and leaving was not an option.

The impending birth provided one glimmer of hope in their midst. Everyone hovered anxiously around Joy. When she sang to her growing belly, they joined in and sang with her. They read books and told stories to entertain the developing baby. They doted on Joy and watched over her to the point that she often pled exhaustion just to gain a few much-needed moments of privacy.

The long-awaited day had arrived earlier than anyone expected. As Robert kissed Joy's hair and rubbed her back, he prayed that God would protect his wife and their child and bring them safely through the birth.

Joy gave a soft moan that cleared Robert's mind as efficiently as a dash of cold water.

"Honey? I love you. I'm here for you. Whatever you need, tell me. If it's in my power to provide it, you'll have it."

"I'm okay." Her laughter was light and breathless. "I believe I'm further along than I thought."

The lights came on, announcing the arrival of day. Robert lingered near Joy while she showered and dressed in a clean shift. Breakfast was delivered, and Robert ate because Joy insisted. After nurses collected the trays, he fumed at the assembly room door. "I know how to get in here from out there," he told Joy. "But I don't see any way to access the wires that would let me open the door from this side once I'm locked in. I'll have to ask Ben if he knows a way."

"The nurses would demand to know how you got out before the doors were opened," Joy pointed out. "You'd risk giving yourself away. It'll open in a few minutes. Be patient, honey. Don't fret so."

The mechanism clicked. Robert turned the lever and

opened the door. He rushed back to his wife for a kiss. "I'll be right back."

"There's no need to hurry."

Robert crossed the assembly room to John and Mary's apartment and rapped sharply against the door.

One glimpse at Robert's expression was enough to bring a slow, wide grin to John's face. "Mary," he called.

"Yes?" She joined her husband in the foyer and looked out at Robert. "Oh," she breathed. "Is it time?"

"It's time," Robert confirmed.

"Oh!" she exclaimed again and gave John a quick hug. She hastened into the common room and preceded Robert to the Lake apartment.

The morning dragged by as Joy labored in vain. Those in the assembly room flipped absently through unread pages, drew abstract designs on the chalk board, and lost track of turns and scores in various games. By noon it was obvious to Mary that Joy was in trouble.

"Please!" Joy gasped. "Just a little longer. I can pretend I'm asleep when they bring the lunch trays. They'll never know the difference..."

"They're going to come and get you at two o'clock anyway for your daily checkup. You've stopped dilating, Joy. You've got to have help."

Fear of endangering the baby prevailed over Joy's mistrust of the medical staff. When lunches were delivered, Mary calmly informed Cheryl of Joy's condition and asked permission to remain with Joy throughout the delivery. Mary's request was denied, as was Robert's when he demanded the right to go with his wife. Robert, however, would not be refused. He insisted over the objections of the medical staff that he would stay with his wife until their baby was born. As Joy was taken away on a gurney, Robert followed her to the door of their room. Dana turned and jabbed a hypodermic needle of fluid into Robert's arm to render him unconscious and thus neutralize his determination to protect his family. Robert managed one frantic swing before the drug dropped him into the arms of his friends. Dana backed into the hall wide-eyed, both hands over her bleeding nose, as Cheryl pulled the door closed behind them.

The afternoon and evening hours were interminable. Tension pervaded the atmosphere as the group hoped, prayed, and waited uneasily for news. Robert sat in a chair just outside his apartment door and stared darkly ahead. Catherine appeared engrossed in the book gripped tightly in her hands, though she had not turned a page in nearly an hour. Elisabeth glanced anxiously back and forth from her father to her sister. She finally sat next to her Uncle Ray and leaned into him for comfort.

Ilya brought the news with only minutes left of the day. Joy's baby had been delivered by Caesarean section earlier in the evening. She and her son were doing fine.

"Take me to them!" Anxious excitement deepened the lines of stress and worry that creased Robert's face.

"I believe you will be allowed to visit Mrs. Lake in the morning," Ilya told him. "Your son is all right, but he is under constant observation. Your visit with the baby will be very brief."

Robert was desperate to see Joy and their baby. He begged shamelessly as Ilya backed through the apartment and out the door, all the while fending him off with shallow excuses that reiterated the nurses' customary helplessness to defy the orders of their superiors.

"I'm sorry, Mr. Lake, I truly am," and she was gone.

Robert wandered back into the assembly room like a

lost child. His friends surrounded him with congratulations and words of encouragement. Ray offered a handshake that became a bear hug. As the curfew chimed over the speakers, the exhausted group straggled to their individual rooms for rest from the suspense of the day. Catherine stalked past Robert into their apartment without a word. Elisabeth hugged her father around the waist as if to support him to his bedside, and he leaned against the slender child without realizing the pressure under which she doggedly endured all their burdens. When Robert sat heavily on the bed, Elisabeth smiled at him.

"What?" he asked.

"I have a baby brother," she said, and Robert couldn't miss the awe in her voice. "I can hardly wait to hold him."

"Neither can I, Lissie."

Elisabeth stared at Robert's haggard face for a moment, and then laughed with delight. It had been years since her father called her that. She and her sister were Lissie and Cat until Catherine decided the endearment was beneath her dignity. In order to be fair, Robert had ceased using both nicknames. Through the fog of exhaustion and lingering worry for his wife and son, it occurred to Robert that Elisabeth had truly missed this simple demonstration of her father's affection.

"I love you, Dad."

"I love you, Elisabeth. Say your prayers."

"I will."

"Goodnight."

§ § § § § §

Robert joined Joy on her bed. He gathered her into his arms and held her tenderly. They clung to each other, loving without words, until the sharpest edge of their longing had softened.

"A son," Robert murmured into Joy's blue-black hair. "We have a little boy. I'm so proud of you, honey. Words won't convey how much I love you."

"And I love you." Joy's vague smile emphasized the dark circles of fatigue under her eyes. "Cheryl says I'll get to move back to our apartment in three or four days. They'll let our baby stay in the room with us as soon as they are sure he is healthy enough."

"You've seen him and held him?"

"I have," Joy said.

"And?" Robert pressed eagerly.

"And he watches me with those big round eyes and nurses without any argument. Cheryl says they are all surprised at how hearty he is. He's smaller than I thought he would be. I was so big, I just expected to have a big baby. Our boy barely weighs six pounds. Isn't that funny?"

"Is he as beautiful..." *as our daughters used to be?*

Joy bowed her head so that Robert could not see her expression. "He looks just like his daddy," she whispered. She hid her face against Robert's chest and sobbed. Robert cuddled her close, his presence a formidable barrier against the residue of fear and anguish that had accompanied the difficult delivery.

"Hang in there, honey. I would stay here with you if I could. I'll visit you every minute they'll let me. I can hardly bear sleeping in that apartment without you. I miss you so."

"I miss you and the girls. I hate being here alone. I

get so scared."

"I'll do all that I can to take care of you," Robert promised. "God will do what I can't. You're never completely alone, Joy. Just remember that." Robert kissed her face, her hair, and she took refuge against him, snuggling under his arm as if to disappear within him. Robert felt his heart would burst with love, longing, and helpless frustration. Joy pressed hot against the full length of his body, and Robert tucked her into the curve of himself. He couldn't hold her close enough.

Joy's trembling gradually abated in response to the security and encouragement of Robert's presence. At length she mopped at her face with a tissue. "How are the girls?"

"Elisabeth is excited. She can hardly wait to get her hands on the baby. I think Catherine is looking forward to it, too."

"I'd like to think so." Joy relaxed against his shoulder. "I worry for her. She won't talk to either of us, and the only contact I ever witness between her and another person is when she occasionally snipes at her sister."

"Maybe her little brother will coax her out of her shell."

"I want to go back with you."

"I wish you could." A thought occurred to Robert as Cheryl entered the room.

"Have you seen Dana?" he asked Joy.

"Not since yesterday. She was among the group that came to get me. I don't remember seeing her after that."

Robert winced but kept the unfortunate details to himself.

"Well, Papa, are you ready?" Cheryl grinned behind

her mask. She waited for Robert to disentangle himself from Joy and move to a chair beside the bed. Cheryl stepped behind him to tie a mask over his nose and mouth. "Congratulations! Your baby represents our first successful birth in this facility." Another nurse walked in carrying a bundle in a pale blue blanket, which she lowered gently into Joy's arms.

"We'll leave you three alone to get acquainted," Cheryl said. "We'll be right through that door. We'll be watching through the glass, so just wave if you need anything."

The nurses slipped away. Joy kissed her baby and rocked him in her arms, humming a melody that only vaguely reminded Robert of the song it was meant to be.

"May I see him?" Robert finally asked.

Joy was doing her best not to cry. As Robert again joined her on the bed, she turned the infant to face him. Joy pulled back the blanket and watched her husband recoil from his first glimpse of their son.

Just like his daddy. Joy had told the truth, and Robert had exulted in proud anticipation of a blonde and blue-eyed child, not comprehending the literal meaning of her words. His most dreaded suspicions about the experiments performed on Joy for months prior to conception and throughout the earliest weeks of her pregnancy could not have prepared him for the frightening truth his wife held in her arms. The baby did indeed look like his father.

"Impossible!" Robert wanted to scream. His voice went flat with shock as he stated the obvious. "I'm not a doctor, but I know certain irrefutable facts. A baby cannot be born with a parent's scars. I've read about such things. If a trait isn't genetic, it can't be reproduced in offspring."

The logic behind his argument only served to confirm the horrible truth he did not want to accept. He and Joy had been used to produce the facility's first successful result of human genetic engineering. Their baby was an infant version of his father and the other Trinity survivors.

Robert collected the baby from his wife and held the distorted miracle in his arms. The infant's eyes opened momentarily and focused on Robert's face before slowly closing once more. The irises of the child's eyes were a smoky shade of deep, dark blue.

"Ethan Robert Lake, Jr.," Robert pronounced brokenly. "My son." He looked into the infant's pitiful face, and the last of his resolve and restraint melted away.

"Time to go," Cheryl said.

"You bet it is," Robert muttered. He yanked off his mask, kissed his son, and passed him to Joy. She held the baby for a moment longer before Cheryl's companion took him away.

"Your turn." Cheryl waved Robert toward the wheelchair. He clung to Joy for an excruciating moment before reluctantly allowing Cheryl to cuff him to the chair for the ride back to his family's apartment.

Robert was too stunned to interact with his friends. He asked Cheryl to close his foyer door so that no one could enter from the assembly room that afternoon. He needed time alone to acclimate himself to the hideous thing that had been done to his wife and son. He needed time to cool rage with rationality, to work as violently as his body would allow in order to expel the tension that threatened to erupt into murderous insanity. He sparred numerous bouts with an imaginary partner and repeated sets of calisthenics until he could hardly stand. He staggered into the bathroom and indulged in a long shower. The water cleansed his body while hot steam rose to clear his mind of the horrors he had been brutally forced to acknowledge and now could not forget. The smell of fear that emanated from every pore washed down the drain, drowning his thirst for revenge. By the time he toweled dry and dressed in clean clothing, Robert's self-control was intact. He did not know how he was going to go about it, but he was also determined to take control of his family's situation and change it, immediately.

When dinner was delivered, Robert requested admission into the assembly room. He ordered his daughters to join him at a table. During the meal he shared with them the details of his visit with their mother. To his surprise, Catherine asked the first question.

"So what does the baby look like?"

Robert had dreaded the question, but he wouldn't lie. His girls deserved the truth and were old enough to hear it. "He has blue eyes," he told them. "He looks like the three of us."

"So he gets to be the gorgeous golden boy of the family," Catherine remarked. "Good for him."

But Elisabeth was watching her father's face. "No, Cat," she said. "That's not what Dad means. He means..." She trailed awkwardly to a stop, hoping Robert would tell her she was wrong, waiting for him to correct her.

Robert nodded slowly. "I'm afraid so. Through the radiation, surgeries, and procedures that were performed on both your mother and me, the medical folks here have caused your little brother to look like us after the Trinity explosion. But except for his appearance, as far as we know, he is a healthy baby boy."

"But Dad," Elisabeth started, and closed her mouth, squirming with discomfort at the thoughts swarming her mind.

"What is it, Lissie?" Robert asked, ignoring Catherine's sharp look of disapproval. "Don't be afraid to ask whatever questions are on your mind. I'll answer them as best I can."

Elisabeth looked up at him with wide, plaintive eyes. "Since they caused the baby to be like us, will they experiment on him like they have on us?"

Robert put everything he had into maintaining control of his emotions and presenting a confident face to his daughters. "Not if I can help it," was the best he could do. It wasn't good enough, and he knew it. Catherine swiftly confirmed it.

"But you can't help it," she snapped. "You couldn't stop the hoods from hurting us. You can't stop these so-called doctors and nurses from having their way with us, and you won't be able to stop them from doing as they please with the baby."

"I didn't excuse you," Robert said as Catherine rose to leave.

The tone of his voice had the desired effect. She sat back in her chair and picked at her food with the flimsy wooden fork.

"Nobody likes to be helpless, Catherine. I certainly didn't choose for my family to be stuck in a situation like this. If there is a way to get us out of it, I will find that way. You know that."

"We know, Dad. We can't blame you for any of this. It's not your fault we're here," Elisabeth said.

Catherine did leave then, rising abruptly and running to their apartment. Robert looked sternly at Elisabeth, who wilted under his glare.

Robert relented a little. "Thank you for trying to make me feel better, Elisabeth, but that was an unnecessary dig at your sister. You've hurt her feelings." He was startled at the anger that clouded Elisabeth's eyes.

"But it is her fault, Dad! We wouldn't be here if it weren't for her! She always had to get her way about everything, and her narcissistic attitude ended up costing her whole family our very lives! She thought if we ran away, she could force you and Mom to do what she wanted you to do."

Robert sighed and laid down his fork. "All right, Elisabeth, I can't argue with that. But there is a detail you are forgetting."

"What?" Elisabeth picked at her napkin.

"You went with her. Catherine might have reasoned with you, threatened you, begged or demanded, but she could not have forced you. You chose to go with her that night."

Elisabeth directed her horrified expression at her plate. "But I didn't know…"

"Neither did Catherine. Regardless of her attempts to get her way, she would not have knowingly walked into a situation like this, nor would she have condemned her entire family to it. She would not have done that any more than you would have."

Elisabeth stared silently at her plate.

"Well?" Robert said.

"I hate her, Dad!" Elisabeth cried. "I can't help it, I

hate her for everything she's always been and still is! I've tried to be nice, but I just can't do it anymore. I wish she wasn't my sister!" And Elisabeth was gone, too, but instead of following Catherine's path to their apartment, she sought refuge with Christine.

Ray approached the table. "In the mood for company?"

Robert stacked the two abandoned plates and slid them to one side. "Have a seat. I was just wondering where my barely-twelve-year-old daughter came up with 'narcissistic.' Guess there's my answer."

Ray followed Robert's gaze to where Elisabeth sat with Christine. "If we had to end up in this institution, at least we were blessed with a schoolteacher."

Robert nodded gravely. "I saw my son today."

"He and Joy are all right?"

"No. They've done things, Ray, things I don't understand, and these things have resulted in genetic mutation. My baby boy looks just like me and you and everyone else who was in the desert when that bomb was detonated." He shoved his plate aside. "I know they did things to Joy's reproductive organs. There were surgeries, exposure to radiation, other things I don't even know about because Joy wouldn't tell me. She excuses it by saying the other women here have been through pretty much the same routine. They did things to me like they've done to you, to Ben, to Tom." He sighed heavily. "Maybe we've all been altered. I guess if the other ladies are able to have children, we'll find out."

Ray was horrified. "I never would have believed..."

"Nor would I. Even after all we've been through, I wouldn't have anticipated this."

"What can I do to help?"

Robert raised his eyes to Ray. "Start making plans to get us out of here. We'll visit Alden a few more times, learn what we need to know. Then we'll set a date and decide who among us will fly out of here on that aircraft to get the help necessary to free those we leave behind."

Ray didn't flinch. "I'll go tonight."

"I'll go with you."

No handshake was necessary to seal the pact. Ray went in search of Tom to tell him of their plans.

Robert excused himself from the others, who all wanted more detail about his son than he could bring himself to share. He went to check on his daughters. Elisabeth had settled into a corner with a book. Catherine was asleep on her bed, or pretending to be. Robert watched her breathe and wondered how they could have lived together for nearly fourteen years and never learned to communicate. He had noticed that Catherine shot him a dirty look when he used Elisabeth's nickname, yet did not retaliate when Elisabeth called her 'Cat.' Elisabeth was the only person with whom Catherine permitted a relationship. Robert wondered if Catherine knew how Elisabeth truly felt.

Somehow he had to pull his family together, and soon. If he was going to lead them out of this place, he had to be certain his daughters would to follow him without allowing their personal battles to disrupt the family's plans and ruin their chance at freedom.

§ § § § § §

"It is my pleasure to introduce Ethan Robert Lake, Jr." Robert proudly pulled the coverlet away from his eight-week-old son as the Trinity survivors crowded around to see the newest member of their family. Robert had told everyone about the child's condition. Nevertheless, he watched their faces and braced for their reaction. Far from being disgusted or appalled, all were eager to caress and hold the baby. Robert's heart melted with gratitude at the family's warm welcome and automatic acceptance of his son.

The infant had been kept in a lab until he was two weeks old. During the next six weeks, a small nursery was arranged in the corner of Robert and Joy's bedroom, and nurses brought him to spend a few hours each day alone with his family within the confines of the apartment. At last Robert and Joy were permitted to keep their baby full time and introduce him to the others.

"May I hold him, Dad?" Elisabeth held out her hands. "Hey, Robin!" she exclaimed as Robert place the baby in her arms.

"He's smiling at her," Christine observed. "Look at that!"

"He loves his sisters," Joy said proudly. "They take turns holding him and keeping him entertained. He knows their voices and looks for them when he hears them in the room."

"I thought you were going to call him Ethan," Mary said.

"We were," Robert said. "Elisabeth took one look at him and called him Robin, and the name stuck."

"How are you doing, Joy?" Callie asked.

"I've recovered just fine from the delivery. They've put me through a weary lot of exams since he was born, but this past week they've only taken me out twice."

Joy glanced at Robert to see if he was listening, but he was paying attention to the baby. "I don't care what they do to me, as long as they leave Robin alone," she confided to Callie. "They give him a checkup every week, but they aren't experimenting on him. If they intend to do that, it will be over my dead body."

Callie shuddered as they turned their attention back to Robin. Everyone had fallen in love with him before they even saw him, this tiny miracle that, despite his appearance or perhaps because of it, was a part of all of them.

Standing a little away from the others, Ray surveyed the happiness that had been born into the group with the arrival of the child. Though he was thrilled for Robert and delighted along with everyone else in the presence of the baby, his enthusiasm was forced. He had not had an opportunity to tell Robert what Ben had learned the night before during his visit with Alden. The information would keep, Ray decided, until tomorrow. Robert deserved to spend time with his family and to be free for at least a short while from other concerns. Ray would pay Alden a visit tonight and discuss what his son had learned.

Don't worry little one, Ray thought, and the smile he directed toward Robin was real. We're going to leave here soon.

Or die trying, came the unbidden taunt, at which Ray stopped speculating and joined in the conversations around him, allowing the ecstatic voices in the assembly room to drown out the ominous whispers in his mind.

Chapter Thirty

"June twenty-third already." Tom tossed a piece of cherry candy onto the table. "Does Alden have any idea at all when it's going to be moved?"

Ray snatched up the candy. "How did you come by this?"

"I have connections." Tom smiled roguishly.

"He has Ilya," Robert corrected with a knowing grin.

"She seems to think a lot of you," Ray observed. "She's a smart lady. Not many women want to study to become a doctor and open their own private practice. She's pretty, too."

"She's a good friend," Tom said.

"Just remember she's one of them." The frown Robert directed at his cards disappeared when he looked over them at Tom. "When it comes to choosing sides, she won't be on ours."

Tom unwrapped a piece of orange candy. "I'd like to think our friendship means enough to her that she would help me as much as she could. I don't believe she would turn against me."

"She may not have a choice," Ray said. "She's answering to real people who can do serious damage to her career if she doesn't follow orders. We need to remember that about all the medical staff. I myself have been mighty quick to pass judgment, but then I remember they are just as human as we are."

"They are now," Robert said. "I haven't forgotten the hoods."

A collective shudder confirmed that the others hadn't, either.

"Robin is eleven weeks old today." Robert smiled.

"Growing like a weed, too," Ray said.

"And putting on weight. I noticed how heavy he was when I held him this morning." Tom briskly sorted his cards as Ray and Robert exchanged a sympathetic glance for the young man who never had the opportunity to hold his own child.

A light "ahem" drew their attention to the foyer.

"Request permission to come aboard," said Ben.

"Permission granted," Ray said. "Come on in and pull up a chair."

"Want we should deal you in?" Robert asked.

"Sure! I brought some stuff." Ben placed five tiny fans that had once been playing cards on the table.

"Where'd you get these?" Tom picked one up for a closer look.

"Sarah made them. The cards are stiff, so they hold a good crease. Sarah's trying to figure out how to fold them into other shapes. Freddy and I have been helping her. Keen, Tom!" He snatched a piece of candy. "Got any grape?"

"You mean you knew Tom was hoarding candy?" Ray demanded.

Ben grinned mischievously. "I don't tell you all everything. A man's got to have a few secrets."

"Well, the four of us have plenty," Robert said.

"And we need to lay them all on the table this evening. Here is what I know: the Council has been working with Alden's notes and diagrams in an effort to build an aircraft similar to the one in the hangar. They've put together several test models at various sites across the country and have actually flown a few of them. This is all done in secret, according to Alden. The general public isn't to be informed due to the nature of the work and the origin of the design. All test flights take place after dark. Our military wants to build an aircraft that is invisible to radar. This has failed because there are still too many unsolved variables. Therefore, those in charge of the project have decided to begin in-depth experiments on our aircraft. Alden says they are going to start their work where he and his team left off. He has heard rumors that the craft will be moved to a location where newer technology and equipment can be used to attempt to disassemble and study it."

"That will end Alden's tenure at this facility," Ben said.

"It will also terminate our one hope for a ride out," Ray added. "What do you say, Robert?"

"Joy has recovered from the delivery, and Robin is thriving. He takes all the formula Joy will give him and asks for more." Robert laid down his cards. "I say we choose our ambassadors to the outside world and go forth to claim our freedom."

"How many?" Tom asked.

"Alden will have to go," Ray said, ignoring his son's determined stare. "He's the only one who can fly the aircraft. One of us needs to go. The other two can stay here and work to keep everyone else calm and focused until we are all rescued."

"That's one pilot, one passenger," Ben said. "The aircraft will hold five, maybe six people."

"Five will fit more comfortably," Robert said. "Alden and me, that makes two." He grinned.

"We'll have to discuss that." Ray smiled, but remained very serious. "If it will carry the weight of six people, we should send six – Alden and five of our own. The more we can get out of here, the better."

"I should go," Ben said. "Before you say no, remember that I'm the one who introduced you and Robert to Alden in the first place. He is my friend. I know just as much as everyone else about everything we've been through here. And I'll be fifteen next month. I'm not a kid anymore."

"We'll have to discuss that, too," Ray said.

"When will we go?" Tom asked.

"We need to visit Alden every night," Robert said. "We don't want to miss an immediate decision by the Council to move the aircraft out and be left with nothing but good intentions. I'll go tonight. Ray, would you mind going tomorrow night?"

"Al finished my chess set a couple of weeks ago," Ben said. "All the pieces have been ready for a while, but he wanted to make me a board. It is a wooden board with light and dark squares. He cut the pieces and glued them together and put them in a vise until they dried. Then he sanded the whole thing smooth and brushed a layer of clear finish over it. It has taken him more than a month to complete it because of the Council's interest in the aircraft. When I was there a couple of days ago, the finish was still tacky. He said the next time I came for a visit, we could start a game on my very own board."

The men fell silent. Ray leaned toward Ben and

draped his arm around his son's shoulders. "Why don't you go tomorrow night instead of me? You can find out what we need to know and get a good start on that game while you're there."

Ben nodded slowly, staring into his hands after the manner of Alden Morrow. "I hope Al will still be my friend after all this is over."

"He will," Robert assured him. "Alden thinks very highly of you. What we are about to do isn't going to change that."

"He might even expect it," Tom said. "From what the three of you have told me, Alden is one of us more than he is one of them. Unlike our nurses, who must obey their orders or deal with the consequences, Alden was set aside for possible punishment if it was determined that he did not fully cooperate with Maslow's desire to destroy the aircraft. He was subsequently forgotten and left to his own devices in the hangar until the Council developed a new interest in the craft. He has to follow orders, of course. I'm just not certain his heart is in it. I wonder if he wouldn't welcome a chance to escape just as much as we would."

"A few of the nurses don't seem too keen on what they have to put us through," Ray said. "But they're scared to contradict their orders."

"I don't think Alden would deliberately disobey and cause problems, but I can't see him getting violent and blowing the whistle on us, either," Robert said.

"Not unless we gave him a reason." Ben scrutinized one of Sarah's fans to avoid meeting the gazes that centered on him. "To disobey or to blow the whistle." Ben managed a sickly grin as he rose to leave. "Tell Al I'll see him tomorrow night," he said to Robert. "Thanks,

Dad." Ben squeezed Ray's shoulder as he walked past him into the foyer and out the door.

"You know, if Alden won't do this willingly, you will have to force him," Tom said. "Are either of you ready to do that?"

"I fought a war." Ray's eyes darkened with the comment. "I know how to make people do things."

"I could handle it." Robert nodded emphatically. "I don't want to hurt Alden, but nothing's going to stand in my way of getting my wife and my children out of this place. Not even him."

Tom nodded. "I'll be in prayer about it. 'Tis all I know to do."

"Your job will be the most difficult of all," Ray said. "Indeed, it already is. I couldn't be the spiritual strength that you are to this group of people. I've questioned God, raged at Him, and argued with Him. I've demanded and begged. He's heard from me plenty. But I don't have the loving relationship with Him that I see in you."

"Don't put me on too high a pedestal," Tom protested. "I'm far from perfect. I just do the best that I can do and leave the rest to God."

"That's all any of us can do," Robert said. "I'm going to go home and take a nap. Ray, tell Belva thanks for giving us run of your apartment, and sorry for the mess we've made on your table."

"What mess? I'll just toss all these things in a drawer," Ray said. "We'll have them for our next game. Like Tom said, I'll be praying about tonight."

"And about the days to come," Tom said. "Don't forget to pray for peace and unity when we tell all our friends what we've been up to for the past year."

§ § § § § §

"Ten July," Alden told Ben. "Two weeks from Thursday. I have orders to fly her to an as-yet-undisclosed location. All that means is that the rumors of Wright Field in Ohio haven't been confirmed yet. I will take two passengers along who are only going in order to keep an eye on me. After I deliver the aircraft, I fully expect to be reassigned. At least I hope that's what they'll do. I haven't disobeyed any orders that would get me into trouble, but Commander Maslow is still annoyed over her survival at Bikini Atoll."

Ben silently advanced a pawn.

"You won't forget me, will you, Ben? You'll remember your old buddy Al and the chess set I made for you and how much fun we had when you came up to see me?"

Ben cleared his throat and blinked hard to control the sadness that burned within his chest. "I will never forget you, Al. Not for as long as I live." He knuckled his eyes. "I wish you didn't have to go. Or that I could go with you."

"Just don't get caught running loose in the institution after I'm gone. I don't know what this hangar will be used for, but it might not be safe to break out and explore anymore. Promise me you'll be careful."

"I promise. You too, Al."

"Ah, don't worry about me." Alden glanced reluctantly at the clock. "It's about time for you to be going. Come and see me as often as you can next week. The stars and stripes and stuffed shirts will show up the weekend after the fourth, and I don't know what my working hours will be from then until I leave."

"I wish I could keep my chess set." Ben turned a rook over and over, examining the miniature parapets Al had carved in intricate detail.

"I'm trying to think of a way for you to have it in your apartment," Al said. "I'm not even supposed to know you exist, so I'm stuck for ideas at the moment. Let me think on it for a few days. I'll do my best to figure something out."

"Do you know any of the medical staff?"

"I know a few by name. They aren't close friends."

"Nurse Thornton takes care of me, but she's an old harridan." Ben thought for a moment. "Do you know the nurse named Ilya?"

Alden nodded. "I sure do. Not personally, like I said, but she's one of the nicest out of the lot of them. She always has a smile."

Ben placed the rook back onto the board. "Ilya is very close to Tom Westfield. He's our preacher. He's her patient, but they spend a lot of extra time together. I'd go so far as to say they love each other."

"Would you now?" Alden grinned with amusement.

Ben nodded gravely and caressed a knight between the horse's flared nostrils. "Just passing on a bit of gossip, as Mama would say." He held out his hand. "Good night, Al. I'll visit again right away."

Alden shook Ben's hand. "Take care, now."

§ § § § § §

Tom restlessly paced the breadth of his room, wall to wall, back and forth. What he wouldn't give to breathe fresh air again, to stroll barefoot across lush green grass under an ocean of blue sky a-sail with fluffy white clouds! His imagination drew out the fantasy and embellished fading memories with beautiful notions that fit the words as best he could recall. Sybil entered his thoughts less vividly these days. Tom still experienced the loss with excruciating clarity from time to time, but he became desperate when he couldn't bring her face clearly into focus or recall the timbre of her voice. What betrayal, that his memory could leave him wanting such precious detail! He supposed it normal after a period of mourning that the heart would explore fulfillment from another. He no longer felt regret about his hopeless attraction to Ilya but was shaken with guilt and remorse at Sybil's vague features and his inability to resurrect her in his mind. He would forever be plagued with questions for which there would never be an answer. Was their child a girl or a boy? Would he and Sybil have had a second child by now? What had become of Sybil's invalid mother? How had the disappearance of twelve people, ten of them teenagers, been explained to the church and to the community – to their families? Tom wrestled with angels of hope and demons of despair until physically exhausted.

Issues that he had previously been able to ignore now demanded consideration. Foremost in his mind was Ilya. He did not feel for her the same transcendent passion he had shared with Sybil. Nothing could compare to the wedded union, the joining of two individuals committed to live as one. Though he had kissed Ilya's hand on several occasions and held her close on several more, that was the extent of the physical contact they had shared. Emotionally, however, they had bonded beyond what Tom would have believed himself capable. The death of his wife and their child and all the events that followed had convinced Tom of the imprudence of ever trusting another person. Ilya had wafted through his walls as though they weren't even there, and he had stood still and allowed her to touch him. Now his dream, the dream shared by all the Trinity survivors, was on the verge of becoming reality. They were going to leave the institution and reclaim their freedom! For Tom the dream was tainted, for it meant sacrificing his relationship with Ilya. He knew that upon his departure he would never see her again. The knowledge ached to the very core of his being, opening wounds that had not completely healed after the loss of his family.

Impossible to say goodbye to Ilya, when he could not even tell her he was leaving. Would she feel betrayed that he had not confided in her? Better that than exploiting her already-divided loyalty by asking her to keep a secret that could cost her everything. His own feelings aside, it was in Ilya's best interest to continue his daily routine as though nothing out of the ordinary were taking place. He could only hope that when all was said and done she would understand.

The one thing he wished above all else was that he could find a way to tell her, before it was too late, that he loved her.

§ § § § § §

Belva slipped her hand into Ray's. "And then what? Where will we go?"

Ray hesitated to admit that he had focused so completely on escape that he had given little thought to how his family would celebrate their hard-earned freedom.

"I don't expect home is an option," Sarah said.

"No," John replied. "We've been here for almost two years. We'd do well to assume that Maslow was telling the truth when he said our families were informed of our demise immediately following the Trinity Test. That being the case, our houses and farms passed into other hands long ago."

They sat in heavy silence until Callie spoke up.

"So we'll start over. We're all strong and capable of working. We've proven, even here, that we have the ability and the determination to make things happen. As soon as we're out of here and have told our story, we'll decide where we want to live and make a home for ourselves there."

"That's going to be more difficult than it sounds," Mary said. "All of us who were exposed to the radiation have scars. We barely look human. A lot of people are going to resist associating with us because of that. People shy away from other people who are different."

"There is also the chance that even if we escape, we won't be allowed to remain free," Ray said. "The government has spent a lot of time and money on us. Assets are worth keeping, but we are about to make liabilities of ourselves by exposing our story to the public. Expanding upon what Mary just said, the government may be able to make a case, based on our appearances and experiences, that we belong in an institution. If that happens, we lose our short-lived freedom, and they regain their assets. We need to tell our story very honestly and sincerely in order to find favor with folks out there who can help us."

The question lingered in Belva's eyes. Ray stroked her hand.

"After that, we'll decide where to go. Kentucky has

always been our home. As far as I'm concerned, we'll return and make it our home again."

Belva leaned against Ray's chest, and he laid his crooked arm across her back.

"Where is Ben?" she asked.

"Robert, Tom, Ben, and I divided the task of telling everyone about the plans for escape. Robert and I are telling our families. Tom is speaking with his friends from the church youth group. Ben is bringing the Pendletons up to date."

"Ben knows about this already?" Sarah asked.

"It was Ben who introduced us to the possibility of escape," Ray said. At their astonished silence, Ray took a deep breath and started at the beginning, at the week the previous September when he had been so ill that Ben, afraid his father might die without outside intervention, had taken Robert to meet Alden Morrow.

Chapter Thirty-One

———◆┝�‒◈‒┥◆———

Sunlight spills across the meadow, awakening her inhabitants to the treasures of a new day. The indescribable, excruciating loveliness of the morning still stirs gratitude in the heart of a woman who learned in her youth that such grace is too precious to ever go unappreciated.

Diamonds glisten on grass, on blooms, on spiders' webs! Only dew, you say, dewdrops in the dawn, and they will evaporate before an hour is gone. But like manna from Heaven, there will be millions glittering fresh across my world tomorrow. I don't have to gather them or buy and sell them or hoard them away. I don't even have to deserve them. They are a gift.

Close your eyes and breathe the scent of a summer morning: mimosa, honeysuckle, wild rose, mint, the sun-warmed aroma of rich, dark earth. Don't miss the music. Listen, really hear the songs of the robin, the meadowlark, and the chick-a-dee, dee-dee-d-dee, dee-dee-d-dee. Savor their colors: the cardinal, the bluebird, the goldfinch, as they lift their songs of praise to the sky.

My reality was once an impossible dream. I yearned for this, I prayed for this, and in times of lesser faith, I despaired of this. Now, as blessings ever fall like rain, I count no privilege greater than greeting the sun as it heralds the creation of a new day.

———◆┝◒◈◒┥◆———

Friday, July fourth, circulated in whispers among twenty-five people desperate to make it a true Independence Day. Excitement and fear, dread and anticipation brewed a general milling about that made Tom think of cattle in the tensely charged moments before a stampede. If some felt indignant about the secret that four of them had kept, they cooled their resentment in the shadow of hope. Wherever individuals balanced on the emotional spectrum, the group had instantly united toward the goal. They were all more than ready to leave. They were ecstatic that plans had been made and a date had been set. They all wanted to be among those chosen for the initial exodus.

For the first time since their incarceration, relationships became strained as heated debates ensued concerning who would take the flight out. They all presented convincing arguments by which they considered themselves uniquely qualified to take the message of their existence to the outside world. Though Ray, Robert, and Tom were held in utmost respect, jealousy arose that the three of them would automatically be the first to leave. On the evening of June twenty-seventh, Freddy broadcast an opinion that resolved the conflict.

"I think we should just draw straws!" he proclaimed hotly to the entire room. "I don't see how else we can possibly be fair about this!" He sat down in a huff, oblivious to the stunned silence that followed his outburst.

Ray stepped in to finish what the boy had started. "That's the most sensible thing any of us has said all week long. I'd like to see a show of hands from all who are willing to draw straws for a ride on that aircraft." He scanned the room. All hands were raised. "Save your forks when you are finished eating," he said. "Give them to Freddy."

Two hours later Ray and Robert called for attention. The Trinity survivors turned to face the two men who had earned their respect and their faith. Ray held up a cluster of wooden sticks.

"These are fork handles, all of them even, with the exception of five that are shorter than the others. Since Robert and I have been meeting with the gentleman who will be persuaded to pilot the craft for us, it is essential that at least one of us be along for the ride. The two of us will draw first."

Freddy offered two sticks, and the men drew from his hands. They showed the result to each other before all the people.

Ray was devastated, but accepted the outcome. "Godspeed," he said to Robert.

Robert nodded. His heart pounded with reluctant anticipation when he looked at Joy and saw the battle between fear and pride that brightened her eyes.

Freddy carried twenty-three sticks down the rows of chairs so that everyone could draw, and the decision was made. Clayton Pendleton would go. Abby McAllister and Ben Davenport would go. The last ticket was drawn by Joy Lake. Robert immediately protested, but she swiftly stood to address her husband and anyone else who might express opposition.

"We agreed to allow the drawing to determine passengers. It is not unfair that I go." She turned to Robert and Ray. "I feel that one of the passengers should be a family member who was not present at the Trinity Test. I am a victim, too, although I carry no outward scars. For that very reason, my voice might be especially important to the success of our mission." Joy placed one hand on Catherine's shoulder and the other on Elisabeth's head. "We will only be away from our children for a short while. I have utmost confidence in Ray and Belva. I ask that they watch over our girls and our baby boy while we are gone." At Belva's nod and gentle smile, Joy played her final card. "I have sisters in New Mexico who can quickly come to my aid, verify my identity to the authorities, and start the support network we will need from all our families and from the general public in order to ensure our uncontested freedom."

Robert hesitated. His wife's arguments made perfect sense, but he did not like the idea of leaving their children without a parent. He knew Ray and Belva would care for Catherine, Elisabeth, and Robin as though they were siblings to Sarah and Ben. For reasons he could not quite put his finger on, he wanted Joy to remain behind. Applause answered Joy's assertion, however, and Robert conceded without sharing his misgivings.

"It is settled, then," Ray said. "Robert and Joy, Clayton, Abby and..." He paused for a troubled sigh. "Ben. Will all of you please join us at the table in the corner now? You too, Tom. We'll discuss the proceedings each day. Tom and I will keep the rest of you updated with any changes in plans as they occur. Remember to discuss this quietly among yourselves. Be careful that none of the nursing staff overhears so much as a word about it."

Joy handed Robin to Belva and joined the others at the table.

"Here's his bottle." Catherine offered it to Belva without looking her in the face.

"Thanks, Catherine. I'm really going to need your help while your parents are gone."

"What for?" Catherine asked suspiciously.

"To help me take care of your baby brother," Belva replied. "I'm not familiar with his feeding schedule or his likes and dislikes. Of course I have two of my own, but my youngest is older than you are. It has been a while since I tended a baby."

Catherine relaxed a little. "Well, feeding him isn't a problem since he was put on formula. He latches on to his bottle and gobbles it all down and then won't let go of it, like he's hoping if he just tries hard enough, he'll get more out of it." She actually smiled.

"Is there a certain way he prefers to be held?" Belva wanted to keep the conversation going while Catherine was open and friendly.

"I always hold him like this," she said, taking Robin from Belva and laying him across her chest with his head on her shoulder. "He'll let me hold him like this for hours," Catherine said proudly. "He likes to be held this way when you walk with him, too."

Catherine suddenly looked into Belva's face. "Isn't it wonderful that we're finally going to get out of here? Now we can get real medical attention and get healed from all our scars. I can hardly wait for that. I don't want any of my friends to see me until my complexion is restored and my hair grows back. After that, I'm going to pretend that these past two years were just one horrendous nightmare. I'm going to forget they ever happened." She handed Robin back to Belva as Belva struggled for a compassionate response. "Dad and 'Lisbeth and little Robin can all be fixed, too. We'll finally look human again, instead of like refugees from outer space. I'll be even more beautiful than I was before all this happened. Don't you look forward to that, Mrs.

Davenport?"

Belva answered carefully. "I was under the impress-sion that our scars are permanent and that we are as healed as we are ever going to be."

"Well, maybe *you* are," Catherine shot back. "You're old anyway, and old people don't care how they look. But I'm not going to look like this for the rest of my life. I'd rather be dead."

She flounced away, leaving Belva caught between pity for the girl's misdirected fantasies and indignation at the insult so carelessly dealt. Belva did not consider herself, at forty-one years of age, to be old. On the other hand, her daughter and son would be nineteen and fifteen, respectively, this year. That knowledge had a way of making her feel very ancient, indeed.

§ § § § § §

"Waiting until four July is pushing our luck," Ray said. "Alden says members of the Council are supposed to show up the following Monday."

"Timing is critical," Robert countered. "And the weekend is to our advantage. More people will be spending leisure time with newspapers and radios. More will be able to come out and see what the fuss is all about because they won't be at work. It's crucial that we get lots of attention quickly."

"Where will we go?" Abby asked.

"That will be up to Alden." Robert glanced at Ben. "Alden has become a good friend to us – hopefully too good of a friend to fly us into danger and turn us all in. We'll provide an alibi so he won't get into trouble. We'll say we forced him to take us out of here. I don't know where we'll land, but I want to set down in a public place, not at a military airport. I want to be seen by the public, to tell our story to whoever will listen before this so-called Council learns where we are and puts in an appearance. I want to contact our families as soon as possible after touching the ground."

"I'll take care of that assignment," Joy said.

"I can contact newspapers and radio stations," Clayton offered.

"I'll call Pastor Clay and Mrs. Fae at the church," Abby said. "They'll explain everything to the entire community for us. With them on our side, we'll surely succeed!"

"I'll stick with Al. Maybe I can help him to not feel so betrayed," Ben said.

Ray laid a hand on Ben's shoulder and squeezed hard. "You know I wish I would have refused to let you draw for this," he said. "And it's not because I don't think you can handle it. I just don't want anything to happen to my boy." He looked at Robert. "I ask the same of you as you have asked of me. Take good care of Ben while you all are out there."

"My life for his," Robert promised. "I won't let any harm befall him."

"I'll be all right, Daddy." Ben laid his hand over his father's. "Please take good care of yourself and Mama and Sarah while I'm gone. And Catherine, Elisabeth, and Robin," he added with a respectful nod at Robert.

Robert laughed. "Your job is more daunting than mine, my friend! I have one young man to my charge. You have four females of different ages and a baby. I don't envy you that."

Ray allowed himself a moment of amusement. "All

the more reason I want you to hurry back." He grimaced as Joy and Abby joined in the laughter.

Clayton cleared his throat. "Would you mind keeping an eye on Freddy, too?" he asked. "Michael's not much with children, and Christine is just the opposite. She might smother the poor kid to death. Freddy's a good boy. He just needs guidance and discipline."

"Be glad to," said Ray.

"All right," Robert said. "We have a week to pull ourselves together. The only getting ready we need to be concerned with is mental preparation. Ray, Ben, and I will take turns visiting with Alden every night until the fourth. The seven of us can meet every morning after breakfast to share any new thoughts, concerns or information we might have." He looked at Tom. "You're awful quiet over there. Are you okay?"

"Sure." Tom nodded. "Looking forward to fresh air and sunshine."

"Oh, yes," sighed Joy.

"I can't wait to see my family, but I dread talking to my parents." Abby's voice was small and sad. "They'll be glad to know I'm alive, but I don't know how they'll handle knowing that Toby really is gone."

Joy put her arm around Abby. "We all have a lot of happiness and sorrow to face when we leave here. It's going to be a trial no matter how we look at it. Each of us has to prove that we are stronger yet than we think we are."

The friends joined hands automatically around the table. Tom bowed his head and led the little group in prayer for the success of the undertaking that they hoped would effect their release.

Chapter Thirty-Two

Robert stepped through the door into the familiar stairwell. Joy followed close as his shadow, pulling Maria along behind her. Clayton stepped in and moved aside for Ben, who slid the door closed behind them. They all held their breaths until they heard the lock click firmly into place.

Maria trembled slightly. Joy held the girl's hand, silently offering comfort and support. Though medications were infrequently administered, the nurse Helen had given Abby injections the day before that left her ill. Robert and Ray decided not to replace her on the flight until Maria shyly approached and asked permission to go in Abby's stead. Recognizing the intense need in Maria's eyes, Tom petitioned Robert and Ray on her behalf, and they agreed. None of the other survivors begrudged Maria the decision. Maria was ecstatic and frightened at her fortune.

"Courage," Joy whispered into Maria's ear. The thread of light went dark, plunging them into utter blackness. Robert guided Joy's hand to the back of his shirt, and she directed Maria to hold onto the sleeve of her shift. Clayton laid a hand lightly on Maria's shoulder, and Ben touched his fingertips to Clayton's back. Thus connected, they ascended the steps and made their way to the hangar.

Alden emerged from his corner office as the five trooped down the stairs to the hangar floor. Clayton, Joy, and Maria gaped at the crouching black aircraft glinting sleekly in the dim light.

"What have we here?" Alden asked the question amiably enough, but Robert and Ben heard the reserve in his voice. Against better judgment, Alden had allowed excursions to the hangar by three of the survivors, usually one at a time. He sympathized with the plight of his new friends and looked forward to their visits. The unexpected presence of five visitors, three of them strangers, placed a strain on Alden's hospitality.

"Tonight is the last night," Ben said.

Alden held out his arms. Ben walked into them and hugged Alden fiercely. Tears dimmed both their eyes when they released one another.

"You've reminded me what it means to be a father," Alden said. "Spending time with you has eased the hurt of not being able to raise my own son. I'm going to miss you, Ben."

Ben stood straight and looked Alden in the face. "I wouldn't have missed knowing you for anything, Al. You're my best friend. I can't stand knowing I'll never see you again."

He took a deep breath and continued. "Al, there's a reason the five of us came to see you tonight. We want to break out of this facility and live free. To do that, we're going to have to take your aircraft. To do that, we're going to have to ask you to fly it for us."

Alden looked from Ben to Robert as the other three Trinity survivors approached and surrounded him. He did a double take when Joy moved into his line of vision. He stared at her for a long moment before clearing his throat and extending a hand. "You must be Robert's wife."

"Joy Lake." She smiled and shook hands with him. "This is Maria Ramirez, and over there is Clayton Pendleton."

"Alden Morrow," he said for the sake of introduction. "I, ah...I understand completely what you all want to do and why you want to do it. If there was any way I could legally help you, believe me, I would not hesitate to do so. What you are proposing is dangerous. I have never flown this craft with more than three people on board. Granting your request would require me to deliberately disobey orders that deny me the use of that aircraft beyond flying it to a new location under cover of darkness. Please understand. My hands are tied."

Clayton moved up behind Alden as he spoke. In one swift move Clayton slipped the pistol from its holster on Alden's belt. Alden stared silently down the barrel of his own gun.

"I'm really sorry, Mr. Morrow." Clayton's voice was shaking as badly as his hands. "But we have no choices left to us in this matter. Either we leave tonight or risk spending the rest of our lives in this vile place. I understand your position, and I hope you understand mine. I heard what you told Ben about your boy. I have three children of my own trapped here with me. Two of them are grown. I haven't been the epitome of upstanding patriotism or responsible living in my time, and it might be too late for me to set a decent example for my oldest son and daughter, but I'd like the chance to prove that people can change. I want the opportunity to be a good father to my youngest boy. I can't do that holed up in a mountain. I can start earning my kids' respect by helping to get them out of here. Please cooperate with us, Mr. Morrow."

Clayton's tone of voice made the words a plea rather than an order. As Alden hesitated, Ben walked to a set of switches mounted on the wall. The little group watched, fascinated, as doors lifted to expose a velvet night swirling with electrified clouds. Lightning ripped the sky, and thunder reverberated in the floor beneath their feet as wind gusted through the hangar.

"The weather is another reason that we should not leave tonight," Alden said. "I don't know how she handles in a storm. Anything could go wrong. No aircraft will survive a high-speed impact from six miles above the earth. What if we crash? How will you help your families then?"

"That's a chance we'll have to take," Robert said. "The night before the Trinity Test was one long series of thunderstorms. We arrived as captives in the aftermath of those storms. Perhaps it's prophetic that we reclaim our freedom in like manner. I'm sorry, Alden, I truly am. If we could have left you out of our plans, we would gladly have done so. Unfortunately, none of us knows how to fly, and even if we did, we wouldn't know how to handle this aircraft. That means that you have to come along and pilot her for us."

Ben watched his friend. He knew Alden was not afraid of Robert. He could tell by Alden's posture that he didn't believe Clayton would actually shoot him, even if they didn't need him alive to fly the aircraft. Al glanced at Joy again. He obviously found her presence disconcerting, though Ben could not have said why. The pivotal moment felt like a lifetime. Alden could yell for help, fight them off, and run away. He could leave them standing in the hangar, reveal their escape attempt to his commander, cause the Trinity survivors to be swept under a rug of secrecy once and for all.

Instead, Alden motioned toward a wheeled ladder. Ben pushed the ladder along behind Alden as they walked to the aircraft. Alden ran his fingers across a series of symbols on the side of the craft as though he were playing an instrument, and the hatch silently raised. Together they rolled the ladder into place. Alden held out a hand to Joy. She graced him with a grateful smile, grasped the handrail, and hurried up the steps to climb aboard. Maria followed. Clayton went next, passing the gun to Robert as he ascended the ladder.

"We'll be your alibi," Robert told Alden. "We'll tell everyone we forced you to take us out of here at gunpoint. We don't want to damage your career. We really are sorry for all the trouble we're putting you through. There just isn't any other way."

Alden directed a wry smile at Robert and a long, forgiving gaze at Ben. He hugged the boy one more time. "It's all right. I understand completely."

"Thanks, Al," Ben said. "For being my friend. For everything. I'm going to miss you."

"Your turn," Robert said, and Alden boarded the craft. As Ben turned to follow him, Robert took the young man by the arm and stepped between him and the ladder.

"Five are plenty," Robert said. His voice was gentle but resolute, and the look in his eyes forbade argument.

Ben tried anyway. "But I drew a short stick. That means I get to go. Please, Robert!"

Robert stood firm. "We need for you to pull the ladder out of the way as soon as I am on board and the hatch is closed. Once we are gone, lower the hangar doors and get back downstairs. You can tell everyone in the morning that we made it out just fine. It will make them feel better to hear it from you, since you saw us leave."

"But..." Ben knew it was pointless to argue. His shoulders sagged with despair.

Robert saw the hurt and resentment in his eyes. "Help your father take care of the others, will you, Ben? They need you."

Ben searched Robert's face and saw the heartfelt sincerity that cushioned the wall of authority. Whether he argued or agreed, the outcome would be the same. Ben pressed a fist firmly against Robert's shoulder. "Be careful."

Robert gave the boy a powerful hug before letting him go. "Be good." He hurried up the steps.

Ben rolled the ladder aside to the wall. He stood safely away as the aircraft breathed alive with the sound of a breeze stirring elm branches in the summer, all but silent against the thunder and wind that disrupted the atmosphere beyond the hangar doors. The craft levitated and hovered, quiet and still. Ben saw that it had been resting on a small platform. It lacked the wheels he had seen as landing gear on other airplanes. Ben wondered how Alden would ever land the thing and then, in an instant, the craft swept out the hangar doors and was gone.

Ben stood in the empty warehouse experiencing deeper loneliness than he had ever known. He felt insignificant and intimidated in the wide-open hangar and already sick with longing for his dearest friends.

Eerie shadows danced in the darkness as veins of lightning ruptured the heavens. Rain abruptly poured from the sky. The hangar vibrated like a live thing as a menacing crash of thunder jarred Ben out of his reverie. He ran to the controls and pressed the buttons. He fled to Alden's office as the doors touched down with a conclusive thump. Ben rapidly called off the chess pieces to ensure he was not leaving any behind as he dropped them into their leather pouch. He drew the strings closed, tucked the wooden board under his arm, and hastened to the stairwell. Ben hurried back to the assembly room and let himself into the apartment he shared with John and Mary. He crept to his room, placed the board and the leather pouch carefully in a drawer, and slipped into bed. Ben pushed aside his bitter disappointment at being left behind and focused on the elation of his family's success – four of the Trinity survivors had escaped from Area L!

The following morning John and Mary were astonished to see him.

"Please don't tell me the mission failed," Mary begged.

"We didn't fail," Ben assured her. "Everything went as planned. Robert thought it best that I let everyone know for sure that Al flew the others out last night. Hopefully they will come back for us before the day is through."

Breakfast was delivered late by nurses who addressed their patients with brisk movements and tight-lipped conversation.

"Where are your parents?" Cheryl demanded of Catherine and Elisabeth.

"They are in the shower." Catherine looked up from changing Robin's diaper. "Elisabeth and I were told not to interrupt them under any circumstances."

"Oh!" Cheryl blushed lightly. "Oh, of course. Well, I'll just leave their breakfasts here on the table."

"Thank you," said Elisabeth.

No one else's presence was questioned, though the undercurrent of tension that drove the nurses was obvious to all. The survivors emerged from their apartments in high spirits. Beside themselves with anticipation, they gathered in constantly shifting groups to share information, hopes and fears, prayers and plans.

Ben sat down with Ray and Belva. "Daddy, I need to ask you something," he began, but Ray held up a hand to stop him.

"No, son. I didn't tell Robert to leave you here. I'll admit I didn't want you to go, but after we drew for the privilege it would have been unfair for me to refuse you the opportunity. I said nothing more to Robert than what you heard me say when I asked him to look out for you."

Ben looked soberly into his hands. "I still don't understand why he left me here. Why not Mrs. Lake or Maria, or even Mr. Pendleton?"

"None of them knew how to get through locked doors. They had never made the trip to the hangar and back and could have easily gotten lost. You were the only one Robert could trust to make it safely back with the news of their escape."

"That makes sense," Ben said. "But it doesn't make me feel any better."

"Got room for one more?" Tom asked.

"Always," said Ray.

"The nurses know the aircraft is missing." Tom kept his voice low as he sat between Ray and Ben. "Ilya was upset this morning. I asked her what was wrong. She said that all personnel are being called forward for a serious dressing down. She said Maslow subjected the nurses to a tremendous verbal beating. It must have been bad, because Ilya was visibly shaken. They were accused of being slack with security and of being too familiar with their test subjects. That's what they call us. The medical staff was informed that there has been an appalling breach of security that resulted in the theft of invaluable equipment by a soldier stationed here. Because of that, all personnel are being raked over the coals to discourage further insubordination. Ilya said Maslow used words like sabotage and treason. I asked her what this trouble had to do with the Trinity survivors. She said it had nothing to do with us, but the nurses will have to get more serious about regular inspections of our rooms and nightly bedtime checks, nevertheless. They'll have to pay closer attention to verifying our ID bracelets, making sure we are all accounted for and in the proper rooms. There will be no more spending the night in a friend's apartment."

"I was afraid of that," Ray said. "We can probably get away with our part in this for the rest of the day, but if they check us into our rooms tonight, we'll not be able to conceal the fact that four of our group are missing."

"Hopefully we'll be rescued before nightfall," Ben said. "When are they going to start going through our rooms?"

"I wouldn't be surprised if they did it today," Tom said.

Ben looked ill.

"What's wrong?" Ray asked.

"My chess set. I collected it after the others had gone and brought it to my room and hid it in a drawer. I didn't want to leave it behind and lose it forever. I thought with us about to be rescued, it wouldn't even be noticed before I left the facility with it."

"Don't worry about it, son," Ray said. "All that means is that if they do search our rooms, they'll learn of our duplicity sooner instead of later."

"Later is better, though." Ben's expression was troubled. "If they find out before Robert's group has a chance to get help for us, Maslow might decide to move us to another place where no one would find us. Our rescuers would arrive too late, and there'd be no sign that we were ever here."

"Let's think positive," Tom urged. "There's no way the staff could know that Alden gave you the chess set. If asked, you could just say it was given to you by facility personnel. That's not a lie. If asked specifically where you got it, you could be evasive and mention that we also have a checker board and card games out here."

"Shrug it off, like it should be common knowledge that it's here."

"Exactly," Tom said, waving for Freddy's attention. When the boy trotted over, Tom requested a favor.

"Sure, Brother Tom. What do you need?"

"Take the checkerboard and checkers from the shelf and put them in a drawer in your room," Tom said. "I'll explain why later. You need to do that right now. Our rooms could be inspected at any time."

Freddy's eyes widened. "You *want* the staff to find the checkers in my room?"

"Please," Tom requested.

"Sure thing. I hope Dad sends help for us soon. The day is crawling by."

"It is," Tom agreed.

Freddy took the checkerboard and the bag of checkers and disappeared into his apartment.

Tom grinned at Ben. "Now you won't be the only one with a game in your room."

"Smart move," Ben said. "Thanks, Brother Tom. I guess I could have just brought my chess set out here and put it on the shelf."

"It could get scratched up that way," Tom said. "The pieces might get scattered around. It's safer in your room."

"I like the way you think," Ray said. "Now if only we could devise a way to get around four missing ID bracelets tonight. It's highly possible Robert's crew won't get us rescued before tomorrow. We'll be in big trouble when we can't explain where they are. I'd just as soon put that off for as long as possible."

§ § § § § §

"Are you asleep?" Callie asked in the darkness.

A deep sigh came from Sarah's bed. "I'm not sleeping. I'm waiting. I'm anxious and excited and afraid."

"Me, too. I expected to be sleeping elsewhere tonight."

"I wonder where Mr. Lake and all of them are right now."

"Some place really nice, I bet. Maybe they're getting so much attention that they aren't sleeping at all. None of us will sleep for a week when we get out of here. We'll be too overwhelmed! I wonder how Catherine and Elisabeth fared with Cheryl at bedtime."

"It wasn't Cheryl." Sarah rolled over to face Callie in the darkness. "Dana showed up for them tonight. I don't think she and Mr. Lake got along. She may have been glad enough not to have to see him, and just hustled the girls to bed. I didn't hear any commotion."

"I saw Aunt Belva carrying Robin into her and Uncle Ray's apartment. Catherine and Elisabeth didn't want to give him up, but I know Aunt Belva feels responsible for him and wants to keep him close by."

"Tom said Ilya told him they were going to crack down on bedtime inspections, but Nancy barely looked at me twice when she stopped by."

"Pat didn't pay any particular attention to me, either. But then, Pat and I don't get along much better than Dana and Robert did."

"Tomorrow," Sarah sighed. "Tomorrow we'll go outdoors. Oh, I hope the sun is shining! I won't complain if it's raining, though. Whatever the weather is like, tomorrow will be the most beautiful day of my entire life. Think of it, Callie: fresh air, the fragrance of flowers, singing birds. And cats! I want so badly to pet a cat, to hear her purr while I run my fingers through her soft fur. I want to eat a home-cooked meal. I want to ride a horse. I want to bake a cake. I want to wear my own clothes, and I won't even complain about feed sack skirts, as long as they're not this shade of blue!"

Callie laughed. "Slow down, girl. That's a big order for one day. You won't get to do all of those things to-morrow. Freedom to do as we please won't follow rescue right away. We'll have to tell our story many times before we'll get to decide where we're going to live."

"But it's nice to have things to look forward to," Sarah dreamily replied. "I know people will look at me funny, but I won't even care. I'll be so friendly they'll have to like me. I'll walk right up and say hello. Do you think a wig would improve my appearance at all? Don't answer that. I look scary and sick. With a wig, I'd look ridiculous and scary and sick."

Callie laughed in spite of herself. "Glad you still have your sense of humor."

"Can't let Fate steal everything away. A smile does get mighty hard to hang onto at times."

"I know."

"I lied, Cal. I do care what people will think. I really am scared. For all of us. I want out of here more than I've ever wanted anything, but I'm frightened of what people will say when they see us. I get jealous of you. I try not to let it show. I'm truly sorry if it ever does. You're more like my sister than my cousin, and I don't ever want to hurt your feelings. It's not that I wish you had been in the desert with us; I don't. I wouldn't wish that on anybody. I just know people are going to stare at me like I'm some sort of freak, and I don't know how I'm going to handle that. It hurts already, and it hasn't even happened yet."

"Just remember that you're not alone. There are twenty-one other people who look like you. They are going to face the same challenges upon returning to society. I know that doesn't make your situation any easier, but at least you aren't an isolated victim with whom no one else in the world can relate. And I know how easy you think it is for me to say that."

"Yes," Sarah admitted.

"There's no way I'll ever know how you feel," Callie continued. "But trust me: there's also no way you will ever know how deeply I hurt for you and our family every minute of every day. I'm frightened, too. How long will it be before I learn the results of the experiments that have been performed on me during the past two years? I get so terrified every time I look at little Robin. What if they've done things to me that will cause my babies to look like that? I don't expect to ever be told the whole truth, because the only people who know it will never tell everything they have done."

"I dread finding out those things, too. Maybe when we get out of here we can see ordinary doctors. Maybe they can figure out what has been done to us and tell us what to expect."

"I doubt it," Callie said. "We've been subjected to experimental practices, remember. The things that take place in this facility aren't procedures that ordinary doctors and nurses are going to know anything about."

"And when we get out of Area L, I don't want to be experimented on anymore, just so one of them can try to figure out what's already been done."

"Amen to that. We'd better try to get some sleep."

"I'm physically exhausted, but my mind is wide awake."

"Same here," Callie said. "But tomorrow is likely to be a very big day. We don't want to yawn our way through any of it."

"I could stay awake all night, and that still wouldn't be a problem!"

"I know. But we still need our sleep. Don't be afraid, Sarah. Everything's going to be all right. You'll see."

Sarah was silent for a moment. "Do you plan on keeping in touch with Michael when our families go their separate ways?"

"I hadn't really thought about it," Callie said. "But probably not. Michael and I don't have much in common. I feel like he's trying to con me every time we talk. Christine has told me a lot about him. She makes excuses for his shortcomings, and I don't argue. We all make less-than-stellar decisions from time to time. It's just that he seems unreliable. Dishonest. Christine makes it sound like life has always been a big joke to Michael, a gamble to see how far he can go beyond acceptable limits. He acts like an overgrown teenager. I would expect more maturity in a man Michael's age."

"Dave's really nice," Sarah said. "I hope he'll want to keep in touch with me. I wish there was a way we could continue to see each other when we get out of here, but Dave's family lives in Utah. Daddy wants to go back to Kentucky."

"Getting out of here is only the first step. We don't know yet what we are going to do or where we are going to go. Go to sleep now, or at least relax and rest."

"I'll try. G'night, Cal."

"Nighty-night," Callie answered. Within moments she was asleep.

Sarah lay awake long into the night imagining their rescue before falling into a fitful slumber.

§ § § § § §

At four o'clock the lights blared to full brilliance, and the door to their room burst open. Nancy, Pat, and two other medical staff rushed through and slammed it closed behind them.

Sarah and Callie sat upright in their beds, terrified at the invasion.

"You're both here," Pat said.

"Excellent powers of observation," Callie retorted.

Pat ignored her. "When was the last time either of you saw Robert Lake and/or his wife, Joy Lake?"

Sarah rubbed her eyes. "We all see each other every day."

Callie shrugged. "What she said."

Pat was undeterred. "Robert and Joy Lake are both missing. Their children deny knowing their whereabouts or the exact moment of their disappearance. We have confirmed that their nurses did not see them at all yesterday. Other apartments are being checked as we speak to account for the rest of you."

Nancy could be heard in the bathroom pushing the shower curtain aside. She returned, shaking droplets of water from her hands. "Just these two," she said.

"Think hard, ladies," Pat ordered. "If the Lakes don't turn up within the next few minutes, count on being questioned in the morning about where and when you last saw them and spoke with them. An answer will be required to every question. I recommend that you both cooperate fully and do exactly as you are told." She motioned for Nancy to open the door. Pat walked through it without waiting for a response. The others followed, and the door banged shut.

Callie fell backward onto the bed as though she'd been shot. "Well, so much for good fortune. We knew it wouldn't last." She yawned widely. "That's what we get for taking nightly bed checks for granted."

"But what'll we do?" Sarah gasped.

"We'll tough it out, that's what." Callie fixed Sarah with a direct gaze. "We'll sit calmly through whatever they throw at us, because we know that help is on the way."

Sarah focused on Callie's face, drawing strength from the indomitable spirit that flashed from those green eyes. At length she nodded. "Yes. Because tomorrow we'll go outdoors."

Callie smiled. "Attagirl. I doubt they'll turn the lights back out, and it's going to be hard to sleep with them on. It's three hours before we normally get up. Would you like to indulge in a game of cards until breakfast?"

Sarah agreed and propped herself up in bed. As Callie dealt the cards, the hope and frustration of the previous day overflowed Sarah's emotions. She hid her face against her knees and cried. Callie rubbed Sarah's back, offering what comfort she could.

"I'm okay," Sarah insisted between sobs. "I'm all right. I'm not losing faith or giving up. It's like you said once before." She accepted a handkerchief and wiped away her tears. "I just get tired sometimes." She looked at Callie, pleading for her to understand. "You know?"

"My little sister Sarah." Callie hugged her cousin close. "Yes. I know."

Chapter Thirty-Three

There is mercy in God's wisdom wherein we are blind to what lies ahead. The future is better a leap of faith than an organized pattern by which we could walk a path clearly seen and never stumble, fall, hurt, learn, and grow.

I wanted so desperately to go with them. I even prayed that I might be allowed the privilege. My petition was denied. Prudence dictated that I exercise patience and maturity and wait with the others for what was to come. Truly we are children, regardless of our years, and helpless but to trust the infinite knowledge that preserves us above and beyond what our simple awareness can comprehend. How often would our wants destroy us, if given into our hands exactly as our will demanded.

Godspeed, I said, and I was glad to see them go, because I knew they would return for those they were leaving behind.

Some day they will.

"I don't know."

Belva gently caressed the taut skin that stretched smooth as warm steel across her husband's clenched jaw. She darted a glance at Sarah, who heeded the message and slipped away from the table her parents shared with Tom Westfield and Russ Winter.

Ray exhaled furiously and forced himself to remain seated. He loathed the harshness of his voice. Sarah would understand and forgive, but Ray would regret snapping at his daughter for much longer than she would feel the sting of his misdirected anger.

"It's been too long." Pointless to repeat what the haunted hope in each survivor's eyes clearly conveyed, but Ray continued. "I knew when they flew out Friday night that it might be a day or two before we were released. But four days!" The thought lingered in the air and completed itself with words that none would say, as if speaking their dread might bring their worst fears to pass.

"I've had my hands full," Tom murmured. "People say to me what they are afraid to say to each other. For all their outward equanimity, their thoughts run wild with speculation. They seem to think I can reach right into Heaven and pull down the answers."

"You are a preacher. Doesn't that mean you know everything about God?" Belva smiled sympathetically.

"In the past certain people have treated me like they think I should be perfect and live always above reproach because I am a Christian. But if I allow myself to be placed on a pedestal, it is to my own eventual fall. I am saved by the same grace, called by the same God, subject to the same commandments. That's why my friends refer to me as a brother, nothing more or less." Tom shook his head. "And yet I feel an overwhelming sense of responsibility toward all of you."

Ray exhaled sharply. "I can relate to that, but not in a spiritual sense. I set everyone up to believe we were about to be rescued. Heck, I believed it myself. Now here we are with nothing but questions. Should we still harbor hope that help is on the way? If it isn't, what happened to our friends? What is going to happen to us? We've been interrogated, threatened, isolated, and then returned to our companions as though nothing out of the ordinary ever occurred. If we're all telling each other the truth, no one mentioned a word about the escape plan. Four of us just disappeared, and we haven't the vaguest notion how or where or why that could have happened. I understand Catherine even behaved indignantly at her questioning. She accused her interrogators of spiriting her parents away and trying to cover their own tracks by transferring the blame. That girl is smart, no doubt about it."

"She's frightened," Belva said. "Catherine holds Robin all the time. She paces the room with him and talks in a voice so low that only he can hear. Elisabeth shadows Christine or clings to me. Both girls are desperate for reassurance we just can't give them."

"I asked Arlene to sing last night, but she and the girls are too apprehensive to make music right now," Russ said. "They won't relax until they know Maria is safe. Kenneth and Dave are beside themselves with concern for Robert and Joy. Freddy can't make up any new stories. He's trying hard to be a young adult, but he's frantic with worry that something terrible has happened to his dad."

"Ben has hardly spoken for the past three days," Belva said.

"He should be sharing our discussion right now." Ray looked across the assembly room for his son. "I don't suppose he feels like joining us. I don't blame him. What is there to say?"

Heavy silence answered his question. Belva gazed absently across the room at Sarah, who appeared deep in conversation with Dave at the table they shared with Nathaniel and Abby. Russ leaned back in his chair and focused on the clock, glaring at time. Even Tom stared off into space, as if listening for an answer their Creator wasn't yet ready to give.

Ray left them and returned to his empty apartment to dispatch stress the way Robert used to do. Despite his bent arm, Ray was capable of strenuous calisthenics. He exercised until tension yielded to exhaustion, then showered, dressed, and pawed through a drawer for his chocolate bar. It was nearly two-thirty when he walked back into the assembly room and slowed to hear news broadcasting from the overhead speakers. As the most recent headline was announced, Ray went cold. He propped against the wall for support.

"The Army Air Forces announced today that the wreckage of a flying disk has been found near Roswell, New Mexico."

The newscast concluded. Ray looked across the room at Tom, who met his eyes for only a moment before hurrying to his apartment. A few of the others looked at each other in amazement at the report, but it appeared that most had not even heard it. Conversations continued as Ray made his way past Christine and her students toward Belva, John, and Mary. Ben headed him off.

"Daddy..."

"You're supposed to be in school."

"Ms. Pendleton excused me. Did you hear the news?"

"I heard."

"Do you think – "

"I don't know." It was all Ray could do to keep from shouting. "I don't know, Ben. If you have any opinions about the matter, keep them to yourself until we know something for certain. Do you understand?"

Ben looked him in the eye as he turned away and slipped quietly back into his chair before the blackboard.

Ray berated himself again for his impatience. 'Provoke not your children to wrath,' the Good Book admonished. Twice in one afternoon Ray had spoken harshly to his children in response to questions born of sincere concern for the very situation that consumed his mind. He wanted to apologize, but hadn't the patience to form the words. Surely they knew he was worried and upset and that he didn't mean to hurt them. It was easy to make that assumption and allow it to relieve him of responsibility for his cruelty. He hoped he was right as he took Belva in his arms, greeted his brother and Mary, and sat with them to wait for what would happen next.

§ § § § § §

"Thanks for coming." Tom hurried to Ilya as she let herself into his room.

"Any time," she said. "Are you all right?" They postponed the answer long enough for her to walk into Tom's open arms and snuggle against his chest. As he held her thus, her hands caressed the hard muscles in his back and began to knead them gently, causing his shoulders to relax and his arms to drape more heavily around her slender frame.

"That feels so good," he murmured against her hair.

"I'll do your whole back if you'll lie down," she offered.

Tom sighed and pulled reluctantly away. He kissed Ilya's hands and held them tightly, entwining his fingers with hers.

"Do you have time to visit? I need to talk with you."

Ilya nodded, and he led her to the foot of his bed. They sat sideways facing one another, still holding hands.

Tom looked around uneasily. "Your commander hasn't started using surveillance against us, has he?"

"No, of course not. It was brought up a long time ago, but you all are so well contained that escape is impossible. We carefully consider the items we make available to you to ensure you have nothing that might be used as a weapon. There's just no reason to go to the trouble and expense of constant monitoring. Granted, now it would be nice because it might give us an idea of where the four missing people have hidden themselves. What makes you ask such a thing?"

Tom took a deep breath and launched into the story he had vowed he would not share with Ilya. He talked for a very long time. He included every detail he could remember from the moment Ben had introduced Robert to Alden Morrow, to the news report that had brought him to the point of confessing that he needed outside help, her help, to find out what had happened to the Trinity survivors who escaped four days ago on the unusual aircraft.

Ilya was silent when he finished. She looked at their hands, hers in his, his in hers, withered gray ash against soft mocha cream. Tom was anxious to glimpse her expression, to discern what she was thinking. When at length she looked up at him, Tom winced at the tide of emotion flooding those depthless dark eyes, at the intensity that laid bare their mutual longing.

"Why have you not shared this with me before now?" Her voice sounded so wistful.

"I didn't want to burden you with a problem that isn't yours. Like you said, yours is a job to do, not a judgment call to make or a situation in which you can make decisions based on sympathy for your patient. I didn't want you to have to choose between betraying your career or my friends and me. Now I don't feel I have a choice. Three children and a baby are without parents, and a group of teenagers are missing a friend because we don't know where that aircraft went after Alden flew it out of here. These people have endured so much already, Ilya. All they want is the freedom to leave here and start new lives for themselves. That's why we took that plane."

"I understand." Ilya spoke in a broken whisper that begged him to believe her. She pressed her hands deeper into his. He held them protectively, loving her, wishing he could love her more. "I'll find out what I can. I'll come back to you tonight." She slipped from his grasp and made for the door.

"Ilya."

She stopped. Tom walked up behind her, put his arms around her and absorbed her trembling against himself.

"Be careful."

She turned to face him and nestled against his chest. He didn't understand her words at first, but she spoke again, and he thought his heart would stop. He clung to her and whispered the vow back into her ear.

"But it doesn't matter," she said, and Tom saw the agony in her expression when she stepped out of his arms. "We can't ever be together. So it doesn't matter."

"It does matter," Tom insisted, caressing her face. "Right here, right now, our love matters. You've made my life worth living, Ilya. I look forward to you, to everything about you, every day. The smooth warmth of your skin, the way you laugh, the way you smell. I'll never understand how you could have lost your heart to the hideous excuse for a man that I am, but I will always be grateful that you did. I'd have been lost without you, Ilya, in ways you don't even know." He hesitated over the next words, but the heart had found its voice and would not be silenced. "I wish we could always be together. I want to leave here, but I don't want to leave you."

He held Ilya's gaze until the emotional storm abated. Her eyes calmed, her breathing slowed and the tears that threatened to spill receded to the well from whence they came.

"I like to think that if we had met in another time and place..." She spoke softly, slowly. "That we might have been a family." With a tremulous smile, Ilya acknowledged defeat. "But even now, after all that has happened, if there was a way, I like to think we still could. You're not hideous, Tom. You are the most beautiful man I have ever met."

Ilya placed her hands behind Tom's neck and pulled his face to hers. The kiss was warm and bittersweet with the taste of now and never again. Ilya smiled, because, "Someday I will be just a memory to you, and I want you to remember me with laughter, not with tears."

Tom held her close, trusting neither his voice nor the words he might say.

"I'll return with news tonight."

The door latched quietly. Tom spent the remainder of the afternoon alone in his apartment letting his emotions freely span the spectrum from heartbreak to elation and back again until, at last, he slept.

Ilya interrupted his nap when she returned breathless and full of information that Tom was ill-prepared to receive.

§ § § § § §

"You look worse than I feel," Ray observed as Tom approached him in the assembly room. "And that's not good, brother, not good at all."

"We need to talk," Tom said. "Now, before the nurses show up with our supper."

Ray followed Tom to the far end of the room away from the others. They had hardly sat down when Tom pulled a newspaper from under his shirt and unrolled it for Ray. The headline of the *Roswell Daily Record* shouted the news: the RAAF had captured a flying saucer on a ranch in the Roswell area.

"Dear God," Ray prayed as he skimmed the page. "It says no details are being revealed. That doesn't mean it's our plane." Ray looked to Tom for concurrence. "Our aircraft doesn't look like a saucer. This could be a different incident altogether." Ray's stomach gripped unpleasantly at Tom's expression, and his mouth went suddenly dry. He laid the paper on the table and turned his chair to face his friend. "Tell me what you know."

"It's our plane." Tom cleared his throat in a futile effort to cover his emotion. "It crashed during the storm the night of July fourth. A rancher found the debris a couple of days ago and reported it. Military personnel from the Roswell Army Air Field are out cleaning up the crash site even as we speak. The bodies – " Tom's voice broke again, and Ray sat silently as Tom pulled himself together. "The bodies have been collected and taken to the RAAF base for autopsies."

"All of them?" Ray's voice faded to a whisper. "There were no survivors?"

Tom shook his head.

"You know this for sure?"

"I confided in Ilya. I asked her if she could find out the fate of our friends. I told her Area L is in New Mexico, and she took the risk of contacting a friend in Roswell. She gleaned what little fact is known so far among all the tales that are circulating. It seems the top brass felt that calling the aircraft a spaceship would generate enough media hysteria to convince even people who saw the debris and handled it that aliens had visited. You know as well as I do that anyone who gets a glimpse of Robert, Clayton, or Maria will erroneously substantiate the alien rumor. The truth has already been obliterated. Our truth will never occur to anyone now because of all attention being directed toward this ... illusion." He swatted the newspaper.

"Dear God. Robert, my buddy, my brother, my friend. What would you do if it had been me?" Ray propped his face on his fists. "All of them. What am I going to tell Catherine and Elisabeth and Freddy?"

"If you want, I will announce it to everyone after we have eaten supper and know for certain that none of the nurses are within earshot."

"Let's do it more quietly. The children should know first," Ray said. "I'll tell them, if you wouldn't mind telling your friends from the church group." He laid a heavy hand against Tom's shoulder as he rose and crossed the room to his apartment. He paused just inside the foyer, overwhelmed by grief and utter defeat. As Ray bowed his head and turned his face to the wall, he felt arms encircle his waist. He looked down into the large, liquid eyes of Elisabeth Lake. Her eyes were beseeching, begging for impossible reassurance, asking the question without words.

Mom and Dad aren't coming back, are they?

Ray looked over her head at Catherine, who watched from just outside the door. Robin slept on her shoulder. When Ray met her eyes, Catherine lowered her head and walked away. Elisabeth started to cry. Ray knelt and put his arms around the child. He drew her close and cried with her.

Ben and Freddy noticed Catherine's vacant expression and Elisabeth's red, swollen face, and sought an explanation from Tom.

"What's happened to Dad?" Freddy demanded.

"Go get Michael and Christine," Tom requested. "Ask them to join us at the table in the corner."

Freddy stood very straight and still and looked at Tom until Tom glanced away. "Dad's dead, isn't he?" The words fell flat and impassive. "I always knew one day he'd leave and never come back."

Russ overheard and caught Freddy as the boy turned away. Freddy stood quietly as if in a daze. Russ looked from Tom to Ben and back again. "Would it help if I told Michael and Christine?"

"Thanks, Russ, but maybe I'd better do it."

"Sure." Russ walked away with Freddy. The boy accompanied him without a trace of emotion.

Tom finally forced himself to look at Ben. The

question hung horrible between them, neither asked nor answered but completely understood. Shattered, Ben turned and numbly made his way to his room. Belva found him two hours later, sitting on the floor staring into an empty drawer.

"Ben? Oh, Ben," she said. "What are you doing in here all by yourself? Supper has just been served. I know it's hard, dear. None of us are of a mind to eat right now."

"Nurse Thornton took it. She searched my room and said she had not seen a chess set that nice in all her career. She said it proved that there were traitors among the staff who have done things for us they weren't supposed to do and who helped four of us escape, whether or not that had anything to do with the theft of other equipment that belonged to Area L." Ben's knuckles turned white as he gripped the drawer. "She took it, and now my friend Al is dead. He made it just for me, and now he's dead, and I don't even have it to remember him by. Robert and Joy are gone, and Clayton and Maria. Nurse Thornton will know we were all in on it. I hope they kill us quickly and get it over with."

"Hush, now! Don't talk like that! We don't know what's going to happen. We don't," Belva insisted. She put her arms around Ben and rocked him back and forth as she had done in years past when her little boy bumped his head or skinned his knee. Ben let her, for both their sakes.

"Does everyone else know?"

"Everyone knows. Your father and Brother Tom shared the telling. Come, now. Join me at the table. Try to eat a little. We all need to be strong."

"What for?" Ben wanted to know.

"For whatever comes next," Belva said. She stood and offered Ben a hand. He got to his feet and draped an arm around his mother's shoulders.

"My goodness." Belva stepped back and looked proudly at her son. "You're taller than I am. When did that happen?"

Belva led Ben out of the apartment to the table she shared with John, Mary, Callie, and Ray. Ben sat and obediently swallowed the food before him, wincing as his stomach cramped in protest. He laid down his fork and glanced around the room. No one else was eating or talking. The evening elapsed in silence as the stunned victims grappled with the meaning of what they had been told.

Wednesday morning the survivors entered the assembly room after breakfast and found chairs arranged in rows before the podium. They sat quietly for the memorial service they had requested of Tom. He loitered in the foyer of his apartment with Ray.

"I feel so inept. This is going to be the hardest thing I've ever done. I know what to say about our friends who are gone. What can I say to those who are still here? How do I give them hope? I know how to give spiritual guidance. I know that faith in God is paramount, regardless of the situation. But sometimes people need tangible reassurance more solid than a promise that if they will just believe, everything will be all right. Yet that's all I have to offer." Tom's shoulders slumped under the weight of his burdens.

"At the risk of teaching the teacher," Ray said, "tell God what you just told me. He knows where we are and what we're going through, and our future is in His hands. We can rest assured of that."

Tom waited until all were in attendance before stepping forward to speak. He looked with compassion at the bereft survivors and prayed for the right words as he moved through eulogies for the five who were no longer with them. He included Alden Morrow. Although only Ray and Ben knew him personally, Alden's relationship with the Trinity survivors had cost him his life. When Tom had spoken his heart, he beckoned Ray to the podium and stepped aside.

Ray stood straight and saluted. His voice deepened, gruff with emotion, as he sang verses to the tune of Taps.

"Day is done, gone the sun,
From the lake, from the hills, from the sky.
All is well, safely rest, God is nigh.

"Then good night, peaceful night,
Till the light of the dawn shineth bright,
God is near, do not fear – Friend, good night."

§ § § § § § §

"The papers have retracted their spaceship story. Now the military claims the thing they found was just a weather balloon. Ilya ran the risk of making a telephone call this morning to her friend in Roswell. Apparently the crash site is closely guarded. Only military clean-up crews are allowed in. Her friend heard that RAAF officials forced the rancher who found the plane to change his story."

"I never would have believed this nightmare could have grown any worse."

"That's not all, Ray. We're being taken out of here.

The Council has decided to shut the seventh floor down. Ilya said all personnel were notified late yesterday and ordered to make preparations for absolute departure within one month. The Council feels that too much attention is being focused on New Mexico. Even though we are a considerable distance from Roswell out here in the mountains, all the commotion is considered a threat to the absolute secrecy of this institution. It appears our bid for liberty may close the curtain on Area L."

"What are they going to do with us?"

"Ilya believes they will move us to either Fort Worth, Texas or Wright Field in Ohio. A lot of the debris from the plane is being sent both places." Tom swallowed hard. "No word on how the medical personnel are to be reassigned."

"I'm sorry, Tom, I truly am. I know you've become fond of Ilya."

Tom stood and headed for the door. "We'd better let everyone know. Things are liable to get scary for a while, and every shred of information we can pass on will help us hold on to our sanity."

Callie nearly ran them over as they emerged from the apartment. "Sorry!" she exclaimed as she stood on her tiptoes to avoid bumping into them. "Pat and Nancy just took Sarah away. Mama and Aunt Belva are gone, too, and so are Christine and the other women. The only females the nurses didn't take are the children and me." She turned worried eyes to Ray. "Have you heard anything about where they've taken them, and why?"

Chapter Thirty-Four

Fate allowed precious little time for tears. In the days following the memorial service, grief became a thing shared through sympathetic glances and murmurs of encouragement. From early in the morning until bedtime, nurses carted the Trinity survivors back and forth between lab facilities and exam rooms where the patients were subjected to blood tests and painstakingly thorough physical examinations. Photographs and x-rays were added to the cumbersome volumes that comprised each survivor's records. Medical staff duplicated every piece of information in those records and carefully documented current information in new files already thick with three days of meticulous detail. Each victim received a clean bill of health. The survivors had healed of that from which they would not recover. The ashen skin and disfiguring scars would ever remain as souvenirs of their experiences in Area L.

There was little chance to talk until after lights-out, when the day's events could at least be discussed between roommates.

"It's not as bad as it used to be," Callie said.

"What do you mean?" Sarah asked.

"The tests. You know. The things they used to do to us. What I went through today was more like a routine medical exam I might get at any doctor's office. It wasn't like before."

"Oh. I know what you mean. I'll never forget those days, but I try not to remember them, either, if I can help it."

"Do you think they'll keep us all together? I hope they won't send us two different places, like Tom said they have done with the wreckage of the aircraft."

Sarah shot Callie a perplexed look of which Callie was unaware in the dark. Callie rarely confessed to worry. Usually Sarah spoke her uncertain mind, and Callie offered a positive point of view. Sarah was glad that Callie had turned to her for encouragement. "I don't think they'll separate us," she offered.

"No? Why not? We are test subjects, remember, and considerably more willful than rodents or frogs. We've caused a lot of trouble. They might find us easier to manage in two or even three smaller groups."

"I don't believe they'll want to spend twice the amount of time and money on preparing more than one place to keep us and carry out their plan for us. Whatever it is."

"I hope you're right," Callie said. "At least, I think I hope you are. Our dead might yet be better off than we are."

The girls fell silent as they contemplated the future that drifted more uncertainly than ever beyond their grasp. Several hours passed before Sarah slept, and she was startled when the lights blared to full brilliance an hour early the following morning.

"But it's Sunday," she protested as Nancy delivered orders.

"Bathe, dress, breakfast," Callie parroted after the nurse was gone. "How is this different from any other morning, except for the time?"

"But breakfast has always been served in our rooms, so why serve it in the assembly room this morning?" Sarah wondered.

"You can go first," Callie ordered, pulling the sheet over her head to block out the light.

Sarah grinned as she padded past her cousin's bed on the way to the bathroom. The smile faded as she looked into the mirror. She had often wondered at the purpose of a mirror in every apartment. Callie, Michael, and Joy needed one, but Sarah would just as soon never have to see her own face again. She kept her eyes downcast as she brushed her teeth, determined to avoid confronting the ugliness that broke her heart. Was it so wrong to wish to be pretty? She stepped into the shower, tugged the curtain closed, and drove the despondency from her thoughts by wondering what the nurses were up to today. Callie's words from the previous night made Sarah shudder at the thought of being sent far away from her family. Searching for comfort, she reached into the past, only to find fading memories of a life forever gone. If the future was too frightening to consider, and if the past was no longer clear, where was she to go? *Dave.* Sarah spent a lot of time talking with Dave, and she thought about him nearly every minute that she wasn't in his presence. He had taken to holding her hand. She wished he would kiss her. Remembering her face in the mirror, she understood completely why he would never want to do that.

Her peace a casualty of circumstances, Sarah leaned against the cool tiled wall and closed her eyes. The water spilled over her face and flowed the length of her body. She imagined it cleansing away each horrible reality that oppressed her spirit until they had all washed out of her mind, off her body, and down the drain. She clung to the refreshing emptiness within, the brief respite from the burden that was her life.

A voice chuckled softly at the fringes of her awareness. *It's not real. It won't last.*

Sarah mentally turned her back on the demon and drowned it along with all the rest.

§ § § § § §

Breakfast was a subdued affair. After everyone had eaten, the nurses lined their patients up against a wall, checked each identification bracelet, and made a final notation in the corresponding file.

Ilya held Tom's hand a little longer than necessary. He looked deeply into her eyes – *like coffee laced with cinnamon* – and visually caressed her café au lait features, committing every detail of her beautiful face to memory. This was their goodbye. Tom could hardly bear it. Ilya remained strong and true to her word. There were no tears. Her smile was genuine, though it trembled and faded quickly. Tom attempted a smile in return. If he could only take her in his arms, kiss her soft and sweet and slow, invoke some miracle by which he could take her with him and never be apart from her again. Ilya entwined her fingers with his for one eternal moment, and then she was gone.

The men who entered the room in the wake of the

nurses were painfully reminiscent of the suits that tended the patients through most of their first year in the institution. Tom backed instinctively away from their approach. They immediately began pairing off the survivors. Ray and Belva held hands and were left alone. Russ and Arlene followed suit. Sarah looked to Dave for comfort as he clasped her hand and offered her a reassuring smile. The men apparently did not care, so long as the people were separated two by two.

Tom felt a hand slip into his and turned, expecting Ilya. With an effort, he voided his expression as Christine's shy glance bounced off the desperate hope in his eyes. She looked startled at what she saw there. She tried to withdraw, as though she had made a terrible mistake, but Tom held onto her hand and gave her a conspiratorial wink. At his encouraging nod, Christine remained by his side, and the men lined them up behind John and Mary.

When their turn came, Tom and Christine followed their escorts into the Lake apartment, where men outfitted them with wrist cuffs and shackles about their ankles. An attendant belted chains around each of their waists and leashed them together with a short chain connecting Tom's belt to Christine's. Thus restrained, the couple followed one of the men into the hallway and onto an elevator. Upon arrival at another floor, the man consigned Tom and Christine to hard wooden chairs alongside other couples to await the rest of the group. When the final two arrived, attendants unceremoniously herded all the survivors down another hallway and into a closed garage. A bus awaited them there.

Ray was the first to be ushered aboard. The men assisted him and Belva onto the bus, settled them onto a seat, and padlocked their shackles to an eye bolt on the floor between their feet.

Ray studied his surroundings as the other survivors were brought aboard. The louvered windows he had seen on the outside of the bus were for appearances only; the walls inside were solid. Dim lights above every other seat illuminated the passengers with a murky yellow glow. A steel panel separated the cab from the passenger seats, broken only by a small square of glass behind a steeply louvered frame, which prevented the driver and his passengers from viewing one another. The normal bus door allowed the driver access to his seat. A second door opened beside the first to admit the passengers, and Ray had noticed that it merged into the side of the vehicle when it was closed, invisible to the casual eye.

As the men locked the last of the survivors into place, one of them pointed to the rear of the bus where a narrow door concealed a toilet. He explained that the guard would unlock anyone who needed to go and escort the prisoner to and from the lavatory.

"Prisoner?" Ray wondered in a low voice, and looked to Belva for the reassurance of her presence.

The door closed, and Ray noted that two people and two keys were required to unlock it from both the inside and the outside. The armed guard who would sit facing them on a short bench beside the louvered window pocketed one key. The driver retained possession of the other.

From the outside, the bus would appear ordinary to the travelers with whom it shared the road. On the inside, it was a portable prison for victims of a war the world never knew took place. Virtually immobilized, chained to each other and to the floor, they were helpless but to wait for the will of an authority whose identity beyond the name of Maslow remained a mystery. Only little Robin was spared manacles and chains. His crib was secured behind the last seat beside the bathroom door. There would be no second chance for escape.

Ray focused on the louvered window. If he slouched in his seat and tilted his head, he could peer from the dark bus into the brighter light of the cab and discern a few details about the driver as the man climbed aboard. He was an unassuming fellow in plain clothes. He appeared to be in his late sixties, Ray thought, possibly a government retiree, and probably ignorant as to the true nature of his cargo. The armed guard might be in his mid-forties. He carried himself with an attitude that invited any opportunity to display his prowess as a fighter. Ray knew the type. He'd fought alongside a few. When the war out-toughed them, they went home in straitjackets. Until then, they were malicious bullies who took pleasure in mistreating those who could not fight back. The guard ran his fingers across the revolver and the club residing on his belt as he sat on the bench and faced his captives. He stretched his long legs out into the aisle and laid his rifle carelessly across his thighs.

Ray stared at the little M1 carbine and thought he might actually drool. As a Marine he had used the heavier M1 Garand and would forever be of the opinion that a man couldn't ask for a better rifle. He'd handled the .30 caliber carbine, too, and been quite impressed with the smaller, lightweight version. The magazine in the guard's rifle would hold fifteen rounds. Between the rifle, the pistol, and the club, the guard wasn't taking any chances with his immobilized prisoners. He probably had a knife, too, Ray thought darkly. His study was disrupted as the bus sputtered to life, flinched into gear, and jolted forward.

Ray recalled Maslow's assurance that personnel arrived and departed under a cloak of obscurity, for it was imperative that they remain ignorant of the facility's location. Ray had assumed that all staff were flown to Area L, that even the Trinity survivors had been flown into the hangar on an airplane and transported deep into the bowels of the mountain fortress. It had not occurred to him that a road might lead across the desert, through the mountains, and onto the base.

His surprise was short-lived. The bus lurched so erratically along the road that Ray entertained a moment of droll gratitude for the chains that kept the survivors from being tossed out of their seats. He quickly decided that the route they traveled must be just adequate enough to permit the passage of an occasional vehicle without maintaining the appearance of a road. Ray bounced in his seat as the wheels beneath him encountered another obstacle. He hoped the rutted trail would prove to be a brief trial between the base and a main road, even as he resigned himself to what he knew was going to be a long trip. Ilya had told Tom that the Trinity survivors were destined for Wright Field.

The children were frightened. Elisabeth was trying hard not to cry. Ray wished he could comfort the girl who had lost both of her parents only to be cast into the unknown with only her sister and infant brother for familial support. The adults wore expressions of despair. Their one hope of freedom was tragically lost, and they wavered on the verge of giving up. Ray had heard furtive conversations all around him at breakfast. Some could see no reason to live if they were living for no reason, and they envied those who had died on their behalf. The dead were at least free. The bus jarred into a higher gear and picked up speed. All around Ray heads bowed, hearts broke, and spirits grieved their very existence.

Have faith, Ray wanted to tell them. We must believe in God and in the strength He has given us. We must be brave. As the guard yawned and settled back into this seat, Ray began an intense visual examination of his surroundings. No fort was impenetrable. There was always an area taken for granted as safe, always an undefended point to be found. Ray started with the guard and concentrated all his efforts toward finding a weakness. The very depths of his soul stirred with the hope and impossible agony of his quest while his spirit prayed that a higher power was working toward the same end.

§ § § § § §

Ben suffered from nausea and severe diarrhea. His nerves had been on edge since the aircraft left without him. He had not had time to cope with the deaths of his friends, especially Robert and Alden. He had endured the last week in a daze, only vaguely aware of the things going on around him, and the twisted knot in his stomach assured that he had not been eating well. Now the bumpy, weaving ride aggravated his already weak stomach until he cramped double. He begged the guard to allow him to use the bathroom. The guard ignored Ben until others spoke up on the boy's behalf. Acting annoyed and horribly put-upon, the guard informed the driver via his handheld radio of what was taking place. He hauled his tall frame off the bench, unlocked Ben's chains and led him, still in wrist and ankle cuffs, to the tiny cubicle. The guard waited by the door until Ben emerged. When Ben asked to go twice more, the guard didn't argue. He could tell Ben wasn't joking, and he didn't want to be trapped inside the stifling bus with the odor of uncontrollable bodily functions.

The bus pulled over twice at remote, prearranged locations where escort vehicles traded shifts. The rests lasted long enough for Belva to give Robin a bottle. The baby, accustomed to constant attention, expressed his dissatisfaction with his unfamiliar surroundings and the lack of human contact. He slept through part of the morning, but when he wasn't sleeping, he cried. He only stopped crying when Belva held him. As the morning hours elapsed, the guard had all he could stand of the incessant wailing. He finally allowed Belva, still in wrist cuffs, to hold Robin in her arms. The baby quieted under her care, and the soft voice Belva used to soothe the child comforted the other passengers as well.

During a stop at noon the guard allowed each person, still shackled, to walk back and forth along the aisle of the bus in order to relieve muscles that were stiff from sitting for hours in the same position. He served the survivors a meager lunch. Belva and Mary encouraged Ben to eat a few bites. When wrappers and napkins were collected and the guard had ensured all bonds were secure, the journey resumed.

A mid-afternoon stop relieved the escorts of their duties. The passengers listened to the bus driver speak with an escort driver about the devastating consequences that could be expected if the specimens aboard the bus were seen in New Mexico in the aftermath of that incident near Roswell. Transporting this particular con-signment away from the area as soon as possible was of utmost importance, and the driver praised the escorts for expediting that effort. The bus driver would continue to check in via telephone calls at regular intervals, but once his cargo was outside New Mexico, the potential for discovery wasn't considered as drastic a threat. An ordinary bus wasn't likely to attract attention on its meandering trip across the country. New drivers would take over at checkpoints along the way so that the trip could be completed without stopping.

"Specimens?" Ray glared at the M1 in the guard's lap.

"The guard referred to us as prisoners, remember." Belva patted Ray on the leg. "There's no telling what the drivers and escorts have been told this bus is hauling."

"Perhaps we should announce our presence and introduce ourselves," he retorted, knowing even as he said it that if he drew a breath to yell, he'd be dead before he made a sound. Ray wondered what the guard told the driver when he had to escort one of the passengers to the bathroom. He could hardly have avoided explaining that the bus was filled with people. The driver had to have heard Robin throughout the morning, and a crying baby just didn't sound like anything else.

Ray laid his hand over Belva's as the driver pulled the bus back onto the road. "I've been losing my temper a lot lately."

"We've been through so many things that if we tried to hide our reactions to all of them, we'd surely lose our minds," Belva said. "Just remember that we're all in this together, and the rest of us share your feelings."

Ray glanced over his fellow passengers. His gaze

lingered on Ben, who dozed with his head uncomfortably reclined against the back of the seat. Several others catnapped in a similar fashion, and Ray caught himself drifting off, despite his efforts to the contrary.

Ben awoke late in the evening. He felt better, but he needed to use the bathroom again. He motioned to the guard, who heaved a sigh of exasperation as he walked back to unlock Ben and escort him to the rear of the bus. The guard didn't bother to inform the driver this time. He had been doing this all day, and he was weary of tending to the sick boy. He pushed Ben into the cubicle and leaned against the door.

The bus swerved slightly, slowed down, and then resumed normal speed. The guard frowned. The vehicle had been thoroughly inspected and found in perfect working order. There should be absolutely no potential for a breakdown. Within the next few moments, it became obvious that the old man was driving erratically. The guard radioed the driver but received no answer. He hesitated. He had orders to stay within an arm's length of any captive not chained in a seat. The bus lurched and tilted at an alarming angle. Something was very wrong. Momentarily disregarding the sickly handcuffed boy in the bathroom, the guard took a step forward, bracing himself against the seats, and again radioed the driver.

The bus swerved sharply and bounced over a series of obstacles that would have hurled the passengers from their seats had they not been tethered in place. After a few seconds of chaos, the bus lurched to a stop leaning drastically to the right. The frightened passengers looked around at one another, wordlessly affirming that each of them was all right. The only sound that broke the silence was that of a baby howling hysterically.

Arlene leaned forward and wiped her bloody nose with the back of her hand. She noticed that Callie's lip was bleeding, and Freddy winced as he attempted to touch his fingertips to the side of his head. Belva had managed to hang on to Robin through the rough ride, and neither appeared to have suffered any injury. Arlene looked around for the guard. He lay face down and motionless in the aisle. She and Russ turned with the others to gaze in astonishment toward the rear of the bus where Ben unsteadily stood, staring in disbelief at the guard's club in his hands.

Ray caught sight of Ben in the instant everyone else realized what had taken place. Though he was bursting with pride for his son, he knew better than to allow the unexpected hero to waste any more time contemplating his actions.

"The keys, Ben!" he ordered. Ben started as though he had been poked in the ribs. He threw down the club and unclipped the keys from the guard's belt. He went to Ray first. They soon found that although the keys unlocked the passengers from the floor and each other and relieved them of the shackles about their ankles, the guard did not have the key that would unlock their handcuffs.

"The driver must have that key," Ray said. "I know he has the key that unlocks the door to the outside, and we can't get out of here without it." He maneuvered to the front of the bus and peered through the louvered window. The driver slumped over the steering wheel with his head turned slightly to one side. His eyes were open, and his face was blue. "Those keys might as well be a million miles away." Ray heaved a frustrated sigh and turned back to his companions. Most were standing or sitting sideways, extending their limbs as far as they could stretch them in so limited a space.

"Help me out here," Ray asked of no one in particular. Russ and Will helped Ray lift the unconscious guard onto one of the seats and shackle him to the bolt in the floor. Ray relieved him of a pocketknife, which he kept, and of a lighter that he tossed to Tom. He passed the guard's revolver to John. "Now we have to get out of here."

A series of panels in the ceiling caught Ray's attention. "Would you all mind sitting down for a moment, please," he requested, and walked under one of the panels. With the blunt edge of a knife blade, he removed the four screws that held it in place and pulled off the cover to reveal a mesh screen. Ray removed that, too. "A vent. Before this bus was modified to carry us, it had a customized ventilation system." Ray looked up at the metal plate that elevated a few inches above the roof in order to permit airflow through the mesh screen. "Listen!" he cried.

Silence settled over the bus. The survivors smiled at the melodic trill of birdsong.

"Look – my God, look at the sky," Tom breathed, pointing to the narrow gap between the metal plate and the roof. "I see a cloud!"

Ray punched at the metal plate. It didn't budge. A hand prevented Ray from a second try.

"If I may, sir?" Will moved in front of Ray and with two solid blows sent the plate flying off the top of the bus. Tom joined them, and others crowded in as best they could, holding onto the seats to remain upright on the sharply angled floor. For a moment, they breathed the fresh air and drank in their first view of the natural world in two years.

"We have to get out of here," Ray said again. A hint of desperation crept into his voice, and the others saw why. None of them was going to fit through the tiny opening in the ceiling. As Ray cast about for another exit, his dismal gaze fell on petite Elisabeth Lake. At twelve, she was still a small girl with a tiny waist, a delicate frame, and dainty features dominated by her father's expressive eyes.

"Elisabeth." Ray hesitated. Robert had left his three children to Ray's care. Upon learning that Robert and Joy had died, Ray's thinking adjusted to count Catherine, Elisabeth, and Robin among his own offspring. He would not willfully endanger any of his children.

Elisabeth watched the battle between responsibility and dire need play out in Ray's eyes for only a moment before she scrambled to his side. "I'll fit, Uncle Ray. Don't worry. This isn't as dangerous as what Mom and Dad did."

Ray hugged Elisabeth and lifted her through the vent, aware that their time was limited.

Elisabeth squeezed out onto the roof and stared at her surroundings. The bus had careened off the road and come to rest with two wheels in a shallow ditch. The narrow two-lane road was, for the moment, deserted. Behind and before her, a thick forest kept pace with the road as far as Elisabeth could see in either direction. She inhaled the fresh air and snapped back to the immediate crisis as Ray tugged her ankle.

"Hold on to the vents," he ordered. "Be careful and go slow."

Elisabeth crept across the roof of the bus by clinging to the other vent covers, much as she had done while playing on monkey bars during long-ago visits to the park with her mother. She climbed down to the window by the driver's seat and lowered herself through. She patted the driver's pockets until she felt a set of keys. She eagerly dug them out. The driver's door on the right side of the bus was angled toward the ground. Elisabeth tugged at the tight handle until the door squealed open, allowing her to slide out onto the grass.

So excited was she to be sitting outdoors on the ground that she almost forgot her mission. The grass felt cool against her bare legs, the air smelled fresh, and birds, lots of birds, flew to and fro among the trees at the forest's edge! Ray called to her from within the bus. She sprang to her feet, looked up at the door that would allow the others to exit, and saw with dismay that she wasn't tall enough to reach the lock. She looked about for something to stand on, but there was nothing within immediate reach.

"I'm trying!" she called back. "I can't reach the lock!"

Silence momentarily settled within the bus, and Elisabeth knew they were desperately thinking of what to do next. Elisabeth thought with them. At length, taking a deep, determined breath, she reached through the driver's door and took hold of the dead man's ankle. Elisabeth braced herself against the steps and pulled with all her might. Aided by gravity and the steep tilt of the bus, she tugged until the man slid down the steps out onto the ground.

With great difficulty caused by the man's weight and the handcuffs she still wore, Elisabeth rolled the body over three times until it lay beneath the lock. She closed her eyes and took a deep breath. Swallowing the lump in her throat, Elisabeth stepped up onto the body, reached up as far as she could, and inserted a key into the lock. The third key she tried turned smoothly. The door fell open and threw her backward into the grass. She lay where she landed, laughing with exhilaration, horror, and relief as Ray retrieved the keys from the lock and set about releasing the survivors from their handcuffs as they emerged from the bus.

Cries of joy softened with wonder and awe.

"Free...we're free..."

"Look at the birds!"

"The sunset...oh, the colors!"

"Take off your slippers! The grass feels so plush and cool!"

"A breeze! Do you feel it?"

"The air smells so clean and fresh..."

Elation was tempered by amazement at the gift of life no longer taken for granted. The Trinity survivors were greeted by a cool evening breeze fresh with the scent of forests that lined both sides of the little two-lane highway. Tears of gratitude flowed across their smiles as they lifted their faces to the violet, crimson, and fiery gold of the evening sky.

"A star! A star! Look, up there, right beside that cloud – our very first star!"

Freedom had been achieved at last, and not by their own hands. Ray acknowledged that their lives would soon be fraught with burdens of which their minds could not immediately conceive. He pushed the premonition aside as his companions hugged one another and thanked God for bringing them out of their own personal Egypt, even as they grieved for those who had laid down their lives for this very moment.

Ray, Russ, and Will hoisted the driver into the back of the bus and laid him in the aisle. Tom, Nathaniel, and Michael searched the bus for anything they might wish to take along. They carried a couple of boxes from under the guard's bench outside onto the grass. Ray cut two strips of material from the guard's shirt. He tied one over the guard's mouth and the second across his eyes.

"We need to get out of here." Ray felt like a record stuck in a monotonous groove. "Let's see what's in those boxes and put some distance between ourselves and this place."

He paused once more as he and Russ stepped outside the bus. The survivors savored the first unmitigated happiness they had experienced in two years. Within moments they would take flight in search of refuge from those who would yet lock them forever away.

For now, they danced with freedom to the melody of nature's song.

Journey of The Dead

I thank my God upon every remembrance of you.
~ Philippians 1:3 KJV

Special thanks to ...

Dr. Ruth Falk Redel, my editor, friend, and prayer warrior. Your expertise and encouragement have made me a better writer and a better person.

Jean Dudgeon, my German language adviser.

Gary Stearns, who talked me through a virtual tour of World War II in the Soviet Union in January 1943.

Keri Knutson of Alchemy Book Covers & Design, who created the outstanding cover art for *Journey of The Dead*.

Author and writing instructor James Brewer; Rita of the Amarillo Globe-News Library; the Alamagordo Chamber of Commerce; the Socorro County Chamber of Commerce; the White Sands Public Information Office; the Music Division staff of the Library of Congress; and Jonathan Gunson of Bestseller Labs.

Bud and Thea Guenther, for a decade of unconditional love, encouragement, prayer, and parental support. I am honored and blessed to be a part of your family.

Katrina Fillo, my sister in spirit, for the beautiful inspiration that you are every day. You are a treasure.

Nine cats for comfort, companionship, and amazing lessons about life.

My Lord and Savior Jesus Christ, for Your constant presence on this incredible journey.

Coming in Autumn 2014

Trinity Road

The Trinity Conspiracy Book Two

Though dead to their families and to the world they once called home, Sarah and her companions savor their freedom as they seek a new beginning and a new life.

As they struggle to survive on the run from the Council, the Trinity family finds that gaining hard-earned liberty is not so much the costly and victorious conclusion of a war as it is the commencement of a lifelong journey … that even freedom has limitations … and that the path home leads straight to one's own heart.

join the conspiracy

www.actownsend.com

www.facebook.com/JoinTheConspiracy

ACTownsend

lives in Kentucky with her husband and six (at the time of the this printing) cats. She is currently writing the fourth and final novel in the Trinity Conspiracy.